THE APP

STUART JAMES

Copyright © 2022 by Stuart James

All rights reserved.

No part of this book may be reproduced in any form or by any electronic or mechanical means, including information storage and retrieval systems, without written permission from the author, except for the use of brief quotations in a book review.

Edited by Rebecca Miller.

Cover design. Thea Magerand.

*To the most amazing people on the planet. My gorgeous wife, Tara, my beautiful children Oli and Ava and incredible parents, Jimmy and Kathleen.
Forever the light in my life.*

A link isn't always a good connection.
	App starts the word, Applause, but it also starts the word, Appalling...

Stuart James.

1

1981

Jonathan Rushmore stared at the TV in the living room as his mother walked in. Her vanilla and rose perfume wafted towards him, making him sneeze.

'Right, we're off. Don't answer the door to anyone, don't leave the house and don't watch too much TV.'

'Mum, I'm sixteen, not six.' Jonathan glanced at her long yellow dress and sensible flat shoes. Her cheeks were dusted with a dark red blusher, and her eyebrows were thick with black pencil. He turned back towards the TV; the next level began, the sound effects blaring as a yellow smiley face raced around collecting pellets.

Gill smirked at the almost comical irritated expression on her son's face. His black, curly hair was messy and spiked at the front, clumped together with gel.

Gill glared at the screen. 'So what's this Pac-Man then?'

Jonathan placed the controller in his lap and turned towards her, his face now bright with excitement. 'Oh, you have to collect all the pellets and avoid the ghosts. You want a go?'

'Another time. We have to leave now if we're going to catch the film. Your father's taking me to see the new Bond film. *For Your Eyes Only*. It's not my thing, but he loves all that macho stuff. But, Jonathan, please don't play computer games all the time. Don't make Dad and I regret getting it for you. There's a reason we bought you that Chopper bike and roller skates. So you could go out with your friends and get some fresh air. It's not healthy being cooped up all your life.'

'All my friends play computer games. I'm not the only one.'

'Right. That's the back door locked. You ready, Gill?' Adam, Jonathan's father, interrupted, walking into the living room, dressed in a loud green jacket, blue jeans and Cuban boots. He'd combed his brown hair over to the right, covering the bald patch, and his moustache had been curled perfectly at each end. His cheap aftershave mixed with Gill's perfume, creating a noxious scent. 'What do you think, son? Your old man's still got it.'

Jonathan wanted to laugh at his father's dress sense, but only just managed to stem the explosion threatening to spill from his lips. Instead, he smiled awkwardly and turned back towards the TV.

'Now, before we go, your mum and I have had a little chat. It's the first time that we're leaving you alone, but you have to earn our trust if you want to keep the freedom.' Pointing his finger, Adam declared, 'Behave. I don't want any of the neighbours complaining to me about the loud music. Don't let us down. We're trusting you. I want you in bed by ten p.m. Understood?'

'Understood,' Jonathan muttered.

Adam stepped forward. 'I didn't quite hear that.'

'Leave it, Adam,' Gill insisted.

'I said, understood.'

'Good lad.' His father left the room, opened the front door and walked out to the brown Ford Cortina parked on the drive.

In the living room, Gill rubbed a hand through Jonathan's black curls. 'We'll be back by eleven thirty. Any problems, go next door to Mavis and wait with her until we return.'

'Nothing's going to happen. Just go. Enjoy the film.'

Gill leant forward, kissed her son on the forehead, then walked down the hallway to the raucous clatter of Pac-Man desperately trying to evade the ghosts.

The front door closed. Through the living room window, Jonathan watched the Ford Cortina spew smoke onto the drive. God, he was so embarrassed to have anything to do with it. A moment later, it was gone.

Picking up the walkie-talkie hidden under the sofa, Jonathan eagerly pressed his thumb against the side button. 'Luke. Over.'

A loud, scrambling noise resounded, and a voice came through. 'Here. Over.'

Again, Jonathan pressed firmly against the side button. 'My parents have gone. Over and out.'

A few minutes later, the doorbell rang out, like an out-of-tune church organ, slowly giving up a fruitless call to its parishioners. It continued to reverberate as Jonathan walked along the hallway and answered the front door.

'Man. You need to do something about that,' Luke stated as he walked inside the house. He looked younger than sixteen. A baseball cap worn backwards hid his long black hair, and his voice was high-pitched and enthusiastic.

'My dad thinks it's cool. I hate it.' Jonathan walked into the living room and sat on the sofa.

Luke joined him. 'Oh wow. You got Pac-Man. Let me have a go.'

Handing the remote control to his friend, Jonathan walked out to the kitchen and filled two glasses with Coke.

Back in the living room, he placed the glasses on the coffee table. Luke was pounding the controller with vigour as he tried to evade the ghosts on the screen. He nearly knocked the drinks with all his enthusiasm.

'Hey, watch it. Don't spill the Coke. Dad will go crazy if we get any on the carpet.'

Luke nodded as the level finished, carefully reaching for a glass.

A white, Austin Morris Mini Van pulled onto the drive. Jonathan stood, peering out of the living room window. 'He's here. I'll grab a video.'

'Get something scary,' Luke called. 'There's that werewolf film in London. That's supposed to be sick.'

Jonathan walked along the hallway and out to the van.

'Hey, Jonathan. You OK?' Harry asked as he opened the van door and stepped onto the drive. As he spoke, a plume of condensation spilt from his mouth, and he zipped his jacket up to his neck with his fingerless gloves to keep warm. His thick black hair was floppy, his brown eyes damp, and his lips were chapped from the cold weather.

Nodding, Jonathan declared, 'We want something scary.' He walked to the back of the van, the familiar smell of damp cardboard invading his senses as he leant over the rows of boxes, his eyes bulging at the array of films. Thrillers, romance, comedies, and some naughtier ones towards the back.

Jonathan knew what he wanted. He'd heard about them. A couple of older kids in the neighbourhood had seen them. He needed to ask. Reaching towards the back of the van, he placed a hand on one of the plain covers. 'What are these?'

The guy looked at Jonathan, somewhat uncomfortable. 'Mate, I don't think you'll like them. They're a bit... what's the word? Warped.'

Picking one of the plain cases out, Jonathan turned it over and read the back. *A crocodile attack, the circus ringleader and the lion and other real-life footage*. 'I want this,' Jonathan confirmed.

Harry turned, rubbing the stubble on his face. 'Mate, your dad will kill me if he finds out. Can't you get something else? I've seen a couple of these. Jonathan, man, they're hideous. I can't let you watch it.'

Jonathan dipped a hand into his pyjama pocket and held out the case to the driver. 'This is the one I want.' The driver hesitated, before sighing and taking the money as the teenager walked inside, closing the front door.

Back in the living room, Jonathan tipped the box on its side, spilling the video cassette into his hand, and then loaded it into the VHS player. Switching the lead in the back of the TV, he hit 'play', then took a seat as white noise and digits displaying the date of the recording appeared on the screen.

'What's this?' Luke asked.

'Just watch. You wanted something scary. This is scary.'

The picture of a man standing by the side of a lake flickered into life. Subtitles confirmed the location to be Florida. The sun gleamed from the sky, and the camera was shaky as it tried to focus on the horizon. It panned over a small mountain in the distance and across yellow-coloured fields stained by the heat until it returned to the man.

'*Are you going in?*' a woman's voice asked from behind the camera.

The man turned, smiling into the lens as the camera zoomed in on his grey hair and down his tanned body. His bright shorts reached his knees, and as he kicked off his sandals, he stepped into the water. Relief from the warm day seemed to wash over him as he lowered himself into the water.

'*Is it nice?*'

A large splash formed as the guy began swimming further into the lake. '*Beautiful!*' he shouted.

'*Don't go too far out, OK?*' the woman said. She tried to focus the camera on the man as he swam, but it became blurry, flickering, dancing between the lake and the sky.

It focused again on the lake, picking out a dark shadow gliding fast through the water towards him.

'*Bert! There's something there,*' the woman shouted. '*Get out of the water!*'

There was a tremendous splash and screams echoed from the TV screen. Bert's hand clasped the air, outstretched and then disappeared as his body was dragged under.

Luke sat on the edge of the sofa, too stunned to talk.

The tape cut to static before focusing again on another scene. A lion in a cage, possibly in a zoo or the back of a circus. Again, the footage was grainy and blurred. But this was more raw and clearer to see. The cage door opened, and the lion looked towards the man entering its space. The cameraman asked what the guy was doing.

'*It's OK, just film. I'm used to this one. He's a big softy. I want people to realise if you treat them with respect, feed them and show them love, they can be tame and love back.*'

As the man edged towards the lion, the camera recorded his every move through the rusty iron bars. The sound of stones crunching under his shoes, his breaths sharp, tension rife in his voice as he told the person to keep filming. The lion pounced; a ferocious roar bellowed from the cage as it leapt on him, pinning him to the ground. The camera spun around, swirling and unfocused, the desperate pleas for help spilling from the cage as the cameraman screamed for help. The camera dropped to the ground, although on its side, it kept filming through the iron bars as the lion began taking chunks from the keeper's limp body.

Luke stood, unsteady on his feet. 'This stuff is twisted. No, you're twisted, Jonathan. I can't believe you like this shit.' He clutched his stomach with one hand, the arm of the chair with the other. His face had gone pale. 'Oh God, I think I'm gonna puke.' He turned and threw up all over the sofa.

'Luke! What the hell? My dad's going to go crazy.' Jonathan looked towards the vomit. 'Clean it up. Clean it now, you idiot.'

'Nah, no way. I need to get out of here.' Racing from the living room, Luke ran out the front door and across the street to his house.

Jonathan turned off the video, cleaned up the vomit and put Pac-Man back on, watching as the yellow circular figure waltzed around the screen, collecting pellets, the ghosts desperate to get out and give chase.

It was all about the hunt.

2

SATURDAY MORNING

The sun glistened on the car bonnet and the warm breeze pushed in through the windows of the BMW as it edged its way through the narrow country roads. The sky was pure blue, almost too blue, as if it had been Photoshopped.

Ed Carter leant forward in the driving seat, and glimpsed above at the single streak of cloud, like a lone splash in a majestic ocean. Wiping the sweat from his face with the sleeve of his T-shirt, he turned to his wife, Cass, in the passenger seat, who was lost in the thriller she was reading on her Kindle.

'I can't stand this heat. It's too much. Give me snow any day of the week.' When no response came, he continued. 'Hun, can we turn the air conditioning on?'

A groan spilt from her mouth. 'No. It dries my skin and plays havoc with my throat. I won't be able to talk by tonight.'

'Suits me.' Ed laughed.

'Oh, you'd love that.' Cass smiled as she shifted in her

seat; her legs felt numb, and the drive was taking its toll on her body. They'd left London hours ago, heading to a holiday cottage in Devon. The Airbnb advert had boasted complete privacy with high fences and a hot tub, and Cass couldn't think of anything she'd like more.

From the corner of his eye, Ed saw Cass lift the Kindle and continue to read. He waited a moment before asking, 'How's the book?'

She placed the Kindle back on her lap harder than she'd intended. 'It would be great if you'd let me read it.' Cass turned her body, eyeing her husband. 'Are you bored?'

He stared out of the window, watching the lush green fields, the empty winding roads and a thatched cottage in the distance, resembling a piece of art exhibited in an expensive gallery. 'Look around us. How could I be bored?'

Tree branches clipped the wing mirror, and the smell of freshly cut grass and pine filled the BMW. Ed inhaled the crisp scent deeply and realised that this was the first time in ages he'd felt happy.

He and Cass had been married for three years. Health complications meant they couldn't have children, and long working hours had been putting a lot of strain on their relationship lately. This weekend was a chance to tend to their relationship, an opportunity for them to go on walks, eat at a nice restaurant, share a bottle of wine with their phones turned off and enjoy some quality time in each other's company.

They'd met at a conference, entitled "Building Your Business Online." Cass owned a florist shop in London and wanted to learn more about selling on the internet, whereas Ed ran a health, training and nutrition course and wanted to take the class to a much wider audience.

After the first lecture had finished and everyone spilt outside, Ed and Cass remained at their desks and began talking. It turned out they had so much in common, and the spark between them was clear. They were both single, attracted to one another and decided to meet again. A year later, they were married.

Seeing a sharp bend ahead, Ed jabbed his foot on the brakes and eased the BMW around the corner. 'I have that meeting on Tuesday.'

'Oh yes, the guy you met at the gym?'

'Yeah, he reckons he can point me in the direction of loads of potential customers. He has a small franchise in Europe. Belgium, France, the Netherlands. Of course, he wants a big cut.'

'Don't they all.'

'I don't mind, though, if he can get people to sign up.'

'How much does he want?'

'Twenty per cent.'

She wiped the fringe of her short blonde hair from her forehead and her hazel-green eyes widened. 'Bloody hell, that's robbery. And you've agreed to it?'

'Well, nothing's signed. We'll meet and see how it—'

Out of the corner of his eye, Ed glimpsed a dark shape, something oddly positioned on the corner of a dirt path leading off the narrow road. They'd been driving too fast to really see, but he was sure his eyes weren't deceiving him. Looking in the rear-view mirror, he touched the brakes and pulled the BMW over to the side of the road. 'Did you see that?'

'What?' Cass asked. She placed the Kindle into the glove compartment, realising Ed seemed determined to stop her from finishing her chapter.

With his hand over his mouth, Ed muttered, 'I don't know. It looked like... It looked like someone was hanging from a tree.'

'Oh, Ed, really? Are you serious? You've been driving too long. It was probably a tyre swing or something.'

'No, I swear.' Ed undid his seat belt and pivoted to the left to see behind him. He peered along the vacant country road. They hadn't seen another vehicle for a while. 'I definitely saw something.'

'Well, do you want to call the police?'

Ed grabbed his phone from the dashboard and tapped the screen. The lone signal bar began flickering in the corner. Was he being paranoid? Had he actually seen something? There was only one way to find out.

Opening the door of the BMW, Ed climbed out onto the road. The heat hit him hard, and it felt like the sun was pushing all its force down on his body. He wiped the dampness from his forehead with his right arm. He could hear Cass removing her seat belt and fiddling with the lock. 'Stay here, please, Cass.' Ed ducked down and spoke through the window of the car. 'If it is bad, I don't want you to see anything.'

She hesitated, then dropped her fingers from the door handle and nodded.

As he walked back along the road, Ed could see the turning for the dirt track to his right up ahead; bushes from the fields loomed over onto the road, and tree branches stretched towards him like sinister fingers. The smell of a distant bonfire filled his lungs; birds squawked from one of the trees as they fought for territory. Ed shivered.

Halfway between the dirt track and the BMW, he hesitated. Breathing slowly, he tried to relax; his body was tense, but his muscles were preparing for the worst. A tractor started up in a field in the distance, and a plume of dark smoke rose into the air. He released his fists, unaware he'd clenched them in the first place, comforted by the knowledge they weren't completely alone.

Ed started walking again, the stony path crunching under his shoes, drowning out the distant tractor engine and the sound of birds fighting in the nearby trees.

On reaching the turning of the dirt track, Ed looked back to the car. Cass had got out, now standing at the side of the BMW, staring at him, but he couldn't make out her facial expression.

The towering hedgerows obscured his view down the dirt road. He took another step forward, turned to Cass, and then, facing forward again, he rounded the hedge, his body taut, his breathing erratic, bracing himself for what awaited along the dirt road.

That's when he saw it. His eyes hadn't been lying.

A large figure with thick rope around its neck and dangling from a tree branch.

Ed stepped towards it, and as his eyes adjusted to the gloom of the tree canopy, he began laughing. Tension poured from his body, his panic washing away and draining.

He walked back onto the road and waved his wife over. 'Cass. Come look.'

'What is it?' she yelled.

Ed remained silent, grinning, and waited for her to approach.

'What's there?' she asked as she arrived beside him. Cass clocked the smirk on her husband's face and tried to read his expression. He pointed down the track, and her eyes followed his fingers.

A papier-mâché figure, roughly the size of a grown man

with a balloon inked with eyes, a nose and lips for a head, hung from a tree. 'What is it? Some kind of freaky scarecrow?' Cass strolled towards it, touching the hard texture under a plain white T-shirt, black tracksuit bottoms and old worn white trainers. 'It doesn't make sense.'

Ed joined his wife and stared up at the figure. 'It's been constructed recently – the balloon is still very much full.'

The distant sound of the tractor suddenly deadened and the cawing birds took flight; the silence hit the couple. It was as if a blanket of nothingness had been pulled over them.

Cass stepped closer to Ed, the hairs on her arms standing on end. Something felt wrong.

Placing his arms around his wife, Ed said, 'Come on, let's go.'

She could hear the agitation in his voice as her husband guided her back to the road.

'Who do you think put it here?' she asked.

'Probably kids fooling around, or something.'

A few metres further down the road, a loud snap sounded from behind them, like a branch being trampled on. They spun around, but no one was there.

Ed reached for his wife's hand, gripping it firmly, and guided her behind him. 'Who's there?'

They walked a few steps backwards, before turning to face the car and picking up their pace.

A few more steps forward and the back of Ed's neck tingled, as if someone was breathing on it. He spun around and caught movement in the corner of his eyes. Something ducked behind the tall hedgerow by the track. Ed's heart almost leapt into his throat.

'Who's there?' he demanded.

Turning to join her husband, Cass's voice was hushed. 'Did you see someone? I'm really freaking out.'

'I don't know. Maybe a shadow, but I can't be certain. On three, we run to the car. OK?'

Cass nodded, gripping her husband's hand tighter.

'One... two... run!'

They spun around in unison, fingers locked tightly together, and raced along the narrow country road towards their vehicle. Their hard breaths spewed into the warm air, panic drenching their bodies, their gasps cutting into the muteness surrounding them.

As they reached the BMW, Cass turned. Behind them, a man was running. He was short, bald, with a pronounced limp that barely hampered his speed as he raced towards them. His right arm was outstretched and holding a mobile phone, as if filming.

'Ed!' Cass screamed.

He looked at where Cass was staring. 'Shit. Get in the car. Quick.' Ed fumbled with the keys, dropping them on the ground.

The man was getting closer. As he approached, they could hear him talking to himself, as if narrating what he was doing.

Cass yanked desperately on the door handle. 'Open the fucking door!' she screamed.

Finding the keys, Ed pressed the fob, and they both plunged into the seats and locked the doors.

Ed's shaking fingers struggled to press the button for the ignition. 'Come on, come on.'

Slam!

Cass screamed.

Their assailant had reached the passenger side, and was hammering at the window, then fiercely pulling the handle to open the door.

'Drive, Ed! For fuck's sake, drive!'

The car started, and Ed wrestled with the gears, fear drenching his body as the fist rained down on the window. The guy pointed the phone into the vehicle, scanning between Ed and Cass. 'I've got her,' he cried. 'It's her! I have her.'

Ed swiped the briefest glance in the wing mirror and hammered his right foot on the accelerator. The gears screamed as the BMW tore onto the road. The attacker fell to the ground, disappearing into the dust kicked up by the tyres.

* * *

Ed drove, the winding country road ahead pushing towards him.

Cass sat in the passenger seat, stunned into silence.

Breaking into the peculiar tension, Ed said, 'I guess he wasn't playing piñata.'

Perturbed by the smirk on her husband's face, Cass peered at his dishevelled black hair, his thick eyebrows high on his forehead, his blue eyes concentrating on the road. 'It's not funny, Ed. Who the fuck was that idiot?'

'Christ knows. It's like he's waiting there, luring people into a trap.'

'We could have been killed,' Cass sniped.

Placing his hand on Cass's lap, Ed took a deep breath. 'Look, let's not let one idiot spoil the weekend. It was probably some wannabe Youtuber with his phone looking for as many hits as possible on his channel. No one was hurt. It could have been just a pra—'

'Been what? A prank? Some bloody prank. The lunatic tried to get into the car – he thumped the glass, for Christ's sake. He would have killed us.'

Ed removed his hand from his wife's leg and placed it back on the steering wheel. As much as he tried to brush off what had happened, visions of the figure hanging from the tree played in his mind.

What had the guy intended to do if he'd got into the car?

3

SATURDAY MORNING

The satnav indicated they were around thirty minutes from the cottage. Tired from driving, Ed's eyes were heavy, his body numb, and he wanted nothing more than to unpack, grab a beer and sink into the hot tub.

Cass held the Kindle in her hands, but the words were just a mass of lines and shapes; her mind couldn't process what was written.

It was getting warmer; sweat trickled down Ed's face and rather than providing relief, the humid air flowing from outside proved more of a nuisance as it funnelled through the window gap and slapped against his skin. He eyed the knob for the air con, wondering if Cass would notice, and reached a hand forward.

'No. I've already told you, Ed.'

He whacked his hand back on the steering wheel. *They were almost there. Would ten minutes be so bad?* he thought.

Ed flicked his eyes to the rear-view mirror. They'd been alone for what seemed like hours, but now there was a large black Jeep sweeping fast along the road behind them.

His gaze returned to the road ahead. 'Is the book any better?'

'I can't concentrate. I keep thinking about the idiot earlier on. What do you think was wrong with him?'

'God knows,' Ed answered.

Cass shifted in her seat. 'Do you think that figure was a trap?'

Not wanting to scare Cass, Ed answered, 'I just think he was sick. Don't worry about it. He's long gone.' Ed wanted to believe his comforting words, but something didn't feel right. Why was the guy filming them? The man's words ran through Ed's mind as he pointed the phone at him and Cass. *I've got her. It's her! I have her. What did he mean?* Ed thought.

Shivering in the seat, Cass stretched her legs and placed her feet on the dashboard. 'I just need to get there?'

Ed looked back in the rear-view mirror. The Jeep was close and he could make out the outline of the driver. 'We're in Devon now. I'd say another half hour or so, depending on traffic.'

'It's like we've been driving for days,' Cass remarked.

'It certainly feels that way.' Ed rolled his shoulders and his joints clicked.

The Jeep was almost touching the back of the BMW. Ed squeezed the steering wheel, keeping silent rather than alarming his wife. He could see the driver clearly now and it wasn't the guy who'd stopped them earlier; this guy was younger and had hair. Probably just some idiot in a rush.

Tapping the brakes, Ed indicated, pulled over to his left-hand side and stopped. Maybe if the guy could overtake, he'd stop hugging his bumper.

But rather than accelerating off, the Jeep rolled to a halt behind them.

Oh, for God's sake. Placing his right arm out of the driver's window, Ed beckoned for the guy to overtake.

Suddenly the driver started flashing.

'What's going on? Why are you stopping?' Cass asked, placing the Kindle onto her lap.

'I'm not sure. The driver behind was right up my arse, in a rush or something. But now he's stopped and is flashing his lights. Maybe we have a flat tyre.'

Undoing her seatbelt, Cass turned her body, looking behind. 'Ed. Can you drive, please?' Her voice was sharp and intense.

'What's up?'

'I don't have a good feeling. He's sat in the Jeep, watching us. If we had a flat tyre, I'm sure he'd tell you as he passed us. Especially if he's in a rush.'

'Good point,' Ed said.

The man remained in the Jeep behind.

Cass twisted her body further around, looking out of the back window. 'I don't have a good feeling about this.'

Lifting his hand and attempting to calm the situation, Ed said, 'OK. Relax. Let's just get out of here.' Watching the road, Ed indicated and pulled out.

The Jeep followed.

Cass watched in the wing mirror, as the Jeep moved closer, almost touching the back of the BMW.

Seeing the same thing in the rear-view mirror, Ed pressed his foot on the accelerator. They were going close to fifty miles an hour; the stretch of road ahead was empty, but it was dangerous to speed.

The Jeep sped up too, clinging to the back of their vehicle.

'What the fuck is his problem?' Ed growled.

'You have to do something.'

'I'm trying.' Hitting the brakes, Ed furiously pushed his arm out of the window and waved for the driver to pass, pulling tight to the ditch. Again, the Jeep pulled up behind the BMW. 'What is this idiot doing?'

Cass looked behind. 'I think he's filming us.'

'What?'

'I mean, he has his phone out, and it looks like he's recording us?'

Ed turned and watched as the driver's door opened and the guy clambered out. He was tall, dressed in a red T-shirt and shorts and, indeed, had his phone in his hand.

Opening the window more, Ed yelled, 'What's the problem?' as the guy moved closer.

The man mumbled something they couldn't hear, but Ed wasn't hanging around to ask him again. As the guy reached the BMW, Ed stamped on the accelerator and pulled away.

The driver raced to the Jeep, closed the door and gave chase.

'Shit, Ed. He's coming,' Cass said. 'We have to lose him.'

'I'm trying. What is his fucking problem?' The figure hanging from the tree from earlier flashed across his mind's eye. 'Has everyone turned into fucking zombies or what? Maybe there's something in the air down here, like it's radioactive or something. Why are people acting so weird?'

'Something's going on, Ed. The figure in the tree, the bald man racing towards us with the mobile phone. The Jeep driver filming us.'

They remained silent, too stunned to talk.

Ed's eyes darted between the rear-view mirror and the windscreen. The long, narrow road suddenly seemed like the eye of a needle. The BMW was the thread, and he was desperately trying to steer through it.

They'd pulled away from the Jeep a few moments ago, and now the road behind them was clear.

'Have we lost him?' Cass asked.

'I hope so.'

They were still speeding, the needle tipping nearly fifty miles per hour, and a sharp bend approached quicker than Ed had anticipated. The wheels slipped under him. 'Shit!'

Cass slammed her right arm on the dashboard, gripping the overhand rail. Ed wrestled with the steering wheel as he tried to guide the large car round the tight corner. With a jolt, the tyres gripped again, and the car righted itself.

Letting go of the overhand rail, her knuckles still white, Cass said, 'Careful, Ed. We've got lunatics chasing after us, we don't need to crash the car too!'

Ed glanced back. The black Jeep suddenly appeared behind them, coming at great speed. 'Oh shit, Cass. He's still following us.'

Turning, she looked along the road. Her voice was raised, panic working through her body. 'Do something, Ed. You have to lose him.'

'I'm trying. What am I supposed to do?'

'Pull off somewhere.'

'There isn't anywhere to turn.'

'Well, go faster.'

'Cass, I'm already doing fifty. It's not saf—'

They jolted forward as the Jeep smashed into the back of the BMW.

With her hands on the dashboard, Cass screamed and panic filled her body. The Jeep backed off and ramped up the speed again. They jolted forward a second time.

Ed yelled out of the window. 'Leave us alone, you fucking nutter. What do you want?' Gripping the steering wheel, he stamped his foot on the accelerator, desperate to gain space between both vehicles. The Jeep was large and powerful, and the driver was determined to stop them.

They approached another sharp bend, and at the speed they were travelling, Ed struggled to manoeuvre the BMW around it; fighting with the steering wheel and jabbing the brakes, he narrowly avoided the ditch. In the wing mirror, he could see the Jeep a little further behind. Ahead, the road stretched for a half-mile or so, and he desperately needed to lose this idiot.

As the speedometer began rising, Ed saw a vehicle to his left, powering down a hill towards the main road. He pointed into the distance. 'Someone's there. Maybe they can help us.'

Cass watched, her fear diluting slightly at the sight of another vehicle. 'Flash your lights. Let them know we're in trouble.'

With his left hand, Ed furiously flicked the switch, trying to alert the other driver.

Again, they jolted forward.

Holding the sides of her head, Cass screeched, crying out in desperation, and grabbed the overhand rail.

'Cass. I'm going to get us out of this. Please keep it together.' He flicked his eyes at the vehicle to his left, close to the main road. 'It's not slowing down.'

'Keep flashing. Maybe they haven't seen us.'

They were around two hundred yards from the turning. The vehicle was almost at the main road, now camouflaged behind the trees. The Jeep was closing behind, and Ed was still flashing his lights. Pounding the horn, he turned to Cass. 'Hold tight. I'll stop that car and get us help. We're going to make it.'

Her terrified expression didn't need any further explanation.

One hundred yards from the turning to their left, the vehicle seemed to have disappeared. The Jeep was almost touching the BMW, and Ed had his foot pressed to the ground on the accelerator. The speedometer read sixty-two miles an hour.

Twenty yards.

Ten.

'Where the hell has the car gone?' Cass asked, gripping the overhand rail tighter.

Ed glanced towards the turning, expecting to see the vehicle stationary, waiting to exit onto the main road. 'I don't know. Please don't say they've U-turned and gone back the other way.'

Suddenly, the vehicle rounded a sharp bend, powering towards the main road. In a matter of seconds, it would be on top of them.

'They're not stopping, Ed!'

The woman in the driver's seat gripped the steering wheel, her face contorted in a sinister, wicked expression.

Ed hit the accelerator, and they rushed forward. The car came hurtling out of the side road, missing their rear bumper by inches and smashing into the side of the Jeep.

A plume of dust rose into the air in the BMW's rear-view mirror, sweeping above the car like an ominous cloud from a nuclear plant spillage.

As Ed hit the brakes and both he and Cass turned to watch the stationary vehicles, the scream of car alarms cut through the air.

Ed looked to the front, glimpsing in the rear-view mirror and then pulled away.

4

A FEW DAYS BEFORE

Her screams ripped through the farmhouse. The smell of damp faeces worked into her nostrils, seeping into her body. It was on her skin, her clothes. She choked on the pungent fumes; she wanted to vomit but only saliva built in her mouth, and she spat it out.

That morning, Corinne Myers had woken, showered, dressed and cooked a fry-up – the full works. She'd had revision to do for her last exam in a few days' time and had decided that a hearty breakfast would be ideal brain food. The sun shone through the window in the kitchen as the eggs, bacon and sausages sizzled in a pan, and although still early, the air that pushed in through the kitchen door was warm.

Looking over her physics books as she ate, Corinne felt good about her revision. Most of the preparation had already been done, so the examination room at Nottingham University wasn't so daunting anymore. She'd worked hard for this, and nothing would get in her way.

As she finished her food, dipping the last piece of bread into the remnants of her egg, she stood and placed the plate and cutlery into the sink. Turning on the tap to wash up, the strange call from her mother last night resurfaced in Corinne's mind.

At just gone 10 p.m. the previous evening, her mobile had rung. Corinne answered her mother's phone call, aware it was late, instantly asking if everything was OK with her father.

Anne, her mother, began telling Corinne about her day; a trip to the shops, the meals she'd cooked and a BBC drama they'd started watching. After a short gap, Anne told her about a weird link she'd received on Facebook Messenger from a friend. Not going into too much detail, it had promised the chance of winning money every Friday.

Curious, Anne put in a few basic details and waited. An hour later, while in her bedroom, she received a sinister message with a load of rules which needed to be followed. But what frightened Anne so much was the picture she'd received.

It was Corinne, her daughter, sitting in her living room, wearing pink pyjamas and watching TV.

The picture had been taken through the window late last night.

Then a threat.

Break any of the rules and we'll kill your daughter.

Corinne asked her mother to send over the picture, but Anne had already deleted the link.

Now, as Corinne looked out into the garden, a shiver punched through her body as she recalled the conversation. It frightened her, knowing someone was watching. Why had they taken her picture and sent it to her mother?' Grabbing her phone, she dialled her mother's number and listened to it ring. '*Hi, you've reached Anne Myers, I can't come to the phone right now, but leave a message and I'll get back to you.*' After dialling a second and third time, Corinne decided to call over to the house.

Something wasn't right.

Placing the phone on the worktop, she peered once again into the garden. Her legs buckled at the sight of two men wearing balaclavas storming along the side entrance. Before she could react, they walked brazenly into the kitchen, and one of them punched her so hard in the face it sent her crashing to the floor. The other assailant grabbed her, stifling her screams with a cloth doused in chloroform as he pinned her to the floor.

The men were professional in their actions, stylish and accurate, and knew what they were doing. They remained silent, calm and in control.

One of them dashed back to the van, parked a few hundred yards away, and reversed along the side entrance to the rear of the house. The details of a false decorating company with a name and phone number were marked across the side door, and a number of ladders were secured on the roof.

No one would question them.

Once the coast was clear, they quickly loaded Corinne into the back of the van and drove away.

'Help me. Someone help!' The room was dark; shadows appeared like a haze of white noise, resembling a TV struggling to pick up a channel, a blur in front of her.

Corinne's head was sore, aching from the substance the kidnappers had used to knock her out. She remembered eating, placing the cutlery and plate into the sink and then seeing two people walk around the side of the house and into the kitchen. Then her world went dark.

Dropping to her knees, Corinne stretched her arms out like someone sinking into quicksand. She shifted on her knees, the cold, stony ground uncomfortable as she pawed into the bleakness. 'Can someone help me? Is anyone there? What do you want?' Turning her head to the side, she listened to the stillness, certain she could hear a voice in the distance. 'Hello?' It sounded like muffled cries coming from the other side of the house. There was definitely someone else there.

Corinne scrambled to her feet, swiping in front of her with her hands. Her legs were heavy, her body tender as she stumbled forward in the darkness and reached a wall on the other side of the room. Slamming her palms against it, Corinne edged to the right and felt a handle. She pulled it down, trying to force the door open.

'Please. What the fuck do you want?' Pounding on the door, panic worked its way through her body. 'I can get you money. My father can transfer it instantly. However much you want. Can you hear me?' Corinne's breaths became erratic; her body seemed to close in on itself, the sense of being crushed now overwhelming. 'I can't be here. I beg you. Please let me go.'

Stepping back from the door, she listened, sure she heard someone in the house. A stifled cry. 'Hello? Can anyone hear me? My name is Corinne Myers, and I've been kidnapped.'

The house was still.

She charged against the door, grabbing the handle and desperately jerking it up and down, banging the palms of her hands against the wood until they burned.

No response.

Falling to the ground, she held the sides of her head and pulled at her long black hair. 'I'm not supposed to be here,' she sobbed. Facing the door, Corinne yelled, 'This isn't fucking happening. Open the door. You have to let me go.'

'Corinne?' a voice whispered.

She looked up. 'Who's there?' Crawling on her hands and knees, her tired body about to collapse with exhaustion, she mustered the strength to push her arms out, pawing into the darkness.

'Corinne?'

The voice was coming from the corner of the room.

5

SATURDAY MORNING

Their hearts soared as Ed and Cass saw a sign declaring Bideford, a historic port town in North Devon, was ten miles ahead.

Cass wiped the tear-smudged mascara from under her eyes, stunned by the events a few minutes ago. While Ed was dazed, glaring at the road, unable to comprehend what had happened. Since they'd witnessed the vehicle racing towards them and smashing into the Jeep, they hadn't said a word to each other.

Ed had his foot firmly to the floor, glimpsing in the wing mirror and wondering if they'd imagined the whole episode. The scenes played out in his mind: the figure hanging from the tree; the guy racing towards them, pointing a camera at them; the Jeep, the crazed woman pulling out of the turning. None of it made sense, like something had seeped into the air, a toxic gas playing with these people's minds and driving them crazy. It had to be a strange cult or a commune that didn't welcome strangers. It was the only explanation he could think of, but he acknowledged how absurd he sounded.

Grabbing her phone from the dashboard, Cass saw she had reception. 'I'm calling the police.'

Nodding, Ed insisted she withheld the number. If there was some kind of cult causing havoc, he didn't want to give the address of the cottage. He listened to Cass explaining what had happened and where to find the crashed vehicles.

'It's on the M5. Around fourteen miles from Bideford.'

'About twelve,' Ed insisted.

Holding up her hand, Cass said, 'My husband reckons twelve... No, we didn't get the registration plates... No, we didn't stay there. It wasn't safe. I told you our lives were in danger. We were under threat... A what?... It most certainly wasn't a hit-and-run. Look, I've told you where to find the vehicles. I've done what I needed to do... No, you can't have our names.' Cass hung up. 'Unreal. She's saying it's a hit-and-run. How dare she!'

Ed placed his hand on Cass's leg. 'It's over now. Let's put it behind us.'

'You're right.' She smiled at her husband, placing her hand over his as she began crying again. 'It's over.'

* * *

Glimpsing at the turning for Bideford Farm and Cottage, Ed pulled the BMW into the drive. A long metal barrier barred their way down the farm track.

'Wait, I have the code.' Ed grabbed his phone from the coffee holder and opened the notes app. He got out of the car and tapped the four-digit code into a small box on the wall and the barrier creaked into life. As it lifted, Ed turned back to the BMW and assessed the damage. It wasn't as bad as he'd expected. The bumper hung lower on one side and was cracked, but there didn't seem to be any dents in the metal. The bumper had taken the brunt of the impact.

Back in the driving seat, he held Cass's hand. 'Are you OK?'

Nodding, she answered, 'What a fucking crazy ride. What happened back there?'

'Hey, we survived. We're here. Look around you – this place is amazing. Let's put it to bed.' Ed leant forward and kissed his wife on the cheek, feeling her hot, sticky face on his lips.

They drove alongside a field full of sheep and cows on their left, and a row of stables lined the slender path, which they guessed housed horses. To their right side was a small lake, trees and bushes shaped into fake animals: a giraffe, a kangaroo and famous landmarks from around the world: Big Ben, the Eiffel Tower, the Leaning Tower Of Pisa and the Arc de Triomphe – either that or Marble Arch, they couldn't tell. A lone cottage sat towards the end of the drive, the only building in the small complex.

Ed tapped the accelerator and drove the BMW along the narrow, stony path, still looking in the rear-view mirror.

'It's amazing, Ed,' Cass declared. As they pulled up outside the cottage, she undid her seatbelt and stepped out of the vehicle. The sun beamed from above, her head began to clear, and she felt her skin tingle. The air smelt so much cleaner than in London. The scent of freshly cut straw, wildflowers and strawberries was apparent. Breathing in the crisp air, Cass's mood lifted. Finally, they could really relax here.

Ed stepped out of the BMW, grabbed the bags from the boot and strolled over to the lockbox to retrieve the keys.

The cottage itself was like something from a Constable painting. The roof was thatched, bright yellow in colour and triangular-shaped. The white painted stone facade peaked out from greenery growing up its walls, and although it must have been centuries old, the building was still in good condition. Eight mullion windows and a red oak door added a touch of elegance.

Turning to Cass, Ed smiled, holding the key up like it was the Holy Grail. 'Ready?'

She nodded.

The key slipped into the lock and the door eased open. The couple gasped as the stunning interior was revealed. A spiral staircase wound up to the first floor, and oak beams hung overhead. The floors were decorated with large black tiles, and frames hung on the walls with photos of the cottage many years ago. The smell was overbearing but pleasant, like burnt coal in a barbecue that had long gone out mixed with freshly ground coffee beans.

Ed closed the door and locked it. Looking through the window, he glanced up towards the farm entrance, breathing a sigh of relief that they were safe.

* * *

After they'd unpacked and showered, Cass's body completely sagged as she relaxed into the hot tub, pleased that her request to lower the water temperature had been honoured. She'd seen weather reports and emailed the owner of the cottage yesterday evening.

Ed, armed with two glasses of chilled champagne, walked out to join her. Cass took the glasses and sipped indulgently as Ed adjusted his knee-length Bermuda swimming shorts, conscious of his stomach hanging over the rim. Once he'd loosened the strings, he felt more comfortable and climbed in beside his wife. Sinking into the warm water, he felt the tension of the earlier dramatic events evaporate from his body. He took his glass back from his wife. 'Cheers.'

'Cheers.' The crystal made a tiny clink as they toasted the start of their weekend break.

Peering beyond their glasses and across the field through the robust fencing surrounding the garden, Ed was struck by the remoteness of the place. Not wanting to say anything to Cass, he merely sipped his champagne, cursing those idiots earlier for putting such a dampener on their holiday. All he wanted was some time to relax, and now he was haunted by images of hanging scarecrows and lunatics in Jeeps.

Cass lay back, careful to keep her hair out of the water, and adjusted the straps of her bikini. Ed took his wife's hand under the water.

'Hey.'

A voice startled them.

Ed looked up to see an elderly man standing by the fence and staring at them. Although the temperature was sweltering outside, he wore a heavy-looking jacket, trousers and boots. A Stetson hat kept his head slightly sheltered from the sun.

'Can I help you? This is private property,' Ed stated. His body tensed. He'd had enough of local weirdos for one day.

Cass gripped his hand tighter under the water, clearly feeling the same.

'Sorry if I startled you. I'm Neville. I work here. I'm off now. So you'll be alone. Any problems, my number is pinned to the fridge door. But be warned, it may be no use to you – the reception is dire here. There's a Wi-Fi code, again pinned to the fridge, but you'll be lucky if it works. Good day to you now.' With his right hand quickly touching the side of his head as if to salute, he walked away.

Cass pushed out a heavy sigh. 'Christ, he's hardly going to win employee of the year.'

Ed laughed, the anxiety seeping from his bones once again. 'Now, let's get back to enjoying our holiday.'

They sipped the champagne and began splashing each other until water covered the decking.

* * *

It was late evening; Ed and Cass had sat in the hot tub for hours until their skin had become wrinkled and itchy, and the growls of their stomachs drew them to the kitchen.

Ed was cooking steak and potatoes; the smell of garlic and onion enticed their appetite tenfold as the pan sizzled on the electric hob.

Cass sat at a small round table, re-reading the chapter that she'd tried to get through in the car, now finally able to digest the words.

Looking out over the fields through the kitchen window, Ed said, 'How beautiful is it here? Such incredible light and no unsightly street lamps or noisy neighbours.'

Cass looked up from her Kindle.

He turned from the cooker to his wife. She looked mesmerising in a white dressing gown, make-up free and the tips of her blonde hair damp from where she'd failed to evade the hot tub water.

'It's stunning—a place you'd never want to leave.' Cass stood and joined her husband at the counter, kissing him firmly on the lips. Grabbing a glass and filling it with water, she followed his gaze out into the garden. The lights of the hot tub peeked out from under the cover, the pump purring gently. Her eyes moved further up over the field, tracing the skyline until—

Cass dropped her glass, shards spraying over the tiled floor.

'Shit, Cass. Are you OK? Here, let me get that. Don't move, you'll cut your feet.'

'I saw someone. Someone is out there,' Cass proclaimed.

Ed bolted upright and looked out the window. 'Where?'

'Across the fields. Look.'

'There's no one there, Cass.'

As she peered through the kitchen window, the figure was gone. 'Ed, I saw someone.'

'It's probably Neville.' Moving out to the garden, Ed walked over to the fence, stood on the rockery and looked into the fields. 'See, there's no one there.'

Cass joined him. 'Someone was. I could see a figure. And it seemed to be staring right at us.'

'Well, it's gone now. Come on, dinner's nearly ready.'

Ed wrapped an arm around his wife's shoulder and guided her back into the kitchen. He'd hoped that it was just a bottle of champagne on an empty stomach and Cass's imagination playing tricks on her, but deep down he feared she'd been right; after this morning's events, anything was possible.

* * *

After they'd eaten, Cass and Ed cleared the plates and cutlery, one washing, the other drying and placing everything in the correct drawers. The cottage had a dishwasher, but they'd forgotten to bring tablets.

When the kitchen was clean, Ed walked over to a cupboard, finding an assortment of board games.

Pulling out a pack of cards, he placed them on the table. 'A game of snap?' he asked.

Cass walked across the tiled floor and sat at the table. 'Snap, indeed.' Her body felt tense, thinking about the figure standing in the field earlier. Today had been so weird, and she needed to talk about it. As Ed shuffled the cards, she placed her hands on his. 'Are we safe?'

Looking up and dropping the cards on the table, Ed stared into her eyes. 'Yes. We're safe. I'm not going to let anything happen to you.' He slid his hands from under Cass's, grabbed the cards and continued shuffling. 'Hun, today was madness. I can't explain or begin to comprehend what happened. If I told someone, they'd struggle to believe me. But it's over. Look around you. We're not in any danger.'

Cass pulled the chair closer to the table. 'So what the fuck was it all about?'

'I don't know. People were behaving so bizarrely. Maybe it's something in the water down here. Best stick to the champagne.' He laughed.

Looking at the cards, Cass asked, 'What are we playing?'

'Poker. Get your money out,' Ed smiled as he began to deal out the cards.

Cass chuckled. Looking at her phone while she waited for Ed to set up the game, she saw the dull Wi-Fi signal blink and go completely empty.

Picking up her cards, she glanced up, and caught sight of movement at the fence through the kitchen window. Panic rose from her stomach and seemed to lodge in her throat.

'Ed,' she choked out. 'Someone's outside.' Kicking the chair from under her, she backed away against the cool stone wall.

Ed stood and turned to the window. 'Are you sure?'

'I saw a shadow. Someone is there.'

Dropping his cards on the table, Ed raced across the kitchen and out to the garden. 'Who's there?' Running to the fence, he stepped on the rockery, the sharp edges cutting into his feet as he peered into the fields. 'Hello? I'm calling the police. Is someone there?' He switched off the hot tub and listened to the silence surrounding them. Ed waited for a few moments and then backed slowly into the kitchen. He pulled the door and locked it. 'No one is out there. Cass, are you sure you saw something? Do you want to go home? We can if you want.'

She stumbled back to the table and began picking the edge of the cards to stop her fingers from shaking. 'I'm so scared.'

Ed reached for her hand, clasped it and pulled it to his chest. 'I'm not going to let anything happen, I promise.'

For the next couple of hours, they sipped wine, played cards, laughing together, enjoying each other's company.

Ed was disgruntled with the lucky hands Cass was getting. He'd have a pair; she'd have two. He'd have a straight, and Cass turned over a flush.

Just before midnight, light-headed with the alcohol and feeling woozy, Cass stood. 'I need my bed. You coming up?'

'Oh, I see, fleece me for all my money and then run. I know your game, missus.'

They embraced, and Ed placed the two empty bottles of red wine and the champagne into the recycling box. Switching off the kitchen light, he followed Cass up the spiral staircase.

After undressing, they brushed their teeth in the en-suite bathroom towards the back of the bedroom, and Ed turned off the light and crawled into the luxurious king-size bed beside his wife. Cass stretched. 'I'm going to sleep for the rest of the weekend. You don't mind, do you?'

Pulling her close, Ed insisted, 'The weekend is yours. Do what you want. We have no one to answer to.'

'What a day,' Cass sighed, snuggling up to Ed's chest. The window behind them was open, and they were thankful for the cool air pushing through the gap.

'It's certainly one we won't forget.'

A few minutes later, the cottage was silent.

The lights were off.

Cass and Ed were asleep.

* * *

Cass woke, her eyes struggling to focus in the pitch-black, forgetting for a moment where she was. Had something woken her? The silence throughout the cottage was unnerving. She turned over in the bed, reaching for her phone on the side unit. Just gone 1 a.m. Still no signal, and the Wi-Fi patchy at best. Returning her phone to the bedside table then closing her eyes, Cass buried herself deeper into the duvet and tried not to think about earlier, desperately trying to push the terror she felt from her mind.

A sudden thump from the floor below caused her to sit bolt upright, eyes wide, her stomach tight, like a fist twisting inside her. Listening hard, she held her breath, too scared to move. Had she imagined it?

Another thump. Like the palm of a hand slapping against the front door.

Her body sprang to life and roused from the temporary paralysis. 'Ed. Ed.' She shook him awake. 'Quick. Someone's downstairs.'

'Huh?'

Reaching for the side light, Ed felt the cord, running his fingers along it and clicked the switch. The room brightened. He shifted his body up the bed, leaning against the headboard and looked at Cass, wondering if her mind was playing tricks. Yes, they'd had a rough day, but was she becoming paranoid? 'Are you sure you weren't dreaming?'

'I know what I heard,' she snapped.

Pivoting his body, Ed placed his feet on the wooden floor and crept to the window. Below, he saw a security light angled and pointing towards the ground. Pushing his face to the glass, he tried to see if anyone was down there. Ed backed away, turning towards the bedroom door. 'I'm going to check.'

Cass climbed out of bed and followed. They stood at the top of the spiral stairs, close together, watching the front door. They'd left the light on in the hallway before going to bed—something which took the edge off the isolation.

Ed crept down the stairs, taking one step at a time; Cass waited in the upstairs hallway.

On the ground floor, he turned back, facing Cass and then looked through the glass of the cottage door. The security light still glared; Ed was unsure if it had been on all evening or if something had stirred its awakening.

Unable to see anything, he grabbed the key from the rack and unlocked the front door, leaving it inside the barrel. His hands shook while his heart felt as if it could stop at any moment. Standing on the front step, Ed called, 'Is anyone out here?'

'Can you see anything?' Cass called from the top of the stairs.

'No—'

A shadow caught the edge of the security light. Something moved in the bushes along the path leading to the cottage. Ed stepped out and walked towards it. 'Neville? Is that you?'

The moon beamed down onto the farm, the stars an incredible spectacle scattered in the clear sky, but Ed didn't want to be here. Not anymore. He and Cass had felt on edge while driving here, and with so much weird shit happening in such a short space of time, and Cass so freaked out, Ed wasn't sure he was enjoying himself anymore.

A silhouette ducked in the bushes before disappearing out of sight.

'Who's there? Neville? Is that you?' Ed stepped forward onto the path, the stones cutting into his feet. 'Neville? Are you here? Stop messing aroun—'

The front door slammed behind him.

Ed turned and raced towards the cottage, barging against the wood. 'Cass. Open the door. Cass, can you hear me?'

Her cries reverberated from within as Ed hammered on the locked door.

6

1981

It was almost a week since Luke had watched the snuff movie at Jonathan's house and vomited on the sofa. Although Jonathan had scrubbed it and doused it with detergent he'd found in the kitchen cupboard, his parents still detected the foul smell as soon as they came home from the cinema. His father had pulled him out of bed and made him scrub it again until his hands were sore.

After insisting no one else had been in the house, Jonathan's father had seen two glasses on the living room table. Because of the lies, Jonathan was banned from going out for a week, and Luke was barred from the house.

Bored, he sat in his bedroom, listening to his mother greet his friends whenever they called over. 'No. Jonathan's not well today.' 'Sorry, he can't play football, his leg's sore.' 'His bike has a puncture.' She used every excuse in the book.

Angry and determined to punish his parents, Jonathan stayed in the bedroom, only coming down for meals. He sat on the bed, reading the *Beano*, laughing to himself at a segment with Dennis the Menace and Gnasher. He dreamed of being like Dennis. With a dog as his loyal best friend. The two of them making as much mischief as possible, winding people up, neighbours, friends, schoolteachers.

Jonathan wanted to be like Dennis so much!

Flipping the page over, he heard shouting coming from across the street. He dropped the comic on his bed and walked to the open window, keeping hidden.

Reaching for the binoculars he kept in his top drawer, Jonathan held them to his eyes and adjusted the focus. He zoomed in, seeing Mr and Mrs Shirland, standing in their living room opposite, arguing with one another.

Jonathan felt excitement; his body flushed with adrenalin as the two adults faced each other; wanting nothing more than to see a savage outburst or a full-blown argument ending in tragedy. Mrs Shirland pushed her husband and charged out of the living room.

Jonathan's heart sank. Hungry for violence, he played out scenarios in his head of all the ways this situation could end. But not this, not Mrs Shirland racing away like a scared rabbit. Boring.

This wouldn't do.

If he was going to invest his time watching them, the least they could do was put on a show for him.

Crossing the bedroom, binoculars in hand, Jonathan opened the door and stood at the top of the stairs. His parents were in the living room with the door closed and the TV loud. He closed his bedroom door and crept down the stairs, easing past the living room, careful not to stand on the creaky floorboards, and opened the front door, leaving it on the latch.

Outside, the cold air hit him; clouds smothered the sun, and the air was a dark grey. Jonathan turned, his body tense as he stared back at the living room window. Thankfully, the curtains were closed, so his parents wouldn't see him leaving the house. Adrenaline pushed him, controlled his puny body and drove him to keep going.

As he crossed the road, staring at the semi-detached house opposite, he saw the gate leading to the back garden was open. He turned, making sure his parents weren't standing at the front door and walked along the side entrance of Mr and Mrs Shirland's house.

A water feature buzzed; a majestic-looking angel placed on a love heart, a bow and arrow in its hands and spilling water from its mouth. Jonathan peered at the shed that looked like it was about to topple any second. The lawn was messy, the grass long and unkempt, and dead flowers drooped over in the flower beds. It smelt of dead leaves. The paving was stained black, and moss had worked into the gaps. The Shirlands clearly weren't green-fingered.

Jonathan turned to face the house and crept towards the kitchen window, his body alive, buzzing, his skin tingling.

Mr and Mrs Shirland stood by the kitchen cupboard. The back door was open, and he could hear everything.

'How dare you do this to me! You bastard. After twenty years? She's a whore. How could you?' She was leaning against the counter and edging her body away from him.

Mr Shirland moved closer to his wife. 'It meant nothing. It was a mistake. How many times do I need to apologise?'

'Where did you do it? In the bed?' she fired back.

'Please. Don't do this.'

Her voice raised to a scream. 'Answer the fucking question?'

'Yes. OK. In the bed, but it meant nothing. It's you, I love. Please, I didn't mean it to happen. You have to believe me.'

'Get out. Get out of this house!'

Mr Shirland stood, opened-mouthed. 'You'll wake the kids. Please, let's sleep on it. We'll talk in the morning.'

'You're not spending another night in this house. I said, get out.'

'Please, Sally. I have nowhere to go.'

'You should have thought about that while you were fucking that whore.'

'Don't call her that. It was me. All me—'

Mrs Shirland raised her fist and punched her husband squarely in the face.

Jonathan watched from the garden, hidden behind a large bush, his body charged with anticipation, watching in awe as Mr Shirland grabbed his wife, spun her around and held her. She shook frantically, screaming for him to let her go, kicking her legs back, saliva spewing from her lips, her face red and twisted with anger. It looked as if she'd explode any second. As she kicked back again, she caught her husband on the shin. Doubling over in pain, he held his leg and lashed out, slapping her across the face.

Jonathan stared through the kitchen window, feeling so many incredible emotions: passion, warmth, amusement, joy, happiness. This was how he wanted to spend every day of the rest of his life. Stood, getting into people's private lives, watching, viewing, practically smelling the fear behind closed doors.

This was him.

It was what made him tick.

As the Shirlands battled, Jonathan peered through the window from the garden, watching as she picked up a knife and rammed it into her husband's stomach.

Jonathan smirked like Dennis The Menace and stepped away, walking casually across the road and up to his bedroom.

7

A FEW DAYS BEFORE

'Corinne?'

A man's voice, coming from the corner of the dank room.

Corinne pushed her arms out, pawing into the darkness, her legs fragile, like twigs supporting a forest. Her breath was jagged, thrusting from her lips; her mouth stale, her throat raw.

As Corinne moved to each corner of the room, bracing herself for an attack, her fingers didn't touch warm flesh, but cold plastic. A speaker? It had to be where the voice was coming from. Her tense body loosened slightly.

'What do you want? Please let me go. I can't be here. I'm begging you.' She turned, listening for a noise, a distant voice, anything to confirm she wasn't alone. 'My name is Corinne Myers. Is anyone else here with me? Don't be frightened. We can do this together. We can help each other.'

Her heart pounded as a remote cry resonated from another part of the house.

Swiping at the dim around her, Corinne charged

towards the door, placing her ear against the cold wood. 'Can you hear me? I'm going to get help.'

Again, another muffled cry. It sounded like it was coming from a basement or well.

Slumping on the ground, Corinne pressed her hands against the sides of her head, screaming, trying desperately to stem the panic attack that was sweeping over her body. Leaning forward, she placed her head against the ground, gulping the foul air and pushing out until her lungs were empty. In for five, out for five.

No. She wasn't here. She was somewhere far away. She allowed her mind to transfer her to a beach. The warm sand under her feet, the strong smell of seaweed, the taste of salt in the air. Children building sandcastles. The sun warming her body, her skin tingling as she walks hand in hand with her parents. In the distance, surfers ride the waves, gliding on their boards; families charge into the cool water, splashing, laughing together; the smell of diesel as jet skis circle close by reminding Corinne of her father's garage; and a large ship looking so elegant as it traces the horizon.

The loud creak of the door opening brought Corinne out of her happy place, casting a shaft of insipid light across the dank floor.

Holding her breath, she waited for a shadow to block the light. But nothing came. Then the light beyond her room disappeared.

She stood, sneaking towards the door and looked out, only a blanket of darkness shrouding her. With her hands held in front, she stepped into the vast space, her breaths light, her body tense. 'Hello?' Someone had opened the door. This was a good sign. Surely she could escape?

Corrine didn't have the luxury to wait. She had to get out; staying in the room would only lead to her demise.

The App

Her hand touched a wall; the smooth surface was solid and cold to the touch. Running her fingers along the surface, Corinne used it as an aid to find the exit. In desperation, she whispered into the bleakness, 'Hello? Is anyone else here? If someone is here, can you bang once?'

A loud noise, like a box dropping to the ground, caused her to jump. Spinning around, Corrine tried to focus on the space around her.

'Who's there? Hello?'

A faint creak, like a door opening, resonated beside her. A floorboard moaned. 'Who's there? Please help me.'

She turned, pawing the wall, her hands jabbing it, sliding along its surface until she felt a door. Searching for the handle, Corrine looked behind her into the dark hallway, her hands grabbing at the cold brass in front of her, and she yanked it downwards. The front door opened, and she sighed with relief as she glimpsed over a farm, aided by a security light facing out.

Feeling the stale odour from inside the farmhouse leave her lungs, she laughed, a release from the torturous hellhole where she'd been held for so many hours.

As she walked along the path, she glanced back, the bright glare from the security light stinging her eyes and the shape of the farmhouse in the shadows becoming distant. She inhaled, walking along the path to freedom.

Reaching the end of the drive, Corrine stared across the fields surrounding her. The air was so fresh; the scent of newly cut grass brought her back to her childhood when her father mowed the lawn, and they'd play football, have family picnics and bounce on the trampoline.

The night was clear, and the moon provided enough light for her to see. Millions of specs across the sky seemed to form the shape of angels, hovering above as if guiding her away from this hellish nightmare.

She had no idea where she was, but instinctively, she followed a path to her left – any place was better than here, even if she got herself lost. Her muscles relaxed and with each step, the anxiety subsided a little more.

The growl of an engine starting up in the distance broke her reverie.

She turned, ducking into the foliage along the path and peering at the farmhouse. Had they found her door open? Were they coming for her?

More security lights flickered into life, pointing at the property.

It looked so threatening.

So alone.

Secluded.

Two bright lights suddenly appeared, blinding her. They'd found her.

'No, no, please,' she whispered. Corrine ran, the path now fully illuminated by the headlights moving towards her.

She sprinted along the path, her legs aching and gasping for breath. The sound of the van's engine grew louder. She had to get off the path. They wouldn't be able to follow her through the field.

Corrine leapt into the ditch that ran alongside the path, but as she hit the ground, a searing pain rushed from her ankle as it twisted, and she hit the hardened dirt with a thud. Above her, the van pulled to a stop. Through the open window, she saw two people sat in the front wearing balaclavas—probably the same people who had come for her earlier. She couldn't be caught again.

Holding her leg and bawling in agony, she desperately

pulled herself to her feet, but her ankle wouldn't bear the weight, and she collapsed down.

'Why? Why the fuck are you doing this?' she screamed above the sound of the engine.

She didn't expect a response, but the person in the driver's seat leered at her and spat out, 'Because your mother deleted The App.'

The person in the passenger seat held his phone out as if recording.

The van revved its engine, then drove forward and rammed into Corrine as she lay on the ground, crushing her in the ditch.

Around Britain, dozens of people stared at their phones in horror; the consequences of deleting The App were now clear.

8

SUNDAY MORNING

Marty Benson sat in the kitchen, listening to the bacon, sausages and eggs sizzling in the pan, the fat spitting like an agitated snake. It was all going swimmingly – bearing in mind his cooking skills normally extended to heating up a microwave meal – the smell of burnt toast wafted into the air. Turning, he yanked out the now cindered pieces of toast while half the kitchen filled with a plume of deathly grey smoke.

Coughing, he walked over to the hob, turned down the gas just as the smoke alarm began wailing. 'Oh, for crying out loud.' Grabbing a tea towel, Marty proceeded to waft the air like a swimmer performing the butterfly stroke.

Just before it felt like his arms would fall off, the beeping stopped.

Bent over, the palms of his hands resting against his thighs, he took a deep breath and called for his family to join him.

'Beth. Abbey. Food's ready.'

Marty forked the burnt sausages, the shrivelled bacon and blackened eggs from the pan and placed them on a plate in the middle of the table, dropping hot oil onto the tiled floor.

The slow footsteps coming down the stairs confirmed Beth was the first to rise. As she walked into the kitchen, her black hair tied up, her deep brown eyes focused on him and a teasing smile; he waited for the harsh critique.

'I don't need to say anything, do I?'

Pouring coffee from a pot into two mugs, Marty looked up. 'I don't have a clue what you're talking about.' The toast – the second round, the first being beyond saving – popped, making him jump.

Beth laughed, eyeing the toaster, which had delivered yet another two burnt slices. 'I'm not that hungry, to be honest.' Her expression was one of awkwardness; even Marty could agree the food looked about as appetising as a wet flip-flop.

Marty walked to the hallway. 'Abbey. The food's getting cold. You're missing out – I've excelled myself this morning.'

Upstairs, a faint groan was heard, followed by the thump of heavy teenage feet, before a bedroom door clicked open, only for the bathroom one to slam shut almost immediately afterwards.

'So, what's your plans for today?' Marty asked Beth as he sat at the table, placing the toast on a plate and smothering them with butter. *If no one else was eating, there was no point wasting it,* he thought.

'I'm meeting Mum – we're going shopping in Oxford Street.' Beth grabbed the least burnt piece of toast, holding it up like a shopkeeper inspecting a fifty-pound note. She took a bite, spilling black crumbs onto the plate.

'Oh, nice. It will be good for her to get out.'

'Yeah, she's bored. I've enticed her with the promise of

lunch as well. She needs to get out more. Since Dad died, she's lost her confidence. I feel so sorry for her.'

'We did ask her to live here,' Marty pointed out.

'We did, but Mum likes her independence. She has a routine. We'll never change her.'

'Routine?' Marty smirked. 'Breakfast TV, followed by *This Morning*, *Loose Women*, reruns of *Columbo* and then old movies. It's a routine, all right. I don't know how her arse isn't blistered.'

'Oh, Marty, I'm eating.'

The stairs pounded, and Abbey's radiant face appeared at the kitchen door.

'You've missed out. Too late, mate,' Marty jested.

'You better be joking.' Abbey walked over to the table and sat down. Staring at the plate of food, she said, 'Christ, Dad, I don't know whether to eat it or bless the ashes.'

'Less of the sarcasm, young lady. I've slaved over this.'

Abbey eyed her mother, and they both laughed.

'We're going into town in a short while. I'm treating, Nan. You fancy it?' Beth asked.

'I would, but I have so much revision. My final exam is this Tuesday.'

'That's sensible.' Beth smiled at her daughter, so proud of the effort she'd put into her school work. Abbey was eighteen and in her final days of sixth form. She was going to the University of Leeds in September after getting an offer to study law, depending on her grades. Her hard work was finally paying off.

'I might come?' Marty said as he stuck his fork into a sausage. One side was black, the other a dull yellow colour.

'No. Not a good idea,' Beth snapped.

'Why?'

Leaning back on the chair, Beth added, 'Because you're a

nightmare to shop with.'

'How so?'

'I can picture it now. You'll moan about carrying our bags, dragging your feet around the shops, bored, whining at the prices, and then you'll want to go home.' She placed her hand on her husband's face, pushing her fingers through his cropped black hair and, gazing into his azure-blue eyes, Beth rubbed his heavy stubble. 'I love you, but you're staying here. End of.'

'Your loss.'

'Maybe so, but I want a relaxing day.'

'I'll get the forklift,' Marty said.

'Forklift? What are you on about?' Beth asked.

'To peel your mother off the sofa.'

Beth broke off a piece of toast and threw it at her husband. 'Git.'

* * *

After breakfast, Beth got ready. Although early, the temperature was already in the late teens, and the sun was so bright, bathing the city in heat from a glorious sky.

She showered, slipped into a bright yellow floral dress and added a touch of blusher to her high cheeks, followed by a smidge of lipstick and eyeliner.

After kissing Abbey and telling her not to put too much pressure on herself, Marty dropped Beth off at Dollis Hill station, picking her mother up on the way.

Back at the house, Marty FaceTimed his parents and then caught up on invoices. He worked for himself, carrying out small building works, and had built up a decent customer base. Beth helped when she could, as well as running her own reflexology and well-being classes.

Once the invoices were updated, Marty debated whether to cut the lawn or sit on the patio and read. He looked at the garden through the kitchen window; until he'd done the former, he knew he'd never be able to enjoy the latter.

Abbey was up in her room, revising; her window was open, and the curtains were gently blowing with the warm breeze.

'Do you want a coffee?' Marty shouted from the patio.

'I'm OK. Thanks, though.'

Marty pulled the lawnmower out of the shed, placed it on the grass, unravelled the long electrical cord and pushed the plug into a socket in the kitchen.

His phone beeped—a WhatsApp message from Davey Hughes. Marty unlocked his phone, expecting to see a joke or a funny picture. He was a little confused by what he saw.

Look at this. Mate, it's incredible. Click the link and download it. You can win huge amounts of money every week.

Marty walked away from the lawnmower and sat on a chair on the patio. The link was short, coloured blue with no gaps; nothing alarming. Davey was his best mate. Marty trusted him and fired a message back.

What's this shit? Is it for real? We need to meet for a beer soon.

Staring at the screen, Marty waited for a reply. The sun was hot, high in the clear sky, and it began to burn his skin.

The idea of winning a shedload of money was alluring; the business was going well, but he'd love to take Abbey and Beth on a holiday when Abbey had finished her exams. With a bit of extra money, he could make it really special. And Davey was as straight as a die, not the type to send junk or spam. They'd been friends since school. If Davey sent the link, it was legitimate.

Impatiently, Marty sent another message.

I'm curious about this link. Can you talk?

He looked to the top of the screen; Davey was offline.

Impatience got the better of him, and he called Davey, listening to the dialling tone and hung up. Hovering his finger over the screen, he jumped as the phone began ringing. Beth.

'Marty. Could you run the mower over the lawn quickly?' his wife asked amidst the background noise of the busy London shopping streets.

'I'm about to do it. How's your mum?'

'She's fine. Hot and bothered, but the shops have air con, so she'll survive.'

'She's missing a great episode of *Columbo*,' Marty chuckled.

'I can hear you,' Ethel croaked. 'Pillock.'

'What's Abbey up to?' Beth asked.

'Revising. She's certainly dedicated, bless her.'

'Tell her I said to take breaks.'

'Will do. Enjoy your day. Speak later.' Marty hung up.

He checked WhatsApp again; Davey was still offline.

With the mobile phone in his left hand, again reading Davey's message, Marty clicked the link.

A screen opened. The word 'Loading' appeared at the top, and a row of dots flashed next to it.

'Come on then. Show me how I can win money' Marty was dubious, and he wasn't stupid; he wasn't going to add credit card details, enrol in bitcoin or anything resembling gambling. Holding the phone screen to his face, he tapped the glass and started shaking the phone as if it would make it load quicker.

Suddenly another screen opened, and a small box appeared, asking simply for his first and surname—nothing else.

'OK. This is straightforward enough, I guess.' Tapping the letters underneath, he proceeded to spell 'Marty Benson' and pressed enter.

'Please Wait' appeared at the top of the screen, and another row of dots continually illuminated and disappeared.

Holding his breath, Marty was now fully invested. The link Davey Hughes had sent was captivating, luring him like a worm on a line. He watched the screen impatiently, his eyes staring as the dots blinked.

'Well, come on then. Show me the money,' Marty laughed.

He placed the phone on the table, 'Please Wait' still showing at the top of the screen. He'd mow the lawn and then come back to it; he had better things to do than stare at a loading screen.

Marty stepped across the patio, seeing the air shimmer with heat. Wiping his forehead with the back of his right hand, he grabbed the lawnmower. The loud whirring noise filled the garden as he glided it over the grass.

* * *

A half hour later, Marty's face was dripping with sweat; his cheeks were flushed, his short black hair damp and perspiration dripped down his neck, staining his T-shirt. He wound the cable around the lawnmower and placed it back in the shed. The WhatsApp link had played on his mind as he mowed, his body tingling at the thought of being able to win some real money.

Marty wasn't a gambling man, and the only time he ever had a bet was at the weekend with a couple of pounds on a football accumulator. He'd invested a few hundred pounds on a pyramid scheme in his late teens, and the loss haunted him for years after. Money was too hard to earn and so easily lost. The motto he reminded himself of if ever tempted.

Walking to the table, those words hung in his mind. Marty picked up the phone, the screen still showing the message to wait. What was the point if the damn link wouldn't open? He placed the phone in his shorts and made his way back inside.

After a cool shower, the cold water easing his hot skin, Marty placed the wet clothes into the laundry basket and grabbed fresh ones from the bedroom upstairs. Tapping the door to Abbey's room, he found her lying on her bed, reading a law book. 'Do you fancy going for a walk?' he asked.

'Maybe later. I'm going to revise for another hour or so, and then I'll come down.'

'Do you want a coffee?'

'No. Ahh, Dad, I know your game. You're bored, aren't you?' Abbey's smile beamed towards him.

'No. I'm good. I'll just mooch downstairs and try and find something to entertain myself. Don't worry about me.'

Abbey laughed. 'Give me an hour. I've revised enough. My flipping eyes are becoming blurry.'

'Whatever you think. Love ya.'

'Love ya, Dad.'

Marty went down the stairs and into the kitchen. As he moved towards the kettle, his phone pinged. For a moment, he'd forgotten about the link Davey Hughes had sent. As he stepped across the floor to the table, he picked up his phone.

The link had downloaded an app. A message popped up on the screen:

. . .

- Do not delete The App.
- Do not tell anyone outside of your family about The App.
- Send the link to one person who is close to you.
* Do not throw your phone away.
* Always narrate while streaming.
- If you break any of the rules, we'll kill a member of your family. Then we'll kill you.

'What the fuck?' Reading it a second time, Marty felt weak, the kitchen a momentary blur. The threat was direct, intense. Suddenly, the words disappeared and another screen loaded automatically, like The App was in charge, seeping through his phone, winding its cogs and enveloping its fingers around his life and squeezing relentlessly.

A photograph appeared, and Marty's legs went weak, like his weight was too much for them to carry. The image was of his wife, Beth and her mother, Ethel, walking along a busy street. Beth was wearing the bright yellow dress with flat shoes she'd left the house in; Ethel wore a simple white blouse and knee-length skirt. The same clothes she'd been wearing when he'd picked her up this morning.

He zoomed in, his fingers spreading over the screen, seeing the two women so clearly. Marty's blood was pinging around his body like a pinball machine; his chest tightened, and despite the heat of the day, his body was suddenly icy cold as a sense of horror enveloped him.

Another screen loaded. Marty watched on in horror as a message appeared in bold, black writing.

You are now part of The App.

Break any of the rules, and we'll kill Beth. Then we'll come for you.

His eyes seemed to bore through the screen, burning a hole in his mobile phone, the contents of The App too terrifying to digest. They'd sent a picture as a threat to follow the rules.

Marty stared as yet another screen appeared.

Thank you for downloading The App. We want to welcome you. This is a one-of-a-kind offer where you will have the chance to win £100,000 every Friday.

This is not a joke. Please don't take it as such. It's a project that's taken some time to develop, and there's nothing else like it in the world. A first of its kind, and you have been chosen to come along for the ride, to be a part of its history.

Let me explain the rules.

Every Friday morning, a person is randomly picked from social media.

They now have a bounty on their head—a death warrant. But they don't know it.

Their profile will appear on The App's main page; all their details will be displayed. We'll give hints in real time as to the whereabouts of this person.

Every app member must follow the rules and play the game at least once a month or face the consequences.

Please remember this.

All you have to do to win £100,000 is be the first to kill the person randomly selected from social media.

Good luck.

9

SUNDAY MORNING

Marty's hands shook as he dialled Beth's number.

She answered on the fourth ring. 'Wow, you can't leave me alone for five minutes. What's up now?'

'Beth. Are you with your mother?'

'Sorry, what? I can't hear you – the traffic is really noisy.'

'I said, are you with Ethel?'

'Of course, who else would I be with?'

Taking a deep breath, struggling to compose himself, Marty spoke. 'Listen, you need to come home.'

A car horn roared in the background, people's voices, conversation. 'Is Abbey OK?'

'Yes. She's fine.'

'We're just about to go for some lunch.'

'Please, I can't talk over the phone. But you need to realise this is urgent.' The threatening words from The App ran through Marty's head. *You are now part of The App. Break any of the rules, and we'll kill Beth. Then we'll come for you.* 'Please, Beth.'

'Marty, you're scaring me. What's wrong?'

'You need to come home.' The rules stated he could share the details with his family and no one else. Marty had no choice but to take the threat seriously. 'Are you listening to me?'

'Yes. Fine,' she snapped. 'Mum won't be happy – she was really looking forward to a lunch out. This better be urgent, Marty.'

As Beth hung up, Marty whispered to himself, 'It is.'

Marty clicked back into The App. The main screen was still open, and the introductory message he'd read a few minutes ago was still displayed. He read over it again, his mouth open, his skin tingling with fear.

The picture of Beth and Ethel, shopping in Oxford Street made him feel sick. Both anger and terror worked through his veins, but this was only the beginning.

At the top of the screen, there was a small square made up of lines. Wrapped in curiosity, he clicked it, and a menu appeared, allowing him to go deeper into The App. The word 'Chase' displayed, and below it a list of different dates.

Taking a huge breath, Marty put his phone down and stood to close the kitchen door. He didn't know what these links would reveal, but his gut told him that he wouldn't want Abbey walking in on it.

He sat back down at the table and opened up his phone again, his sweat-drenched grip loose on the device.

Under the first link:

This is what happens if you don't participate.

Marty clicked it, and after a brief pause, a video clip loaded.

Phone camera footage. The camera lens was pointed to the ground then slowly lifted to reveal a house surrounded by fields. It must have been early evening, still bright. The building stood alone, isolated. The screen panned the area, wild and remote. The lens was blurred by rain, and whoever was holding the camera was struggling to keep the image clear.

Then, over the sound of thundering rain, a woman began to speak, her voice breathless and tense. '*Narrate? The pressure I'm under, and you want me to fucking talk? Fine, I'll narrate all right, so others can see the torment I'm going through and maybe do something to get me out of this hell. OK. You sick bastards have forced me into this — I don't want to be here. I'm not a killer. Everything I live for and believe in, my morals and values are the opposite of what you want to turn me into.*'

'*See, I got a link a few days ago from a friend. I don't blame her. After reading the rules and seeing the hideous crimes within The App, I know she had no choice. I've learned how you force people into doing things they don't want to participate in, and I ask anyone watching this, you deluded fucks, would you take part or risk the consequences? Imagine you click the link sent to you by a friend with the promise of winning vast amounts of money, and an hour later, you get a picture — say it's your parents, daughter, son, husband or someone else who you couldn't live without, who you'd die for — and these people send a fucking picture with horrendous threats against that person.*

'*It happened to me. I signed up after a friend sent the link. I received a photograph of my parents, sitting at home, watching TV. I'd literally just spoken to them on FaceTime. I'd asked them about their day and how they were. Then the picture came through.*

'*My mother was wearing the same cream-coloured cardigan I'd seen in our earlier conversation—my father in his favourite chair, a pipe in his hand and a newspaper on his lap. I knew then that this was no prank.*

'*So yes, well done, you've forced me into this. Ask yourself, if your family were at risk and the only way you could save them was by taking part in the hunt, would you do it? Well, would you?'*

The phone camera flicked to the ground, the grass long on the narrow road and the wind loud as it pushed into the speaker. Her voice was muffled for a few moments as she made her way along the path towards the house. The woman who'd been speaking began sobbing as she lifted the camera to focus on the huge windows at the front of the building; a figure briefly appeared , silhouetted against the cosy lights as someone strolled around inside.

Through her cries, the narrator began speaking again.

'I don't know if she's inside. I can see a kitchen. So this is it. Shall I knock? Maybe break a window? Or go around the back and hope there's a door open?'

The phone camera focused on the terracotta brickwork, lifting to the first floor then scanning over the rest of the structure. A security light above the front door sprung to life. The camera swung around in a blur.

'Shit. I thought I heard someone behind me.'

Washing over the fields and the dark grey sky, the camera turned back to the kitchen window before moving forward, focusing on the inside of the property. Dirty dishes and cutlery sat on the counter, a TV on the wall showed a news bulletin, magnets stuck to a chrome fridge, an electric hob and a shelf with a few pictures in wooden frames.

The narrator gasped, and the camera ducked below the line of the window as a man and woman entered the kitchen.

'It's her. I can see the woman picked from social media. She's so beautiful... So young...'

Tentatively, the camera rose up again to reveal a man wearing a crisp white shirt and a pair of jeans, standing in his bare feet. The woman wore a blouse, a pair of shorts and white slippers. The man leant against the counter and pulled the woman close into an intimate embrace. He tucked a strand of loose hair behind her ear then drew the woman into a kiss. It started as affectionate, the couple clearly very much in love, before climbing in passion as hands started to explore.

Suddenly, the camera pulled away from the window and the view dropped to the ground again. *'I can't do it,'* the narrator said, sobbing. *'I'm not supposed to be here. I can't fucking do this. I hope you burn in hell.'*

The screen went blank.

Marty's right hand trembled as he held the phone. Dropping his head into his left hand, he rubbed the stress knot from his forehead, trying to digest the horror, fear, despair and every other emotion this woman felt. He could feel it pouring from her body as she stood outside the kitchen window. It seemed to seep from the screen and fester in his own veins. He'd never seen someone so frightened.

The kitchen was silent, and the only sound was his heart pumping hard in his chest.

Holding the phone out and preparing himself, Marty clicked the second link.

A woman stood in the kitchen, drying plates. It seemed she was unaware of being filmed. He could hear the heavy breaths of the camera holder. Suddenly, her mobile phone rang.

'Hello? Who is it? Hello?'

As she placed the phone back on the worktop and turned, Marty froze, recognising her voice.

The camera zoomed in. It was the same woman who'd been outside the house in the first video.

'No, no, no, no...' Marty muttered under his breath as the

woman in the footage walked towards the camera, oblivious of its presence, and turned in the hallway, out of sight.

Marty guessed the person recording must have been hidden in a storeroom or cupboard.

A few moments later, a toilet flushed, and the woman came back into shot. Then the camera dropped to the floor, only showing footage of the hallway. Footsteps pounded, causing the screen to vibrate, followed by a woman's scream off camera. Then silence, as the recording finished.

Another link showed yesterday's date. Marty clicked it and waited for it to load.

The camera was jumpy, the footage slightly grainy. Marty jolted in his seat as the image swung round to reveal a figure hanging from a tree. The camera zoomed in, and he was somewhat relieved to see it had a balloon head. The dummy was dressed in a pair of tracksuit bottoms, a T-shirt and white trainers and swayed gently in a breeze.

Someone started speaking.

'I've set this up to lure Cass Carter into a trap. I haven't done this yet; it's the fourth week since signing up to The App, and I know the consequences if I don't participate. I understand the rules. I had a picture sent to me via The App. My daughter, my beautiful baby. They'll kill her if I don't play the game.

'She was pictured at school, in the classroom. Kate has her whole life in front of her, her dreams and aspirations. She will be a success and wants to study psychology at university. She's been accepted. I won't say which one, not here.

'I remember the day she got her offer – the excitement, anticipation. I ran towards her, lifting her in the air and swung her around the kitchen. That night, we celebrated. My daughter, my wife and me.

'I can't jeopardise her life, her happiness. I can't do that. So here I am, a part of this barbaric game.'

The stream cut in and out, the phone camera moved around, unfocused, pointing at the figure dangling from a tree. A dirt track became visible, shrubs, bushes; the man was on a country road. Marty could hear him breathing; he sounded unfit, tired, and most definitely didn't want to be there.

'*I learned from the clues posted on The App that Cass is driving towards a particular place. Again, I'm not going to give anything away; I can't share hints as I don't want anyone else to win the money. It may sound wicked, even selfish, but if I have to do this, there has to be something in it for me.*

'*Don't get me wrong, a hundred thousand pounds is life-changing; it will allow my wife and I to live comfortably, afford holidays and weekends away, and help my daughter get through uni. But I'm not a killer. I wouldn't harm a fly. Ask any of my friends; they'll tell you the same. I am not a murderer. I am doing this solely because my daughter's life depends on it. Kate is in danger. The rules state you must participate at least once a month in the hunt. So here I am. Fuck the money. This is to save my daughter's life. They'll kill her if I don't do it, or at least try. I don't know how I'll deal with it afterwards. How will I sleep at night?*

'*If you're watching this, please know, it's the only reason why I have to kill Cass Carter.*'

The phone camera spun around to the empty main road, before swinging back and focusing on the figure hanging from the tree.

'*OK, I can hear a car in the distance, and I'm hoping Cass Carter is inside it.*'

The camera flicked to a BMW in the distance, driving along the country road.

'*Let me see if I can focus this thing. There, can you see it? The car is coming this way, and it's the correct number plate. I have Cass Carter in my sight. Right, let's do this.'*

He ran to the figure, pushed it and the papier-mâché man swung like a pendulum on a clock. Marty heard the branch bearing its weight begin to creak.

'I'm going to hide behind this bush. Hopefully, she'll stop. I haven't figured out how I will kill Cass. I'm thinking, either with the rock I found earlier – wait, let me show you.' The camera focused on the ground, and a man's hand holding a large stone came into view. *'Or I will strangle her – one of the two. The car is getting closer. I can hear it as it tears along the road. It's almost here. I hope she stops. She has to stop.'*

The camera began shaking in the man's hand, his heavy breaths sharp and erratic. Then laughter. Why was this man laughing? Nerves, terror, excitement? Marty couldn't tell which.

'It's stopped. Yes. The BMW has pulled over. It's worked. OK, bear with me as I figure out my next steps. I'll narrate quietly. Oh shit, I can hear a man's voice. Fuck. She has someone with her. Well, this has thrown a spanner in the works. The footsteps are closer – I need to hide.'

Marty could hear voices, a man calling to his partner and asking her to come over. She joined him, seeing the papier-mâché sculpture. After inspecting it, the woman began to freak out, and they moved away.

The camera holder started to speak again.

'I have to do it now. It's my only chance. If I'm forced to kill, I might as well win a hundred grand for it. I have to try.'

Watching as the camera jumped up, Marty heard footsteps heavy on the ground as the man ran towards the BMW. The woman stood by the passenger door, screaming her husband's name, before scrambling into the car. The camera holder caught up to the vehicle and desperately tried to get inside. As he pulled the handle and slammed his fists against the glass, the vehicle pulled away, and the screen went blank.

Marty threw the phone down onto the table as the reality hit him like a sledgehammer. This guy holding his camera phone and trying to lure Cass Carter into a trap, waiting out on the lonely road to kill an innocent woman in a brutal act, was persecuted. He'd downloaded The App and had been forced into this inhumane situation.

A chill worked through Marty's body, and his skin stung as he desperately tried to digest what he'd seen. He inhaled deeply, and the kitchen became a blur, reaching for the arms of the chair to right himself. Standing for a moment, steadying his body, he blinked, trying to focus. After a moment, he walked to the sink, grabbed a glass from the cupboard and filled it with water from the tap. Slugging the first one, Marty had a second glass and pondered whether to fill it with whisky.

Marty had never been so frightened in his life; The App's content was horrific, and he was now a pawn in the twisted competition.

He sat again, pulling the chair closer to the table, and dialled Davey's number. He listened as it rang, hung up and dialled again, leaving a voice message. 'What the fuck is wrong with you?' he shouted before realising Abbey might hear him and ask what was happening.

Like morbid curiosity, passengers in a vehicle staring out at an accident, cars wrapped around each other and everyone gasping, Marty had to keep looking at the links, trying to understand and digest what he'd been drawn into. He clicked the next link. Also dated yesterday. The stream began with an excited voice, loud and boisterous.

'I have her in my sights. The BMW is around five hundred

yards along the road. I can see the vehicle. I haven't a clue what I'm going to do, I'll play it by ear, but I think I have Cass Carter.'

The phone dropped, and the screen went blank.

'*Shit, hang on.*' The long stretch of country road reappeared as the person filming placed the phone back on the dashboard. His voice was deep, and he seemed eager, as if the ethics of the game didn't greatly concern him. Marty wondered what kind of person was behind the camera.

'*I'm gaining on her. I can see the vehicle ahead, maybe a couple of hundred yards away now. I'm getting closer; I can see the number plate. Hang on, oh shit. She's got someone with her.*'

Marty could see the road, the BMW ahead, the picture jumping as the driver seemed to speed up.

'*I intended to overtake her, stand in the middle of the road and pretend I'd broken down. But I'm not sure what to do now. Plan B, I'm thinking. Ram them off the fucking road? This is my second time participating in the chase. The first one was a month ago after getting a threat they'd murder my wife. I almost had the last guy, Paul Adams. This time, I'm determined to succeed. The money's in the bank already. I've committed to the idea. I saw a link, what they do if you don't take part in the chase. Christ, they broke into his house and strung him up, beating him to death. I can't let that happen to me. I refuse, so this is me now, my life, as a hunter. There's no other choice. I'm a part of this sick game.*'

As the guy spoke, honesty evident in his voice, he rammed the BMW from behind.

'*Come on, pull over, you bastards! I have you, Cass. I have you.*' His voice suddenly became loud and perverse as he rammed the BMW again.

The noise was overbearing; Marty had to turn the phone down, frightened Abbey would hear. How the hell would he begin explaining the contents of The App to his daughter?

Marty continued listening as the guy narrated, thrill in his voice, shouting, telling Cass to pull over.

Again, the phone dropped, and the sounds of car alarms rang out as the stream finished.

The audio cut out just as Marty heard a key twisting in the front door.

10

A FEW HOURS EARLIER

Fists thumped on the front door as Ben Ward stood in the hallway of the cottage. He'd been watching the couple from a field, waiting patiently for the right moment but jumping at every vehicle that drove past, worried someone else would come and steal the trophy.

Ben lived in Devon and had worked out where Cass Carter was staying from the clues posted on The App. While watching others try to get to her, he recognised the road leading into Bideford. Then the next clue led him straight to the cottage.

Parking his car on the side of the road, he walked around the barrier and hid in the fields, watching them in the hot tub and seeing an elderly man standing by the fence, talking to the couple.

At the sight of Cass so close, Ben's heart jumped with anticipation, knowing what he had to do and how close he was to the prize.

He'd signed up to The App after receiving the link from a close friend and adding his details. The next thing he knew, there was a photo of his daughter out with her friends and a threat that she'd be killed if he didn't take part in the hunt. He knew what he had to do to keep her alive. He'd watched the streams, the outcome of not taking part. Ben had no choice. It had been four weeks, and this was his last chance.

After hiding for hours, his body restless, his knees sore, Ben had to draw them out and get into the cottage. At one stage, he thought the game was up when Cass saw him in the distance and her partner came out into the garden and looked over the fence.

He remained tucked away until the man had returned inside, locked the kitchen door and moved to another part of the cottage. Then Ben became desperate and agitated; time was running out.

Later, when the lights went off and Cass and her partner had gone to bed, he crept to the front door, and waited, pacing back and forth, his stomach sick with worry. At any moment, someone could jump him and secure the prize for themselves, and he couldn't have that.

Ben banged on the door and then ran to hide in the bushes, listening to the key fumble in the lock and the panicked voices inside.

Cass's partner opened the front door and stepped along the path. 'Neville? Is that you?'

Ducking out from behind the bush, Ben slipped inside the cottage. He hid in the shadows and checked out his surroundings. Then he heard her voice, coming from upstairs.

'Ed, come back. I'm frightened. Ed. Can you hear me?'

This was his chance. He removed the key, slammed the cottage door shut and stepped into the moonlight cast across the black tiles.

Cass gasped as she saw a figure in the hallway. Her legs

The App

gave way under her and her body dropped onto the stairs. 'Leave me alone!' she screamed, desperately backing away. Her eyes were wild and filled with terror as she watched the man climbing the stairs; Ed's voice and his thumps on the door seemed so distant. Turning, Cass charged along the upstairs hallway. She had to get away.

Ben listened as her light footsteps raced across the ceiling, followed by a door slamming. He wanted to hold her hand, tell her his predicament, and assure her he didn't want to be here either, but he had to be strong and take charge. Removing the phone from his trouser pocket, seeing there was no reception, Ben decided to make a video recording and load it to The App later.

'One of the rules states we must narrate, make it exciting for the people watching. So fuck it, here goes. I'm not giving my name for fear of backlash; The App's creator, whoever you are, has my ID number. If I win, and I have no doubt it will happen within the next few minutes, I'll send my bank details and this whole mess will be over. That's what they've promised.

'Cass is upstairs on the first floor, and I think she may have locked herself in a room. I'm uncertain whether she's got a phone and has called the police. If she has, I will run as soon as I hear the sirens. There's the possibility they will still kill my daughter if I'm caught, so I will do everything possible to avert being arrested.'

Cass's partner continued to pound on the front door, shouting for Cass to hide, but Ben ignored him as he continued to stalk up the stairs. The phone shook in his hand as the camera focused along the floor and across the hallway and then on a room to his right side. The door was closed.

As he searched for Cass, Ben guided the camera over the

thick oak floor, the white walls, and the triangular arch constructed with wooden beams that lead to what must be the main bedroom at the back of the cottage.

Creeping along the upstairs hallway, Ben walked through the arch and into the bedroom. Panting, loud wheezing sounds emanated from his chest as he scanned over to the units on either side of the bed. There were two mobile phones which put him at ease; they wouldn't be able to call without their phones.

There was only one door left on the floor, and Ben pointed the camera towards the bathroom at the back of the bedroom. He reached out for the handle.

'I'm so sorry for what I'm about to do. God forgive me.'

On the other side of the door, Cass cowered beside the bath, curled into the foetal position, her head down, her hands clutched to the sides of her face. She'd locked the door from the inside, but when the handle shook, she feared how long it would hold. As the crunching sounds began, and someone threw their weight against the door panel, she screamed so hard her throat felt raw.

Ben held the phone camera, showing the bedroom wall as he barged his shoulder against the door, thrusting his body with as much force as he could muster. He thought about the many people who'd watch the stream, wondering what they could be thinking.

The vibration of the impact against the wood caused his back to ache; he was tired and suddenly weak and didn't know if he had the energy to go through with this. The cracking sound of the wood as it splintered was loud in his ears, Cass's cries became more amplified as if puncturing his brain. It was now or never.

The bathroom door gave way, falling off its hinges, and Ben shoved it back, dashing to where Cass was lying. As she screamed, he balanced the phone on the edge of the bath and grabbed her, turning her body, forcing her onto her front and kneeling on her back with all his weight as she fought beneath him. Reaching over the bath, Ben fitted the rubber plug into the waste and turned on the taps. The flow of water was strong, and it wouldn't take long before there was enough for what he needed to do.

Cass tried to lift her body off the floor, but the man was too heavy.

'What the fuck do you want with me?' Her voice was raspy and weak as she struggled to breathe. 'Help. Someone help me. Help.'

The water splashed loudly into the bath, as were the screams, but Ben kept silent. He was already a nervous wreck, and speaking with Cass would surely give away his vulnerable state of mind.

Grabbing the phone, the video recorder still running, he pointed at her as she struggled to get up; Ben pressed his leg harder against her back. Cass, pleading for her life, begged him to let her go, but Ben remained muted, concentrating, focused on what had to happen.

The minutes waiting for the bath to fill seemed like hours to both Ben and Cass. Once half full, he dropped the phone camera face down on the floor, gripped her hair tightly in his right hand, and pulled her to her knees, forcing her body over the edge of the bath.

'Please don't do this. I'm begging you,' Cass screamed.

Remaining silent, Ben forced himself to concentrate and stay in the zone; if he acknowledged her as a person, another human being, with a life, a family, Ben wasn't sure he could do this. With all his strength, he silenced her screams and pushed her face into the warm water. As he held her there, he grabbed the camera and continued to film.

Waving her arms, trying to hit out at her assailant, Cass desperately tried to escape, thumping her fists against the bathtub, bubbles pushing to the surface as she screamed under the water.

'This is to spare the life of my daughter,' Ben said over and over, filming Cass struggling against him.

Feeling the life drain out of her, Cass had one last shot. Her vision was already blacking out and she only had seconds left. With what little strength she had left, she swung her leg back, catching Ben in the groin. The blow was hard, and he whipped back his hands, as he stumbled and dropped to the floor, the phone landing next to him.

Cass turned and using the bath to help her stand, still coughing up the bath water, she lifted her leg and stamped on the man's groin again.

Doubled over in pain, Ben turned onto his side and howled.

Cass charged out of the bathroom, but he was too quick and reached behind him, grabbing her ankle and forcing her to the floor.

Again, she kicked out, catching him in the face, and crawled on her hands and knees into the bedroom.

The pain in Ben's groin was almost unbearable, but he forced himself to stand, grabbing the mobile phone and shoving it in his pocket. Half hobbling, he reached Cass and pulled her up by the hair, yanking her head back, to make her stand and face him. He swapped his grip and wrapped his fingers around her throat, then pulled out the phone again and pointed the camera. Marching her backwards across the room, he pinned her head against the wall, his hand like a vice around her throat, squeezing with everything he had. Holding his phone with his other hand, he filmed it all, as the blood seemed to drain from her face and she gasped for breath, but he couldn't watch and turned his head away.

Cass brought her hands to Ben's arms, clawing at the skin with her nails. Her vision was hazy and unfocused, darkness creeping in. This was it. Her body was about to pass out. This was how she was going to die—

Then, suddenly, with a roar, Ed burst into the room. 'Get off her!' The air rushed into her lungs as Ben released his grip and Ed barrelled into him, shoving him against the window pane. The glass shattered and Ben dropped to the ground outside.

* * *

Cass's body gave out, and she crashed on to her hands and knees. Even though her airway was no longer restricted, she still struggled to draw in air, and strange wheezing noises came from her mouth as she tried to clear her throat.

'Cass, Cass, are you OK?' Ed knelt beside his wife, rubbing her back to help her breathe. She vomited on the floor, her face ghostly white, the veins in her neck protruding. When her stomach felt empty, and she couldn't puke anymore, Ed handed her a tissue from the side unit, and she dabbed it on her lips, leaning back against the wall for support.

Ed stood and stepped over to the window, avoiding the shards of glass on the floor with his bare feet. He leant over the ledge, his hands placed on the window sill, careful not to cut himself and saw the mangled body of the intruder, awkwardly positioned and motionless.

Turning back towards his wife, he helped her to stand

and guided her over to the bed. She was still holding her throat, her eyes wild and fearful. Placing his arms around her, Ed kissed her face. 'Are you OK?' he asked again.

Her throat was raw, dry, and her head was pounding. 'I... I survived. But what the fuck is going on?' she asked with a bewildered expression. Her eyebrows knotted, her mouth was open, and she searched Ed's face for an answer.

'I don't know. Nothing about the last few hours makes any sense. I just want to take you home. But' – gesturing towards the window with his head – 'we need to call the police. There's a dead body outside the cottage.'

Cass reached her hand to the side of Ed's face. 'It was self-defence. You saved my life. They'll understand that.'

He stood up and wrapped his wife in one of the many blankets on the bed and then grabbed his mobile phone from the side unit. He found the weakest Wi-Fi signal in the corner of the room and dialled 999. 'Hi, yes, police please... There's been a break-in...'

As Ed explained the situation to the emergency services call handler, Cass pulled the blanket around her tighter. What had happened? They'd been plagued with stalkers and weirdos all day, and then to be attacked, nearly killed in a place they knew no one? It didn't make sense.

She stood and walked on unsteady legs, stepping through the glass to the window.

'Right, Cass. The operator said to stay in the bedroom and to not touch anything if we can help it. Officers are on their way. Come away from there, you'll cut yourself.'

Cass leant over the window, peering into the half-light. Her heart nearly stopped at what she saw below.

'Ed, the body's gone.'

11

SUNDAY MORNING

'Marty, this better be good,' Beth called from the hallway. 'Abbey, is everything OK?'

'Yeah. You're back early. What's happened?' Abbey called from her bedroom, where she was still looking over her law books.

'Your father is what's happened. He can't survive without me for a second. Nan had to go home and she's not pleased.' Opening the kitchen door, Beth dropped the two bags on the floor; the tips of her fingers had turned red with the weight and strap marks appeared across the skin. She peered at her husband. 'So go on then, what's the emergency? Oh, hang on, wait, I know. You can't find the remote control. We've run out of teabags. Am I getting warm?'

Marty stood, trying to remain as calm as possible. His stomach churned as if his insides were rolling over, and he felt weak. The heat drove in from the garden; his skin was sticky and damp, and he felt like he needed another shower. 'Can you please sit?'

Pulling a chair from under the table and dragging its legs along the tiles, Beth sat, watching her husband's face.

'What is it, Marty? I dragged my poor mother down to Oxford Street on a stuffy train with the promise of lunch, only to drop her home without even a cup of tea because you insist there's an emergency you can't discuss over the phone. Give me strength. What's so important?' Beth looked up into Marty's face; come to think of it, his skin did look a bit pale, and there was genuine anguish in his eyes. She hoped he wasn't coming down with something; she couldn't take the drama of nursing him through another bout of man flu.

'Earlier, I got a message from Davey Hughes.'

'Right.'

Passing the phone to her, Marty showed Beth the picture of her and her mother walking along Oxford Street.

Beth looked at the photo. 'Who took this? Was it Davey? If he was in London, he should have said.'

Leaning into the table, Marty rubbed his fingers against the side of his head. 'No. You don't understand. I got a link from Davey sent to my WhatsApp with the promise of winning one hundred thousand pounds. You know Davey, he's not a bullshitter. If he sends something, it's legit. So, I open it, sign up for free with no apparent strings attached, and I see this. Beth, you need to brace yourself.'

Her eyes jumped between her husband and the phone screen as Marty clicked link after link, showing his wife the true horror of The App. They watched recordings of recent live streams. The figure hanging from the tree. The Jeep in pursuit of the BMW. The crash, the car alarms ringing out in the air and even some which Marty hadn't yet seen.

The latest link showed a man trying to drown Cass Carter in a bath of water, and the recording ended with him being pushed out of a window.

Beth dropped Marty's phone on the table. What the hell

was going on? The content of The App was too much to digest. Grabbing her phone, she began dialling 999.

Marty reached for the phone and snatched it from her hand. 'What are you doing?'

'I'm calling the police. This twisted... app, has to be reported. Can you imagine if Abbey found this? Would you want her seeing this?'

'Are you mad? You don't understand, do you?'

'Give me my phone.'

Standing again, unable to keep still, Marty leant on the back of his chair, needing Beth to understand the consequences. 'Haven't you seen the streams? Don't you get it?'

Her eyes widened, focusing on her husband. It felt like she was suspended above the kitchen, removed from reality and too stunned to listen. 'Get what, Marty?'

He sat back down, placing her phone on the table and taking Beth's hands in his. 'I'm a part of this now. The pictures sent of you and your mother... They weren't Davey, nor Abbey or me. We were here, Beth, all the time. You've watched the streams and seen how it works. As soon as people sign up to The App, a picture is sent of their loved ones, with the threats. It's a way to get them to obey the rules. Beth,' Marty continued, watching as his wife digested everything, 'An hour after I signed up to The App, I was sent threats of a family member being killed if I don't follow the rules, and this picture. You and your mother. It's not a wind-up.'

'What are we going to do?' Beth whispered. Tears formed in her eyes. In the short time she'd been home, it felt like her world had come crashing down.

Marty reached over the table and wiped the stream of water that rolled down her cheeks. 'We can't call the police. I've seen what these people do. I mean, I showed you. Their threats are genuine. The woman stood by the window of a house, tasked with killing someone inside. Shit, Beth, you could hear the terror in her voice – it's something you can't fake.' Marty recalled a link they'd just watched. 'Someone was filming the same woman and hiding in her home. You saw how it finished with this person racing towards her. They didn't show it, but I know they killed her. I can still hear the scream. If we call the police, we're signing our own death warrants.'

'Are they listening to us now?' Beth grabbed Marty's hand, squeezing it tight.

'I don't think so, no, but Beth, the horror I felt when they sent the picture was beyond words. I couldn't leave the house until I knew what was going on. That's why I rang for you to come home. I couldn't leave Abbey alone.'

'What about Mum? And your parents?'

'Oh shit, I don't know. Dad's practically bedridden. Mum won't like leaving the house due to his dementia. I don't want to frighten them. I think I need to see how it plays out first. Where's your mum?'

'I dropped her home on the way. Should we call her and tell her what's going on?'

'You've seen the rules. We can't talk about it, especially over the phone. And I can't throw my phone away. I'm not tech savvy in the slightest, but I'm guessing if they need to, they can track us through location services. I can't arouse suspicion, tampering with my phone. We have to get used to this and act as normal as possible. At least until we figure out what we're going to do?'

Beth looked her husband in the eyes. 'Tell me again – I need to get this straight in my head.'

Marty explained how he had the lawnmower out, Abbey was upstairs, and a message came through on WhatsApp.

How he clicked the link sent by Davey Hughes, added his details, and later a picture was sent of Beth and her mother with the chilling threats.

'They're forcing people to kill. Every Friday, a person is picked randomly from social media as the target. And now that I've downloaded The App, I'm part of it. I have to join the hunt, or they'll kill you. Then they'll kill me.'

Beth stood, trying to understand what was going on. 'Have you called Davey?'

'Yes. A few times. He's not answering.'

Beth was getting more agitated by the second. 'So let's go over there. He can fill us in.'

'Beth, you're not getting it. We can't go over there, not until we understand how it works. They could be watching.' Standing, Marty peered into the garden and at the disused railway tracks at the back of the house. 'They could be hiding, waiting.'

Beth followed her husband's eyes, and a chill ran through her body.

The kitchen door flung open, causing them both to jump.

'Mum, why are you back so soon?'

Beth glanced at Marty and then looked at her daughter. 'Umm, I didn't feel well, sweetheart. Oxford Street was so busy, and I had a funny turn.'

Abbey crossed the kitchen, her eyebrows knotted and her green eyes filled with concern as she blew her long, brown hair from her face. She placed her hands on her mother's shoulders and squeezed them encouragingly. 'Maybe you're dehydrated. It's so hot. Let me get you some water.' Abbey went over to the sink, grabbed a glass from the cupboard and ran the cold tap. 'Here, sit down – you do look pale.'

With the fuss, Beth regretted making up an excuse. 'I'm fine. Stop worrying. How's the revision going?'

'If I'm not ready now, I never will be. My eyes are heavy. I need a break. Dad said we'd go for a walk.'

Beth spat out her water.

'No,' Marty spouted, realising he sounded too forceful. He was still trying to understand the situation. The more he thought about it, the threats, the links he'd watched and what they did if people broke the rules, the more careful he realised they had to be. For now, Marty needed to keep under the radar as much as possible. And that meant staying inside the house.

'Bloody hell, what's wrong with you two? It's just a walk. I need some air.'

Another awkward glance passed between Beth and Marty.

'Go into the garden. There's loads of air out there,' Marty insisted.

'Whatever.' Turning to her mother, Beth asked, 'How's nan?'

'She's OK. She was asking after you.'

'I'll drop over to hers once I'm done with this exam. It's taking up so much of my time – I hope the hard work is worth it.' Abbey stepped out of the kitchen and into the garden; a few seconds later, she was lying on a deck chair.

Turning to Marty, Beth whispered, 'I can't deal with this. Should we tell her?'

'How can we? She's got her law exam on Tuesday and needs all her attention on that.'

Beth inhaled and sighed loudly. 'This is crazy. I can't believe what's happening. How are we going to resolve this?'

Marty looked towards his daughter, lying in the sun, knowing there was only one way to protect his family.

* * *

The humid day had turned into a chilly evening. After a light snack, Abbey had declared she was going up to do another hour of revision before having a cool shower to soothe her tight skin – she'd accidentally burned her forearms and chest relaxing in the afternoon sun. Whereas Marty and Beth had retreated to the living room. They'd put on their favourite show, but neither was concentrating, their minds more concerned with what they'd do about The App than the period drama they normally loved. They couldn't call the police or ask anyone else for advice. Together, they'd have to figure it out between them.

Marty's phone pinged from the coffee table.

'Who's that?' Beth asked, adjusting her body and peering through the living room window and onto the street, wondering if they were being watched.

Picking up the phone, Marty saw there were new notifications. Staring at the screen, his hands shaking, his world seemed to pause.

'What is it, Marty?'

Beth's voice brought him out of his stupor. 'There's... There's more links.' Slamming the phone on the sofa, Marty looked at his wife. 'I can't do this, Beth, it's too much.'

She stood, walking over to where Marty was sitting. 'Open it!'

'What?'

'We have to see what we're dealing with here. Click the link.'

'Beth, It's sick. I don't want to see—'

'Click it.'

His hand hovered over the screen, and he opened The App, clicking the latest link.

12

A FEW HOURS EARLIER

Cass was still in shock when the police arrived at the cottage. Ed had given the call handler the code for the gate, and they watched the blue lights illuminating the sky as the police car steered along the drive. A few minutes later, an ambulance followed and pulled up to the cottage too.

Cass sat on the edge of the bed, her body shaking and weird moaning noises spilling from her mouth. She rocked back and forth and stared at the floor.

Ed held her, kissing her forehead, telling her it was over and that they were safe.

While the police officers questioned them, Ed looked over the window ledge. He couldn't work it out. How could the man who'd attacked them be gone? He'd seen the body lying there, limp and contorted. There was no possible way he could have got off the ground and run into the night. There had to be more to it. But what? Nothing had made sense since they'd left London earlier the previous day.

The paramedics checked Cass over, taking her blood pressure, shining a torch in her eyes and asking questions. She was in shock but aware of her surroundings. They carried out the same checks on Ed, and tried to convince them to go to the hospital, but all Cass wanted was to go home.

He'd told the officers about the attack, how someone had knocked on the door, Ed going out in the dark and the intruder getting into the cottage. He also explained the strange events that unfolded during the trip here. But Ed kept quiet about the man lying on the ground outside and hadn't told the call handler at the time. The last thing he needed was a manslaughter charge. As far as the police knew, the intruder got off the ground and ran. Ed had to keep quiet. But there was no way around it, the disappearance of the body unnerved him. There was no way he could have got up.

Ed watched from the window as officers shone torches through the fields, their lights flickering in the distance.

Once the officers had checked the area and returned to the cottage, the police told them they could return to London. Now, as they drove, Cass sleeping in the passenger seat, Ed looked at the dashboard. 03.43.

His frustration was building, his eyes heavy with lack of sleep; the road seemed like one continuous conveyor belt pulling towards the full lights. His body felt cold, and an ache developed behind his eyes like they were attached to heavy weights.

He glanced at Cass, the passenger seat back and a light jacket covering her body. She looked so peaceful. Their weekend was meant to be perfect. How could a man have broken into the cottage and almost murdered his wife, forcing them to go home less than twenty-four hours after they'd arrived? His agitation neared boiling point, and he wanted to pull the BMW over and scream until his throat inflamed and his lungs emptied.

As Ed stared ahead and took long calming breaths, he thought about the figure hanging in the tree, the Jeep which had followed them and rammed them from behind. Could they still be following him? Fear engulfed his body as he looked back; the bleak void behind offered no reassurance.

Holding the steering wheel, Ed tried desperately to work out what had happened. How could two people have such bad luck? It felt like he and Cass were the main characters in a game, something from a horror movie. It didn't feel real.

Needing a distraction, Ed put the radio on quietly; the soothing voices of the late-night presenters allowed his body to relax slightly.

Cass began to stir, talking to herself. 'No, leave me alone. Ed. Run. You have to run.'

Her head turned left and right and her body twitched. Ed placed his hand on her leg until she turned into the passenger door. 'It's OK. I'm here. It's just a nightmare.' Ed wanted to believe the words, but somehow he couldn't accept that all this was just bad luck.

* * *

They arrived home at just gone eight on Sunday morning. The traffic was light as they drove through London and Ed watched everyone with suspicion.

Once they'd pulled up outside the house in Finsbury Park, North London, he gently woke Cass. She stretched, uncertain where she was for a moment, her eyes peering towards the house. 'We're home. You drove all night? Oh, Ed, you must be shattered.' Her body shivered with the coldness of the morning and the disturbed sleep.

'I'm OK. But I'm going straight to bed.' He looked at Cass. 'We had no choice. We had to leave.'

Moving the jacket off her body, she said, 'I know. It was horrible. But we're home now.' Gently, she opened the passenger door and stood on the road. Her body was numb, like it had been drained of blood, and she ached everywhere. Events from earlier played in her mind; the man in the cottage, holding her under the water. She'd never been more frightened. Glancing towards the semi-detached house, the sun glistening off the windows, the familiarity gave her comfort.

Locking the BMW, Ed took Cass by the hand and walked to the house. As they opened the front door, Ed couldn't help glancing back onto the street. Certain there was no one watching them, he closed the door behind them, put on the Chubb lock and secured the chain.

* * *

They slept most of the day. Ed had woken up a few times. A car horn outside on the street. A parcel being delivered, and a couple of times to use the bathroom.

It was about five in the evening when Ed pushed his body up against the headboard and watched his wife, her chest moving in and out, her lips flapping with her breaths and listening to the words she said while dreaming. Realising how close he was to losing her, Ed slid back down the bed and placed his arm around her body. A few more minutes wouldn't hurt. Her skin felt hot, and her face was damp with sweat.

On feeling Ed's embrace, Cass woke with a start. She sprang up, throwing her arms in the air and screaming.

Ed jumped out of the way and put a reassuring hand on

her arm. 'Hey, Cass, it's all right. It's just a nightmare. I'm here – you're safe.'

Turning to her husband, her panicked expression melted into a smile as she lay her head back on the pillow. She felt safe with Ed there, but terrifying images plagued her mind as she stared at the ceiling, the figure in the tree, the Jeep, the cottage. No, she couldn't let it beat her. The intruder had shattered their weekend, but Cass wasn't going to let it ruin her life too. Pushing her hands into the soft mattress, she swung her body out of bed. 'Right, I'm hungry. Take me out.'

'What?'

'I'm not going to let this beat me. I want to go out. We're meant to be having a weekend away, but a staycation will have to do. We're going to eat, drink and enjoy each other's company.'

'Cass, I don't think—'

'We're home. We're in North London. It's my happy place. I can't lie in bed, hidden from the world. What we went through was awful, but it's over now. That's what you keep telling me, so let's face it head-on. I want to go out.'

Ed watched Cass stroll over to the en-suite, listening to the shower door open and the water begin to run, fearing they were making a grave mistake.

13

SUNDAY EVENING

'Well?' Beth asked, anxious to see the new live stream.

'It's loading. I can't bear this.' Marty's hands were shaking as he held the phone. A new link had been uploaded within The App, and both he and Beth hovered over the screen. 'Beth, I don't want—'

'We need to see what's going on. And then we can work out how to get out of it.'

Suddenly, an image of a wall appeared on the screen and a man started speaking.

'I hope you can see the screen. I've wiped the camera to make it more clear. You'll understand if it starts shaking – my nerves are shattered. I haven't slept since I clicked the link and put in my details. I don't know how this is going to end. For now, I have to take part. I received The App from my best mate almost four weeks ago; I'm trying to work it out. Two days ago was the fourth Friday. Which means it's my last chance. If you're watching, if you're a part of this fucked-up shit show, I didn't want this; it landed on my doorstep. My best friend hasn't returned any of my calls, and I'm alone. I haven't told my wife through fear. Fear that

she'll go to the police. I've seen what these animals do, how they force people into murder. I can't believe I'm saying that word, "murder". I can't even come to terms with what I'm about to do. I'm a family man. I adore my son and daughter – I'd do anything for them. I married the woman of my dreams nineteen years ago and cannot imagine life without her or my family.

'After loading my name, I became so excited. We have money, we're doing OK, but who'd turn down the chance of winning all that money every Friday? Especially when your best mate sends you the details, and you think there's no strings attached. A chance to have a better life. If only I knew. But hey, hindsight is a bitch.'

Beth was stunned. Marty had showed her the videos before, but watching it live, her heart raced and she felt nauseous. Whispering to Marty, she said, 'My heart bleeds for this guy. He's terrified.'

'He can't hear you,' Marty whispered back.

The phone camera moved across the room and out to a hallway. They could hear his footsteps as he walked over the floor. A hand reached out and opened the front door. Then the footage skimmed over the ground, shaking and unfocused. As the man filming stepped along the path and out to the street, they could hear a car door open. The man pointed the phone camera towards the sky, careful not to show his vehicle.

'I have no choice, I have to try. I hope you can see I'm doing it. You've forced me, my hands are tied. I received a photo of my daughter – she was at a friend's house, jumping on a trampoline, a huge smile on her face and without a care in the world. The morning the picture came through, followed by the horrific threat, my world fell apart. I remember it felt like my heart had dropped from my body, out of my fucking arse. I raced over to her friend's house so fast I thought I'd have a heart attack. I

can't even recall the excuse I used and how rude I must have sounded when I knocked on their door. The friend's father answered, and I think I pushed passed him into the garden. I grabbed my princess by the hand and led her out. I recall my wife being livid, but my head is too confused to tell you what I said.'

The phone was placed on the dashboard; the picture went fuzzy and then cleared up as the camera focused on the road in front.

'I have no one to talk to, no one with whom to vent my frustration. One of the stupid fucking rules is to narrate. Oh, I'll talk. I hope at least one of you watching this has empathy for me. I'm just a normal guy who adores his family, driven to murder an innocent woman.'

Beth and Marty watched, stunned as the events played out on the live stream. The atmosphere was thick with anxiety as the screen displayed a main road, vehicles sweeping towards the camera, and groups of people walking along the pavement.

As he started talking again, they could hear a change in the man's voice, weak and unsteady. He sniffed hard, inhaling deeply then holding his breath before releasing it.

'I haven't planned this. How does a normal person who's about to kill someone decide how they're going to do it? I don't know the answer. I have thoughts, ideas I never dreamed I'd have to consider. Before I left the house, I went to the toolbox and grabbed a hammer. I held it in my hands, gripping the rubber handle and imagined smashing her over the head. The thought made me want to vomit. Not just the act —coming up behind her, lifting my hand and then, bang – but the sound it would make. The crunch. The damage. The sight of her lying on the floor. If she gets up, do I hit her again? Is the second time easier? And how the fuck would her head look?'

Beth looked at Marty with pity in her eyes. Words weren't needed.

The screen showed the car turning left into a side street, and his driving became more erratic. As the camera neared parked vehicles, the man began to cry.

'Whoa, sorry... I nearly clipped the mirror of a parked car. I'm almost here, so, there's your narration of how an innocent man has been forced to murder an innocent woman. If you're watching this and thinking about your turn, I have no fucking advice. None whatsoever. The threat is enough to drive me over the edge, that's all I know. How do you turn a lover into a fighter? How do you get someone to perform one of the worst acts imaginable, like the most contented person in the world jumping off a cliff, or the wealthiest person stealing from the corner shop? Threaten a member of their family. That's enough to drive you insane.'

As he reached the end of the road, Beth and Marty could see shops opposite. The guy streaming turned right and parked in a bay along the main road.

The camera lifted, turning towards the passenger seat.

'I'm here. I hope this is the right place. I'm going to turn the camera off and go inside. I can't narrate, as I'll draw attention to myself, but I'll film when the time is right. I'm going to kill Cass Carter.'

The screen went blank.

Beth sat next to Marty, her body shaking and her head cloudy. 'I know where he is? He's on Holloway Road. There's an Italian restaurant there. I've gone with Mum a few times.'

As Marty looked at the blank screen, stunned by the latest stream, he said, 'What has our life become?'

Beth stood abruptly and announced, 'I'm going to stop this.'

'Are you mad? What are you talking about?' Marty stood too, as Beth began pacing the floor and turning in circles. 'I have to do something, Marty. I won't let this happen. I, I just can't.'

Reaching out, Marty placed his arms around Beth's waist, and held her. Tears formed in her eyes, and she struggled to catch her breath as she sobbed.

'Please, I'm here. I won't let anything happen to you,' he promised.

Her face looked so pitiful.

'We're part of this.' Pulling away, Beth placed her hands on the arm of the sofa. 'We've been dragged into this fucking mess.'

'Beth, please hold it together. We can work it out – we'll get through this.'

'How?' she said firmly. 'Did you hear the fear in his voice, explaining how much he loved his family? What he's been driven to do? Could you do it? That man, holding the phone camera, waiting at the restaurant in Holloway Road, could be you.' Beth straightened her body, her mind dazed. 'Could you do it, Marty?'

'I'd do anything to save my family. Anything.'

'And what? Face the rest of your life in prison, all the sleepless nights as the images circle around your mind, the nightmare, the sheer torment. You're not a murderer. I won't let you take part in this. I'd rather die than see you go through the aftermath.'

Marty broke down. The tension which had built, the stress his body carried, poured from his eyes as he wept.

Beth held him, kissing his damp hair, running her fingertips along his warm skin. 'You're such an amazing man, Marty. I couldn't find a better husband, and Abbey couldn't have a better father. I won't let you go through this. We need to stop it.'

Marty took a huge gulp of air. 'How?'

Beth moved away and walked out to the hallway, grabbing the car keys from a rack on the wall. 'I'm going to Holloway Road. You stay here. I need to stop this. If we call the police, they'll know. This is the only way.'

'Beth. Listen to yourself,' Marty said as he followed her down the corridor. 'Do you know how dangerous this is? We can't leave the house until we know what's going on. It's too risky.'

Kissing his face, she said, 'That's why you're staying here with Abbey. You received The App this morning, but since getting the picture of Mum and me, there's been nothing else to make us suspect they're watching us. As far as The App goes, we're spectators waiting for our turn. They have no reason to come for us.'

'Beth, this is absolute madness. What are you going to do? You can't stop this. Please, you're not thinking straight.'

'I'm going to drive over there and get a message to this Cass Carter. If she's at the restaurant, I need to let her know she's in danger. I can't message her online as they've probably hacked her social media. It has to be in person.' Beth stepped towards the front door.

'I can't let you go on your own,' Marty insisted. Turning towards the stairs, he yelled, 'Abbey, we're going for something to eat.'

14

1981

'Something terrible must have happened.' Gill stood by the living-room window, watching the row of police cars lined along the street. Male and female officers stood on the pavement, others moved in and out of the house. Neighbours were standing on the pavement, clusters of people on the road staring at the house, and police officers were pleading for them to step back.

Adam joined his wife. 'It's the Shirlands' place. It must be serious with the number of officers.'

As they watched the carnage, more people gathered on the street, hands over their mouths and shocked faces.

Upstairs, Jonathan was also standing at the window as Mrs Shirland was led out of the house in handcuffs; her long, greasy black hair and wild eyes amplified her evil appearance.

'I did it!' she screamed. 'I fucking did it, OK. So you can all go about your business.' The officers lowered her into a police car and closed the back door. The crowds of people began to disperse, and Jonathan's body tingled at the memory of the murder.

He felt privileged, honoured to have witnessed such a horrific act. As he'd watched Mrs Shirland plunging the knife into her husband from the garden, Jonathan should have been appalled, disgusted to see something so repulsive. But on the contrary, the excitement only enticed his appetite.

Jonathan wasn't a cruel person as such; he didn't act violently, but it inspired his senses when he witnessed something wicked. It stimulated him, making him feel alive and dynamic.

Moving back to the bed, he grabbed his latest *Beano*, re-reading the escapades of Dennis and Gnasher. Boredom was setting in; he stared at the posters on his wall – *Friday The 13th* and The *Texas Chainsaw Massacre* – his collection of Star Wars toys lined up along the shelf and the Rubik's cube. Placing the comic on the bed, Jonathan walked to the shelf, grabbed the cube and began twisting the edges. Luke had said if you turn two rows for long enough, one vertical, one horizontal, the colours would eventually match. It didn't nearly resemble anywhere near completion after spending an hour a day for the first few weeks since he'd bought it, but he wouldn't give up. Others at school took the cube apart or peeled off the stickers, but Jonathan never understood the logic of cheating; if he were to conquer the cube, he'd do it properly.

He sat, turning the edges, watching the colours blink in front of him.

Downstairs, someone knocked at the front door. Jonathan tossed the cube on the bed and moved to the upstairs hallway and peered through the banister.

Mrs Hatton, a neighbour, had called over with the news of Mr Shirland's death. His mother and father stood by the front door, and Jonathan could hear their gasps. They invited Mavis in, and the three of them walked through to the kitchen.

A minute later, Jonathan could hear the kettle whistling on the stove. He smirked, basking in the feeling of superiority over his parents, the neighbours, the police and paramedics as he imagined the conversation, all of them trying to guess what had happened. Jonathan wondered how to utilise this for his gratification.

If only he could predict where and when disaster struck.

* * *

'Jonathan, can you come down, please?' Jonathan's father called from the hallway.

Mrs Hatton had just left, and his father's voice sounded regretful, not the normal stern tone he'd use.

'Coming.' Jonathan placed his *Beano* on the bed and strolled out of the room and down the stairs. 'Yeah?' he asked awkwardly when he arrived in the kitchen.

Adam wore a thin shirt and shorts, his brown hair was messy, and he had tomato ketchup on his moustache. 'I've made you a fish-finger sandwich. Mum and I want to chat with you.'

His mother was standing by the stove, her face slightly red, and it looked like she'd been crying. The kitchen was humid, and the smell of fish was overbearing.

As they explained what had happened across the road, Jonathan feigned shock, as if hearing it for the first time. His parents spoke over each other, and once finished, his mother stepped towards Jonathan and held him tight.

'It's so devastating. I was only talking to her yesterday.

I'm sorry, Jonathan. We'll deal with this together, OK? It's tragic. I don't know the proper story, but it looks like she may have killed him. Neighbours heard her admit it as the police drove her away.'

'Oh my goodness. That's awful,' Jonathan announced, trying his utmost to fake an appalled response.

'It is, Jonathan, it's horrible,' Adam said. 'And well, your mother and I have been chatting, and although we're still annoyed with you for opening the door while we were out and letting your friend in the house – Luke's a good lad, but the lies annoyed us the most – we wanted to draw a line under it, in light of what's just happened. We could all do with a break, so, as it's half term and you've been grounded for almost five days, how about a camping trip? We could set off now, if you want?'

'Oh yes, Dad, I'd like that.'

Eyeing his mother, Jonathan saw the delight on her face. He knew she worried about their father/son relationship and often had to stop Adam from going too far with his punishments. Jonathan admired his mother so much, always dressed elegantly, had time to listen and rarely judged her son. On the other hand, his father was often brutish and seemed to hate when Jonathan spoke to him. This was good though, even if it was such bleak news that had changed his father's mind on Jonathan being grounded.

Once the bags and tent were loaded into the boot of the Ford Cortina, Adam ran around the house to ensure everything was locked.

Jonathan sat in the back of the car, while his mother was in the passenger seat. He could see her looking over to the Shirlands' house, where police officers were standing outside, guarding the crime scene.

'I still can't believe what's happened,' she said, her voice fragile.

With the house finally secured, Adam came out and got into the driver's seat. 'OK, are we set?'

They both nodded, and the Ford Cortina pulled off the drive, heading for Surrey.

* * *

Two hours later, they arrived at the campsite. An old wooden sign displayed the name. 'Camp Grey Oak', written in bright red letters.

As Jonathan looked over the rugged fields and the dirt track leading to the edge of a hill, he couldn't help but think of the movie, *Friday The 13th*.

They drove up to the main hut and spoke to the security guard, who told them where to park and said someone would be around later to collect the cash for their stay.

The barrier lifted and they drove forward. Jonathan turned, watching the security guard's peeved expression as the Ford Cortina spewed black smoke over the hut. They followed the dirt track along the side of the hill, taking in the beautiful landscape and they gasped at the vast lake, the sun shimmering on the water's edge and the tree branches tilting in the warm breeze.

'Wow, look at this. Amazing, isn't it?' Gill said.

Once they'd parked up, they got out of the car, grabbed the bags and tent and walked along the side of the hill.

It was pretty much a free-for-all, and you could pitch up camp wherever you liked. Small barbecue grills were set on metal units at regular intervals across the campsite, the legs dug into the ground, and logs were stacked in neat piles so you could make campfires. Signs showed a map of the area and others promoting the use of hired canoes and fishing rods.

Adam and Jonathan grabbed the tent, unzipped the bag and proceeded to build their shelter for the night. Jonathan hated this part. They'd been camping several times before but not for a few years. He recalled it taking hours to set up the tent and the heavy rain soaking their bodies as he and his father tried to put it together. Looking to the sky, Jonathan saw patches of cloud, the sun struggling to push through and no sign of rain. They should be OK for now. He peered at his mother, who wore a light green dress and sat on the grass, reading a horror novel called *The Shining*. Occasionally, her face lifted towards the sky and her eyes closed. She looked so content.

'Jonathan, are you listening? Grab the hammer from the bag and start knocking the pegs in.'

'Oh, sorry.'

'You're in your own world sometimes. Where does your mind drift to?'

'Adam,' Gill warned. 'We're going to have a nice trip. Come on, he's trying to help.'

Looking up, Adam said, 'Trying to help? I have to tell him five or six times before it sinks into his head.'

I wish it were you who Mrs Shirland murdered, Jonathan thought to himself. Knocking in the pegs, he mused over his father's lack of patience, his aggressive behaviour and how angry he was all the time. God, he hated him. His father was never there, never listened when he spoke to him and mostly dismissed his views, laughing at him. He recalled so many times when his father's friends had come over and how he'd mock Jonathan, ordering him around like a robot, his little lapdog, showing off and looking at his friends for a reaction.

Whereas his mother did everything with him, including his homework, taking him to football practice, martial arts and would always wait patiently in the car when he had after-school rehearsals without shouting that he was late or lecturing him on the way home with a sermon about how precious her time was. She asked him questions and always gave Jonathan her time. He loved how she listened, holding his face, crouching down, her eyes beaming. Like she was proud of everything that came out of his mouth.

She gave him courage, strength and determination. But most of all, her time.

As he knelt, banging the next peg into the ground, he wondered how it would feel to whack his father on the side of the head. Watch the blood drain from his body as he lay on the ground, his eyes full of pity, his body quivering, his arms out, reaching for help. He tightened his grip on the hammer. Would Jonathan enjoy watching his father die? Would he even miss him?

'I'll say it one last time, you idiot. Bang them harder.'

Jonathan looked up. 'Huh? Oh, sorry.'

'Sorry,' his father mimicked. 'That's the usual response. You need to think for yourself. If you see something needs doing, then take control and do it. Christ, your grandfather wouldn't have been able to bear you for a second. It's just as well he died before you came along. God help you when you start working. You won't last five minutes in a job.'

Gill stood, her voice raised. 'I told you to leave him alone, Adam. How do you ever expect him to gain confidence when you never stop having a go at him? He's trying.'

Adam flashed her an aggravated look as he wiped sweat from his face. 'Gill—'

'Gill nothing,' she fired back. 'If it carries on, I promise the two of us will leave you here on your own.'

Adam continued working in silence.

Jonathan wished he had the same control over his father that his mother had. He never answered her back, and when she barked an order, he listened. How could she command so much respect?

Jonathan needed to gain people's respect.

He needed people to be fearful of him too.

* * *

The smell of burgers and sausages seeped into the air while the intense sizzling noise enticed the Rushmores' appetites. Adam stood by the barbecue, flipping them every few minutes as smoke rose above them.

Gill was still reading, her body leaning against a tree, the sun on her face as it began to set in the distance. Jonathan sat next to her, flipping the pages of his *Beano*, again reading the same story of Dennis and Gnasher, as they walk along the pavement, aware of the puddle caused by a heavy downpour of rain. A young woman walks towards them. Dennis hears a car in the distance. At the last second, he and Gnasher hide behind a bush, laughing uncontrollably as the woman gets soaked.

Stepping away from the heat of the flames, Adam turned and saw his son smile. 'What is so amusing?'

'Oh, nothing,' Jonathan answered.

Peering at the comic, Adam said, 'You won't make anything of your life reading comics. A young boy like you should read history books, geography, science – try learning about the world for once.'

Jonathan slammed the comic on the ground in frustration. This was meant to be a holiday, wasn't it? Why wouldn't his father stop having a go, just for once? His mother shook her head, discreetly warning him against saying anything. It wasn't worth it.

Once the food was cooked, they sat together around the tree, the rough bark uncomfortable against their backs. It was dark; the clouds had cleared, making way for millions of beautiful stars spread across the sky—a peaceful, harmonious spectacle above them. As Jonathan looked up, biting into his burger, his mind drifted to films his mother had taken him to see. *Star Wars* and *Superman*, he hoped if he stared long enough, he might see something from those movies.

'You don't know how lucky you are,' Adam insisted as he bit into a sausage. My father never took us anywhere. You're spoilt, Jonathan. Look around you, breathe in the fresh air, take time with nature. You're a lucky lad. There's not many parents who'd do this for their child.' Adam grabbed a bottle of white wine from one of the bags and a plastic cup, filling it to the brim and passing it to Gill. A loud crack sounded as Adam opened a beer for himself.

'Thank you,' Gill said. 'So Jonathan, you have a choice. We can either sing or tell ghost stories.'

'Er, sing? No way. I'm not five anymore,' Jonathan said. 'Let's go with the ghost stories.' Looking around the camp as darkness began to draw in, a chill ran through his body. He began with a few spooky tales he'd read in comics and stories he'd heard from his school friends. Then Gill told a couple.

His wife and son soon became absorbed in their own amusement, while Adam sat, staring out at the trees, only their shadows visible, as he swigged his beer with relief. It was so nice to have some time to himself. His son irritated him, and he wished they'd left him at home.

*   *   *

Jonathan woke in the middle of the night. An owl or other creature must have woken him and sounded as if it was right outside. He pawed the ground for his small torch, and when he found it, he shone it towards his parents, wrapped in their sleeping bags and fast asleep.

Jonathan felt for the zip on his own sleeping bag and gently slid it along the length of his body, careful not to make too much noise. Anxious to see what was causing the strange noise and in need of adventure, he stood and crept towards the opening of the tent, pushing his thin body through the gap and shining the dim light at the trees, The night air was cold, but it wasn't that which made him shiver. He had a distinct sense of being watched. Of someone out there, hiding, observing them. Jonathan whispered, 'Hello?'

A twig snapped close to where he stood, causing him to jump. He wanted to back off and wake his father, but already he could hear his nagging voice, asking why he'd left the tent in the first place and insisting what an idiot his son was. It wasn't worth the grief.

Jonathan could smell pine trees and the remnants of the barbecue earlier on the cool breeze as he walked further from the tent.

Then, out of the darkness, something growled beside him. It sounded like a bear or other large animal. He froze, his body trembling, and the opening scenes of *An American Werewolf In London* played out in his mind, of David and Jack leaving The Slaughtered Lamb pub and walking across the moors. Only this was happening to him, and for the first time in ages, Jonathan was scared. He wanted to charge into the tent, wake his father and feel safe in his arms. But that would never happen. His father would shout, get in his face and call him an idiot. He'd laugh and mock his pathetic son for weeks.

As Jonathan stared towards the trees, his body taut, he backed away.

More noises filled the air. Another growl, possibly a second animal. Then a shriek as they began fighting. Shining the torch back and forth through the trees, Jonathan listened to the horrific noises echoing through the night.

But something excited him, out there alone, listening as they fought for territory.

He waited in the darkness until it went silent.

* * *

'Morning, how did you sleep?' Gill was already up and dressed when her son woke. The smell of bacon and eggs filled the tent.

Wiping his eyes, Jonathan glanced over at the empty sleeping bag. Not seeing his father gave him hope; maybe he'd had enough and gone home. 'Good. I thought it would be uncomfortable, but I slept fine. How are you, Mum? Where's Dad?'

'Great. How nice is it waking up with all that fresh air? He's got a surprise for you. He's going to hire a canoe and take you fishing. He spoke with the security guard.'

No such luck then. But Jonathan knew it would have been his mother who had organised this attempt at father/son bonding. Still, it would be nice to get out on the lake. Although... 'I didn't think Dad could swim. He hates the water.'

'He does, but he's willing to face that challenge.'

* * *

After they'd eaten, Adam and Jonathan walked down to the water's edge, unlocked the padlock on the canoe shed and pulled one of the canoes away.

Although early, it was warm; the sun was high, and Adam's shirt was already sticking to his back, wet with sweat.

'OK, we'll go out, but not too far. The security guard gave us a fishing rod we can share and some bait. Every father and son should experience this at least once.'

'So, are you going to give me a beer as well?' Jonathan asked cheekily.

'Don't wind me up. Not today. Right, climb aboard – I'll hold it still.'

Jonathan stepped over and into the canoe, feeling it rock slightly. His father joined him.

'OK, pick up the oar and let's go,' Adam demanded.

'Urgh, do I have to do all the hard work?' Jonathan asked.

'Hey, you're privileged to be here; not every child has been camping and gets to fish on the water. Don't start with the cheek, Jonathan, or I'll drive us straight home.'

Begrudgingly, Jonathan picked up the oar and dipped it into the water, skimming the edge and sweeping.

'Put your bloody back into it. Dig the water – imagine you have a shovel and you want to make a hole.'

As he dug and swept the end of the oar into the water, Jonathon watched his father smirk, the delight on his face as his son struggled. Jonathan thought how he'd love to lift the end out and whack his father across the head, wiping the smug grin from his face. That's what Dennis The Menace would do. He'd splash his father while Gnasher laughed in the corner of the canoe. Maybe he'd try doing that, but he knew already that his father wouldn't see the funny side.

He'd been rowing for fifteen minutes. The life jacket exposed Jonathan's arms to the sun, and his skin had already started to burn. Jonathan turned his head, seeing the tent in the distance as sweat dripped off his face. Breathless, he watched his father lying back, one of his legs dangling in the cold water.

'That will do,' his father ordered. 'We're far enough.' Sitting upright again, Adam grabbed the fishing rod and awkwardly opened the plastic container holding the maggots and placed one on the end of the line. The smell was hideous. As he cast out, the canoe rocked, and Jonathan grabbed the edge.

'It's all about patience,' Adam pointed out. 'We could be here all day without so much as a bite.'

They watched the line, ready to act if it moved.

'Have you ever caught anything?' Jonathan asked.

'Yeah. Old boots and a cold.' Adam laughed hard as he slapped his son on the back. 'Here, take the rod. See this on the side? Wind it slowly if you have a bite. It's all about the battle.'

Grabbing the rod, Jonathan sat in the canoe, watching the line, waiting patiently for something to happen. After a few minutes, it started dipping.

'Yes, that's it. You got something,' his father said excitedly. 'OK, don't lose it now – keep focused.'

Gently spinning the handle, Jonathan reeled the line in towards the canoe.

'Slower. You're going too fast. You'll lose it.'

'I won't,' Jonathan fired back. 'It's fine.'

'Slower,' his father shouted. 'Why don't you listen?'

'Dad, I can do this.'

As the empty line came out of the water, his father looked at him. 'See, I told you. I knew you'd lost it.'

'OK, I can go again.'

Grabbing the rod from his son's hands, Adam continued with a tirade of abuse. 'I knew it. I could guarantee the line was empty. You don't listen, that's the problem. If you'd gone easy as I'd said—'

'I did go easy. I went easy, Dad.'

Adam placed another maggot on the end of the line and again cast out into the lake.

'You're such an idiot. Your mother and I should have come alone. You ruin everything.'

Jonathan felt the rush of blood as if his body would explode. 'I'm not an idiot.'

Smirking, Adam turned to his son. 'Wow. Hit a nerve, have I? Don't act like such a baby. Start listening to me, and we'll get along fine.'

'We've never got along.'

Adam looked back at the water. 'Well, whose fault is that?'

'Not mine.' Jonathan wondered how far to push it. He needed to say all he could without his father lashing out. 'I hate you sometimes.'

As the words resonated, Adam threw the rod into the water. 'Is that so? Well, you know what, I hate—' Adam brought his hand to his chest, the pain unbearable. His face went bright red as he gasped for breath.

The canoe rocked as Jonathan watched his father stagger and drop into the ice-cold water.

Adam's body turned face up, the life jacket keeping him afloat, and he reached his hands towards his son, pleading with his eyes for help.

Jonathan sat there, calmly staring at his father, watching as he struggled, and finally, Adam took his last breath.

His only regret was that he didn't have it recorded so he could watch it over and over. Twenty minutes later, Jonathan began rowing to the shore.

15

SUNDAY EVENING

'Where are we going?' Abbey asked, sitting in the back of the Kia Sorento. She'd only had moments to get ready, throwing on a light brown dress and mascara. Holding a small mirror to her face in the back seat, she applied bright red lipstick and blusher. Then placed the mirror in her handbag.

Marty drove, listening to the satnav navigate them through London. He peered at Beth, his daughter's question resonating in his mind. They couldn't tell her. It wasn't fair. In two days, she was taking her final exam.

'We're going for a bite to eat,' Marty answered.

Abbey sat back in the seat, welcoming the cool breeze from the air con. 'That's a little spontaneous.'

'Well, your mother had to rush home and missed out on lunch, so I thought I'd make it up to her.'

Concerned, Abbey placed her hand on her mother's shoulder. 'Are you feeling better?'

Reaching her arm back, she held her daughter's hand. 'I am. I'm not sure what was wrong earlier,' Beth lied. She thought about Cass Carter. The guy who was going to stream her murder. The App that Marty had received. So many consequences raced through her mind. Would they find Cass? Was Beth's rash decision putting her family at risk? While watching the stream earlier, she could hear the torment in the man's voice; a tortured soul forced into a horrific situation to save his daughter's life. He'd had a picture sent through of his little girl bouncing on a trampoline, threatening her life; they'd kill her if he didn't do what they asked. Any parent would do the same to save their child.

Tears filled her eyes, and she tried to swallow the lump in her throat, fighting the urge to cry the stress away until no tears were left.

She looked through the windscreen at the people's lives playing out in front of her. She was just a mere spectator, and it reminded her of The App, watching from the safety of her house, while others were forced to play their part in this horrendous game. She tried to imagine the sick bastards who'd developed it, how they spoke, their mannerisms and beliefs. The more she thought about it, the angrier Beth became. They were evil, getting off on the anguish of others, wallowing in people's torment.

As Marty drove in silence along a quiet side road, Beth gripped the sides of the seat, feeling like she'd pass out; although the air con blew an ice-cold gust on her body, it felt like her skin was on fire.

'What are you thinking?' Marty asked.

'Huh? Oh, nothing.'

With his hand on hers, squeezing gently, both of them knew what had to be done.

His voice was low as he angled his head towards her. 'Are you sure about this?'

'What choice do we have?' Beth whispered.

From the back of the car, Abbey asked, 'What's going on with you two? You're acting weird. I've never known you to be so quiet.'

Closing her eyes, Beth struggled to stem the threatening outburst, wanting to hold her daughter, to tell her about the terrible predicament which had landed on their door. How they'd planned to visit a restaurant in Archway to stop an innocent man from killing a guiltless woman. Instead, she shifted her body, facing her daughter. 'We're fine. What do you mean?'

'I mean, most of the time I have to fight to get a bloody word in. I don't like this. It's not the natural way you are together.'

Needing to change the subject, Beth asked, 'How is the revising going? Do you feel confident?'

'I do, but... How do I explain it? The more you look over something, the more you wonder if you understand it. Do you know what I mean?'

'Yes,' Marty piped up. 'That's how I feel with your mother.'

Beth jokingly slapped him on the forearm. 'You're the most complex person I've ever met.'

'Me? I'm an open book.'

'Yeah, with no words,' Abbey laughed.

Looking at Beth, he said, 'Can you believe the hassle I'm getting?'

Beth smiled. 'You bring it on yourself.'

At that moment, Marty wished his life would freeze, the banter with his family, under The App's radar and safe inside their vehicle where nothing and no one could hurt them. He had a dreadful feeling they were at hell's door, about to enter. Beth wanted to help, and no amount of words would sway her mind.

He would back her decision a hundred per cent. But it was the possible repercussions that terrified him the most.

* * *

As they pulled up at traffic lights on Holloway Road in North London, Beth pointed ahead. 'There it is.'

With a deep breath, struggling to draw air into his lungs, Marty pulled the car over to the pavement and parked up.

'Why this place?' Abbey asked as she undid her seatbelt. 'It's a long way to come to eat.' Her phone rang, and Abbey stepped out of the car. It gave Beth and Marty a few seconds to talk alone.

'Right. We need to turn off Wi-Fi on our phones,' Marty insisted. 'The restaurant's router will give our IP address, which means they can trace us. We can't risk them knowing where we are.'

'Look at you. Did you see that on Google?'

Nodding, Marty smiled and looked out of the windows onto the street. 'Technology goes over my head, but I understand that once we keep off their internet, we should be all right.'

'What about location services?' Beth asked.

Sighing, Marty said, 'If The App has a tracker, they'll know where we are. As far as they're concerned, we're just a normal family going for a meal. Turning off Wi-Fi is a regular occurrence, but it might alarm them if I disable location services. I don't want to tamper with the phone and cause alarm or a spotlight on us for no reason. I couldn't leave my phone at home as I need to see how this situation plays out. There's no reason for them to watch us at the moment. We just need to act normal and take our chances.'

'What if there are cameras?'

'Shit. I didn't think of that. The App's developers can easily hack into those. There are apps which allow anyone to view public security cameras. Are there any inside the restaurant?'

'I don't remember. Mum and I came here a while ago, and I wasn't really paying attention.'

'We have to be certain, Beth.' Looking along the road from the driver's seat, Marty glimpsed at the buildings on either side. He couldn't see any CCTV from where he sat, but it didn't mean anything. Cameras were often small and hidden. He reached for Beth's hand and looked into her eyes. 'We're in this together. Are you certain it's what you want?'

Beth nodded, unable to muster the strength to speak.

As Marty opened the driver's door and climbed out the car, he looked over at his daughter as she continued her call. He took in her long brown hair, her deep green eyes, the way she itched her nose with the back of her hand, deep in conversation and unaware of the hell that had landed on their doorstep. He'd do anything for his daughter. The scene of the man holding the phone and making his way to the restaurant to murder Cass Carter replayed in his mind. He could feel the man's angst, as if Marty knew him, feeling his emotion, his apprehension. Swiping his mobile phone screen, Marty disabled Wi-Fi. Beth joined him on the pavement and did the same.

Abbey looked at her parents waiting patiently on the kerb and flicked her eyes upwards as if apologising. A minute later, she ended the call. 'Sorry, It was Michael from school. We're helping each other revise. He's having a panic attack about the exam.'

'Abbey, can you turn off Wi-Fi?' Marty requested.

Looking at her phone, she declared. 'It's off. Why do you want Wi-Fi disabled? You guys are getting more weird by the second.'

It sounded suspicious, Marty knew it, but he had little choice. 'Just keep it off. I'll explain later,' he lied, hoping she wouldn't ask again.

The three of them walked away from the car. Marty and Beth held hands, feeling each other's damp, clammy skin. Abbey strolled behind them, placing her phone in her handbag.

An Italian flag hung above the restaurant door, and beside it, the name emblazoned in cursive script. They were at the right place. Through the large window, Beth looked inside at what looked like a restauranteur's dream; staff were waltzing around with trays delivering drinks and food; a couple of guests stood beside the till waiting to be seated. Families sat at tables, laughing, jovial and deep in conversation.

Beth's stomach began to ache, not from hunger, but like a piece of string was pulling at her insides. For a moment, her world became blurry, and she placed her hands against the glass.

'Mum. What's wrong? Are you OK?'

'I'm fine. I just feel dizzy. I think I might still be a bit dehydrated with the heat.'

Marty moved his face close to Beth and whispered, 'We can still go home.'

Beth knew how stupid it was, coming here after witnessing everything that had happened to Cass Carter over the last day, how people had tried to end her life to save their families. It was all so wrong. When she'd looked at the latest stream, sat on the sofa with Marty, adrenaline kicked in, taking over her body amid tragedy and spurring her on. At that moment, everything else seemed meaningless, and the danger was trivial. On the drive over, her conviction had faltered, and she'd wondered whether this was the right choice, but looking at the innocent people in the restaurant, she thought of how this could be happening to any one of them. Something stirred her emotions, charged her body; she had to act.

She had to save Cass Carter.

'I'm going inside,' she confirmed.

Kissing his wife on the cheek, Marty pulled the door open to the restaurant. As Beth and Abbey walked through, he scanned everyone's faces. The music was loud – an old Dean Martin song bellowed from the speakers. The smell of garlic and dough from the kitchen was welcoming and enticed their appetite.

Marty looked to the ceiling and along the walls searching for a security camera. So far, he saw nothing to indicate they were being watched. The conversation from the tables was boisterous, families laughing hard and shouting over the music. The air conditioning whirred above his head, the old rickety-looking unit fixed to the ceiling. Staff balanced drinks and plates on trays held high in the air as they waltzed passed customers, and the sound of pans clattered in the kitchen behind the steam.

'Can I help you?' a large man wearing a tight black suit asked. Recognising Beth, he shook her hand, kissing her on both cheeks. 'Ahh, welcome back! So lovely to have you with us.'

'Thank you, Roberto, it's good to be back. This is my husband and daughter,' Beth confirmed.

Roberto shook their hands. 'It's good to see you. How is your *mamma*?' he asked in a strong Italian accent. His thick grey hair was messy, and his cheeks were full of broken veins.

'She's good – she can't complain.'

'She bloody can – it's just we choose not to listen,' Marty said, and Roberto laughed. 'We'd like a table for three, please.'

His chin dropped to his chest as his eyes scanned over a book resting on the counter. 'Have you booked?' Roberto asked.

'I'm sorry, we haven't,' Marty fired back. His heart sank for a moment.

'I can fit you in the corner at the far end. But we have another sitting at 10pm. Otherwise, you can move to another table if we have a cancellation. How does that sound?'

'Perfect,' Marty answered.

'Follow me.' Roberto led them past the kitchen, checking in with his customers as they walked to the far corner.

A candle sat in the middle of the table; the flame seemed to dance as it flickered in the soft light. The table was set with shiny cutlery, and the tablecloth was elegant, draped over the edges.

Roberto pulled the chairs out, first for Beth and Abbey and then for Marty.

They sat, all of them facing the front.

'Well, this is nice. Thank you both so much. It's been a while since we've done this,' Abbey stated.

Marty ignored his daughter and picked up the menu, unable to concentrate. The words seemed like scribbles, and the pictures were one big haze that morphed into one another. Dropping the menu, he peered around the room. Any one of the men who sat eating could be the person who was streaming earlier. He searched for Cass but couldn't see her, praying she didn't turn up. Could something happen here? Surely not. There would be too many witnesses. But too much pressure could do things to people. It drove them insane. If anything were about to happen, he would do all he could to shield Beth and Abbey from it.

As he sat with his family, surrounded by others blissfully ignorant of the weight of the ridiculous decision they'd made being here, apprehension addled his mind.

They were in a restaurant with someone possibly driven to kill.

* * *

A couple of tables away, a man reached for his phone and brought the screen to his face.

Gripping the edge of the table, Marty watched in horror. He looked around but everyone was oblivious. Beth's eyes were still glancing over the menu. Abbey was tapping on her phone, texting her friend, Michael, who was probably still stressing about the exam. The staff were attending to the guests, the chefs busy in the kitchen as another Dean Martin song came on, blaring from the speakers.

Was the man streaming? Was it the same guy he and Beth had watched as he left his house and drove over here?

With his fingers squeezing the edge of the table, Marty watched as the man began speaking.

'Hey. How is everything?' Bringing the phone away from his face, the man put on a pair of glasses and smiled at the screen. A woman was talking through the loudspeaker, but Marty couldn't make out the words. A waiter walked to the man's table and placed two takeaway boxes in front of him.

'It's here now. I'll be home in twenty minutes. Love you both.'

The call ended.

The man tapped a card against the reader, the waiter handed him a receipt, and he gently pushed his chair back and left.

A huge sigh pushed through Marty's lips. His body relaxed slightly.

'Dad.'

'Yes.'

'You haven't looked at the menu,' Abbey stated.

'Oh, sorry.'

'Are you OK?' Beth asked, her voice low as she placed her hand on Marty's lap under the table.

He smiled. All he wanted to do was grab her and Abbey, race across the restaurant floor and out onto the road. They'd pile into the car, lock the doors and drive until all this was over. He felt so frightened as they sat, vulnerable and exposed, wondering whether The App's creator was watching them. Was there more than one? A team of psychopaths turning the cogs from behind the scenes. The longer they sat, the more Marty thought they were making a dreadful mistake.

'What would you like to drink, sir?'

Marty hadn't even seen the waitress approaching. How the hell was he going to stop anything from happening if he hadn't even noticed the serving staff? Turning, he smiled at her. 'Just a Coke, please.'

'Very good, sir.'

Beth ordered a large wine and Abbey a sparkling water.

'I need it for my nerves,' Beth whispered.

'It's OK. Enjoy it,' Marty insisted.

'Nerves?' Abbey asked, concern in her voice.

The front door opened, and a man and woman stepped into the restaurant.

Marty and Beth knew who they were. They'd been watching the streams.

Their hearts sunk in unison as the couple were shown to their table at the back.

The woman with a one-hundred-thousand-pound bounty on her head was walking towards them.

16

SUNDAY EVENING

The legs scraped along the tiled floor as a waiter pulled out a chair, inviting Cass to sit down at their table in the Italian restaurant they'd chosen.

'This is nice,' Cass said as Ed took the seat next to her. She glanced around the room, smiling at a family sitting next to them and noticing their concerned faces. She hoped it wasn't a reflection of the food.

'I'm so sorry about the weekend. What a fuck-up,' Ed stated.

'Let's just try to forget about it.' Cass was still getting flashbacks. The crazy antics that had happened on the way to Devon and the guy breaking into the cottage had plagued any rest she'd tried to get since she got home, but as she looked around the restaurant, music playing from the speakers and the sound of laughter, the beaming smiles, couples holding hands, and clinking glasses, she couldn't feel safer. Whatever happened in Devon, whatever craziness she and Ed had been through, was over. This was her way of dealing with it, getting up and out, pushing the trauma from her mind.

'What would you like to drink?' Ed asked.

Cass looked at the menu. 'Shall we share a bottle of wine?'

'Sounds good.' The waiter came over, and Ed ordered the wine and garlic bread to start. Cass went for a large pepperoni pizza on thin bread, and Ed ordered a plate of pasta.

The air con machine whirred above their heads, pushing ice-cold air in their direction. Cass couldn't believe that after the heat of the previous day she was actually cold.

Reaching round to get the cardigan on the back of her chair, she caught the eyes of the couple next to them with a younger woman who kept staring. They were staring at her. Did she have something on her face? Her top? Cass suddenly felt very uncomfortable. She wanted to say something and ask what was wrong, but it had been such a weekend so far, the last thing she needed was more aggravation. No, she was just being paranoid. Cass drew her eyes away from their table and back to Ed.

The waiter returned with a bottle of red wine, struggling to remove the cork and clamping the bottle between his legs. His face turned a weird purple colour as he struggled, and the popping sound caused Ed to jerk in his seat. The waiter poured a small glass and let both Cass and Ed have a taste before filling the glasses.

Clinking them together, Cass downed her drink in one.

'Woah. Go easy. I don't want to have to carry you home,' Ed joked before topping up the glass with more wine.

'I don't care. Here's to the past being the past. The shit show of the last twenty-four hours is behind us.' Sipping more wine, Cass continued. 'Where the hell do you think he went?'

'Who? The guy from the cottage? I thought you wanted to forget about it.'

'I know, but I'm just asking.'

'God knows. I saw his body, the way he landed – there's no possible way he could have got up.'

'Do you think he's still out there?' Cass said.

'I don't know. Let's not think about it. Oh, I emailed the landlady about the window. And breaking the glass in the utility room to get in after the guy locked the front door. She hasn't got back to me yet, but I think she'll waive the bill – "nearly strangled to death by a raving lunatic" wouldn't do her reviews any good.' He laughed.

Cass looked up. Someone was walking towards their table.

17

SUNDAY EVENING

Cass Carter had walked into the restaurant a few minutes ago. She was here with a man, presumably her partner, and as they followed the waiter to their seats, Marty and Beth felt like they were watching celebrities. In a way they were: the woman, everyone on The App was watching, picked from social media.

They'd tried to smile at Cass and get her attention. But after all she'd been through, Marty and Beth could understand her suspicious glances.

Once Cass had arrived, the man's behaviour became even more erratic, and it confirmed to Marty and Beth that it had to be the hunter from the livestream they'd watched earlier. They looked at each other, glanced at Cass and then back again.

'What do we do?' Beth whispered.

'Are you going to tell me what's going on?' Abbey had had enough.

'What do you mean?' Beth fired back, startled by her daughter's blunt question.

With a sarcastic smirk, Abbey stated, 'The whispers,

how unsettled you both are. Mum coming home early from Oxford Street, the dash to this restaurant. Don't get me wrong, it's beautiful here, and the food's great, but a long way to come for an Italian.'

Marty wanted to tell her, to explain everything, but it wasn't fair. Abbey didn't need to know what was happening. She'd freak out, possibly make a scene. He had to think of something. A way to get the message to Cass before the guy sitting at the table came over. Surely he wouldn't try something here, in front of everyone. But they'd watched the stream; a person under such pressure was capable of anything. Smiling at Abbey, he said, 'Nothing is going on. Your mother loves this place. Like I said, I felt bad when she came home earlier from Oxford Street, so I suggested we go out this evening.'

'Yeah. All right. Whatever.'

A man stood up, looking around the restaurant.

Rife with uncertainty, Marty and Beth glanced across the room.

'What is it?' Abbey peeked over to the man standing at the table, seeing him unsteady on his feet. 'Do you know him?'

Averting her eyes, Beth said, 'Who?'

'Oh, come on. The guy looking like he's about to explode. I don't think he's well.'

He turned, looking directly at Cass. Wiping the sweat from his forehead, he grabbed his phone from the table and pointed it around the restaurant.

Beth eyed Cass, sat at the next table, deep in conversation, and glanced back to the man holding the mobile phone. 'What's he doing?' Beth whispered to her husband.

'He's streaming,' Marty stated a little too loud.

'Streaming? What do you mean? Streaming what? This is so weird. Who is he?'

Ignoring the question from his daughter, Marty glimpsed the other tables. The man holding the mobile phone was the only customer alone.

Abbey's phone beeped, and she flipped it over to check who it was. Michael again. Leaning forward, elbows on the table, she began tapping.

'Take Abbey to the toilet,' Marty mouthed silently.

Nodding, Beth pushed her chair back and stood. 'I need the loo. Will you come with me, Abbey?'

She placed the phone into her handbag and got up. 'No problem. Dad, will you order me another sparkling water? I'm still thirsty.'

'Of course.'

As Beth and Abbey strolled across the floor towards the toilets, the guy holding the mobile phone was approached by a waitress, perhaps asking if he was OK. He sat back down and the conversation seemed jovial. She'd inadvertently bought Cass more time.

Soon enough, the waitress nodded and walked over to the bar. Marty observed, seeing her return with a large whisky. The man's phone was placed on the table in front of him, and he kept turning, looking at Cass. So far, she hadn't noticed.

The tension was unnerving. Marty's body trembled, his heart raced and his hands were clammy. Beth and Abbey could be back from the toilet any moment. He prayed she'd keep Abbey in there as long as possible. There wasn't time. He had to do something now.

Pushing the chair back, Marty stood. The restaurant oozed a relaxed atmosphere; the empty plates, staff with trays of alcohol, smiles on their faces and soft music playing through the speakers, but he'd never felt so tense.

It was now or never. Marty strolled towards Cass.

She looked up, a smile thinly veiling a concerned demeanour. 'Can I help you?' she asked.

Her partner looked at Marty, his eyes almost piercing his soul, and reached for Cass's hand. 'What is it, mate?'

'You're—'

'There she is!' A voice practically exploded. 'OK. This is it. I'm streaming. I can't wait any longer. I'm so sorry.' Grabbing a steak knife from the table next to him, the man ran at Cass, his eyes wild and focused as he charged along the tiled floor.

'Quick,' Marty shouted, lifting the cloth. 'Under there.'

Cass heaved her body backwards, her chair falling against the wall. Screaming, she dropped to the floor and crawled under the table.

Her partner jumped up, frozen in terror as the hunter, now inches from their table, pointed his phone at him.

Instinctively, Marty rushed forward, barging the man with the phone with such force he hit his head on the edge of a table and collapsed to the ground.

Staff came rushing over, guests dropped their cutlery and the place fell deathly silent.

The bathroom door opened, and Beth froze, holding Abbey back.

'Dad,' Abbey called out over her mum's shoulder. 'What's happened?'

The sound of Cass's sobs rose from under the table. While her partner leant against the back wall, completely stunned.

As Marty backed away, Abbey rushed to him, placing

her arms around his waist. 'Are you OK? What happened, Dad?'

'I'm fine.'

Beth joined her family, and the three of them huddled together.

More staff stood over the man lying on the floor, and guests came over, crowding him. A chef asked if anyone knew first aid.

'Who is he?' Abbey asked.

Her parents didn't answer, but it would only be a matter of minutes before Abbey would find out the true horror that had landed at their door.

* * *

Walking back to their table, Marty saw the blank, vacant expression on Ed's face as he leant against the wall. 'Are you all right?' Marty asked.

'Yes. Thank you for... You know.' Ed crouched and tried to coax Cass out, who was cowering under the table. 'You're safe now. It's over.'

Her eyes were wide and empty; mascara smudged across her face, her expression dazed. As she crawled out from under the table, sharp, whimpering noises came from her mouth; she looked between the two men, so lost and confused.

'Has anyone called the police?' a voice called out. 'Look, he's coming round.'

The man who'd attacked Cass sat up. For a moment, he looked bewildered as he glanced around, seeing people gathered, staring at him. He reached for his phone then touched the cut on the side of his head, wincing, before inspecting his bloodstained fingers. Suddenly, he stumbled up, guilt-ridden and angry, placing the knife in his pocket and running across the restaurant, charging through the door and out onto the street.

Having lured her out from under the table, Ed helped Cass to her feet, holding her tight and never wanting to let go. She shook in his arms, her stunned body so fragile and vulnerable, and he eased her into a chair.

They watched nervous guests filtering out as the owner, Roberto, apologised and shook hands with everyone as they left. Then he came over to the back of the restaurant and knelt down beside Cass, offering her a napkin. 'Please accept my apologies, *signora*. Nothing like this has happened before. I've called the police. They should be here soon. Would you like a drink? For the shock? On the house, of course.'

Lifting a hand, Ed said, 'There's no need, really. But thank you.'

Most of the guests had now left. The chefs tidied the kitchen, and the staff wiped surfaces and turned chairs upside down, placing them on the tables.

Cass looked up at her saviour, dabbing the napkin that the owner had given her on her eyes. 'Thank you... for earlier'

'It's OK,' Marty answered as gently as possible.

'Dad, what happened?' Abbey asked her father. 'Who was that guy lying on the floor? Why did he just run out?'

Marty looked at Beth, seeing her nod. They couldn't keep it from her any longer.

'I need to—' A tap on the glass doors caused Marty to stop mid-sentence.

'The police are here.' Roberto rushed to the front and let them inside.

They made their way over to Cass, who watched them sceptically, unsure if she could trust anyone at this moment.

The male officer was in his thirties. He was tall with pale skin and a heavy blond stubble. He looked at Cass, smiling, presumably to ease her tension. His partner was much shorter with wavy black hair, a pleasant face and was much younger. The female officer took charge, asking if they could sit, going through a series of questions. 'Can you explain what happened in your own words?'

'I... I don't know. It happened so fast.'

'What did he look like?'

'I'm not sure. I didn't get a proper look at him.'

'OK, Do you know him? I mean, did you recognise the attacker, perhaps someone you know from social media or work perhaps?'

'No. I don't think so. I... I don't know. I'm sorry. My head is so confused,' Cass mustered. As she struggled, Ed gave most of the answers.

Turning to Marty, Beth and Abbey, the female officer asked what they'd seen.

Marty told the story exactly how Ed had explained it. The guy walked over to the table with a knife, and Marty barged him to the floor.

Reassuring them that they'd look for the man, the officer took Cass and Ed's details and said they'd be in touch with any news.

Once the police had gone, Abbey looked at her father. 'Dad, please tell me what's going on?'

Again, Beth nodded and Marty braced himself. It was time. Addressing Cass and Ed, he began to speak. 'Please listen and, although it's going to sound like madness, take this seriously. You are both in severe danger.'

'What do you mean?' Ed asked, his voice filled with concern.

Looking at Cass, Marty continued. 'You may think this is ludicrous, that I'm winding you up or something. But I've never been more serious. People are trying to kill you.'

'Oh God,' Cass replied. Glancing at Ed, she recalled all the incidents from the last twenty-four hours, everything racing through her mind. It didn't come as the biggest shock. 'Why? Why is this happening?'

'I received a link from a friend this morning. It promised a chance of winning one hundred thousand pounds.'

Again, Cass dabbed the tissue against her eyes and sniffed hard. 'What has this got to do with me?'

'I clicked the link and it downloaded an app. An hour later, I received a picture of my wife shopping in Oxford Street with her mother.' Marty saw the faces, studying him, sceptical, the eyes almost boring a hole in his skin. 'Then the threats came through; I'm not supposed to talk about The App or delete it. Everyone who has The App, must participate in a hunt at least once a month or a family member is murdered. Then they come for the person who has The App.'

'I still don't understand. What app? A hunt? What has this got to do with me?' Cass insisted.

Marty continued. 'Every Friday morning, a person is randomly selected from social media. Their picture and details are displayed across The App. The first person to kill them wins a hundred thousand pounds. It's you, Cass. You've been selected.'

Marty was expecting Cass to break down on the spot. But instead, she remained still, except for her hands shaking as she reached out to her husband. 'I, I don't understand. Why me? Who would do such a thing? What have I done?'

Ed knelt beside his wife and pulled her close. Rocking in his arms, she sobbed into her husband's shirt, repeating the same words over and over. 'I don't understand.'

'I'm so sorry to have to tell you,' Marty offered. 'It's your choice now whether to tell the police, but please be aware, it's breaking the rules, and they may kill you both.'

'Dad, are we in danger? What's going on?' Abbey asked, her voice quiet and grave.

The words almost broke his heart; his daughter, so innocent, so ambitious and learning of the horror her parents were going through.

'I will do everything to bring this person or persons down.'

'Let me see it, Dad. Let me see The App.'

Looking at Beth for approval, Marty reluctantly grabbed his phone, opened The App to Cass's profile and passed it to his daughter. 'Don't click on any of the links. Do you hear me? I don't want you watching any of the videos.' She didn't need to see the full horror if he could help it.

Abbey sat, opened-mouthed, a ball of stress developing in her stomach as she read Cass's profile. She looked across to their table, unable to believe what was happening.

Pulling her face from Ed's chest, her voice weak, Cass asked, 'Can I see?'

'I'm not sure that's a good idea—' Ed began to protest, but Abbey handed Cass the phone. The sounds of her gasps filled the restaurant as staff members looked over.

'This is so fucked up,' Ed announced, after looking over Cass's shoulder at the footage on The App. 'How do we stop this? Is it one person? A few? How many?'

'I'm not sure,' Marty said from his table. 'It could be one person or a group of fucking psychos involved. It's hard to say.'

Ed clicked on a recent link, watching him and Cass walking to their BMW along the quiet country road. 'Oh my God, this was the piñata. The guy who chased us.'

Another link showed the Jeep, ramming them from behind, the driver filming with his mobile phone camera.

Ed looked at Cass. 'This explains everything. We need to give this to the police.'

Marty took back his phone and said gravely, 'It's your call. If you tell the police, they may try and kill you both. But I wouldn't blame you. I'm already breaking their rules by being here, but we couldn't stand by and watch you being murdered. Before coming, we watched the stream of the man who attacked you leaving his house. Beth recognised the restaurant. That's why we're here. I'm hoping at this moment, we're off the radar. Roberto has no security cameras, but they're watching you both.'

Abbey glanced at Cass and Ed, then her mum and dad, the true terror of The App finally registering. 'How are we going to get out of this?'

They fell silent, the sense of dread washing over each of them as they sat at the back of the restaurant. Marty, Beth and Abbey held each other's hands, feeling so sorry for the woman sitting at the next table, while Ed and Cass just stared into nothingness, numb.

Eventually, Marty broke the silence. 'I think you should speak with the police.' As the words left his lips, he realised how ludicrous the idea was. But he'd said it; it may be their only chance of survival. 'You're in danger.'

'I agree with Marty,' Beth added. 'It may be your only way out.'

'No,' Ed insisted. 'Cass has been selected, so they can probably see everything through The App. If she's been chosen, we're on the radar. So I'm guessing they'll be giving clues to our whereabouts. The only way out of this for us is to keep moving and hide. Maybe it will blow over.'

'I don't think it will blow over,' Marty said with a concerned voice. Someone is chosen every Friday. Their profile is possibly left on The App until—' He couldn't finish the sentence.

'We'll take our chances and keep moving.'

Marty stood, Beth and Abbey, followed. 'OK, I understand. But we have to go. I can't risk my family being here any longer. Please be careful. I hope you both make it out alive,' Marty stated.

Placing his arm out, Ed shook hands with Marty. 'Thank you for your help.'

Roberto held the door open, and he thanked them for everything.

As they stepped onto the warm street, Marty heard Roberto lock the front door. Turning, he gazed into the restaurant at Ed and Cass. They were standing, embracing each other. His heart went out to them.

Roberto waved as he stepped away from the front door.

Then, a chef came out of the kitchen, holding a mobile phone in front of him. Marty could see his lips moving as he spoke. The edge of the knife he was carrying glistened as it caught the light.

'No!' Marty screamed, banging his fists against the glass, helpless as he watched the chef approach Cass and stab her multiple times in the neck.

18

1981

As Jonathan rowed back to the shore, he saw the shock on his mother's face as she stood by the water's edge.

'Where's your father?' she yelled. 'Jonathan, where is he?'

'There's been an accident. He fell into the water.' Stepping out of the canoe, he ran to her. She shook uncontrollably, gasping, unable to get her words out as the horror oozed from her body. Jonathan held her tight, breathing in the familiar scent of vanilla and rose.

Gill struggled to pull her son away, Jonathan's powerful arms gripping tightly around her waist. 'Go and... Go and tell the security guard to call an ambulance. Go, Jonathan. Be quick.' She pushed Jonathan towards the security hut, and then stepped into the canoe he'd just come from, pushing off then ferociously dipping and sweeping the water with the oar, trying desperately to get to her husband. Gill glanced back over her shoulder at her son running to fetch help. Although she didn't want to give it light, she couldn't help but wonder whether Jonathan had done everything he could to rescue his father. She'd witnessed his mood swings, how he looked at Adam while being remonstrated, the eyes a window to his wicked thoughts.

She stopped rowing, the heat from the sun tiring her arms quicker than she thought. The only sounds she could hear were the lake lapping at the canoe and a flock of birds taking to the sky. At any other time, they'd be soothing, but Gill knew something was amiss. She could feel the tension exuding from her surroundings.

Standing, she looked out over the vacant lake, stunned, terrified at what she'd find. 'Adam!' she screamed. The canoe rocked, and Gill fell forward, gripping the edge of the wood. Getting back up, she turned, trying to balance, and saw Jonathan and the security guard racing towards the water. A couple of minutes later, they were inside a canoe and heading towards her.

Gill searched the water for any sign of her husband, and soon saw a figure wearing a bright red lifejacket floating in the water. A deathly roar ripped from her mouth. 'Adam. Are you OK? Please, God, someone help us. Adam.' She sat back in the canoe and continued to row, desperately whining as she approached his lifeless body.

Jonathan watched from the canoe behind, trying to make sense of his mixed emotions. He was elated that his father was finally out of his life but devastated for his mother. She didn't deserve this.

He hadn't thought it through at the time, while he sat, watching his father die. He'd make it up to her. He had to. Jonathan was the man of the house now.

The security guard held the oars, wiping sweat from his face between strokes, panting for breath as he cut through the water.

In his mind, Jonathan heard the sound of his father, his voice harsh, raw with so much anger.

Then it disappeared.

* * *

Over the next few weeks, Jonathan witnessed his mother's decline. She was devastated, beyond broken at the death of her husband.

Adam's funeral was difficult for Jonathan. Not because he had to look at the coffin displayed in the church, but because of the relations queuing to shake his hand, telling them how sorry they were for his loss, and him having to fawn sadness, thanking people for their prayers. That was a hard act to pull off. Inside, he wanted everyone to disappear and to spend the rest of his life with his mother, just the two of them, safe in her arms.

Night after night, Jonathan stood outside her bedroom, listening to her wailing as she sobbed into her pillow. Often, he'd enter the room and try to talk to her, but seeing her blank expression, the way she looked at him as if she knew what he'd done, would have him leaving again soon after.

But how could she know?

Then came the phone call. They'd just had dinner – Jonathan's favourite, ham, egg and chips – and he was playing Frogger, trying to steer the amphibian through the traffic without being hit. His mother seemed more cheerful this evening and shimmered in a plain red dress and matching shoes. As she tidied up the kitchen, she hummed 'Tainted Love' by Soft Cell, which they'd heard a few times on the radio. How very fitting, Jonathan thought when he pictured his father.

As Jonathan held the controller in his hand, sitting on

the sofa in the living room, he heard the house phone ring. Standing, he turned the TV down and listened through the open door to the hallway.

His mother was whispering, her voice hushed and exhausted.

'I'm OK, Joyce. It gets a little easier to tolerate day by day... What choice do I have?... Jonathan? He's all right. I haven't spoken to him about Adam's death, if I'm honest. It's tough for him being a teenager. The passing of a parent is hard to take.' Her voice lowered. Jonathan sat back on the sofa as he heard her walking towards the living room door and pushing it closed, but not completely, so that he could still hear his mother's conversation with her sister, Aunty Joyce. Listening to her footsteps move along the hallway, he stood and crept to the living room door.

Gill continued. 'I have to talk to someone, Joyce. I'm going mad inside.' She burst into tears, wheezing as she caught her breath. 'I... I think Jonathan let him die. I think he's responsible. He could have done something to help.'

Jonathan stepped away from the door, feeling like he'd been hit with a bat; the shock drove a surge of anguish through his body. He fell against the living room door and slid down, collapsing into a pile on the floor.

* * *

His mother's conversation with his aunt played over and over in his mind as Jonathan lay on his bed. How could she know he was responsible? He couldn't hide it any longer. Jonathan had to talk to her. He had to convince her that somehow he never had an option.

Standing in the upstairs hallway, he listened hard for his mother's voice. The phone call had finished; he'd heard her climbing the stairs, closing her bedroom door, her voice replaced by the mumblings of the TV.

Inhaling, ready to confront her, he suddenly felt dizzy; his eyes blurred as he rehearsed what to say. Should he admit it? Should he tell her and apologise? How would she take it? His mind was overloaded with questions.

As he stood outside her bedroom, he tapped his knuckles against the wood, braced himself and opened the door.

Gill was hanging from a rafter, the rope tight around her neck, her body dangling in mid-air, and a chair resting on its side.

'No. Mum, what have you done? I'm so sorry.' He tried desperately to release her, lifting her body and struggling to get the rope from around her neck. But it was no use.

The only person he ever loved had killed herself.

Because of him.

19

SUNDAY EVENING

It was the second time Gary Miller had killed since downloading The App, and it felt good to take the prize again. Two weeks ago, Stephen Power, a middle-aged man who'd been selected from social media, had his profile and photo splashed on The App's main page.

There were clues, the first being a picture of Lady Godiva riding naked on a horse; a historical figure mainly remembered for a legend dating back to at least the thirteenth century in which she rode naked – covered only in her long hair – through the streets of Coventry to protest the oppressive taxation that her husband, Leofric, imposed on his tenants.

As Gary researched further, he also found out the term 'peeping Tom' also originated from later versions of this legend, in which a man named Thomas watched her ride and was struck blind. In other versions of the story, Thomas died on the spot.

A very fitting story for the way The App operated.

Gary thought it a safe bet that Stephen Power resided in Coventry, and so he took a short drive along the M1 from

London, eagerly glimpsing at his phone on the passenger seat and listening for a new message providing the next clue.

As he drove, glancing at people in their vehicles, he wondered if any of them were doing the same as him – whether driven by the dollar signs in their eyes or by fear to protect their loved ones, maybe both – forced to do something they'd never normally consider.

For Gary, it was the money. As simple as that. He'd received a picture of his son, taken from outside a restaurant in Swiss Cottage, North West London. Rory was sitting at a table, holding a woman's hand, a bottle of wine perched in the middle with two full glasses.

Gary hated his son and smirked when the picture came through, unable to forgive Rory for convincing his mother to kick him out after his infidelity. Rose never took Gary back. That, and Rory accusing his father of trying it on with his ex-wife, Helen, after they'd split up. OK, Gary had been a comforting shoulder to cry on, calling over to the flat to check how she was doing, and as he made love to his son's ex-wife, he couldn't help feeling a small victory. If his son was going to fire accusations, there may as well be probable cause.

Gary knew he was the lowest of the low. Sitting in the driver's seat of his transit van, he fought the stirring in his groin, thinking about Helen's body and what he'd like to do with her. He hadn't called her for a few months; maybe it was time to rekindle their acquaintance.

After serving in the army for a few years as a mechanic, he was discharged for bad behaviour; now a nightclub bouncer, Gary was paid to beat the shit out of low-life drunks.

The App was going to be his new venture, a way to make serious money.

If people had to die, Gary might as well be the master of their fate. And be paid to do it too.

His phone pinged, vibrating on the passenger seat. Pulling to the inside lane, he slowed the van, picked up the mobile phone and saw the latest clue. A picture of Robin Hood, dressed in green and holding a bow and arrow.

'Find Robin Hood Lane in Coventry,' Gary instructed the satnav. No results were found. 'Find Robin Hood Way.' Again, no results. Frustrated, Gary shouted, 'Find Robin Hood Road!' Bingo. The address was just over thirty minutes away.

As he pulled off the motorway, following the A45, his phone pinged again.

Another clue.

The square root of eighty-one.

Hopeful the target lived at 9 Robin Hood Road, Gary suddenly felt unstoppable.

He was going to make shitloads of money.

* * *

Gary pulled up outside the house, a tired looking semi-detached building, the red brickwork crumbling and patchy, wisteria crawling along its surface. Reaching for the rope in the footwell, he stepped out of the van, gently closing the door and slid around the side entrance.

Unaware he was being watched, Stephen Power sat in the kitchen, tapping keys on his laptop, oblivious to his profile splashed over The App's main page and the hundred-thousand-pound bounty on his head.

Creeping back along the side entrance to the front of the

house, Gary noticed a window cleaner, a ladder under his arm and a sign-written van parked at the top of the street, and he was struck by an idea. Gary marched up to the front door with confidence and rang the doorbell. It was a risk if Stephen Power didn't actually have his windows cleaned, but he'd cross that bridge if it came to it.

His target opened the door moments after the doorbell stopped, and Gary declared that he was collecting the money while pointing to the window cleaner. 'Oh, course. Just give me a sec.' Stephen walked back into the kitchen to search for cash.

Gary stepped in and closed the door behind him.

Stephen turned, perturbed at his rudeness. 'Er, excuse me. Would you mind—?'

Gary punched him in the face before he could finish his sentence and watched him drop to the floor. As he turned his body over, Stephen cried for help but Gary just dug his knee harder into his back, making his victim cry out in pain, placed the rope around his neck and pulled hard. Filming everything with the phone held in his right hand, Gary watched as Stephen's body arched and twisted until it fell limp against the taut rope.

The money was transferred to his bank account the following morning.

This time around, the clues to locate Cass Carter were proving more tricky. The previous morning, the clue had stated:

A county in England starting with a letter which, if on its side, resembles a tongue.

Gary had that one. The letter 'D'. But which county?

Derbyshire, Dorset, Devon, Durham?

In the hope she was a social media user and had posted something about her weekend plans, Gary had pulled up

Cass's Facebook page, but there was nothing. Her Twitter account hadn't been active for a couple of years, and she didn't have Instagram. Other Cass Carters appeared, but the photos weren't her.

Taking a wild stab at it, he drove to Dorset, waiting for another hint.

After spending hours cruising the streets and knowing how conspicuous he looked, Gary pulled into a side road and parked, waiting impatiently for something to reveal her whereabouts. His phone pinged—another clue.

A town. Take the 'E' out of this eight-letter word, and you could be making an offer for a type of British car.

This stumped him. Gary tried everything, sat in his van, wracking his brain, Googling towns and trying to dissect the clue. Frustrated, he punched the steering wheel, banging his fist on the dashboard.

'Come on, think.' His brain struggled to function; the more he guessed, the more frustrated he became, reminding him of Rumpelstiltskin.

Deciding to call it a day and give up on this hunt, Gary drove back to London, the latest clue mulling over in his mind.

A town. Take the 'E' out of this eight-letter word, and you could be making an offer for a make of British car. What did it even mean?

Nearly three hours later, as he pulled off the M1 at Brent Cross in North West London, he figured it out.

Bideford.

* * *

Gary's misfortune changed when he saw another hint. He'd got home late last night, having decided that driving all the way back to Devon would have been a waste of time, and had slept most of Sunday. As he lay in bed, watching recent streams within The App, the words appeared on the main page.

A street in North London which sounds similar to the Christmas song, Holiday Road.

And then another clue appeared.

A famous Italian footballer with the surname, Baggio.

Roberto's on Holloway Road.

Now, Gary had another chance at Cass Carter.

* * *

As Gary drove along Holloway Road, his phone sounded from the passenger seat. Before leaving the flat, he'd watched the live feed of a man narrating as he drove over here, and Gary feared he was too late. But this second stream, which he opened once he'd parked up, showed the inside of Roberto's restaurant, the same terrified voice narrating.

Gary watched with anticipation, seeing the streamer run towards Cass, he wanted the money for himself, but watching the hunt was just as exciting. But just as the man barrelled towards the target, another customer barged him, knocking him to the floor. The picture went blank, and a minute later, Gary saw a man running along the street from the direction of the restaurant. It must have been him.

It was time.

Stepping out of the van, Gary walked along the side entrance to the back of the restaurant. Customers and staff were standing, grouped together, and the kitchen was empty. Gary grabbed a knife from the worktop and a chef's hat from a shelf above his head to camouflage himself, then side-footed it to the toilet along the corridor, waiting in a cubicle. He listened as staff came in, talking about the incident, followed by the noise of the hand dryer blowing warm air before they bid goodnight to one another.

Once it was silent, Gary opened the cubicle door and walked out to the restaurant. Soft voices were coming from the back of the room, and a man was locking the front door, waving to the people who'd just left.

There she was. Cass Carter, sitting at a table towards the back with another man sat next to her. She looked up, seeing the chef's hat and looked away.

Gary felt his heart literally bounce as he tried to stem his growing excitement. As he removed his phone, opened The App and began streaming, he narrated, his voice energised, animated and full of passion. 'I have her. It took patience and a little working out, but I finally found Cass Carter.' Gripping the knife in his hand, he raced towards her.

Cass screamed, desperately trying to run, but Gary plunged the knife into the side of her neck, pulling it out and stabbing Cass four more times before she was able to escape.

Her body slumped to the floor, knocking against a table.

The man at her table was too stunned to move, and watched dumbfounded and impotent as Gary raced out through the back door, got into his van and drove away.

* * *

Kneeling on the floor, sobbing, Ed stared at his beautiful wife. He lifted her lifeless head, praying she'd look at him, longing for her chest to move, to talk to him, wanting desperately to tell her he loved her and that everything would be OK.

He pleaded with God, begging for one more hour with her, he'd hold her in his arms and never let go, tell her how incredible she was and how she made his life complete. His soulmate, life partner. How could he function without her in his world?

Roberto was still standing at the front of the restaurant, leaning against the glass door, his face drawn and pale, breathing hard. His words stumbled as they left his mouth. 'I'll... I'll call the police.'

Outside, Marty banged on the glass after witnessing the brutal attack on Cass. 'Open the door, Roberto.'

The restaurant owner responded, placing the key in the lock, but before he could open the door, two men with balaclavas rushed into the restaurant from the back.

Thinking instinctively, Roberto dropped to the floor and crawled to the side of the bar, unsure if he'd been seen.

The taller of the two men, Gus, pointed a handgun at Ed, his arm steady as his muscles bulged through his tight black T-shirt. 'If you do anything stupid, I'll drop you where you stand.'

Ed froze, watching the gun pointed at his head. He was petrified, paralysed with shock.

'What a mess, eh?' Stevo said, strolling over to Cass's body. He was the shorter of the pair, unfit and overweight, but he was capable of keeping the operation running smoothly. His main concern was hiding the bodies. He and Gus had just driven back from Devon, after digging a grave in the woods and burying a man who'd been hurled out of a cottage window.

As he placed his hands under Cass's neck, Ed shouted, 'Don't you fucking touch her! That's my wife. Get away from her. You bastards have done enough damage.'

Gus slowly walked over to Ed, weapon still pointed, and

whacked him on the side of the face, knocking him over a table. 'Another word, and I promise I'll kill you.'

Ed cowered on the ground and simply nodded; his jaw felt like it was broken, and he was too frightened to answer back.

A whisper came from the front of the restaurant.

Stevo was crouched by Cass Carter's dead body, and flicked his gaze to Gus, placing a stubby finger over his lips. The two men paused, trying to hear where it was coming from.

'No, I can't talk louder...'

They crept across the floor, keeping as silent as possible, heading towards the voice.

'I said I need the police.' Roberto lay on his stomach, his phone to his ear having called 999. 'I can't speak any louder. There are—'

Reaching for the phone in Roberto's hand, Gus spoke into the mouthpiece. 'Sorry, a false alarm. Everything is resolved now.' Ending the call, he shook his head at Roberto. 'You've made such a stupid mistake.'

Gus grabbed the back of Roberto's head and began slamming it against the tiled floor.

The sound of his skull smashing against the ground reverberated through the restaurant.

The moment that the two men were distracted by Roberto, Ed crawled on his hands and knees towards the back door. His body jolted with every crack of bone against porcelain, and Ed struggled to not pass out. Once he reached the corridor, Ed got up and raced through the back exit of the restaurant, glancing behind to ensure he wasn't being followed.

But he only got as far as the bins. He was riddled with guilt for leaving Cass, and yet too petrified to go back inside as Roberto's head smashing against the tiled floor and the knife plunging into Cass's neck ran over and over in his mind. He felt he was breaking, his body closing down and unable to make a decision.

Ed clenched his fists as his stomach flipped over, and he vomited on the ground. Using the wall for support, his hand pressed against the rough brick, he tried to work out what to do. If he went back inside to the restaurant, they'd kill him. If he called the police, they'd kill him. The family had told him about The App; how people stream the murder of others. Would they know his face now too? He searched up and down the street. Was he being watched?

Suddenly, there were voices behind him and he span around.

'Get him, for fuck's sake. How did you not see him leaving?'

Ed could see the smaller of the two men racing along the corridor through the side window. There were only moments before they'd reach him, kill him the same way they'd murdered Roberto.

Backing away, Ed tried to command his legs to obey his orders, but they felt like they'd buckle under him. Like a newborn deer, unsteady and gaining in confidence, Ed raced along the pavement and onto the main road.

Suddenly, brakes screeched around him. Ed jumped as a vehicle slammed to a halt beside him.

'Quick, get in!' Marty ordered from the driver's seat, Beth beside him. Abbey threw open the door from the back.

Ed didn't need to think and threw himself into the car. Turning in his seat, he saw the smaller of the two men, stood at the back door to the kitchen, the menacing balaclava covering his face, watching them drive away.

* * *

'What am I doing? Please, can you turn around?' Ed sat in the back of the Kia Sorento as it whizzed along Holloway Road. His face ached from where he'd been hit and a throbbing pain was developing above his eyes. 'I need to go back to Cass. Please, pull over.'

Ed had told them what had happened to Cass. How a man dressed as a chef had stabbed her and how two men wearing balaclavas had entered from the back, finding Roberto on the phone and smashing his head against the tiled floor. Everyone had been stunned into silence.

'Listen to me,' Marty ordered from the driver's seat. 'It's not safe. They'll kill you. We don't want another unnecessary death.'

'You can't go back there, Ed. It's too dangerous.' Beth stated. 'Please listen to us.'

'Let me out.'

'Ed, you know what these people are capable of now.' Beth turned around, peering at him. His complexion was ghostly white, like the blood had drained entirely from his body, leaving only a corpse. His eyes were cold, and he stared at the floor, blank, lost. 'I'm so sorry for your loss,' she said, although the words seemed empty, even to her.

'In her hour of need, I just stood there and watched her die.'

Abbey shook her head, placing her hand on Ed's shoulder. 'No, you did look after her. She was so lucky to have someone like you to share her life with.'

Ed nodded, and then broke down, sobbing like a child, his body shaking. 'I can't carry on – let me out of the car. I can't do this.'

Indicating, Marty pulled the Kia Sorento into a side

street and parked by the kerb. Ed climbed out, but rather than driving away, Marty joined him, and the two men stood at the back of the car. Vehicles swept along the high street, the muggy evening air still uncomfortable.

'What do you want to do?' Marty asked, trying to be as sensitive as possible.

With his cheeks now flushed, tears ran down Ed's face, and he sniffed hard. 'I don't know. I want to go back to Cass.'

Taking a deep breath, Marty said, 'OK, if you go back to Cass, in the same room as those two fucking animals, what do you think will happen? You watched them murder Roberto, pounding his fucking head against the ground because he attempted to make a phone call to the police. They're a part of this sick fucking show. If you go back now, you're going to die.'

Ed stared straight through Marty. 'What are they going to do with Cass? Hide her body? How can I say goodbye? I can't let them take her.'

'Please,' Marty said. 'Do it for Cass and keep her spirit going inside you. Don't allow them to kill you too; we're nothing to them, just an obstacle they will very easily work around.'

The two men hugged.

Opening the car door, Ed looked at Marty. 'Thanks, mate. I appreciate your help.'

As Marty got into the driver's seat, Ed turned and raced along the street away from the Kia Sorento.

20

1981

Jonathan woke, his eyes trying to focus in the surrounding blackness. The alarm clock blinked red with neon digits: *03.14*. His skin felt hot and clammy as he tried to remember where he was. The horrid nightmare that plagued his sleep had seemed so real. A shadow formed as he sat up in his bed, and Jonathan could hear his mother's voice. Her beautiful vision appeared beside him, gleaming in the darkness, her hand outstretched, her mouth open, calling for her husband.

The death of his mother had destroyed him. The visions of her body hanging from the rafters in his bedroom haunted him night after night. It cut into his sleep, invading his rest, causing him to wake hour after hour, her body often over him, drifting, floating like a helium balloon. He'd reach out, trying to touch her face, but as soon as he got close, it would twist and morph into a demon from another world. Sweat dripped from his face, soaking his bedding. As Jonathan blinked, his mother disappeared.

With his body pressed against the headboard, Jonathan

twisted his knuckles into his eye sockets to ease the strain, feeling like they'd pop out at any moment.

A sense of haziness engulfed him, his head dizzy and disorientated.

Finally, Jonathan could see across the room, the shape of the door and the heavy curtains blowing over the window.

His head hurt, confused by the visions that haunted his mind. He wanted to see his mother exactly how he remembered her; the beautiful, elegant, gentle soul who'd guided him, nurtured him and made everything better. But the wicked apparitions that swarmed his thoughts were so far removed from the person he knew. It scared him seeing her like that, with her head tilted to the side by the knot in the rope around her neck, her legs dangling underneath her contorted body. His mind misinterpreted the memories, distorting them and spitting out offensive images.

He lay back down, craving the sweet oblivion of dreamless sleep.

* * *

The morning brought comfort as he opened the curtains; the light soaked his bedroom, a warm breeze seeped in through the window, and birdsong filled the air.

The alarm clock blinked, the neon lights displaying *10.01*. Finally, he felt safe, but it would only be a matter of hours before he returned, lying on the bed and waiting for the hideous nightmares to return.

A shiver powered through his body as his mother's image entered his head. This time she was hanging mid-air, her arms outstretched and calling for help.

Tears formed in his eyes, and he blinked them away,

determined not to let them affect his mood. He'd deal with it when the time was right.

'Jonathan,' Aunty Joyce called from the ground floor.

'Coming.'

Putting on a clean T-shirt and jeans, Jonathan made his way downstairs. As he reached the ground floor, the smell of bacon and toast was pleasing. 'Morning.' He looked at Joyce, suddenly stunned at how much she resembled his mother. For a moment, he wanted to race across the kitchen, lift her and swirl her in the air. But it wasn't her. Jonathan felt sick as he watched his aunt standing by the cooker. The heat from the flames caused her to sweat, damp patches under the arms of her yellow dress. His mother's dress. He peered at the brown slip-on shoes and smelt the familiar perfume. Jonathan wanted to confront her, ask why she'd stolen his mother's things, but it wasn't the time. She'd come back with something stupid, like how his mother would love to see that her possessions weren't going to waste. That she'd smile down, knowing her memory was living on and that Joyce was making good use of her things.

He wanted to strangle her as he stood by the kitchen door, watching the smile on her face as she placed the eggs on a plate.

'How did you sleep?'

Smirking, Jonathan answered, 'Fine, thank you.' Aunt Joyce slept in the upstairs box room, and he was thankful she hadn't taken his parent's bedroom. It wouldn't seem right.

'Take a seat. You don't need an invitation.'

As Jonathan pulled out a chair, he felt the anger subside. He hated feeling this way, but he had to remember this was only temporary. His aunt was a good person, kind and softly spoken, caring and sympathetic.

She just wasn't his mother.

Joyce made a pot of tea, placed it on the table and joined her nephew. 'How do you think yesterday went?'

Awkwardly picking up his knife and fork, the memories of his mother's funeral flooded Jonathan's head. 'I think she'd be pleased. I can't believe so many people turned out.'

Joyce reached forward, placing her hand on Jonathan's arm. 'You did well. The speech was just right, and she would be really proud of how you kept it all together.'

Tears spilt from his eyes and rolled down his cheeks, the memories still too raw.

Pouring tea into two mugs, she looked at her nephew. 'It's so difficult for you, losing both parents weeks apart. But I'm here – I'll take care of you. It will seem strange, me living here with you, but you'll get used to it. You know that, don't you?'

Jonathan nodded and pushed his breakfast around his plate. 'I'm looking forward to starting work tomorrow,' he announced, changing the conversation.

'Oh yes, I forgot. Tomorrow's the big day. Fantastic news. Tell me what it involves again?' She placed the teapot down and began cutting her bacon and eggs.

'Well, they're a computer firm. My friend Luke works there. The money isn't great to start with, but the training will be excellent. They're going to teach me everything. I want to build them, develop them myself and eventually have my own firm.'

'Wow, look at you! That's amazing, Jonathan. Your parents would be so proud.'

Well, one of them would be, he thought.

* * *

Jonathan and his aunt spent the evening in the living room, watching highlights from a snooker match on BBC1: Alex Higgins versus John Spencer.

Jonathan sat on the sofa while Joyce was perched in a worn-looking orange-coloured armchair she'd taken from her house, reading a magazine. Every few minutes, she looked at her nephew as if she wanted to say something.

Finally, she placed the magazine down on her lap, and steered her eyes towards Jonathan.

'I need to talk to you,' she said. An uncomfortable silence followed; the atmosphere dropped and became awkward, almost hostile, seeing a grimace develop on his aunt's face.

Jonathan smiled embarrassingly, feeling his face flush. 'About what?'

'Why didn't you help?' she asked.

There it was. The line of questioning he most dreaded. His mind cast back to the night he found his mother's body. She'd been on the phone, talking to Joyce. He remembered her exact words, her voice hushed and frightened. She'd pushed the door, so Jonathan couldn't hear and said, *I have to talk to someone. I'm going mad inside.* She'd burst into tears, wheezing as she struggled to speak. *I think Jonathan let him die. I think he's responsible. He could have done something to help.*

He looked towards his aunt, at the sadness in her eyes, her grey hair tied back, loose strands hanging over her face, the high, hollow cheekbones, her bitter expression, and he felt uneasy. He imagined grabbing a pillow and placing it over her face until she couldn't breathe, feeling her struggle, her hands on his body as she squirmed in desperation. At this moment, Jonathan wanted so badly to smother her, feel his power over her as she sprawled out on the armchair, feeling her body jolting and going limp.

What was wrong with him? Why did he think this way? Since his mother died, he'd had the most horrifying thoughts. Before, he loved to see tragedy play out, to develop in front of him – the snuff movies, Mrs Shirland stabbing her husband, his father dying in the water – but now, the urges were more sinister, like he wanted to create the situations.

Composing himself, he peered at his aunt and simply answered, 'I did help.'

'I think you could have done more.' Joyce began coughing uncontrollably, her face went a deep red colour, the veins in her neck protruded, and a rash developed on her chest.

'I'll get you some water.' Jonathan hurried into the kitchen and filled a glass, bringing it back and touching it to her lips.

'Thank you.' Sipping the water, she looked into his eyes. 'Jonathan, your mother wanted answers. I need to tell you something. I've had a couple of doctor's appointments lately. It wasn't just check-ups. I have cancer. It's too far gone, and there's not much time left. Jonathan, your mother phoned me the night she—' Joyce couldn't say it. 'I'm a religious woman, as you know. I believe in absolution for any sin. But to be forgiven, you need to seek mercy for your actions. So I'm asking you, did you let your father die?'

The words hit him like a sledgehammer. The room began to spin. Anger raced through his body, his heart beating so fast it felt like it would explode.

When he'd finally composed himself, he stood and walked across the room, pausing in the doorway. 'I'm going to bed. Sorry to hear of your illness.' Closing the living room door, he stomped up the stairs and went to his room.

That night, the horrific nightmares were among the worst he'd ever experienced. His mother was hanging from a rope, screaming at her son to save his father. The red life jacket was visible in the water, and as his father turned, his face was skeletal with no skin.

Jonathan woke, his face sticky with sweat, trying to reach his mother.

But he would never be sorry for watching his father die.

* * *

His first week at work had been enjoyable. He'd dressed in a black suit that Joyce had bought for him, along with five crisp white shirts, stating that Jonathan could pay her back when he'd made his first millions.

He met with Luke on the first morning, and his friend had showed him around the office, introducing Jonathan to his colleagues. He was placed with a tech guy who promised to show him how to repair, programme and build computers. Jonathan couldn't be happier; a step closer to his dream of one day owning and building his own software.

Meanwhile, his aunt Joyce slowly deteriorated, and one evening, when he came home from work, she was lying on the kitchen floor.

'Oh my goodness. What happened?'

'I'm sorry, I fainted. I feel so sick.'

Slowly lifting his aunt, Jonathan gently guided her into the living room. 'How long have you been lying there?'

Joyce placed her hand on her head, too addled to think. 'I don't know.' As she sat on the armchair, she looked at her nephew. 'You look so smart. Your parents would be proud.'

The App

'I'll get you some tea. Don't move.' Jonathan walked to the kitchen, boiling the kettle. He could hear Joyce calling but he couldn't make out the words over the hiss of the boiling water. He placed a teabag in each cup, poured the water and dabbed them with a spoon, adding milk and sugar. As he returned to the living room, Joyce was slumped on the armchair. 'Here, let me sit you up.'

Grasping his arm, she looked into his eyes. 'This can't go on, Jonathan. I'm going to stay in a hospice. I have money. I can't continue like this. I'm getting weaker, and soon I won't be able to move.'

'I'll take care of you, Aunty Joyce. I don't want to see you in a hospice. You'll get depressed and die before your time. This is your home now.'

Her voice was frail, and she whispered, 'They'll look after me. Please. Let me do this, Jonathan.'

He sat with her for the evening, watching a film and wondering how he'd cope if Joyce went to a hospice.

He wouldn't let it happen.

Over the next few days, Jonathan spent his spare time setting up the room for his aunt. He made it as comfortable as possible using his DIY skills, which Luke's father had taught him the many times Jonathan had gone over to the house. His own father had never bothered, even though he spent hours in the shed working on small projects. There were drills, a hammer, nails, a wrench, everything he needed. He was determined to make it as easy as possible for her to live with cancer. He couldn't bear the thought of her dying in a hospice.

One evening, he'd come home early from work, and as he entered the house, he was certain she'd passed away. 'Aunty, I'm home. Aunty? Aunty, are you OK?' Standing in the hallway, he removed his tie and placed his black suit jacket on the coat stand. There had been no answer. Jonathan walked along the hallway and made his way upstairs.

In her room, Joyce lay on the mattress, her body turned towards the wall.

Shaking her gently, he asked, 'Are you OK?'

'I'm fine. I'm resting.'

'I'll fix us something to eat. It won't be long. Ham, eggs and chips. You like that, don't you?'

Joyce turned, the agony evident on her face. 'I don't want to eat. I can't manage it this evening.'

He placed his hand on her warm, clammy skin. She looked so ill, her complexion was pale, her lips a deep purple colour, and it looked like she was foaming at the mouth. 'You need to try and eat, Aunty, or you'll just get weaker. I'm looking after you, with, you know... everything you've done for me. It's the least I can do. Please try and eat.'

Closing her eyes, she pushed out a heavy sigh.

Jonathan went back downstairs and started cooking, cracking some eggs into a pan and placing a tray of chips in the oven. As he waited, he thought about his mother, how pleased she'd be with his new job and how he was caring for his aunty. He imagined her sitting wherever she was, looking down, so proud of the man he'd become.

When the food was ready, Jonathan grabbed two plates from the cupboard, loaded them with chips, ham and eggs, all neatly displayed.

As he climbed the stairs, he called out, 'Aunty, I've cooked. Please eat – it's for your own good.' He placed a plate on the flimsy unit and observed as she struggled to sit up. 'Here, I've got you.' Placing his hands under her arms, he gently lifted her frail body.

'Thank you,' she mustered. 'How was work?'

Sitting on the edge of the mattress, he placed her plate on the floor. Cutting the ham, he added a couple of chips and lifted the fork to Joyce's mouth. 'Here, it's your favourite.'

Smiling, Joyce mustered a response. 'Thank you, Jonathan.' She opened her mouth to receive the food, her breath rancid, and began slowly chewing.

'See, that's it. You can do it. We need to get you strong.'

'I don't have long left. Please, Jonathan, call the hospice. I have money – I want to die with dignity.'

Upset with her last comment, Jonathan placed more food on the fork and brought it to her lips. 'Dignity? Are you serious? This is your house now, where you live, your home. What's dignified about being left in a chair to rot? To lie in your own excrement for hours on end and be spoken to with no respect like you're a piece of trash. Look, there's a bucket there which I clean for you. I bring you food, tea, I talk to you, look after you. You're not paying a hospice to let you fucking rot.'

Joyce looked at her nephew with distaste for the first time since she'd moved in. 'Do not use that language, Jonathan Rushmore.'

Dropping his head to his chest, Jonathan apologised. 'I'm sorry. But this is your home now, Aunty.'

'I need the loo.' Joyce insisted.

Turning away, he listened as his aunty peed in the bucket. When she'd finished, he washed it out in the bathroom sink.

'Why don't you want me in a hospice?' she asked on his return.

'Because you're my mother's sister. I owe it to you both. Now, I'm leaving the food here if you want any more. You have a clean bucket, as I know you struggle to walk. I'll be downstairs – call me if you need anything.'

As Jonathan stepped away from the mattress, he heard the chain rattling.

He turned and watched Aunty Joyce pulling at the cuff on her hand, which he'd attached to a wooden railing.

'You can't keep me locked up here. Let me go, do you hear me?' Joyce screamed. 'For the love of God, let me go.'

Ignoring her, he peered at the Betacam video recorder he'd set up to film his aunt slowly dying, grabbed the latest tape and climbed down the ladder from the loft.

21

SUNDAY NIGHT

As he raced along the street, the warm evening air pushed against Ed's face. His skin was itchy and uncomfortable, stinging under his shirt. He ducked and dived between groups of people stood on the pavement of Holloway Road. He could smell a barbecue coming from a roof terrace across the street; a couple sat in chairs, clinking beer bottles together and laughing. Further along, music began pumping from a car, the driver dancing in her seat, unaware of the torment Ed was feeling.

Wiping tears from his eyes, Ed pictured Cass, his beautiful wife, lying on the restaurant floor, blood pumping from her neck and dying in his arms.

After watching the two men in balaclavas kill Roberto, he panicked and shot out the back door onto the street. How could he leave her? Marty and his family might have saved his life by picking him up, but he couldn't just leave her there. He had to do something.

As he ran along the pavement, tackling his conscience, his thoughts turned to anger. Anger at himself for not doing more. He was going to put a stop to it. First, he'd take revenge on the men who'd burst into the restaurant and then hunt down the man responsible for stabbing his wife.

When Ed caught sight of the Italian flag hung above the restaurant, the front door closed and only darkness through the glass, he stopped and placed his hands on his thighs, struggling to catch his breath. Almost choking, he gasped, filling his lungs with the rancid vehicle fumes in the air. Once he'd gained control of his breathing, he stood up, just in time to see a van pulling out of a side street. On the side of the van was signage displaying a company name and phone number, and two men sat in the front. Ed stepped back, hiding by a shop front, and waited until the van pulled onto the high street.

As he watched it pull away, Ed rushed to his BMW parked a few streets away.

He was going to follow them and make them pay.

As Ed drove, seeing the van slowly crawl along the London streets, the tyres spinning and the lights blinking as it slowed, he imagined ways to kill both men. He couldn't call the police. Marty and his family had told him that.

But just as they had selected Cass, now Ed had selected them.

His eyes were glued to the van in front as it weaved along the London roads and onto the M25 motorway.

* * *

He'd driven for around thirty minutes on the inside lane. The van was a hundred yards in front, keeping conspicuous so as not to draw attention.

Vehicles sped along other lanes, and a large truck caused a wind tunnel as Ed gripped the steering wheel. His body was so tired, and he struggled to keep his eyes open.

His mind went back to the weekend, everything that had happened, and to Cass, his beautiful wife, the last vision he had was of blood gushing from her neck. Thumping the steering wheel with his hand, he screamed. As his lungs emptied, the strain momentarily faded. His cheeks were damp and sticky with the tears from his eyes, and the road became a blur. The lights in front were hazy, appearing like heavy fog, blurry and clouded.

Switching the radio on, the voices discussing the latest news topics soothed his mind. Ed slapped his face, trying to force life into his body. He had to keep going and avenge the horror those lunatics had brought to his world.

The van pulled off at the junction for Essex. Ed followed but dropped further back, knowing the slightest mistake could give him away. He needed to keep concealed. When the time was right, he'd strike.

The van pushed along narrow country lanes, going much faster now. The driver was confident and seemed to know the roads.

Tapping the brakes, Ed kept his distance, aware the full lights from the BMW may give him away. He was patient, waiting until the van rounded the sharp corners before pressing hard on the accelerator, watching the glare in the distance, a glow cutting through the countryside.

When he got closer, he dropped the lights from full to dim and sometimes off completely. It was dangerous, but hatred drove him to act this way.

The flat road suddenly became a steep hill. The BMW was noisy as the tyres gripped the tarmac.

Suddenly, as he rounded a bend, the tail lights of the van were gone.

'No!' Ed cried. What was going on? Where is the van? Had they turned off? Ed muted the voices on the radio and opened the driver's window; the warm breeze had turned into a chilly draft. He pressed the accelerator to the floor, reaching the top of the hill, peering along the road hundreds of yards ahead. It was total darkness.

The lights had completely disappeared.

* * *

Ed cut the engine and sat for a few moments with the full lights of the BMW piercing into the darkness ahead. His body was suddenly cold, the tension taking its toll as fatigue worked through his veins. He'd been following the van for over an hour since it left North London. He'd been diligent, making sure not to be spotted, hanging back, driving as carefully as possible.

And now, the van was gone.

Opening the driver's door, Ed stood out on the road, listening to the silence around him, needing to hear the engine as the van manoeuvred along the desolate road. Guided by the full beams, he edged forward, walking down the brow of the hill.

The van had to be here, he thought. He saw it reach the top of the hill. He screamed, 'Where are you?' Realising his mistake and being too conspicuous through sheer grief, Ed backed away and got into the driver's seat, watching for any movement in the rear-view mirror. It seemed he was all alone. But Ed was certain the van had pulled over, turned the lights out to keep hidden and were waiting.

He debated whether to turn back, try another route and surprise them but the uncertainty of being seen halted the idea. He only had one way to go: forward. Maybe it was a trap, perhaps they were waiting, but Ed had no choice. The only way this could end was for him to avenge Cass's death.

Gently touching the accelerator with his right foot, Ed steered the BMW along the road. A whipping sound continually reverberated as tree branches lashed against the screen; dark shadows formed from the fields, creating sinister-looking shapes dancing in the distance, figures pointing, urging Ed to turn back.

Once again, the image of his beautiful wife, screaming in terror as she was attacked plagued his mind. He forced his brain to remember something, anything from their past. The more he thought, the harder the blood pumped from her arteries. Again, Ed screamed, gripping the steering wheel and digging his nails into the texture, the veins protruding in his hands. The car swerved, and Ed grappled with the wheel and spun it back onto the road. He straightened his back, hearing a click, and breathed hard into his lungs.

There was a light in the distance. Ed slammed his foot on the brake.

Through a gap in the bushes, it shone dimly towards him. Ed parked close to the bushes, pressing the bonnet into the shrubs.

There was a lone cottage, isolated in the shadows.

It had to be where they were hiding.

22

SUNDAY NIGHT

'What was he thinking, Dad?' Abbey still pictured Ed racing away from their car as she sat in the back seat. It was dark, the streets were quiet, and she worried for him.

'I don't know, Abbey, I just hope he doesn't do anything stupid.' As Marty watched the road, he reached for Beth's hand. 'Are you all right?'

'I'm so sorry.' Her voice was low and sluggish due to the exhaustion from the strenuous day.

The traffic lights ahead turned red, and Marty tapped the brakes. It worried him that the two men who broke into the restaurant could be watching and jump out at any moment. 'You have nothing to be sorry about, Beth.'

Abbey leant forward, touching her mother's shoulder. 'You are both heroes.'

'It's the most stupid thing I've ever done. I put our lives in danger. Christ, what was I thinking?'

'I would have done the same. Please don't beat yourself up about it, Mum. You and Dad were so brave.'

Beth sniffed hard, fighting the lump in her throat and trying to contain the tears that threatened to spill.

'You're incredible. Honestly,' Marty stated. 'You saw Cass in danger and took it into your own hands. You tried to save a woman from being murdered. I'm so proud of you. And you, Abbey.'

'I didn't save her though, did I?' Beth sighed.

The car fell silent for a moment, a mark of respect for what had happened.

'Ed said Roberto was attacked. Do you think—?' It was too tough for Beth to finish the sentence.

Marty pressed down on the accelerator and brought his hand back to the steering wheel. 'I tried to get inside. A guy entered from the back and stabbed Cass.' Marty was careful about going into too much detail. 'I'm just glad you'd both made it to the car already – I didn't want you witnessing anything else. It was horrific. Should we call the police?' As the words left his lips, he realised how ludicrous the idea sounded.

'Are you serious?' Abbey intervened. 'We'll be dead by midnight.' Looking out of the window, she wondered if *they* were out there, watching.

* * *

It was late when they arrived back home in Dollis Hill. Marty pulled the Kia Sorento into the drive and got out. Beth and Abbey followed, and they all stood by the front door; the air had turned cooler and more tolerable, the street was silent, tranquil, and they hugged each other, forming a small circle.

'We're going to get through this, you hear,' Marty said.

'We're a team. No one fucks with the Bensons.' Marty saw his daughter smile. 'What?' he asked.

'You're just funny, Dad. You sound like the lead actor in an eighties action film.'

'I'd give any of them a run for their money.' Marty looked at the front door, pleased to see there was no damage. He feared someone may have entered the house while they were away. Pushing the key into the lock, he gently twisted and pushed the door back. The hallway was dark; the only light came from upstairs.

Beth and Abbey's breath on his back revealed their anxiety as they followed him closely.

'Is anyone here?' Beth shouted.

Marty was startled. 'What? As if someone is going to answer. "Oh yeah, I'm in the living room, just helping myself to the TV. Ignore me; I'll be done in a second."'

The light switch clicked behind them. Beth jumped.

'There. Now we can see.' Abbey peered upstairs, her eyes scanning for shadows.

Filled with anxiety, Marty struggled to push the image of Cass Carter from his mind, needing to be strong for his family. He feared tonight would have repercussions.

Although he wouldn't say it, Beth's actions could have put them at risk. At this moment, he was unsure if they were still under the radar. If he followed the rules and kept his head down, hopefully, they'd be safe. 'I'll make some tea.' Marty moved to the kitchen, grabbed the kettle, filled it with water and flicked the switch to turn it on.

Abbey sat at the table, gently pulling out a chair, where Beth joined her.

'I need to get my head around today. I'm sorry to bring it up. It's a little surreal. Tell me again, Dad. What the hell happened?'

Marty dropped three teabags into mugs, poured hot water over them and placed them on the table. He sat, running his hand through his hair, taking a deep breath and began talking, explaining everything that happened, from receiving the link from Davey Hughes, to the last stream he and Beth watched before leaving the house. As he finished explaining, one of the rules churned in his mind. *Send the link to someone close to you.*

Abbey thought about the streams her father had described and how the two men had turned up at the restaurant. Looking to the front door, she whispered, 'Do you think they can see us?'

'I don't think so,' Marty insisted. 'There's no reason for them to watch us.'

A noise came from upstairs, sounding like a large object falling onto the floor.

Marty, Beth and Abbey snapped their heads towards the hallway, too frightened to move.

'What was that?' Abbey whispered. Uncertainty formed in her stomach and worked through her body.

'I don't know.' Marty slid the chair back and stood. He crept to the back door, making sure it was locked. Cupping his face to the glass, he saw only darkness. His mind went to earlier in the day; the sun was shining, Abbey was revising, and Beth was out shopping with her mum. The smell of newly cut grass as he ran the mower over the lawn and the sun warming his skin was such a beautiful memory. He couldn't remember being happier. But how it had all changed in a few hours. How could he be in this predicament? How the hell was he going to deal with it? His mind raced; scenarios plagued his brain of how it would end. Turning, he faced Beth and Abbey. 'I'm going to check upstairs. Keep the kitchen door closed. Sit tight. Don't open the back door. I need to make sure we're safe.'

Grabbing a knife from the drawer, Marty walked out to the hallway and opened the living room door on his right. Flicking the light switch, he peered across the room. The flat-screen TV was hanging on the wall opposite; the unit adorned with family photos stood on the left near the window. Beside him, the large black four-seater sofa was tight against the wall. Marty crept further into the room, seeing their wedding photos in large frames hung on rusted nails, a bookshelf with the authors in alphabetical order and Beth's home improvement magazines placed neatly in a rack, which she hadn't looked at for years.

Next, Marty looked in the small bathroom; a corner sink attached to the wall and a toilet. No one hiding. He pushed the door to the utility room; a washing machine in the left corner, a tumble dryer next to it—the boiler hanging above and in standby mode. Outside, the side entrance to the house looked dark through the window. But then, a spotlight came on, cutting into the gloom. Grabbing the sideboard, Marty tensed, still and motionless, like an animal in the headlights. Catching his breath, he held it, closing his eyes, panic gnawing at his skin, a sharp breath, and when his eyes opened, the light was off. Marty pushed out a heavy sigh, dread working from the pit of his stomach. Was someone out there? The sound of screeches made him jump, possibly a catfight. Waiting until his heart slowed, he backed out of the room and into the hallway.

Beth and Abbey were in the kitchen, looking towards him. Their anticipation was evident on their faces. He shook his head at them. *Nothing so far.*

Smiling to ease the tension, Marty began climbing the stairs. At the top, he pushed Abbey's bedroom door open, bracing himself, his body sore from stress. Flicking the light switch, he gazed across the room. The bed was made, a light sheet tucked into the mattress, her revision books neatly stacked on a unit. At this moment, he thought of how incredible his daughter was – polite, intelligent, graceful, sincere, and such a beautiful human being. Dropping to the floor, Marty looked under the bed. Nothing. He stood and crossed the room, lifting the curtains. Still nothing.

Back in the hallway, he opened the door to the spare room. Again, it was completely empty.

Just one room left.

Finally, Marty opened the door to their bedroom, his hand trembling as he pushed it back. Flicking the light switch, he saw a hairdryer lying on the floor, which had fallen from the unit. Relief washed over him, and it felt like his body was springing back into shape, like air in a balloon, the sense of dread replaced by comfort. Quickly, Marty walked around the room and finished in the en-suite.

Only for him and his family, he was confident the house was empty.

* * *

'A hairdryer. It fell off the unit. No one got inside,' Marty confirmed.

'Oh, thank God.' Beth rushed to her husband, placing her arms around his waist and holding him tight. She broke down, sobbing into his shirt.

'Hey, come on. We can deal with this.' Marty pulled back and rubbed away the stream of tears. 'Beth. Listen to me. We're alive. We're going to get through this, you hear?' His fingers traced her jawline, high cheekbones, and he looked into her beautiful brown eyes.

Abbey joined them, again, the three of them huddled together in the kitchen.

'Dad's right– we'll get through this. We need to stay strong,' Abbey ordered. She glanced at her wristwatch. 'Wow, look at the time. I have to get up early and revise. I only have one day left.'

'You'll smash it.' Marty stood back. 'I think it's time to tell you how proud your Mum and I are. You're truly an amazing young lady.'

'Aw, thanks. I love you both, but it's bedtime. I'll see you guys in the morning.'

Marty peered at Beth, then back to his daughter. 'Erm, I think you should sleep in our room. I'll get the mattress from under the bed. It's just until... you know.'

'Please, Abbey. Do you mind? We'd feel so much better.'

'Fine,' she snapped, perturbed at her sleeping arrangements. Go and get the mattress. I don't mind listening to you both snoring one bit.'

* * *

Marty and Beth lay on the bed, their hands clasped together under the sheet, fingers entwined. Abbey was asleep on the mattress, and the rest of the house was still and motionless.

But Marty couldn't sleep. Pushing his head deeper into the pillow, he thought about The App, wondering the kind of psychopath who could have invented it and what made them tick. He tried to picture the person, watching all those innocent people drawn into such a wicked game, wallowing in the torment, the pain and suffering of others meaning nothing to them. Were they watching Marty and his family? Surely there'd be no reason to at this moment?

Before they came upstairs, Marty had again gone around

the house, checking cupboards, under beds, behind curtains and that every door and window was locked. Nothing showed they'd had an intruder. But what if cameras were pointing at them now, someone watching as they lay in bed? Maybe everyone who received the link could be found and detected in a moment. Perhaps everyone could be seen. But if *they* hadn't got into the house, surely his family were safe for now?

His mind raced, the streams from The App working in his brain, agitating him, those poor people innocently filling out their details with the chance of winning money, only for their world to turn upside down.

It was happening to him. He was a part of it, and Marty needed to do something. What had the rules said?

Do not delete The App.
Do not tell anyone outside of your family about The App.
Send the link to one person who is close to you.
Do not throw your phone away.
Always narrate while streaming.

His phone pinged on the sideboard. Pushing his hands into the mattress, careful not to wake Beth, Marty sat up and reached for his mobile.

Two terrifying things happened in the space of minutes.

A new link had appeared within The App. Marty turned the volume down on his phone and clicked the screen.

A light shone over a cottage in the woods. It went off a few seconds later, and the screen went dark. Marty could hear a car in the distance. Someone was streaming. There were voices in the background as a live feed showed a car pulling into the ditch.

'I think he's going into Dag cottage.'

Another voice. 'Have you started streaming yet?'

'Just about to. Why is it called Dag cottage?'

'His tribute to Dennis and Gnasher. D and G. He's going in. Right, keep quiet, I think we're live.'

The driver got out, unaware he was being recorded. As he looked at the cottage, his nervous behaviour was obvious. The man walked along the path, continually checking behind him, and then stood in front of the full lights of his vehicle. To the left-hand side, a sign declared Chigwell Row.

Marty recognised him.

The man was Ed Carter. But he wasn't the person streaming.

A second link came through. Marty's hands shook as he pressed the screen. He felt his body tense as he fought the urge to click the next link.

As he pressed it, a picture appeared on the screen.

His world came crashing in as Marty glanced at the photo.

It was him, barging the guy in the restaurant and knocking him over the table.

23

SUNDAY NIGHT

The glare of the full lights from the BMW pushed into his eyes as Ed peered along the desolate road. As he'd approached the brow of the hill, he could see far into the distance, but the van he'd been following had vanished, and the lights evaporated along the stretch of road. It had to be here.

As he walked towards the cottage, guided by the full beams of his BMW, he thought for a moment how ludicrous this was. These men were dangerous, part of the wicked hunt within The App. Ed was driven by hatred; the anger worked through his veins, spreading around his body, moving like shit in a sewer pipe, and at this moment, he didn't care what happened to him. They'd murdered his best friend, his companion and soulmate. Cass Carter. His beautiful Cass. They were going to pay. Regardless of what happened to him, he was going to avenge her death.

A rusty old gate stood between the cottage and the road. Ed placed his hand down and pushed it open, the hinges shrieking loud and raucous, then moved towards the door.

The cottage was an ancient building, stood alone and

appeared menacing against the dark night. Peering through the window at the front, he could see only a pitch-black void, like the souls of the people driving this vile, wicked game.

Placing his hand on the door, his body numb and cold from exhaustion, Ed pushed and was stunned that it opened. The rotting wood caused it to bow as he shoved it back, like it were elastic and would spring forward and whack him in the face.

Inside, he placed the palm of his hand against the wall, dabbing over its surface to feel for a light switch, knowing his phone torch wouldn't be enough if someone came at him. The texture was cold, rough and paint crumbled onto the floor. Finding one, he wasted no time. The switch clicked loudly and seemed to wake the cottage. The ground floor was suddenly soaked in light.

Ed was standing in the living room, and he took in the tired, distressed decor. The walls were sodden with damp; large bubbles had formed, and were doused with gaping holes. The skirting boards were cracked and had long come away. Oak beams which once hung proudly had become a feeding ground for woodworms, and the smell of damp and rotting wood was a testament that the cottage was deserted.

The floorboards bowed as Ed walked to the kitchen at the back. Each step was tentative, fearful that at any moment he'd drop through them and into a world in which there was no escape.

The kitchen was a dank pit and smelled of vomit. Stained bowls, plates and cutlery were strewn on the worktop. Cupboard doors hung on their sides, and dark patches coated the once-white walls. The smell of excrement was noticeable and caused Ed to almost empty the contents of his stomach. He covered his mouth with his shirt, retching as he backed into the living room.

Through the window, Ed caught the glimpse of a light glistening outside. Only a short, sharp punch, then it went out.

Ed crouched and positioned himself on the floor, his chest against the cold wood. Someone was outside. Waiting, he listened hard. Were the men he'd followed here coming into the cottage? He had to hide.

Crawling on all fours, he worked his way across the ground floor and onto the stairs. Ed stood, grabbed the handrail and gently made his way to the first floor. Upstairs, it was dark; if the men were outside, he couldn't risk putting the lights on up here.

Another blink of light. Ed held his breath for a moment, waiting for a sign they were inside. He walked to the window, positioned at the front of the cottage, but it was too dark to see anything. Ed ducked under the window sill as his heart pumped hard.

A thump at the front door jolted his body. Stepping back, Ed reached behind and pushed a door leading to a bedroom. There was no plan, no idea of how to kill these bastards. Driven by despair, Ed had been too hasty in his vengeance. Now, he could die here, and no one would know.

Gently, he pushed the door and stepped inside, his movement slow, like an action replay. He stemmed his breathing until the moment the door clicked shut. The sounds had seemed noisier than it should in the eerie quiet. Had they heard him? Were they coming up the stairs? Was this how he was going to die? Scenarios played through his mind, and Ed's imagination ran riot. He needed an escape. There was no choice. The light needed to go on. There'd be a window, and maybe he could jump.

Another loud thump on the door.

Leaning his body against the wall, feeling for the light switch, Ed flicked it on and a scream exploded from his mouth.

Cass, his wonderful Cass, was hanging on the wall, placed on a hook which penetrated through the back of her skull. Her mouth was widened for effect, with long nails pushed between her lips to elevate the terrifying appearance. Her eyes were taped open, giving a shocked expression.

Ed dropped to the floor, screaming so hard his throat hurt. 'What have you done? Bastards. What the fuck have you done to her?' He turned, silent for a moment, looking at the other hooks twisted into the brickwork, the bloodstains on the walls and floor, a bed frame lying in the corner with a soiled mattress and a pair of handcuffs attached to one corner.

It was a torture room. Probably for the punishment of individuals who didn't follow the rules.

A woman cried out in the distance, sounding like a lone voice in a well.

'Help me. Someone, please help me.'

Ed froze, like his feet were stuck to the floor, unable to command his body to move, the sheer terror he felt taking over causing paralysis.

Another thump at the door and a loud, penetrating crack.

Were they inside? Were they coming for him?

Petrified, he grabbed the phone from his pocket and cried at the empty signal bar. He wanted to hurl it against the wall.

Instead, he opened the window and jumped.

* * *

Ed's fall had been broken by a tall hedge separating the cottage and a field. His body was badly scratched, his clothes torn, and he'd hurt his ankle as he'd landed on the ground. But he was alive. He lay there for a few minutes, gripping his foot, trying to turn it and relieve the pain. He was sure it was only a sprain, but it was painful, and he knew he wouldn't be able to walk fast let alone run. Glaring towards the cottage, he saw a light dancing around in the upstairs hallway. He had to get out of there. Once they realised he had jumped, it would only be seconds before they found him.

Driving over here earlier, Ed had made so many plans, fantasising what he'd do, how he'd avenge Cass's death. Now, his main concern was keeping alive. Murdering the people responsible would have to go on the back burner.

Heaving himself up and wincing at the pain in his ankle, Ed stepped out onto the deserted road. A security light sprung to life. A barn that had been shielded in the black of night was suddenly illuminated along with a gravel drive. The door to the outbuilding swung open and the noise of a vehicle revving drowned the stillness.

Ed started to run, but the pain in his ankle was too severe. Instead, he dropped behind the bush, resting for a moment, watching as the van he'd followed pulled out from the side of the cottage and along the quiet road.

Fighting the pain, Ed hobbled to the BMW, opened the driver's door, carefully supporting his foot with both hands and started the car.

Driving along the road, he saw only bleakness, no lights, no sign of life. As he rounded a bend and the road dipped, he saw the van. The brake lights flickering in the distance.

Punching the roof of the BMW, Ed yelled with his achievement. His determination was paying off, and excitement flooded his body.

'Yes, I have you now. You'll fucking pay.' He was going to smash them from behind and ram them off the road. Anger, hatred and frustration fired him up, like he'd lost his mind and his soul purpose was ending their lives. He envisioned how they'd end up, left on the road and unrecognisable.

Nearing the van, he steadied himself, his leg throbbing as it jammed the accelerator. His body shuddered as he rammed the van for the first time, the BMW jerking on the road. Ed was laughing, thumping his fist on the dashboard. Another hard slam into the back of the van caused the driver to lose control and crash into a rock wall.

Ed hit the brakes and stared out through the cracked windscreen, his mouth open, waiting for the men to get out. He planned to run them over one by one, leaving their dead bodies on the road.

Watching the doors, waiting as minutes passed, Ed sat, patient, the serenity of vengeance daunting. 'Come on, get out of the van. You didn't crash that hard. Get out.' His eyes were hazy, tired from watching the doors; the scene became blurred from the intensity of his stare. Enough of waiting. Wiping his eyes, Ed grabbed the driver's door, pushed it open and stood out on the road.

His ankle ached – it felt swollen and throbbed under his trousers – but he hobbled over to the van, regardless.

As he approached, ready to get back in the BMW and mow them down, he looked into the window. A man sat, his seatbelt strapped around him. When he saw Ed, he started pulling at the jammed strap, terror in his eyes.

'Please don't kill me. I'm not a part of this.'

Unsure whether to believe him, Ed stepped back. 'Where are they? I followed two men here. Where are they?'

The guy began crying. 'I don't know, man. These guys, they held me at the cottage and ordered me to get into the van and drive. I deleted The App. They came for me. You have to help me.'

Ed waited, letting his story sink in, and then he crept around the van towards the driver's side.

The back door burst open, and a man wearing a balaclava lifted a bat and hit Ed over the head.

A few seconds later, Ed's body was loaded into the van.

24

SUNDAY NIGHT

Pushing the sheet back, careful not to wake Beth and Abbey, Marty pulled on a pair of pyjama bottoms, pocketing his mobile phone and crept out of the bedroom.

Downstairs in the kitchen, he grabbed a glass from the unit above the sink, filled it with water and slugged it in one. Marty moved to the kitchen door, cupping his hands against the glass and testing the handle to ensure it was locked. Then he sat, his body trembling, the picture he'd seen moments ago plaguing his mind.

Grabbing his phone, Marty opened The App and stared again at the photo of him pushing the attacker in the restaurant. His face was clear for everyone to see.

They had him.

But what did it mean? Why was his picture posted? Was it a warning, letting him know they were watching? With his heart in his mouth, Marty scrolled down the page, seeing if there were other posts. He couldn't see anything. He pressed the back arrow, coming out of the page and onto the main site, wanting to see if this had happened before.

There were so many links, and it would take all night to go through them. But as far as he could recall, Marty hadn't seen any other photos posted of app members.

It meant they knew he was there, at the restaurant and helping. They'd seen him. Roberto had stated they didn't have cameras, but the picture was taken inside. So they must have taken it from the live stream and posted the photo.

Marty had to hope it was just a warning and nothing else.

The other link he'd clicked, which showed Ed standing in full lights, ended before he got out of bed. As Marty placed the phone on the table, wondering what happened to Ed, another link appeared.

'Oh no, can't it just stop?' he whispered. However much he tried, he couldn't draw himself away. However much it pained him, Marty had to see what was going on within The App. Pressing the link, he waited with bated breath, full of apprehension, as concern began saturating his body. Marty checked behind him, making sure the kitchen door was closed and looked out into the garden through the window, seeing only a blanket of darkness.

It loaded after a few seconds, and a black screen appeared. There was a shuffling noise in the background, possibly moaning sounds, muffled, but Marty couldn't tell what it was. As he held the phone, his hands shook violently, placing his elbows on the table to steady them. His heart jumped inside his chest as a torchlight came on momentarily and then went off. Another few seconds and the light came on, showing something in the corner of a dark room. Marty struggled to determine what it was. Again, the light from a torch came on for a couple of seconds and off again. Visions of a lighthouse flooded his mind, stood proud, illustrious, the bright lights serving to warn mariners of dangerous shallows and perilous rocky coasts. But Marty knew this was no helpful warning; this was a threat.

He swallowed hard, his throat dry, his chest tight, unable to draw himself away. As the torchlight flicked into life again, Marty jumped. For a moment, his eyes were drawn to outside, wondering if someone was watching him, sat, vulnerable at the kitchen table with the light on, so exposed. This time, the torchlight stayed on in the footage, drawing closer to the figure slumped in the corner. The floorboards creaked, heavy breathing hissed through the phone speaker, the person holding the camera gaining slowly, prowling like a predator in the night.

Wiping his eyes with his hand to relieve the strain, the camera was finally close enough for Marty to see the figure. Ed Carter was slumped against the wall, a gag tied around his mouth and rope wrapped around his body, crushing his arms and legs. The light moved closer to his face, and Marty could feel the fear, the sheer terror this man was going through. Ed moaned loudly, trying to speak. The person holding the camera remained calm and composed, keeping silent. Muffled cries burst from Ed's mouth, wailing noises from deep within his lungs. As the torchlight skimmed over the floor, cutting into the bleakness, another figure appeared, tied to a robust hook hanging on a wall.

Marty dropped the phone. His heart pounded so hard he thought it would burst. Gripping the table, he fought the panic rushing through his veins; the terror he was feeling almost drowned his body.

Ed Carter was in a room, held captive. And his wife had been strung up like a trophy for everyone to see.

Suddenly a voice sounded, deep and poised.

'Interfere in any way, delete The App or talk to the police and there will be consequences. You have been warned,' he said.

Picking up the phone again, Marty held it in front of him, wanting to turn the stream off, to delete The App and forget it had ever happened. He'd never seen anything so cruel, so wicked. At this moment, he wanted to visit Davey Hughes and ram the phone down his throat until he choked. But how could he blame his friend? This is what happens if you don't follow the rules.

He stared at the blank screen. Suddenly, the torchlight drenched Ed's body. His gaze caught the camera, and the fear in his eyes was something that would haunt Marty forever. Moans echoed through the room, and in desperation, Ed wriggled his body like a fish on a line and slumped sideways on the floor. But it was futile. He lay there, lost and alone.

Again, darkness. The heavy breaths disappeared, as did the wailing cries. Now, only silence.

Moments passed, and Marty sat, his mouth open, anticipating the next move. Had they left the room? Muted the sound? Left Ed alone with the hope of being rescued? So many questions formed in Marty's mind as he watched the blank screen.

Heavy footsteps penetrated over the floorboards. Another light flickered. The room illuminated as someone crouched, turning the flint of a lighter with their thumb and holding the flame to the floor. The path lit up, fire tearing towards Ed's body, and soon he was engulfed in flames.

A door slammed, and all Marty could hear were Ed's deathly screams.

25

SUNDAY NIGHT

The hiss of fire extinguishers rang out from the speakers hanging on the wall. Jonathan watched the screen, showing an upstairs bedroom of a cottage in Essex, from his penthouse apartment in Mayfair, London. 'OK, good work. Show me the bodies,' he ordered.

The torch worked along the floor, up the wall and onto Cass Carter. Then it illuminated Ed's body. Only charcoaled remains were left, but it was enough to satisfy Jonathan's appetite.

He stepped up to the large monitor, placed his hand on the glass, stroking it, and delicately caressed his fingers from the top of the screen to the bottom. 'Oh, that's it—what a work of art. They really are beautiful. Keep the torch shining on the bodies.' Excitement powered through his body, and he fought the stirring in his groin. He would deal with his arousal later. Now was the time to savour the moment, relish what he had accomplished and appreciate all he'd developed.

Moving to the enormous window, Jonathan looked out over London, draped in the night light. Below, minuscule objects pushed along the winding road, like a child's toy set, reminding him of Christmas, he and his mother shopping for a Scalextric set. Jonathan would spend hours driving the cars around the circuit, frustrated whenever they fell off, or the track came apart.

He felt like a king in his castle, high above the most amazing city in the world. On a clear day, he could see for miles. The arch at Wembley Stadium, the London Eye and the tip of the Shard.

He stepped back from the window and turned, seeing the tall, elegant unit filled with DVDs. Placing his arm out, Jonathan ran the tips of his fingers over them and read some of the titles. *Death by Chocolate*. This was one he'd managed to get hold of while living with his aunt Joyce. A friend lent it to him, and it showed an overweight man, basically killing himself by eating as much chocolate as possible while documenting it.

Jonathan never returned it, and it took pride of place in his collection. He'd managed to transfer it to DVD and later save it on his phone.

A Crocodile Attack, the Circus Ringleader and the Lion, and Other Real-Life Footage. A snuff movie that was still close to his heart and the first one he and Luke had watched as kids.

Further up, he saw the first one he'd ever filmed himself. This was one of Jonathan's favourites, and he still watched the collection from time to time.

The Death of Aunt Joyce.

There were many clips saved on the DVD; Jonathan had edited the boring parts, and the later footage was harrowing once Joyce was chained and held in the loft. She'd questioned Jonathan about his father's death, and when she'd insisted on going to a hospice, he had no choice but to keep her locked away. He couldn't have her tell people of her suspicions. Watching her death was a bonus.

How he wished his father's passing, floating in the water with a life jacket, pleading for his son to help, had been documented.

It all seemed so long ago, but Jonathan was still bitter that he had nothing recorded. He'd accomplished many great things since it happened, and that was something he was proud of. He knew if his father was still alive, he'd laugh at his achievements and mock him, however successful he became. Well, Jonathan had the last laugh; that was something he'd always have on his father.

As he stood in the living room, his mother's vision came into his mind. The nightmares had long passed, and Jonathan could now remember her beautiful face without the hideous memory of her hanging in the bedroom. It had taken years for that to dissolve. Occasionally, she haunted his dreams, but he could deal with that.

'Is that enough now, Mr Rushmore?' The voice came through the phone's speaker.

Jonathan suddenly realised the screen was still showing the charred remains of Cass and Ed Carter. 'Oh, yeah, sorry. That's all I need. Good work, you can go home. Keep your phones on in case I need you.'

'Will do, Mr Rushmore. Thanks. Sleep well.'

Jonathan ended the call.

It was late, but the excitement the evening had brought would heighten his insomnia. It happened more with every success.

When Aunt Joyce died, Jonathan contacted the funeral directors, who removed the body. First, he lifted her down from the loft, balancing her over his shoulders and gently stepped down the ladder, placing Joyce in her bedroom.

Jonathan burned the mattress in the garden to rid any evidence of his foul play and hid the Betacam video recorder. Worried that the coroner would ask about the bruises on her ankles and wrists and an investigation taking place, Jonathan had a story ready and would insist he tied his aunt to a bed to stop her from falling out of it. In hindsight, he laughed at how ridiculous that excuse would have sounded, and nothing was ever said. In any case, Jonathan's perversions were so outrageous, that no one would believe how sick he was and the lengths he would go to in order to indulge in his depraved fetish.

As Jonathan was completely orphaned, with no relatives willing to step up, he continued living in the family home, a two-bedroom detached building in Highbury, North London. But alone in the house, when he slept, not only did he have to deal with his mother, her twisted body floating in the air and plaguing his dreams, but he could also hear Aunt Joyce calling from the loft.

His father never once visited. Jonathan was pleased about that.

He progressed at great speed within the company, learning everything to do with computers, eventually starting his own business, becoming a lead player in the tech market, and developing mobile phones and apps.

A couple of years ago, Jonathan hit *The Times*'s Rich List of the wealthiest people in England. His success was down to hard work and sheer commitment to better himself and break many boundaries. But he was careful. Never once did he allow his photo to be taken, and he never posted on social media.

From early morning to late into the night, Jonathan devised ways to bring technology to the masses; the more ideas he had, the more apps he created.

Almost a year ago, Jonathan sold the business for an undisclosed figure, enough to retire for a hundred lifetimes.

But now, he was bored. There were only so many recordings he could watch, only so many disasters he'd seen numerous times, knowing what happened and how the end result played out.

Thinking back to hiding in the garden while watching the heated argument between Mr Shirland and his wife, her stabbing him, the feeling as he dropped to the floor, the police arriving, people gathering on the street, whispers carrying in the air of what had happened, Jonathan held onto that sensation and the powerful feeling it created.

His father drowning in the lake had been one of the lowest points in his life. Not the fact that he'd died, as Jonathan despised him, but the fact that he couldn't watch it over and over, wallowing in the visual spectacle.

Watching Aunty Joyce dying, her body decaying every day, was such a high point in his life. Jonathan could still feel the emotion and excitement coming home from work, climbing the loft ladder, feeding her, listening to her pleas for him to let her down, how she screamed out through the night, shouting for help. He had to stem that soon enough by gagging her, not wanting the neighbours to hear. Finally, he had power over the situation.

After she'd eat, he'd go back up, clear the plates, uncuff her so she could go to the toilet in a bucket and wash her soiled nighties.

The evenings he'd spent in front of the TV, watching the recordings of her deterioration, were memories he'd always treasure.

There had to be a way for Jonathan to see into the future. Even his creative brain struggled to devise a plan. Time travel was impossible, so how could he produce something where he could watch, be there in the moment and see people's pain in real time?

Then it came to him.

The App.

It was perfect.

* * *

The penthouse apartment, high over the London streets, was fitted with the latest technology and all the gadgets you'd ever need. Jonathan looked towards the enormous double-glazed window, and with a simple command, the blinds folded in, giving him complete privacy. The underfloor heating, music and entertainment were all voice-controlled, and the apartment's security was state of the art.

The Italian restaurant had been a disaster. First, the idiot arriving, trying to murder Cass in full view, putting everything Jonathan had worked so hard to develop in jeopardy. Thankfully, he had Gus and Stevo to clear up the mess. They were invaluable and worth every penny he paid them.

After screenshotting the live stream, Jonathan stared hard at the picture. A man barged the hunter over a table. The same man who'd signed up for The App this morning. He smiled, knowing punishment would follow; he was unsure of what he'd do, but there'd be consequences.

Marty Benson could be certain of that.

The guy who'd finally killed Cass Carter had been clever. Jonathan respected that. He'd waited outside, calm and calculated, biding his time, and remained hidden until people filtered out. He'd pretended to be one of the chefs, before finally pouncing then making his escape out the back. Genius.

Looking at the flat-screen TV, Jonathan tapped the keys

on his laptop, editing the footage from earlier. The trail of flames charging towards Ed and Cass Carter, their charred bodies on display, now ran on a loop.

Entering his bedroom, Jonathan walked to the en-suite toilet, took a piss and washed his hands. Grabbing a toilet roll, he got into bed and turned on the TV.

Ed's muffled cries rang out through the speakers as he huddled in the corner of the room, followed by the flames, then their burnt bodies. Ed's cries, the flames, their burnt bodies, over and over it displayed.

Jonathan worked his hands under the sheet, down his body and began to play with himself.

26

MONDAY MORNING

Marty lay in bed, staring at the ceiling; his pillow was damp from sweat but his body was cold and stiff. Beside him, Beth's light breaths pushed from her lips, and she muttered something in her sleep, turning away and facing the wall.

He sat up, his eyes so heavy from tiredness, but his head busy with the latest updates from The App.

Abbey's eyes opened as she stretched on the mattress, her face swollen from tiredness. She smiled as she saw her father. 'Morning,' she whispered. 'Did you sleep OK?'

'Yeah, like a baby,' he lied. Marty had decided not to tell Beth and Abbey about his picture appearing on The App. It would only scare them, and besides, nothing was attached, no warning. He hoped it was simply a caution.

'I need to revise. I'll be in my room,' Abbey said, crawling out of bed and making her way to the bedroom door.

'Wait,' Marty insisted. Pushing the sheet off his body, he got out of bed, walked along the upstairs hallway and checked Abbey's room. Once he was certain it was empty, he called for her to come out.

'Dad, really? Do we need to go to these lengths? They have no reason to come for us.'

Again, his photo, barging the man over the table, flashed in his mind. 'We have to be careful. I'm just taking precautions.'

'How about doing me a coffee? See that as a precaution in making your day more tolerable. You know what I'm like until I get caffeine.'

Smiling, Marty went back into the master bedroom.

Beth had just woken and was sitting against the headboard, scrolling through her phone. 'Hey. How did you sleep?' she asked, not looking up.

At this moment, he wanted to pour his heart out, to tell his wife of the wicked things he'd witnessed. How he'd sat in the kitchen, his body trembling with fear, Ed's cries for help pushing through the mobile phone speaker as his body was set alight. And the picture of him protecting Cass Carter displayed for everyone to see. But he couldn't. Beth looked comfortable, rested, and Marty wouldn't cause her more concern. He'd made a dreadful mistake in signing up to The App, and he was going to deal with it, find a way out of this mess. 'I slept well. Do you want a coffee?'

'You know I do. Oh, make it strong and bring a couple of chocolate biscuits too.'

'You got it.'

In the kitchen, Marty Facetimed his mother, again pleading for his parents to come over to the house but not wanting to alarm them. 'I'll pick you up, Mum. It's not a problem.'

'Why the sudden emergency, Marty? Is everything OK?'

'Yes, why wouldn't it be?'

'You know your father's condition. It's too much for him. He's resting at the moment, and he doesn't need the pressure of disruption. We can't come over.'

Needing to drive home the emergency, Marty didn't know what else to say without alarming her. If he forced them into a decision, she'd get suspicious and ask a barrage of questions.

'Look,' she continued. 'Let's see how your father is in a few days. I love you, Son. Speak later.'

Filling the kettle with water, Marty flicked the switch and looked out at the lawn through the window. The sky was heavily clouded, the sun hidden. He opened the back door; the gentle breeze was much cooler today and refreshing as it tickled his skin. Marty thought about how much had happened in the last twenty-four hours, how he'd started yesterday with a fry-up, Beth and her mother going to Oxford Street, Abbey lying in her room revising, while he tackled the lawn, feeling so good about life. He wished he could rewind the clock, see the link and delete it. His body felt frail; exhaustion caused his eyes to blur, and for a moment, he felt like he'd collapse.

Anger worked through his veins as he sat at the table, and Marty grabbed the phone, again dialling Davey Hughes. It rang for almost a minute. Redialling, he listened to the ringing sound, frustrated.

Slamming the phone on the table, Marty thrust the chair back and made the coffee.

* * *

'I'm going over there.' Marty had just given Abbey her coffee. She'd thanked him, her eyes glued to her books, and he had retreated to their master bedroom, armed with two more coffees and chocolate biscuits, as requested.

Beth sat on the edge of the bed, blowing into her cup. 'Going where?'

'To see Davey Hughes,' Marty announced. The picture gnawed at his brain; they'd loaded it onto The App, knowing what Marty had done in the restaurant, but the fact they hadn't messaged surely meant he was safe for now.

Placing the cup on the side unit, Beth looked into Marty's eyes. 'Are you serious? What if they get into the house while we're gone?' She hesitated momentarily, searching his face for signs he was joking.

'Beth, I need answers. We can't live like prisoners, frightened in our own home. We can't. We may as well give up if that's the case. Davey is the only person who I can talk to.'

'But he's not taking your calls. So he doesn't want to talk.'

'That's precisely why I have to go over there. If I can make him speak, I'll get a better understanding of what's happening. I have to go, Beth – there's no choice.' Marty watched her eyes soften, her confused expression turning to acceptance. 'Have you called your mother today?' he asked.

Beth jumped to her feet. 'Oh my goodness. I didn't think, what with everything that's happened.'

'I think we need to bring her here. Just until it blows over.'

Beth stepped towards her husband. 'You don't think they'll go after her, surely?'

'We can't take any chances. She's alone and vulnerable. It's better if she's here.'

'Are you sure?' Beth asked. 'I know how you two bicker.'

'Look, let's grab Abbey. She can revise in the car. We'll pick your mother up, go to Davey and come home. I know he's frightened, but he's part of this. We can talk about how to proceed and hopefully beat them. I have to make him talk, no matter how scared he is.'

Beth got dressed, worried about how Davey would react to seeing Marty at his door. Leaving their home unoccupied was also a concern. Her mother wouldn't be best pleased either, having to live with Marty until their predicament was sorted. But Marty was right. If they were at risk, her mother would be safer moving in with them until it all blew over.

It was going to be a long day.

* * *

'Don't knock so loudly – you'll frighten her.' Beth stood beside her husband, his agitation noticeable as he stepped from one foot to the other, continually glancing over his shoulder to check on Abbey at the gate, paranoid that someone would jump out.

'She's not going to answer. She's probably wedged on the sofa. Have you got a key?' Marty asked.

Beth eyed him; her scowl was enough to warn him from saying anything else. 'Really, Marty? Do you have to make stupid comments like that? Be nice to her. She's lonely and isn't used to visitors.'

'I wonder why,' he whispered under his breath. Marty knocked again, hearing a voice calling from along the hallway.

'I'm not bloody deaf. Have some patience. Who is it anyway?'

'Mum, it's us. Take your time.'

'Any slower, and she'll go backwards.'

With a closed fist, Beth dug Marty in the ribs.

A fumbling sound came from the other side of the door

as Ethel tried to take the chain off. 'There. That's it. Hold on. Wait there. Oh, I haven't got the key. It's on a rack in the kitchen. Sorry, I'll be back in a minute.'

'Oh, for God's sake.' Marty saw the figure disappearing from the door and along the hall. 'There goes our day.'

'I said stop it,' Beth ordered, with a playful look on her face.

Ethel returned a few minutes later and eventually opened the door. 'Oh, I'm bloody knackered, traipsing up and down the hallway like that.'

'Move the key rack closer to the door then,' Marty suggested. 'Have you ever thought about that?'

'The battery's run out on my drill.' Ethel smiled. 'There's nothing stopping you from coming around and doing it for me.' She turned around in the hallway, touching the sides of her newly rinsed hair. 'Do you like it, Beth? I had it done early this morning. Purple is the new me.'

'Yes, it's lovely. Listen, Mum, I need you to pack a bag.'

'Why? What's wrong? Are we going away?'

'Not as such. We'll explain in the car.'

'Hi, Nan,' Abbey called from the front gate.

'Ahh, Abbey, dear. It's so good to see you.'

'You too, Nan.'

'I can't pack a bag; one of those house improvement shows is about to start.'

'Ethel, you can watch all the TV you want at our house. Please, we need to be quick.' Marty spoke forcefully but was careful not to scare her. 'Beth can help you, but we need to hurry.'

'What's going on? You're all acting weird.' Ethel stepped forward, looking deep into Marty's eyes. 'We had to come home yesterday from London. Beth was about to treat me. You're not dying, are you?'

'I'm not dying, much to your disappointment.' *Yet, he thought.* 'Just get ready as quick as you can. We'll explain on the way.'

Beth walked into the house and closed the front door.

Turning, Marty walked over to his daughter. 'I'm so sorry about this.' He placed his hands on her shoulders.

'Dad, we'll work it out. Worst-case scenario, we'll call the police. Let's not let them beat us. You're doing a great thing picking Nan up – I think it's for the best. These people won't get away with it, and I'm sure they've been reported.'

'I hope so.' He had to keep his fears to himself; somehow, Marty thought this was only the beginning. He had to keep his head down and ride the storm.

* * *

Twenty minutes later, Marty pulled the Kia Sorento onto the road, leaving Ethel's house in Willesden Green. He drove, with Beth in the passenger seat and Abbey and Ethel in the back. Every few seconds, he watched the rear-view mirror. As far as Marty could tell, there was no one following. But they needed to be cautious. Any vehicle in front or behind would now be questionable. Gripping the steering wheel and controlling his speed, Marty was careful not to look conspicuous.

'What are you going to say to Davey?' Beth asked, placing her hand on his arm.

'I need to talk to him. Get a gist of how he's playing it. I want to know if he's taken part in the hunt.'

'He's not going to tell you that.'

'I have to ask him. In less than a month, according to the rules, they're going to expect me to—-' His words trailed off.

'I'm sure the bastards will be caught by then,' Beth confirmed.

Turning to face his wife, Marty said, 'And if they're not?'

'Then they'll come for us. And all we can do is hide.'

'Slow down, Marty – you drive like a maniac.'

Ethel's deep, croaky voice frightened Marty, as he'd forgotten she was in the car. 'Sorry. We're in a rush. We'll explain everything shortly.'

'Where are we going anyway? This could be constituted as kidnap, you know.' Turning to her granddaughter, Ethel smiled. 'Chance would be a fine thing. Only I'd expect a hunk, not that pillock in the front.'

Abbey placed her law book on her lap, knowing she'd get no revising done with her nan in the car. She kept her voice low. 'We're in a bit of trouble. Dad downloaded a link on his phone, and it wasn't what he'd expected.'

'A link. What was it? One of those mucky films? Your granddad, Ted, bless his soul used to watch those. Big hairy arses and bits on show. I never saw the appeal.'

'Maybe you'd have learned something,' Marty added.

Ethel leant forward. 'From what I hear, it's you who needs to learn.'

'Mum. What are you like?'

'Well, it's true. One child. Call yourself a man. You should have an army.'

Abbey laughed, signing for her nan to keep quiet, knowing her father would snap.

'How's life off the sofa, Ethel? You missing it yet?'

Playfully, she slapped his shoulder.

Marty continued. 'Seriously though, we want you to stay for a few days. However much it pains me to say it.' He glanced at Beth, preparing to deliver the reason they picked her up. There was no easy way to say it. 'Ethel, it's not safe for you to stay at the house.'

'Why?'

'It's just not.'

'But why? Is it to do with that mucky link?'

'Oh, for goodness' sake. It wasn't a mucky link.'

'You men are all the same.'

Straightening his back, Marty sighed, trying to be patient. He could tolerate Ethel, but often she didn't know where the off switch was located.

* * *

The traffic was unusually quiet for a Monday morning as they drove along Kingsbury High Road.

Beth wondered how much she should tell her mother. It could go one of two ways. She'd either laugh it off and say Marty brought it on himself, signing up to The App, or cower in a corner and insist she wanted to go home. The more Beth thought, the more sensible it seemed not to say too much. It was better to drive home the urgency in a delicate manner.

Marty indicated, pulling into a side street before taking the first parking space he saw. Pointing to the maisonette, he said, 'There. That's where Davey lives. The ground floor.'

Beth hadn't seen him since he'd split from his wife a few weeks ago. 'That's a downsize from the house in Maida Vale.'

'I guess it's what happens when you have a gambling addiction,' Marty insisted. 'He almost lost the family house. I think he's cleaned up his act since Tina kicked him out. I speak with him most days, but he hasn't answered the phone since... you know.' Marty didn't want to mention The App.

'Shall I come in with you?'

'It's best not to. He could get violent. Seeing it as forceful, us being here.'

'Davey? Really?' Beth asked.

'I don't know. Just wait here. Call me if you see anything suspicious and pull the car away. I won't be long.'

A chill rushed through Beth's body. As Marty got out of the car, she locked the doors, trying to ignore the fact that she felt like a sitting duck.

* * *

Marty climbed the crumbling stone steps, leading to the house. The cracks resembling a smashed mirror. He peered up at the property, seeing the windows covered with wooden boards. Rubbish bags were strewn over the front lawn, encircled with flies, and the smell of rotten eggs spilt from the overflowing drain. The short, yellow grass contained animal faeces, and Marty had to step over it.

He stood by the front door, bracing himself, and tapped the knocker. When there was no response, he listened for anyone inside and tapped again, waiting in anticipation. Opening the letter box and fighting through the cobwebs, Marty called out. 'Davey. It's me. Open the door. We need to talk.' The hallway was bleak, with piles of books, magazines and cardboard boxes piled halfway to the ceiling. The rank odour of rotten food and mildew pushed into his lungs, and for a moment, Marty feared his friend was dead inside, lying somewhere on the floor. His stomach began churning, and he wanted to vomit. How would he deal with seeing Davey Hughes, prone, decomposing, maggots feasting on his body? He heaved, desperately trying to stem the sick feeling.

'Open the fucking door, Davey! Davey? Are you in there?' He stepped back, then spun around, certain he heard a twig snap behind him.

Get it together, Marty. You're hearing things. If Davey has done a runner, you'll have to deal with it. Your family is the most important thing.

One last time, he called through the letter box and walked around the back of the house.

The garden was even worse. An old moth-ridden mattress lay against the back wall. Rubbish bags overflowed with beer cans and takeaway food cartons, spilling out onto the path. The back drain was also flooded, and a greasy substance gave off an odour like death. The outside toilet had water dripping off the felt from an overflow pipe above it, and the back door was missing its handle. Marty had never seen a property more hideous. How could his friend live like this?

A shadow moved from inside the kitchen. Marty jolted, his body rigid, preparing for an attack. He waited, but when nothing came, he stepped towards the door, pushing his face against the glass.

His friend was cowering in the kitchen corner, curled into a ball on the floor.

Banging the glass, Marty shouted, 'Open the fucking door, Davey. It's me. Open up.'

Hesitating, Davey stood; his body seemed to manoeuvre in slow motion, like a man in severe pain. He held his hand in front of his eyes, as if he wasn't used to daylight. His hair looked greasy, and his beard was heavy on his face. Slowly, he unlocked the kitchen door, his tired eyes seemed full of embarrassment.

Marty stepped into the house, gazing around and worried for his poor lungs, having to take in the stench of the place. The kitchen was a health hazard; the walls were covered in deep black patches of mould, and the smell of sweat and gone-off food hit him hard. 'For fuck's sake, mate. What's happened to you?'

Davey stood in front of Marty for a moment and resumed the fetal position on the floor. 'Did you download the link?' He stared at the ground, looking sombre. His voice was low and weak, like it pained him to communicate.

'Yes, I downloaded the link. By the way, I forgot to thank you for sending it to me. Who needs enemies?'

'I had no choice, man. They're coming for me. This Friday is the fourth week – after that, I'm finished.'

Marty joined him on the floor, almost slipping on the grease stains on the lino.

'I need to ask you some questions,' Marty said. 'Please be straight with me – I haven't got anywhere else to turn.'

'You can turn around and back out the same way you came in. I don't have anything to say to you.'

Shifting his body, Marty stared into Davey's deep brown eyes; once full of ambition and optimism, now, they seemed like a gateway to a callous pit. It was obvious his friend had given up, holed up in his maisonette, hiding from the horror of The App.

When Marty had called to see him a few weeks ago, yes, Davey had been saddened by his family booting him out of the house, but he was optimistic for the future. He'd promised Marty he'd given up the gambling and taken control of his life, gripping it head-on, and would face the future with a smile and a jump in his step. But the Davey of weeks ago had long gone, and Marty hardly recognised his old friend.

'Davey, I'm in a fucking terrifying position here. My family are in danger, as am I. I need your help. I'm asking you as a friend. For Christ's sake, you got me into this shit. I need answers. I need to know if they're coming for me, who I send the link to and if they're watching. You've been a part of it for almost a month. You told me yourself that this Friday you are taking part in the hunt. Your last chance. Have they communicated with you at all?'

Heaving himself away from the wall, his breath putrid, lips dry and crusted, and eyes menacing, Davey shouted, 'Fuck off! Get out of my house.'

Marty got on his knees, grabbed Davey's grubby T-shirt and rammed his body against the wall, his elbow crushing his friend's neck. 'I swear to God, if you don't talk, I'll beat the living shit out of you.' He pulled Davey towards him, and then slammed him so hard against the wall he thought he'd broken Davey's back. Again, he pulled him away from the wall, lying him down and placing his knee on his chest.

'OK, OK, get off me.'

Shifting off the floor, Marty stood over him as Davey choked, his face bright red, hand clasped around his neck. Marty was surprised Davey was so weak. Any other time, he'd have given a good fight. This was him at rock bottom. 'Start talking.'

'I got the link on my phone almost a month ago. I didn't know, man—a close friend who we used to meet in Maida Vale for the odd pint sent it to me. I should have known. The bastard hasn't contacted me since Tina kicked me out.' Davey pushed his skinny arms against the floor, hoisting his body up, and then he sat on a rickety chair by the table.

Marty joined him. 'What did it say?'

'Adam Simpson sent it via Instagram. He added a message, saying that he hoped I was well and how sorry he was to hear Tina and I had split, but that's beside the point. He added that this would cheer me up, or words to that extent—a chance to win a hundred thousand pounds every Friday. Well, you know about my... problem. So I couldn't resist. I messaged back, asking why he'd sent this. His answer, "You don't have to spend a penny". Can you believe the callous bastard?'

Marty wanted to tear into Davey, who'd done basically the same thing. He chose to leave it alone. He looked at his phone, ensuring he had service in case Beth rang. 'What then?'

'Well, I signed up to The App. I thought all my dreams had come true. I filled out my details and waited for it to load. An hour later, I got a picture. Tina was in the kitchen; my youngest son was in the high chair playing with a toy. Then the threat, a list of rules and how they'd kill Tina if I broke any of their fucking laws. I still love her, Marty. I miss her so much. I couldn't bear anything happening to her. You have to help me.'

Marty leant forward, the creak of the chair as loud as if it were about to break, and pulled Davey close, listening as he cried uncontrollably into his chest.

When he composed himself, Davey stood, walked to the cupboard and poured a large whisky. 'Hey, you want one, man?'

'No. It's too early for me. Although I'd love to sit here and get smashed – I can't think of anything better at this moment.'

After downing the drink, Davey poured a second one to the brim of the glass. Again, he slugged the entire contents. Placing the bottle on the kitchen counter, he held his arm out. 'Look. As steady as a rock. It's only alcohol that gives me relief from this hell. What are we going to do? I have to take part in three days, or they'll kill Tina, then they'll come for me. Have you seen the streams? There are loads of links inside The App.'

Marty nodded. 'Yes, I've seen them.'

'Who have you sent the link to?'

The question took Marty off guard. He'd forgotten about that rule. 'I don't know. I haven't sent it yet. Maybe I'll pass it on to the mother-in-law.'

Since receiving The App, Davey struggled to remember the last time he'd smiled. It felt good, and suddenly guilt began to fester inside his body. 'I'm sorry, man. I couldn't think of anyone else. They pressured me. It had been a few days. Like maybe a week. I thought if I held back and kept The App on my phone but didn't send the link, I'd go under the radar. But they know, Marty. A timer started. Big fucking numbers appearing on the screen. I was under so much pressure, that's when I sent it to you. They know. I think they're watching us. Through The App.'

Marty had wanted to leave his mobile phone at home, aware they could track his movements, but he had to have it with him, knowing it could make him and his family powerless missing notifications. It was the only way to stay mindful of how this situation progressed. 'Pack a bag. Something for a few nights. You can stay with us.'

Davey shook his head, eyes filled with terror and said, 'No can do, I'm afraid. I'm staying put. Thanks for the offer. I haven't left the house since getting The App. I'm not leaving now, either.'

'Please, Davey.'

'No way, Pedro.'

'It's José.'

'Whatever, man. I'm safer here, but you can call me when you've worked something out.'

'You don't bloody answer.'

Looking at his phone on the table, Davey said, 'I will. I promise.'

'Look. I have to go. Beth, Abbey and Ethel are in the car. But I'll be in touch.'

The men embraced, and Marty climbed over the obstacle course in the garden. As he stood by the front gate, he looked back at the house, trying to understand how his friend had deteriorated so badly. He barely recognised him.

Marty turned to face the street. The car was gone.

27

MONDAY MORNING

'Are you inside?' Jonathan was speaking to Gus from his penthouse on FaceTime.

'Yeah, piece of cake. A coat hanger through the letter box, and I hooked the door handle. No problem. In their haste, they'd forgotten to Chubb lock it. Saved me time having to pick the lock. People are foolish under pressure. They're still out.'

'OK. You know what to do. Hide them well. I don't want the devices being found. I'll stay on the phone.'

'Got ya.' Gus flipped his camera view, so Jonathan could see what he could, and stepped along the kitchen floor and into the living room. He couldn't believe how stupid Marty Benson had been, leaving the house unoccupied. But while Gus had been working for Jonathan, he'd seen people acting out of desperation, doing things without thinking, frantically trying to stay alive and making hideous mistakes in the process. But Marty was just another simple player who'd be easy to deal with. He knew his boss was pissed off that he'd intervened at the restaurant, knocking the guy over the table while live streaming; it made Mr Rushmore look weak and amateurish.

Gripping the phone between his chin and his chest, Gus strolled over to the four-seater sofa, grabbing one end and standing it up. Removing a knife from his pocket, he cut a small hole in the material and slipped one of the monitoring devices inside. Then he placed the sofa back on the floor, carefully positioning it in exactly the same spot. Glancing at the ceiling, he saw a large, antique chandelier with crystal leaves surrounding the underside. Grabbing a chair, he planted another device in the ceiling, ensuring it was camouflaged and invisible from underneath. He wiped the chair of footprints and placed it back under the table. 'Where else?' Gus asked.

'I'd say the main bedroom. A camera. It will be useful being able to see them.'

'Consider it done.' Gus grabbed the rucksack, placed it on his shoulder and climbed the stairs. On the first floor, he opened one of the bedrooms. Law books were stacked on the floor, and posters of boy bands were Blu-Tacked to the wall. Backing out, he turned and strolled to the bedroom at the end of the hall. The door was closed. Gus slowly pushed it back, bracing himself even though he was confident that no one was inside. Before entering, he'd checked over the house, searching for any security cameras or smart doorbells. There was nothing. These people were like an open book, on show and exposed for all to see. He laughed to himself at how easy this was.

The bed was made, and an empty cup was placed on the bedside unit. Clothes were neatly folded and piled on a chest of drawers, and dressing gowns hung on the back of the door.

Gus crept inside and found a vent high on the ceiling,

possibly used with an old gas fire as the chimney had been sealed and boxed up. Perfect.

Tapping the screen of his mobile phone, he texted Stevo. *Bring a ladder. We need to be quick.*

Through the bedroom window, he watched as Stevo clambered out of the passenger seat and moved to the back of the van. A few minutes later, he could hear heavy panting as he climbed the stairs.

'Nice one. You need to get more exercise,' Gus said as his friend bent forward and wheezed after delivering the ladder. 'I've found a vent. I'm placing a monitor inside it. Can you go down and keep watch?'

'No worries. I'll buzz you if I see anything.' Stevo left the room, returning to the street.

Removing a small battery drill from his rucksack, Gus started undoing the screws, removing the vent and planting the monitoring device. As he positioned it, he asked his boss, 'Can you see the room?'

'Only darkness,' Jonathan insisted. 'Turn it slightly. There, that's it. Perfect.'

Gus placed the cover back, aware the paint had split around the sides. There wasn't enough time to deal with it now. He just had to hope they didn't notice. He grabbed a small battery-powered vacuum from his rucksack and swept up the crumbs. Then he crept back downstairs and left the house.

***

Back in Mayfair, Jonathan thanked Gus for his great work and hung up.

The bedroom in the cottage, the trail of flames and the aftermath showing Cass and Ed Carter's charred bodies still played on a loop on the TV in his bedroom. Again, Jonathan felt the arousal in his pants, the excitement. But it would have to wait. He had decisions to make.

Pushing the sheet back, he stepped out of bed, put on jogging bottoms and a T-shirt and walked into the living room.

On his command, the blinds opened, and he looked over London. The clouds were dark grey and thick, and a faint mist clung to the air. The light was alluring as he gazed towards the Shard.

'Switch on the monitors.' Jonathan turned back into the room and glared at the huge flat-screen TV. Hundreds of boxes appeared, each one displaying live feeds of people who were part of The App. His empire. Gus and Stevo had been busy. It had been so easy gaining entry to all those properties, disabling the alarms and watching. His dream for so long was now a reality—a way of getting into people's lives and wreaking havoc.

Jonathan had learned quickly all the techniques which he now used in his work. The skills he needed to hack into computers, emails, mobile phones and CCTV cameras across Britain. He was an expert, working on many of the programmes developed for the government and British intelligence services. As Jonathan progressed, his company was at the forefront of the software used to infiltrate criminal organisations.

For so long, he'd dreamed of devising a way to be in the moment, the ability to watch the horror unfold, the torment, anguish and pain of others in real time.

Then came the idea of The App.

A dark web-style forum, under the radar, undetected and wholly for his pleasure.

'Next page.' The screen slid to the right; more people at

home, in their bedrooms, bathrooms and kitchens, unaware they were being monitored. 'Next page.'

In the bottom right-hand corner, an empty bedroom.

A monitoring device sat in the vent.

Watching.

28

MONDAY MORNING

As Marty ran along the street, his heartbeat pushed hard through his neck, fear swarming his brain. He searched for the Kia Sorento, glaring at the empty space on the road. 'No, no, no, no, no. Where are they? Please don't do this to me.' Reaching the corner of the side street, the raucous sound of vehicles pushing along the main road grated in his ears. He stood for a moment, his eyes peering across the road. His breaths were sharp, feeling like his lungs were blocked as he struggled to operate his body.

His eyes became blurry, his head ached, and Marty thought he would collapse. He turned and his heart soared at the sight of their car parked by a pay meter. Leaning forward, Marty laughed to release the stress, the tension drifting from his body. He jogged over and opened the car door, delight on his face. Before he had a chance to sit down, he heard Ethel's voice from the back.

'Well, you took your time. We're baking in here.' Her purple hair was styled neatly, the wrinkles on her face more pronounced as she grimaced, her blue eyes squinting with her irritation.

At this moment, he'd never been so delighted to see her. Looking at Beth, he said, 'What happened? I thought you'd been—' He stopped, as not to frighten his daughter and mother-in-law.

'A traffic warden was prowling around. I could only hold him off for so long. So, how's Davey?'

'He's in such a state. I've never seen anyone decline so quickly. You don't want to see the squalor where he's living.'

'You can join him if you leave us like that again,' Ethel piped up.

Abbey signed for her nan to stop, although conscious Ethel was unaware of their predicament and the pressure they were under.

'Dad, is Davey OK?'

Shifting his body, Marty faced the back of the car and held his daughter's hand. 'Not really. He's holed up in a squat, too frightened to leave.' Marty had to drive the harsh reality home, needing his daughter to understand the seriousness of their situation. Later, he'd sit her down and have a chat to ensure she appreciated what was going on, but to reassure that he'd keep them safe.

'Can you take me home?' Ethel insisted. '*A Place In The Sun* is on shortly, and it's in Ireland.'

'Nan, Ireland is wetter than here.'

'Is it, dear? Maybe it's Iceland, then. I get them mixed up.'

Marty started the car, wondering if he could drop Ethel home. Did he really need the added pressure of his irritating mother-in-law? Saying that, at least she brought entertainment.

* * *

Marty pulled the Kia Sorento into the drive and looked up at their home. The house seemed different. Like it was pushing out signs and trying to say something.

He was unable to put his finger on it. It seemed tainted, almost alien, but he didn't know why. 'Wait here a moment. I need to check the place over.'

'Oh, for heaven's sake. What's wrong now? Don't tidy it up, for my sake. I'm used to seeing the house in a state,' Ethel barked.

'Mum, please have patience,' Beth said as Marty stepped out and walked up the drive. 'He's being careful.'

Abbey had her fingers in her ears, her law book resting on her lap, unable to concentrate. She chose to remain silent, not wanting to insult her nan.

The windows were closed. The front door was still in one piece, and nothing was damaged. Marty placed his hand against the lock, pushing it and thinking it might drop out if it had been drilled, but Marty was no expert. It seemed sturdy. Stepping away from the front door, he glanced to the first floor; again, all the windows were closed and intact. He looked at Beth, seeing the turmoil in her eyes, and smiled to ease her tension. Ethel was mouthing something he couldn't make out, and Abbey sat patiently next to her.

As Marty walked around the side entrance, he prepared himself for an attack. If anyone jumped him, he'd shout for Beth to drive away. His family were his priority. Looking over the garden – the fresh air, the sweet smell of tulips and roses he and Beth had planted recently and the spacious area with an orderly lawn – Marty realised how lucky they were. His mind drifted to Davey's place and the dire pit he called home. Marty felt so sorry for him. How he'd declined in the space of a few weeks. Would The App cause him to take the same route? His body jolted at the thought, and Marty pushed his shoulders back to deal with the build-up of stress.

The back door was closed and locked. Marty pressed the handle down and leant against the thick glass, glancing at the frame to see if there were any signs a sharp tool had been used. Nothing seemed out of place.

Finally, he checked the fence to ensure it was sturdy and in place. He felt paranoid, wondering if any of the neighbours were watching. But he had to be sure it was safe.

Back on the drive, Marty signed for his family to join him.

As Beth opened the car door, she asked, 'Are you sure no one got inside?'

With a thumbs up, Marty walked to the car and opened the back door, helping Ethel to her feet.

'Thank goodness for that. My arthritis is playing havoc. Any longer and you'd have had to carry me out.'

'Next time, why don't we bring the sofa?'

'There's no room, you pillock.'

'There is if we tow it with rope,' Marty added. 'We can strap you into it and pull you along the road.'

Beth slapped his wrist, letting him know to stop.

Abbey grabbed her law book, anxious to get some revising done. Her big exam was at 9 a.m. tomorrow, and despite her initial confidence only days before, now she was nervous that she'd flunk it. But her parents' predicament was playing havoc with her mind, thinking back to last night, driving over to North London, how brave they were and how her father had saved that woman's life. Although they hadn't said too much about it, she knew they were scared.

Placing his key in the front door, Marty gently twisted it and pushed the door back. 'Wait there a second,' he instructed. The house seemed to whisper, voices rising from the floors, spreading over the walls and ceilings. Was it possible someone had been inside while they were gone? Were they watching, monitoring their every move?

Careful not to make any noise, Marty crept to the kitchen, opening the living room door on the way. *Come on. This is ludicrous. My paranoia is going to cause everyone concern,* he thought. But Marty had an excuse. The photo he was sent last night was still strong in his mind, although he hadn't mentioned it to Beth and Abbey. Why had they done it? What the hell did it mean? Were they coming for him?

He jumped as Abbey called from behind.

'I'm going to my room. I have to get some revision done. I'll be down later.'

Watching as she climbed the stairs, Marty wanted to plead with her to stay with them. But how did he keep them safe without alarming them? Abbey, Beth and now Ethel could all be in danger.

Again, he thought about the picture.

It had to have been a warning.

Marty needed to be vigilant, keep under the radar and not do anything else to piss them off.

Otherwise, next time, it could be a hell of a lot worse.

But something told him it might already be too late.

29

MONDAY EVENING

'We need to talk,' Beth announced, looking at her mother.

Ethel sat in the living room, the TV on loud, holding a mug, puffing vigorously onto the black coffee to cool it down.

'Why don't you just add some water?' Marty suggested standing at the living room door.

'I don't want water in my coffee,' she sniped.

'But there's already... You know what? Never mind.' The words slipped off; now was not the time to start an argument.

Beth sat beside her mother, needing to drive home their urgency, but ever since she could remember, conversation was difficult with Ethel; she was in her own world, almost oblivious to her surroundings. It was like she was in a bubble, and no one could ever get inside.

'Can you turn that down, Mum?' she asked.

'Huh? What did you say?'

'Oh, for heaven's sake.' Grabbing the remote control

from the edge of the sofa, Marty hit the mute button. He didn't dare turn it off for the sake of his sanity.

'Mum, listen to me.' Beth looked at the frail old lady in front of her. The newly rinsed hair, her crisp white blouse, the long grey skirt and sensible shoes. Her face was gaunt; her cheeks hollow and her once sparkling eyes had long darkened. Looking at her, Beth breathed deeply, straightened her body and said, 'Mum, we're in a bit of a situation.'

Ethel's eyes flicked between her daughter and son-in-law. 'Go on. What kind of situation?'

'A couple of days ago, Marty received a link. It was sent by Davey Hughes, hence the reason we went over to his house earlier.'

'I'm with you.' Ethel glared at the TV, wanting the volume back up.

Beth explained what had happened and Ethel's eyebrows knotted into a shocked expression on her face, mouth wide and wild eyes, as she listened silently to everything she said. Beth finished with them, arriving at the Italian restaurant, the death of Cass Carter, the attack on Roberto and why they'd visited Davey Hughes, needing advice from him.

'Then we need to stop it,' Ethel insisted.

'Yes, but we don't know how,' Beth said.

Sitting on the sofa, Ethel pushed her body back, making herself comfortable. 'I remember a day trip to Margate once. Oh, way before you both were born. Your father, rest his soul, drove there in an old Morris Minor. I can still remember him smoking in the driver's seat, coughing like a lunatic and unable to open the windows. Back then, we had to wind them down manually. But for some reason, they were stuck.'

'All of them?' Marty asked.

'Yes, all of them. That's beside the point and not the main reason for the story. I suppose we were lucky the windows were jammed, as it rained.'

Beth and Marty peered at each other, not wanting to laugh.

'Anyway, when we arrived, Ted went to pay to get us into the funfair. Well, there were one-pound notes back then, and Ted had a fistful. Anyway, he paid, and as we walked through the gates and into the main area, a security guard grabbed him. Huge, he was. He'd said that Ted hadn't paid enough money. Well, as you can imagine, I was furious. We went back to the till. Your father had a habit of putting black dots in the corner of the notes with a felt-tip pen for that very reason.'

'So what happened?' Marty asked.

'Well, they counted the money, saw the black dots and realised he'd paid enough after all.'

'Then what?' Marty asked.

'Well, then we went inside, to the funfair.'

Marty stood, open-mouthed, after listening to Ethel and the story of getting into Bembom Brothers in Margate, wondering whether to laugh or cry.

Ethel continued. 'All I'm saying is don't let people get away with things. Take a lesson from my dear Ted. He never let anyone shit on him.'

Marty sighed hard. 'Good old Ted. I feel such inspiration listening to that. What a story. You must have been so proud of him,' Marty said, sarcastically.

'Oh, I was dear. No one took my Ted for a mug. You could take a leaf out of his book.'

'You know, I think I might. Beth, have we any felt-tip pens?'

Beth smirked over her mother but knew no amount of

markers or any other clever schemes would help them. They needed a miracle to get out of this situation.

* * *

Later, Marty made a dinner of pasta with a spicy tomato sauce while Beth, Ethel and Abbey sat at the table in the kitchen. The door was open leading to the garden, and although the sun had set, the light was beautiful in the red sky.

Every few seconds, Marty peered towards the fence and the back, checking to make sure the garden was empty. He listened to the laughter coming from behind him as Ethel recited a story of her TV breaking down and a blank picture for three days before realising it was unplugged.

For a moment, he felt safe and secure, the sound of his family's voices ringing out over the kitchen, their smiles, the company he thrived on being part of and the people he loved most in this world—even Ethel. Although they were often at each other's throats, it was good to have her here. Turning, he looked at Abbey. 'How's the revising going?'

She smiled. 'Good. That's me, though. If I'm not ready for it now, I never will be.' She stood and walked to the fridge, grabbing a chilled bottle of white wine.

'Oh, I shouldn't,' Ethel insisted. 'But if you're opening it, I won't waste it.'

'I bet you won't.' Marty laughed. He set four plates on the table and filled them with pasta coated in a thick sauce, then grabbed some wine glasses from the cupboard. The aroma of garlic and tomatoes was so appetising, and his mouth began watering.

Abbey opened the cap and filled each glass a quarter way.

'Cheers,' Marty said, watching everyone clink their glasses. 'To Abbey's exam tomorrow. May you shine like the incredible light you are. Here's to smashing it.'

'"Smashing it", indeed. You lot with your weird language. It meant "breaking things" when I was younger.' Looking at Abbey, Ethel continued. 'Go in there with your head held high, do your best. That's all you can do. And bloody smash it.'

They all laughed.

'How is Michael? Is he still panicking?' Marty asked Abbey.

'He's all right. I called him earlier and went over some questions. He stresses out. The thing is, he knows what he's doing.'

'It's a tough time. As Nan said, all you can do is your best. Wow, the pasta's great,' Beth confirmed.

Marty watched her fork the food into her mouth, the joy evident on Beth's face. 'You look surprised.'

'Well, after yesterday's breakfast attempt... All I'm saying is it would be nice if you did it more often.'

'My Ted was great in the kitchen. He loved to cook. Always had a smile on his face.'

'You could see it from the sofa, could you?' Marty asked.

Ethel shot him a look as if to say the comment didn't go unnoticed. 'His favourite was a beef casserole, and he loved Indian food too. I found it spicy, and it played havoc with my digestive system. Gave me the right shits.'

'We're trying to eat. Christ, you'd be great if someone wanted to lose weight,' Marty snapped.

'Coma, that was his favourite. A chicken coma.'

'It's korma, Ethel,' Marty corrected.

'He'd do rice, potatoes and that fancy bread.'

'Naan,' Abbey said.

'Yes, dear?'

Abbey laughed. 'No, it's called naan bread.'

'Oh, I don't know the fancy names.'

'How's the pasta?' Beth asked. 'It's not too hot, is it?'

Ethel looked at her plate. 'It tastes rusty.'

Marty eyed his daughter, watching the smirk on her face.

When they'd finished eating, Beth and Abbey cleared the plates and loaded them into the dishwasher.

Ethel walked into the living room and perched on the corner of the sofa, and Marty followed, turning the channel to an old quiz show from the eighties on a repeats channel.

'Oh, look, it's Bruce Forsyth. I thought he'd died.'

Marty didn't answer. His phone pinged from his jeans pocket. Holding it in front of his face, he saw a message on WhatsApp. Although it pained him to click the link, he had to keep up to date with everything that was going on. It was the only way he'd be able to deal with it. As he clicked, his heart fell through his body.

A clock appeared and began counting down forty-eight hours.

It was the time he had to send the link to someone.

It was starting.

30

TUESDAY MORNING

'Are you serious? What time is it?' Ethel looked around the bedroom, struggling to get her bearings. As she lifted her head off the pillow, removing her eye mask, she looked at Beth, suddenly remembering where she was.

Beth opened the curtains, drenching the bedroom with light. 'How did you sleep, Mum?'

'I don't know yet. How early is it, for goodness' sake?'

'Seven thirty. Sorry, Mum. We're dropping Beth into her exam – because of our predicament, you'll have to come with us. We need to make sure you're safe.'

'I was safe at home.'

As Beth walked out of the room, she called out, 'We're not taking no for an answer. You're not a teenager. Up you get.'

Marty was making coffee in the kitchen. He stared at the screen of his phone and clicked the link that had been sent via WhatsApp the previous evening. The timer displayed thirty-nine hours and sixteen minutes.

His brain was foggy, a stress knot had developed in his

neck, and he felt sick with worry. There was no one he hated enough to send The App to. How could he? To put another poor fucker through the torment he was experiencing. Marty thought about Davey, then anger festered inside him. He imagined his friend, someone Marty had known since school, gone on holiday with and shared so many great times and memories, receiving the link, clicking it, putting in his details and then, when realising what he had to do, sending it to Marty. That was cold, heartless.

Slamming his fist on the kitchen worktop, he was annoyed for feeling this way. He had to let the anger go, try to look forward, remain focused, and work out his next step.

A voice at the kitchen door caused Marty to jump.

'Dad, where's Nan? We have to leave.'

'Err, she's upstairs.'

Stepping closer to her father, she asked, 'Are you all right?'

'Me? Yes, I'm good. Great, in fact. Don't worry. You have an exam to go to, and you'll do amazing. I'm so proud of you, Abbey.'

She leant back. 'And I'm so proud of you, too.'

'Taking me from my home, waking me up at an ungodly hour, dragging me from pillar to post like a bloody broken parcel,' Ethel grumbled as she padded into the kitchen in her slippers.

'Morning, Ethel. How was the bed? Comfy?' Marty asked.

'I don't know. I wasn't in it for long.'

Marty stepped towards his mother-in-law, her face swollen from sleep, her eyes puffy and watering. 'Look, it's not for long. We're doing this for you as much as us. We have to keep you safe. Please understand.'

Ethel looked hard into his eyes, a scowl on her face, the

bottom half of her teeth protruding, and she sighed heavily. 'I was safe at home. I've lived in Willesden for over fifty years. In all that time, we've never once been burgled.'

'They wouldn't dare.'

'Right. Are we ready?' Beth rushed into the kitchen, grabbing her handbag from the worktop. She looked flustered, her cheeks were bright pink, and a rash had developed on her chest due to stress.

'Yes. Come on – I'll be late.'

Reaching her arms out, Beth held her daughter. 'I know how important today is. Do your best – that's all anyone asks. You've revised so hard for this final exam, and we know you'll do amazing. We're all with you.'

'Thanks, Mum. I know.' Her eyes browsed the room. 'I just want to say thanks for all the support. It means so much. Right, let's go.'

As they walked out through the front door, Marty turned around, glancing along the hallway and up to the first floor.

The timer was ticking, and he didn't know who to send the link to.

It wouldn't be long until it reached zero.

* * *

The school building was sleek and modern. They'd recently refurbished it; the old grey brickwork was painted white, and the windows were replaced with double glazing. The roof had been refelted after it leaked and rain had dripped through to the classrooms several times. The field surrounding it had been returfed and fitted with goalposts.

Further along the road, Marty glared at the lollipop lady standing on the pavement outside the junior school, memories flooding his mind of the school run when Abbey was a child. His eyes began watering, and he wiped them with the back of his hands. His daughter had become a beautiful, intelligent woman, of which he was so proud, but the time seemed to have passed so quickly. Coughing to stem the threat of the tears, knowing his family would laugh, Marty realised how sentimental and nostalgic he'd suddenly become.

'Oh, God. Right, OK, this is it. Wish me luck.' Placing her bag over her shoulder, Abbey opened the door and kissed Beth, Ethel and finally, her father. She held his hand, squeezing it as if to say everything would be all right.

They watched as she walked along the pavement and disappeared into school.

'I need some air. Christ, it's like a coffin in here.' Ethel struggled with the door, pulled the lock and stood out on the pavement.

Beth followed.

Marty heard them chatting, Ethel moaning about her back and being cooped up in the car. Leaning back in the driver's seat, he tried to figure out what to do about the timer, almost hearing it tick in his ears, booming inside the Kia Sorento.

Bang.

Another second gone.

Bang.

Bang.

* * *

His body jolting in the driver's seat, Marty turned on the car and eyed the dashboard. 9.39 a.m. He'd been asleep for almost thirty minutes. Ethel and Beth were still outside on the pavement chatting. Glancing towards the school, he thought about Abbey and her final exam. He didn't want to let her out of his sight, but there was no choice. Marty listened to Beth's voice, again the events of the last couple of days driving through his mind, and he wondered if it was possible to keep her safe. Ethel, as stubborn and awkward as she was, would have to follow their instructions and to understand the seriousness of the situation.

His mind cast back to Sunday morning, the picture taken of Beth and Ethel in Oxford Street; someone had been standing there, watching them. The threat to their life was very real; Marty didn't doubt it for a second after what he'd seen unfold on The App. For a moment, he considered deleting it, wiping it from his phone and brushing it under the carpet, dealing with whatever they threw at him like a man, in the knowledge he'd die for his family.

A thump on the window caused his body to jerk. Marty saw Beth, her body bent forward, and he opened the window.

'Mum needs a wee.'

'Oh, for goodness' sake. Can't she go in the field?'

'No, she can't. She's not an animal.'

Marty gave a look as if to disagree, then regretted it. 'Why don't you take her to the school? I'm sure they won't mind.' He watched as the two women walked along the pavement, pressing the security button on the gate.

Suddenly, Marty's phone pinged. He grabbed it off the dashboard, looking at the screen—a new notification. Clicking on it, Marty was directed to a page within The App.

The strain of the last couple of days was taking over, and it seemed every muscle in his body ached. He'd never boxed, but he imagined this is what a ten-rounder felt like.

His breathing became difficult, his eyes blurred, and the

words resembled an array of fuzzy lines, like scratches on the glass.

With his hand shaking, his mind blurry, Marty read the message.

As you are aware, we have rules. Granted, you haven't spoken to anyone outside of The App – family is permissible – and you haven't deleted it either. But you did interfere with the hunt, and for that, there are consequences. Regretfully, we've made a decision.

It felt like his heart would explode as it thumped under his T-shirt and panic drowned his body. Placing his hand on the driver's seat, straightening his body, Marty looked behind and across the street, certain he was alone.

But was he? Were they watching him now? Sat, alone in the car. So exposed.

Staring at the screen, Marty re-read the message. The last line grating so hard in his brain.

Regretfully, we've made a decision.

As Marty waited, the anticipation almost too much to tolerate, the phone pinged again. A link on WhatsApp.

Earlier, while in the kitchen, the timer had shown thirty-nine hours and sixteen minutes. Now, as he pressed the link in the corner of the screen, it had decreased to nine hours.

Again, the phone pinged. Marty read the message inside The App.

One more thing. You must take part in the hunt this Friday.

The phone dropped from his hands into the footwell.

* * *

Just after eleven, Abbey practically waltzed out of the school gates beaming. Michael walked with her, clutching his revision books. He was much taller than Abbey, with thick black hair pulled back into a ponytail. He had a pleasant face, and Marty wondered if they were more than friends. He'd met him a couple of times and liked him, but Abbey hadn't implied that their relationship was anything more.

'She's here. By the grin on her face, I think it went well.' Beth opened the passenger door and stood on the pavement. Marty and Ethel followed.

'Well?' Beth called out.

With slight embarrassment, Abbey smiled. 'It was amazing. I can't believe how easy it was. We answered all the questions.' She gripped Michael's hand, and they raised them in the air.

'Fantastic, you guys. That's amazing.' The messages he'd received earlier ran through Marty's mind, and images of the clock counting down. How could he send The App to someone? How could he take part in the hunt? Marty stepped towards his daughter, and Beth followed. They could see the strain practically release from Abbey's body like a waterfall; the worry on her face had melted away.

Beth grabbed her daughter, holding her so close she almost crushed her. Then she turned to Michael and did the same. 'I'm so proud of you both. Congratulations.'

'Thanks, Mrs Benson. So glad to have it over with.'

Abbey kissed Michael on the cheek. 'I'll call you tonight.' Maybe, they weren't just friends, after all. Abbey would tell them in her own time, though.

'Thanks for everything. I mean it, Abbey. At my lowest times, you were there for me, my rock. I'll never forget how you carried me these last few days. I'll be forever grateful.' Michael turned to Beth and Marty. 'You really have a special daughter. She's one in a million.'

Smiling, Marty said, 'I know. She's an absolute blessing.'

* * *

'Right then. I'm doing something special for dinner tonight.' Beth was in the kitchen, removing some fillet steaks from the freezer. Marty and Abbey were sat at the table, talking about the exam and Ethel was perched on the sofa in the living room, watching a home-improvement show.

'There's no need to go to all that trouble, really. I'm happy with a takeaway.'

'It's no problem.' Beth turned. 'We're so proud of you.'

'Ahh, thank you both. I just hope the results are enough to get into uni.'

Marty held his daughter's hand. 'I'm sure they will. Christ, if anyone deserves the grades, it's you. The revision you put in, the hours spent in your bedroom, looking over your books, the dedication and commitment – if you flunk it, then the exam was impossible.'

Laughing, Abbey said, 'Exactly, Dad. If I fail, you can call the uni and speak to the head of law. Tell them straight.'

'You think I won't?'

'Oh, I know you will.'

They heard the sound of slippered feet dragging in the hallway. Ethel was making her way to the kitchen, her eyes surveying everyone looking at her.

'Have you shit the sofa?' Marty asked.

'There's an ad break. I don't give them time of day. Actors drivelling on about washing tablets, dishwasher tablets, tablets for the over-fifties, they're even calling computers tablets now. Tablets to help in the bedroom. What a load of baloney. My Ted didn't need any tablets in the bedroom.'

Marty almost spat out his coffee, shocked to hear what Ethel had said. He looked at her. 'I doubt that very much.'

With her hand resting on the table, supporting her thin

frame, Ethel announced, 'I'll have you know, I was a real sort in my younger days. All the fellas were after me.'

'Why? Did you owe them money?' Marty watched as Abbey placed her hand over her mouth, restraining the threatened burst of laughter.

'Ted was lucky to bag me. I can't say the same for my daughter.'

Ethel smiled as if to say, *'Come back from that.'*

His mood instantly changed as his phone pinged. Marty opened the screen, tapped the link on WhatsApp and looked at the timer. There were only a few hours left before he'd have to send The App to someone close to him and ruin their lives.

* * *

Later that evening, Marty, Beth, Abbey and Ethel sat around the table, drinking white wine and eating the most fabulous fillet steak in celebration of Abbey finishing her exams.

The atmosphere was jubilant, but Marty's mood was sombre as he watched his family smile, the conversation flowing, laughter filling the room. It seemed like they'd forgotten the threat, but it was down to Marty keeping silent. He wasn't going to ruin the ambience. It was something he had to deal with; it was his responsibility to find a way out of the hellhole he'd fallen into.

It wasn't fair to tell them of the recent developments. The photo of him in the restaurant, the timer almost out, and having to take part in the hunt in three days' time. The image of Davey Hughes, holed up in a maisonette, plagued his mind. How his friend had been affected since receiving the link and signing up. The repercussions it brought. Although earlier that day, he'd been consumed with anger at the situation his friend had put him in, now he felt sad for Davey. There was no one he could turn to, no one to give him advice and help with his predicament.

Peering around the kitchen, Marty was thankful for his family, watching their beaming faces, the warm smiles, the genuine love and support they showed each other.

His eyes blurry with tears and fighting the lump that felt like a stone in his throat, Marty heard Beth's voice.

'Hey, are you OK?'

Smiling, Marty answered, 'Yes. Don't worry about me. I'm good.'

She reached over, grabbing his hand. 'We'll get through this, you hear? It will all blow over in a few days. Have you heard anything since?'

His face flushed, and it felt like a gate had opened, the blood shoving through and filling his head like a tsunami, devouring everything in its path. His world paused for a moment, as if he were outside of his body, glaring from above, unable to control his thoughts and emotions, a mere observer of what was happening around him. His body seemed paralysed, his mind unable to process the questions. Breathing deep, forcing air into his lungs, Marty lied, 'Nothing. There hasn't been any activity within The App since Sunday night. I'm sure it will blow over like you say.' Guilt ate at him, festering and working its way around Marty's body, but he wouldn't ruin this moment. Not for anything.

Maybe Beth was right.

Maybe it would all go away.

As Ethel recounted another story, Marty's phone vibrated while on silent. Reaching for the phone and pressing the link on WhatsApp, the timer displayed zero.

31

THURSDAY

The next couple of days dragged, like watching a clock, but with the second hand wearing cement-filled boots.

Ignoring the timer, Marty threw himself into work, as he'd neglected it recently. There were jobs to sort out and invoices that needed chasing.

Abbey spent most of her time in the garden, reading and sunbathing after the months of revising in her bedroom. It was good to feel the sun on her skin.

Ethel mainly sat in the living room, either screaming at the remote control to get it to work, or shouting for more coffee.

And Beth decluttered the bedrooms upstairs, finding old photos and placing them in an album, bagging hers and Marty's old clothes ready to go to the local charity shop and organising the mess.

Marty sat at the laptop in the office at the front of the house, trying to work, but every time the phone pinged, his body froze.

Nothing had come through since Tuesday evening. No

link inside The App, no picture and no threatening message. It was the calm before the storm. Tomorrow morning, he'd be ordered to take part in the hunt. Otherwise, according to the rules, they'd kill Beth, then come for him. He wanted to grab his family and transport to another world; a place without worry or fear, somewhere they'd be safe.

Tapping his fingers on the keyboard, Marty opened Google and typed in the name 'Cass Carter'. Had it all been a nightmare? Had it really happened? It seemed so long ago they'd gone to the restaurant on Beth's orders, trying to stop her murder.

Marty had watched the live stream; her and Ed's bodies set on fire, the sickening act filmed by the people running The App. So much had happened in a few days, but it seemed a lifetime ago that Marty stood in the garden and filled out his details on receiving the link.

The TV was loud in the living room, and the hoover roared from upstairs.

A Google search bought him to a page on Facebook with a headline:

Missing. Have you seen Cass and Ed Carter?

Concerns are growing for Cass, 43, and Ed Carter, 47, of Finsbury Park, North London, who haven't been seen since Sunday evening. Both Cass and her husband Ed, had visited Roberto's Italian restaurant in Archway, North London on Sunday night and haven't been seen since.

A couple of eyewitnesses, who choose to remain anonymous, described how a man in his early forties wearing a green T-shirt and blue jeans approached Cass and was knocked to the ground by a man sitting at the next table. In a bizarre twist of events, the restaurant owner, Roberto Rossi, is also missing. Staff said they left after the incident Sunday night and on returning

Monday lunchtime, Roberto's daughter informed them he was missing.

Family and friends are concerned for their safety. Please call the number below or email if you have any information on Cass or Ed Carter, or Roberto Rossi.

Marty hovered his finger over the keys. His body ached to comment on what happened, to tell the horrendous account of how Cass and Ed were murdered, their bodies set alight and burned in the bedroom of an isolated cottage. And how Roberto died such a violent death.

He slammed the lid of the laptop, praying for a way out of this mess.

* * *

As he lay in bed that night, a fan whirring in the background blowing warm air onto his skin, a light sheet draped over his body, Marty stared at the ceiling, his eyes still and his mind overloaded with noise. He thought about Cass Carter. The connection was weird; even though he and Beth had known her no more than an hour, it almost felt like Marty was grieving for her, like she was a friend, someone he knew.

Beth's breathing was soft beside him, and knowing in a few hours he would have to take part in the hunt, Marty's body began to tremble, and he fought to keep the panic attack at bay. The room started to shift, circling around him, faster and faster as his eyes became blurry and unfocused.

Sitting up, Marty leant against the headboard, gasping for breath. His face felt so hot and his skin was suddenly wringing wet. As he controlled his breaths, the panic attack subsided, it felt like his body melted, sweeping gently in the air and drifting to the ground. Closing his eyes, Marty pushed his hands into the mattress and slid down the bed, laying his head on the pillow, his body straight, the fan blowing air on his face. As he lay still, desperately trying to rid his mind of the horrendous visions within The App, he prayed for a way out. Marty wouldn't participate, opening his phone and streaming, narrating as he tried to end another person's life. It couldn't happen.

Turning in the bed, he placed an arm around Beth; his world, his soulmate and best friend.

He couldn't lose her.

But if he didn't take part, that's what would happen.

Wiping the stream of tears from his face, he closed his eyes.

32

FRIDAY MORNING

Loud beeps ripped through the room, and the alarm clock displayed 7.40 a.m. Marty opened his eyes, the light beaming in through the slight gap in the curtains over the bedroom window.

On the wall opposite, the camera hidden in the vent watched his every move.

Shifting his body, Marty placed his feet on the floor and stretched to rid his aching back. Beth was still asleep and he didn't want to wake her. Whatever horror unfolded today, he'd deal with alone.

Reaching for his phone, Marty touched the screen, apprehensive about whether he'd received another notification. Nothing had come through, and for a moment, he hoped it was all over, that the last few days hadn't happened; a terrible nightmare that ended as he woke.

Slipping into a clean pair of jeans and a T-shirt, Marty walked out of the bedroom. Along the hallway, he tapped his knuckles against Abbey's door, pushing it back and seeing her asleep. Lastly, he checked Ethel, who was snoring loudly in the spare room.

He stood at the top of the stairs, steadying himself, fearful of what the day would bring: people streaming, trying to take the trophy, the heartache, suffering and all of them terrified for their loved ones. It was cruel beyond belief, and they expected Marty to take part.

Anger roared through his body; his skin itched and an ache developed on the side of his face. It felt like he was having a stroke. Reaching for the stair rail, he gripped hard, his fingers numb, veins popping through his skin. After a moment, the ache passed, and Marty took a deep breath, pushing out hard before going downstairs.

In the kitchen, he closed the door, pulled out his mobile and dialled Davey's number. After four rings, his friend answered in a low, troubled voice.

'Hey, man. You shouldn't be calling. They could be listening.'

'Look, it's too late for that. They've told me I have to take part, as I helped Cass Carter. I'm in deep and I don't know what the fuck to do.' There was a pause; Marty could hear Davey breathing down the phone, agitated and restless. 'What are you going to do? Haven't they told you to take part as well? It's your fourth week.'

'Yeah, I have to, Marty – the threats are real. Like you, I've seen the live streams and what they do if you don't take part. I can't let that happen.'

'So you're going to do it?'

'I have to, man. What choice have I got?'

'There has to be another way. I'm in trouble, Davey. I got the timer sent on WhatsApp.'

'The timer telling you to send the link?'

'Yes.'

'How long have you got?'

Marty paused. 'The timer's run out.'

'You didn't send it?'

'No.'

'Marty, you've broken one of the rules.'

His hand began shaking as he held the phone; Marty turned towards the kitchen window and looked out into the garden. Backing away, he spun around and walked into the living room and stared out the window. Were they out there, watching? 'Look, I have to go. I have so much to think about.'

'To think about? Marty, you've got to take part. There's no other choice. However much it goes against your principles, whatever your integrity and beliefs, you have to take part.'

Marty could hear his friend sucking on something and imagined it was a joint. 'Are you high?'

'Yeah, I need something to dull the pain. I'm ready, Marty. I have reasoned with myself. I got to do what I got to do.'

Listening to Davey take another drag on the joint caused Marty irritation as he walked back to the kitchen. 'I'll speak to you later. Whatever you choose, I wish you luck.'

'You too, man. Be safe.'

Marty moved into the garden, thinking about the phone call with Davey and how he was adamant he'd take part in the hunt. He imagined his skinny, puny body racing out of the maisonette, over the mess in the front garden, stoned and unable to focus, participating to protect his family as he held his phone and tried to narrate his actions. Then Marty imagined himself doing the same. He looked at the clear blue sky, the heat already uncomfortable; the only sound was a plane's engine in the distance.

His phone pinged at exactly 8 a.m. Marty pulled it from his pocket, seeing a notification appear on his screen. His body began trembling, his chest became hot, and his fingers tingled as he pressed the screen and went into The App's main page.

His world collapsed around him as he saw the picture of today's target.

Welcome one and all. Happy Friday. The following person has been chosen from social media. Clues will follow. As usual, £100,000 is on offer for the first person to kill her.

Good luck, everyone.

Abbey Benson

Age: 18

Height: 5ft 3in

Hair colour: Brown.

Likes: Reading. Exercise. Socialising. Netflix/box sets.

Occupation: Sixth-form student. Hoping to read law at university.

Address: North West London.

33

FRIDAY MORNING

Jonathan cheated. Abbey wasn't picked at random from social media.

But to watch Marty Benson sign up to The App, a life-changing opportunity to make huge amounts of cash, and then instantly interfere was a slap in the face. A kick while lying unconscious on the ground. That's how Jonathan saw it.

Over the past few days, he'd heard Marty and Beth talking in the bedroom, unaware of the camera in the vent. He'd watched them and got to know their peculiar habits – Beth sounding like a baby lamb when she snored, Marty calling his daughter's name in his sleep.

On numerous occasions, they'd spoken about The App, trying to work out a way to deal with their predicament. Marty, struggling to deal with the consequences of downloading The App. Beth consoling her husband and sweeping it under the carpet, thinking it would blow over and disappear like a puff of smoke. How very wrong they were.

Earlier, Jonathan had sat at the laptop, looking at Abbey's Facebook profile, and selected a recent picture before loading it onto The App's main page.

Now, he stood in the living room and commanded the blinds to open.

Looking down onto the street, a surge of energy shot through his veins. Any minute, people would receive the notification, see Abbey's picture, her profile, and begin waiting for the first clue.

Moving back to the laptop, he went into a programme and saw the first person click.

Davey Hughes.

Wow, I'd forgotten about Marty's friend. It's his last opportunity to save his family's life. The fourth Friday. Well, this should be fun, he thought.

Another click showed Davey's maisonette, the hidden camera capturing his every move.

'Go on, up you get. You realise it's Abbey, don't you? Look at your face – if a picture could paint words, you'd have a book—a whole fucking library.'

Davey picked up the mobile phone.

Jonathan narrated out loud what he saw. 'Your breathing is heavy, and excitement fills your body. You want to call Marty and let him know, but you're an addict. Gambling, drugs and alcohol. The money is too much to pass, the allure so tempting, plus the fact you still love your ex-wife. It would be so easy. It would sort all your problems. Go on, what are you waiting for? You have a head start over everyone else, an advantage. I won't wait for long. They'll be clues, and you'll miss out.'

Tapping keys on his laptop, Jonathan viewed more people in their homes, clicking the notification, seeing Abbey Benson's picture, waiting for a clue.

The App

Davey Hughes was the first to leave the house and get into his car.

34

FRIDAY MORNING

'No. Please, God, no. No, no, no! This has to be some kind of fucking joke.' Staring at Abbey's picture displayed inside The App, Marty expected a camera crew to arrive with lights shining on his face, people laughing, Beth and Abbey standing by the kitchen door.

Yeah. We got you. Would you take a look at your face? It's a picture, Marty. We got you so good. This is one to tell the grandchildren.

He fell to his knees, slapping his hands to the side of his head. Strange noises came from his mouth as he tried to breathe. He reached for the back-door handle to support himself, but his hand missed, as his eyes became blurry and unfocused, and slapped down on the floor again.

Ethel's voice startled him from the kitchen window.

'What on earth are you doing?'

'I'm fine. I fell over.'

'Oh, do be careful, Marty.' She rushed to the back door and helped steady him, using all her strength to help Marty to his feet.

'Thank you, Ethel, but you have to leave.'

'Oh no, you don't. I've just settled here. You're not kicking me out. And besides, your TV's bigger than mine. You haven't been on the juice already? I'll tell Beth.'

Placing his hands on Ethel's shoulders, his eyes pleading for her to be quiet, Marty said, 'Ethel, I haven't been drinking. Have you seen anyone in the house?'

'No. I've just got up. Whatever's the matter?'

'I'll explain in a minute. Are Beth and Abbey still in bed?'

'I think so. Marty, you're scaring me.'

'I'm sorry.' Urging himself to keep calm, Marty stepped into the kitchen, and Ethel followed. He closed the back door and told her to remain still.

Turning, he charged through the house, up the stairs and checked Abbey. She was stirring and looked like she was about to wake.

'Abbey, you need to get up. Quickly. Come on.'

'Huh?'

'Please. Get dressed and don't leave your room.'

Then he ran along the hall and into their bedroom. Beth was lying on her side, her feet sticking out of the sheet. Marty gently stepped across the wooden floor and knelt by her side. He forced himself to remain subdued, not wanting to shake her or scream at the top of his lungs and cause mass hysteria. They'd deal with this. There was no choice. 'Beth.' Marty placed his hand on her shoulder, gently rocking her. 'Beth.'

Her eyes opened, and she looked at her husband, disorientated with sleep. 'Hey.' Her smile was soft and comforting. 'What's going on?'

'Beth. I have something to tell you. Please don't panic. Don't scream and try not to lose your shit.'

Pressing her fists into the mattress, she lifted her body against the headboard. 'What is it?'

Inhaling deeply, Marty braced himself for her reaction. 'I opened The App. It's Friday morning. They want me to take part.' Creases developed on her forehead, her lips dropped, and sadness enveloped her face. 'Listen, I was in the garden. A notification came through. I clicked on it, and it brought me into The App. Beth... Beth, it's showing a picture of Abbey.'

'What do you mean? How? Why is Abbey's photo on The App?'

Tears spilt down his cheeks, dropping onto his T-shirt. He looked away, embarrassed for a moment and then back to his wife. Extending his arms, he pulled Beth close, breaking down as he kissed her forehead.

'Marty, what's going on? I don't understand.'

'Abbey has been chosen. They're coming for her.'

'Coming for her? Who? Who's coming for her?'

'Listen. There was another link. I opened The App. You know the rules. I've explained them to you. Every Friday, they pick someone from social media. At random. People take part in the hunt.'

'I know all that. But why's Abbey's picture on there?'

'She's the target.'

Suddenly, he saw it dawn on her, her brain registering Marty's words as they slowly filtered through.

Beth sat up further against the headboard. She went to speak, but it was like her tongue had stuck behind her teeth, unable to say the words. She sat, open-mouthed like she'd had a stroke.

'Beth, are you hearing me?'

'This isn't happening. It can't be.' She grabbed Marty's

face, clamping his cheeks with her hands. Coughing, she lost her breath, struggling for air; fear had struck her mute.

Pulling her close, he looked deep into her eyes. 'We're going to fix this. No one is going to hurt Abbey. Beth, are you hearing me? Beth?'

'They're coming for our daughter. Are they, Marty? Are they coming for her?'

'We need to get out of here. We'll take Abbey, your mum, my parents and go to the police. In fact, I'll call them now. Fuck it. I don't care about the rules anymore. If they're doing this, putting my daughter as the target, then I have nothing else to lose.'

Marty grabbed his mobile phone from his pocket. As he went to dial 999, A picture came through on WhatsApp. His parents were in their bedroom, both of them sat up on the bed. As he zoomed in, spreading his fingers on the screen, Marty could see gags around their mouths, their faces contorted with fear as they sat, held captive. Then a message.

Go to the police, and we'll kill them both.

The front door opened. Ethel's voice rang out from downstairs. 'Christ, Davey, you frightened me. All I could see was a shadow beyond the glass. They'll be down in a minute... No. Don't go up. Davey.'

35

FRIDAY MORNING

Footsteps pounded up the stairs. Marty raced to the bedroom door and saw Davey at the top step. He wore a grubby T-shirt, khaki shorts and shabby Nike trainers. He peered at Marty through hazy, distorted eyes.

The toilet flushed and the bathroom door opened. Abbey saw Davey.

'Hey, Davey, what are you doing here so early?'

Pulling his phone from his pocket, Davey shouted, 'Don't move, Abbey!'

Marty charged along the upstairs hallway, but before he reached his daughter, Davey grabbed Abbey, shoving her back into the bathroom and locking it behind them.

'Open the door, Davey – I'm fucking warning you. Lay a finger on her, and I swear to God, I'll rip you apart. Open the fucking door.' Restricted by the width of the hallway, Marty took a short run-up and barged his shoulders against the wood. He stepped back and charged again. The lock cracked. In desperation, Marty pounded the door with his fists.

'What on earth is that racket?' Ethel was standing at the bottom of the stairs. 'There are two toilets, you know, if you're that impatient.'

'Ethel, go into the living room. Wait there and do not, under any circumstances, open the front or back door. Not to anyone.' He heard her disgruntled mutterings fade as she sauntered away.

Beth was standing at the bedroom door, wearing a dressing gown and fluffy slippers. Her hand was over her mouth, unable to comprehend what was happening. She crept towards her husband, almost in slow motion, careful, deliberate steps, like a tortoise. Her mind was addled, and she was in meltdown.

'Davey's in the bathroom with Abbey. I have to get in there.' The pounding noise bounced off the hallway walls as Marty desperately slammed his body against the door.

They could hear Abbey whimpering, pleading for Davey to let her go. 'Put the phone away and open the door. Davey, can you hear me?' Beth shouted, 'Davey, what are you doing?'

Davey spoke, as if narrating.

Memories pushed through Marty's mind, the links within The App as he slammed his fists against the wood, but the door was so strong.

From the bathroom, Abbey pleaded with Davey. 'Put the phone down, and we'll talk.'

'I want to show you something,' Davey insisted, turning the screen towards her. 'Look.' Clicking into The App, thrusting his arm out, he showed Abbey her picture and profile.

Standing in the bath and peering at the screen, she tried to control her breathing, her body relaxed slightly, and she took the phone. 'What? What are you showing me?' Her eyes were blurry through the tears.

'It's you, Abbey. They've picked you. I'm not going to let anything happen to you. I have to protect you. You're safe in here.' Davey could hear the wood crack as Marty rammed his body against it.

'Open the door, Davey. I'm warning you.'

'She's safer in here, man. I got this.'

'Are you stoned?'

'No,' Davey called out. 'I've never had a clearer head.' He looked towards Abbey, shock etched on her face; raised eyebrows, open mouth and wild eyes staring at the phone screen.

'How? How have I been picked? Am I going to die?' she said.

Davey stepped forward, pulling Abbey tight to him, listening to her sob into his chest. He'd known the Bensons all his life, Marty was his best friend, and he loved Beth and Abbey. This was his way to try to protect her. To give something back after sending Marty the link. Twisting the key in the lock, Davey opened the door.

Marty charged towards him, pushing him over and into the bath, listening to his pleas as his hand grabbed Davey's throat. His face turned red, his lips a deep purple as Marty squeezed his fingers on his throat. 'You stupid bastard. Don't ever do that again. I should strangle you where you lie.'

'I'm, I'm sorry,' he said with a strained voice. 'I'm... I'm trying to keep her safe. I needed to be here. To help. After... I'm so sorry.'

Releasing his grip, Marty stood back and sat on the edge of the bath.

'Dad, am I going to die?'

Marty turned to his daughter. Her face was smudged

with last night's mascara; her eyes appeared so frightened as they darted around the bathroom. He pulled her to him and held her tight, feeling her body quiver, so weak and lifeless, like she'd slump to the floor any second. Standing back but still holding her face, Marty insisted, 'No one is going to get you, you hear? No one.'

Davey scrambled around in the bath, like a deer on ice, trying to stand. 'Your father's right. We will lay our lives down before letting anything happen to you. We've got your back. Them fuckers don't know who they're messing with.'

'Am I missing something? What's so special about that loo?' Ethel was standing at the top of the stairs, looking at the eyes directed towards her.

* * *

In the master bedroom, Beth, Marty, Abbey, Ethel and Davey sat on the bed, trying to figure out what to do. The atmosphere was one of despair.

Marty choked back tears, thinking about his parents, the picture he'd received and how he'd keep his daughter safe. But he couldn't fall to pieces now, needing to be stronger than ever. 'We have the upper hand,' he said, forcing hope into his voice.

'How? How the hell do we have the upper hand, Marty?' Beth asked, her face resting on the palms of her hands.

'No, Marty's right. We do. It's like a film you've watched dozens of times. You can see the scenes before they happen. It's memory, familiarity, you know. We can see it before it happens. The live streams, they'll play out on The App. It gives us the opportunity to see them coming.'

Abbey jumped up. 'I'm so scared. I don't want to die. Please, I have to get out of here.' Her heart thumped, the room began to spin, and she stumbled backwards onto the bed again, trying to take a breath.

Beth sat on the edge of the bed, placing her hand on her daughter's chest. 'Abbey, nothing is going to happen to you. Breathe in, ten seconds – come on, do it.' Opening her mouth, Abbey drew air deep into her lungs. 'That's it. Now, look at me. Look into my eyes. That's it, hold the breath, now out, slowly.'

The room became clear as her eyes focused, the comfort of her mother's hand aiding her as she repeated the technique. After a minute, the panic attack faded, and her body was more composed.

Looking around the room, Marty said, 'They're watching us.'

'How do you know?' Beth whispered, her voice hushed.

'When I went to dial 999, the first time I came up to the bedroom after seeing Abbey's picture, I got a message on WhatsApp. My parents are being held hostage. Someone saw me, about to make the call.'

Marty raced out of the bedroom and returned a minute later with a tool bag and small ladder. With his hands on the wall, he crept around the room, looking up at the vent. Spreading the ladder, Marty stood on the fourth step, opening the screws. Shining his phone torch into the vent, he saw the recording device, removed it and threw it to the floor, crushing it with a hammer from his toolbox. 'There. I knew it. They've been watching us all the time. How the heck did they get inside?'

'Maybe when we went to the restaurant or visited Davey?' Beth piped up.

Marty and Davey's phones pinged in unison. Marty jabbed the screen with his finger.

The first hint had been posted under Abbey's picture.

The clue is in the sentence below—a town in North West London:

(A bee) flies over a collection of toys, concerned that the (doll is ill.)

Turning to Abbey, then addressing the rest of the room, Marty said, 'We need to go.'

36

FRIDAY MORNING

'I think it's safe. I can't see anyone outside.' Marty was standing by the living room window, looking out onto the street. Davey and Beth stood next to him, and Abbey and Ethel were in the hallway.

Marty turned around, looking at the sofa, the large armchair sat next to it, then along the walls and over the ceiling. 'They've probably got listening devices everywhere.' Lowering his voice, he continued in a whisper, 'We don't stand a chance here.' Again, he pulled out his phone and dialled his mum's number, wiping the tears from his eyes. 'If those fuckers hurt my parents, I'll devote my life to finding them. They must be terrified.' He faced Davey, who was still looking out of the window. 'My father has dementia. He must be so frightened.' Listening to the dialling tone, Marty cancelled the call and dialled again. 'Come on, pick up the phone.' He wondered if someone was there now, watching his parents as they lay, tied up in the bed, hearing the phone ring. 'If you're holding my parents captive, the least you can do is answer and let me know your fucking demands.'

Ending the call, Marty slammed the palm of his hand against the wall. 'I have to go over there.'

'Mate, it's pointless. They'll see you coming and end your folks instantly.' Davey placed his arm on his friend's shoulder, trying to console him. 'We need to follow their orders and keep safe. There's no other choice.'

As Marty began tapping on his phone and writing a message to his mother to tell her he loved her, Davey pushed his face to the window.

'Hold up – we may have encountered our first problem.'

'What?' Marty joined him and peered across the front garden out onto the road.

'There's a black car – it looks new, one of those flash ones. An Audi.'

'What about it?'

'Well, it passed a few minutes ago, going slowly along the road.'

'Right?'

'And now it's just passed again, going the other way.'

Silence drenched the room as Marty and Beth stared out of the window.

An elderly couple walked along the pavement, linking arms; a woman with a buggy stopped on the other side of the road, adjusted the sun visor over her baby and placed her hands on her hips. She waited a couple of seconds and continued jogging along the road with the pram.

'Well, that isn't right.' Ethel joined them, seeing the woman running along the road.

'What, Mum? What have you seen?' Beth asked.

'That woman. It's not right.'

They all turned, looking at Ethel.

'That poor baba will be as sick as a dog, bouncing all

over the place in the pushchair – it's got a wonky wheel. Then she'll wonder why she has to clean up all that vomit.'

Sighing, Marty requested, 'Ethel. Please. Can you go and stand with Abbey?'

'No need to bite my head off.'

'I didn't bite your—'

'There it is again.' Davey pointed towards the road.

The black Audi crawled passed the house; the driver had his phone in his hand, like he was ready to stream.

Marty looked at his mobile, expecting to see a notification, the first live footage. There was nothing. 'We'd see something come through, surely?' His shoulders felt tight, and his back ached from the strain.

'You'd think so,' Davey answered.

Suddenly, almost like his brain hadn't processed the words he was about to say, Marty spoke. 'They can do whatever the fuck they like. It's their rules. We're dead people walking! It's like a fucking zombie infestation, the walkers being The App members, and we're the lone survivors, desperate to keep alive, hiding and waiting for the attack. How are we going to keep everyone at bay?'

'Mate, that's deep. But I like the way you put it,' Davey answered. 'I think we're safe at the moment. The App has Abbey's picture, a clue to her name and location, but not the home address.'

The street was vacant; Marty, Beth and Davey gazed out of the window, and watched the black Audi pull up by the kerb on the other side of the road.

Behind them, Abbey whimpered from the hallway, unable to speak with distress.

The man sat in the driver's seat, his phone held in front of his face. As he looked across the street towards the house, everyone ducked.

'Shit. What's he doing? Why hasn't a notification come through?' Marty asked.

'I say we wait until he crosses the road. Let him come to the house. We can go around the side entrance and jump him.' Beth ordered.

Clenching his fists, Marty wanted to tear the man in the Audi limb from limb, to slam his body against the wall until he resembled a rag doll. When his family were threatened, he'd lay down his life, no question.

Marty's phone pinged, and he swallowed hard as he looked at the screen.

Beth and Davey peered at him, too frightened to ask what it was.

With a heavy sigh, Marty's shoulders dropped. 'It's Andy Rothan sending a joke. It's all good.'

Outside, the Audi driver opened the car door and stood on the pavement. Their gasps filled the living room. The man was talking on the phone, glimpsing along the street. Suddenly, a front door opened, and a middle-aged woman wearing an apron over her dress walked out onto the steps. The man grabbed a handful of brochures from the passenger seat and entered the house.

Marty looked around the room, seeing the relieved faces. 'OK, it's time. We have to leave.'

* * *

After looking through the glass of the front door to ensure the drive was empty, Marty wrenched the handle and glimpsed at the petrified eyes and despondent expressions behind him. He nodded his head to give them encouragement, then pulled the door back and walked along the driveway. Birds sang, filling the air with hope; the smell of burning wood was noticeable from a neighbour's bonfire. A truck sounded in the background as it shifted along the road.

Moving behind a bush, Marty watched it pass and stepped onto the pavement. A mother and child walked hand in hand in the distance; two elderly men stood on a street corner, one with a newspaper tucked under his arm, both deep in conversation. Turning, he glanced the other way and saw a car coming towards him. Marty ducked behind their Kia Sorento, his paranoia rife, ebbing at his bones and causing panic to rise slowly from his stomach, enveloping his body. The sound of tyres gripping the road as stones danced, the raucous engine grated in his ears. Was this him, his life now? Frightened to live, wary of every cough and spit, and wondering if anyone they encountered would be a part of this monstrosity? How would he know?

How could he stop a murder, when everyone could be the killer?

The lights of the Kia Sorento blinked and the alarm bleeped as Marty unlocked the car. Dropping to the ground, he crawled under the vehicle, searching for a tracking device. Once he was certain nothing had been planted, he slid back out. 'Let's go – we need to be quick. Everyone needs to turn off Wi-Fi and location services. He can't track us that way. We need to be on high alert. Whatever you see, however strange, it could be an attack. Keep your eyes wide open and be vigilant.'

Watching Beth, Abbey, Ethel and Davey walk along the drive, muted with fear, the sense of responsibility was daunting. He hadn't a clue how to play this. Their future was filled with uncertainty and all they could do was desperately try to avoid an attack; the possibility was rife with every step they took, around every corner.

'No good looking at me – Why-Fi sounds like a question,' Ethel stated. Placing her arm around her granddaughter, Ethel held her tight. 'All these flash words and terminology, it's beyond me, dear. How are you, Abbey? I still don't understand what's going on, but I'll not let anyone harm you.'

'I know, Nan. I love you.'

'I love you too, dear.' Looking at Marty, she snapped, 'In, out, in, out. Make your bloody mind up. I feel like I'm doing the Hokey Cokey.' Ethel opened the back door and manoeuvred her body along the seat. Abbey and Davey sat beside her, and Beth got into the passenger seat.

Beth, Abbey and Davey went into their settings and closed down Wi-Fi and location services, Beth doing Marty's phone as well.

Images of his poor parents, bound and gagged on the bed, roared through Marty's mind. He rang the number again and listened to the dialling tone blasting through the Sorento's speakers.

Unexpectedly, the phone was answered. A deathly silence fell.

Marty waited a moment, listening to the muffled sounds in the background. 'Mum? Can you hear me? You're going to be OK. Nothing is going to happen. I love you both so much.'

Suddenly, he saw a FaceTime request pop up on his phone screen. Glimpsing at Beth, his heart felt like it would burst through his lips. He pressed the screen and answered the call.

'I'm here. It's Marty. Is that you, Mum?' Waiting for a reply, he felt helpless, like he was stuck in a pit without a ladder, or lying at the bottom of the ocean with a ball and chain attached to his ankle.

A familiar picture appeared on the screen, images of his parents' wedding day, set in a wooden frame and hanging on the upstairs hallway wall. Further along, he saw a sign on the bedroom door reading, *Where We Sleep.* Marty had written it in large, black letters to aid his father's memory. The door creaked, the sound loud as it spilt from the car speakers.

'Who's there? I want to see my parents.' Raising his voice and gripping the steering wheel in frustration, Marty shouted, 'Let me see my parents. If you lay a finger on them, I swear to fuck, I'll never stop until I hunt you down.'

Heavy breathing pushed out of the speakers as the camera scanned the bedroom. Marty saw the old chest of drawers with clothes neatly folded on top, the washing basket, the old cream-coloured wallpaper and the coving design on the ceiling. It was like his regular video chat with his parents, they'd talk for ages as his mother set the phone down, the camera pointing to the ceiling. They'd laugh at how she never got used to technology before Marty asked how they were doing, speaking to his father in the hope that today he recognised him. Except now, he feared the worst, knowing his parents were at risk.

The camera slowly scanned the room, and then his parents appeared, lying slumped against the headboard, their hands tied and resting on their laps, gags tight around their mouths.

'You bastard. Why? Why are you doing this? Please, let me take their place.' Marty burst into tears, listening to the gasps coming from behind him. Beth grabbed his hand, squeezing it tightly.

'Hey there, Gracie. Hey Albert. Nice to see you both,' Ethel shouted.

The camera swiftly darted to the ceiling and seemed to

freeze. Then a voice, calm and calculated spoke. 'I've thought long and hard, Marty Benson. You broke the rules, more than once, and there are consequences and repercussions for your actions. You need to understand how it works. I'm a fair man, Marty Benson. I give and take, I understand decency, but there are rules – which were stated quite clearly the first time you clicked the link and entered your details, and yet, you chose to disobey my orders.'

'Fuck your orders. You hear me?'

'Tut, tut, that won't do, Marty. Not at all. I've worked my arse off to develop this project. A way I, and only I, control things, not you. I could have ended your life at the drop of a hat when you first started interfering, but where's the fun in that?'

Muffled cries pushed through the speakers, and again, Marty begged for him to let his parents go. He knew how terrified they would be, how traumatised his father was, not knowing what was happening. It felt like he was there, feeling their pain, every thought, every emotion.

The camera jerked and suddenly pointed towards Marty's mother, lying on the bed, leaning against the headboard in her dressing gown, then to his father, the wild, empty eyes, his face so gaunt and pale.

'I swear I'll kill you. I'll be the last person you think of as you take your final breath, knowing I'm responsible,' Marty threatened.

There was a short pause as the voice on the line seemed unaffected, his breathing controlled throughout, and then he spoke again. 'As I was saying, this plan is much better. A genius idea, don't you think? Putting young Abbey in the spotlight. I'm going to enjoy watching her die.'

The screen went blank as the call ended.

* * *

Marty sat in the driver's seat, his head resting in the palms of his hands, crying tears of frustration. He'd never been more angry or disturbed. He felt useless and insignificant, like a chess piece waiting to be lifted by this evil bastard pulling the strings.

As he went to start the car, a message came through on WhatsApp. Marty felt like he was about to vomit. A picture showed a knife, held to his mother's throat.

Underneath, eight words.

If you come here, I'll kill them instantly.

Turning to Beth, Marty said, 'There's no way out. What are we going to do?'

'Hey, don't think like that. You got this, mate,' Davey said from the back. 'Remember when I was bullied at school? Who was the person that made it stop? Or when I used to go with that married woman and her husband was looking for me? You, Marty. You sorted it. You're a brave soul. You'll find a way.'

Abbey leant forward, kissing her father on the cheek. 'Whatever happens, whatever the outcome, I love you so much. You're my hero, Dad.'

'They're right. You'll find a way. We're in this together,' Beth confirmed.

His eyes were blurry from crying, and his head ached. 'You're all heroes—each one of you,' Marty said.

'My Ted was a hero,' Ethel piped up. 'One time at a dance, oh many years ago, it was, I remember this big beast of a man. Boy, did he stink. I could smell him from across the hall. Anyway, back in those days, the fellas would stand on one side of the hall, the ladies on the other. The walk of shame it was called. This great oaf walked across the floor, like the big I am and asked me to dance. I refused, and Ted was standing behind him. When the stinker stepped to the side, Ted asked me to dance. The bravest thing I ever saw.'

'So what happened?' Marty asked. 'Was there a fight?'

'Oh goodness no, Ted would have run a mile. We danced. That night, I swear I felt my heart melt.'

Marty turned, looking at Ethel. 'That's a brave thing to do, all right.' He saw Abbey smirking and continued. 'Dancing with you, I mean.'

Turning to the front, Marty started the Kia Sorento, uncertain of where to go, hoping his instincts would keep his daughter alive.

37

FRIDAY MORNING

'I say we book into a lodge, somewhere quiet where we can hide, until we find a way to deal with this.' Marty looked at the signs for St Albans as they drove along the A405 in Hertfordshire. 'I think a hotel leaves us too vulnerable, too many people posing a threat, and we can't keep driving – we're too exposed.'

'Good shout, mate. I like your way of thinking.' Davey turned to Abbey, his voice low. 'How you holding up, kiddo?'

Abbey hadn't spoken for a few minutes; the sense of dread she was feeling left her fragile, and her brain was struggling to process what was happening. Her voice was weak and broken. 'I... I'm so scared. What's going to happen?'

Davey grabbed her hand. 'What's going to happen is we're getting you out of this hellhole, you hear me? Me, your mum and your dad.' Looking at Ethel, he included her name too. 'We're going to protect you. We won't let anything happen.'

Abbey shifted in the seat, looking at Davey. 'Honestly? You promise?'

The sadness on her face, the despondency, made his heart melt. He thought about Tina, his ex-wife, how they'd split up, and her last words as he walked out of the house. *You're a total loser.* Maybe he was, but this was his time to be courageous, to do something heroic and be a proud man again. He'd spoken to Tina last night, keeping The App a secret, not wanting to cause her concern. It wasn't fair. He still cared deeply for her and hoped one day she'd give him another chance. Now, he had to keep strong for his best friend and help protect Abbey.

'I promise,' he answered.

In the front seat, Beth searched Google on her phone for a last-minute lodge in Hertfordshire. Marty and Davey's phones were hacked, The App's creator was possibly able to watch their every move. So far, there was nothing to suggest Beth's phone had been tampered with. No strange links or notifications and none of her friends had messaged to ask about weird messages she'd sent on social media. A page opened, and she scrolled, putting in today's date, unable to think of an end time or how long they'd need it for. 'There's a couple we can have. One looks deep in the woods, private and secluded. What do you think?'

'Wow, you found that quick,' Marty noted.

'You haven't seen the price – that's why I found it so quick.'

'However expensive it is, it sounds perfect. Book it. We can hide out there.'

Beth put in her card details, deciding to book the lodge until Sunday. A confirmation email arrived a few minutes later, confirming the booking and check-in time. Midday. It was ideal.

Marty and Davey's phones beeped together. A new message inside The App. They were a mile from St Albans, and Marty slowed the car, turning to look at his friend. 'What is it, Davey?'

'Wait a second, let me check.' Shifting his body to the side, Davey reached for his mobile phone. 'Oh shit, man. It's another clue.' Davey began reading the text. '"A roman city close to H H, in H."' Scratching his head, he asked, 'What's that mean?'

'Hemel Hempstead. Hertfordshire.' Pounding his fist on the wheel as he drove, Marty shouted, 'How does he know? We've turned everything off.'

'Even so, Dad, he may still have a way to see us,' Abbey stated.

'With everything off? How. How is that possible?

'I don't know. Possibly through The App. I haven't got a clue how it works. Maybe the only thing is for you and Davey to turn your phones off.'

'How can we? It's the only way we can see the threat of attack. Our only advantage.' He looked towards the shops and the quiet main road, searching for cameras. There was nothing visible. 'He can watch security monitors, CCTV. There are apps available which allow people to view live footage on the streets. But it seems he sees our every move.'

The phones pinged again. 'This is all too much to take' Marty whispered to Beth.

She clicked into The App on Marty's phone, her hand trembling as she read the Kia Sorento's registration plate. Beth looked out of the window, vehicles coming towards them, people strolling along the street, dubious of everyone. 'There's nowhere to hide.'

'We need to keep going.' Marty looked at the road behind, watching for an ambush. It was them against the world, unsure where the danger would come from next. As he pulled onto the road, a horn blasted behind them, causing Marty to swerve.

'Whoa.' Davey turned his body and knelt on the seat, looking out the back window. A car pulled around them, the driver giving them the finger, and faded into the distance. 'It's OK. Just a knobhead driver.'

As he drove, he fought the image of his parents, the sounds of their muffled cries, the whimpering playing loud in his ears, the knife at his mother's throat. He pushed his body forward on the seat, straightening his frame and trying to ease the painful knot at the bottom of his back. His brain went to happier times, forcing the cruel images from his mind. A recent holiday in Greece; he, Beth and Abbey walking along the beach, their toes sinking into the warm sand with the sun on their skin. The sound of waves gently caressing the shore, children's laughter, the smell of seaweed in the air and the boats on the horizon. He hoped they'd spend time like that again, the three of them without a care in the world.

Beth looked out of the passenger window, her body rigid and her mind busy. She reached behind, grabbing her daughter's hand, feeling the clammy skin, and gently squeezing it to let Abbey know everything would be OK. But would it? Regret filled her body; it had been her decision to try to help Cass Carter. Little did she know the consequences of her actions. Her heart pained for Marty; his parents held captive, unable to do anything about it. She blamed herself, and for Abbey being chosen too, knowing it wasn't a coincidence after listening to the voice on FaceTime. She tried to work out how this man, this creator of The App, could do such a wicked thing, tormenting others, ruining people's lives, and for what? Sick, twisted kicks?

Her head slumped against the passenger window and

she peered down the street, noticing an Italian restaurant – a flag outside and signage similar to Roberto's. Closing her eyes, riddled with guilt, she prayed they'd survive this hideous situation.

Marty's voice interrupted her thoughts.

'Where's the lodge?'

'Oh, let me look. Near Hatfield. I'd say another half hour.'

A red light came on, indicating they needed petrol. A mile up the road, Marty swung left and pulled up by a pump. Two other vehicles were on the forecourt; an elderly man shook the nozzle and replaced it, fitted the cap back onto his Jaguar and headed into the shop. Further along, a red Ford Orion pulled out onto the road. Glimpsing the right-side wing mirror, Marty opened the driver's door. 'Any requests?'

'Mint humbugs. Get me a large bag,' Ethel ordered.

Marty looked behind him and back into the car. 'Anyone else?'

'Err, I could use a Coke,' Davey suggested.

'Yeah, I'll have one, Dad.'

'Mint humbugs and two cokes. Beth?'

'I'm good. Oh, no, a sandwich. Cheese and ham.'

'Right.' Marty pulled out the nozzle, opened the cap and began filling.

The elderly gentleman returned to his Jaguar, nodding at Marty and driving away.

Peering over the Kia Sorento, Marty watched vehicles power along the road. Suddenly, an old camper van pulled in and crawled onto the forecourt, stopping a few yards from the petrol pumps. The sun glimmered on the windscreen, making it awkward for Marty to see the driver. He knew stopping would make them vulnerable, but had someone found them already? His breath was choppy as it filled his lungs, his fingers numb as he pulled on the handle, the strong smell of petrol overpowering. Gazing at Beth, he steadied himself, resting a hand on the Sorento; around him, the forecourt became a haze of cloud.

The camper van sat stationary, Marty still unable to see the driver.

The handle became limp, announcing the tank was full. The door of the camper van opened, and a tall, skinny guy in his early twenties stepped out.

Marty replaced the nozzle, glancing between Beth and the driver of the camper van. She was chatting to her mother, unaware of the sudden threat.

He saw the driver standing by the camper van, looking bemused, turning around to possibly check his bearings. Waiting at the petrol pump, Marty's pulse raced as he began to approach.

His accent was from the Midlands, possibly Birmingham. 'Hey, my phone's dead, and the charger in the van doesn't work. Am I on the right road for Hatfield? My partner and I are checking out the Galleria. A bit of shopping.'

Marty stepped back, glancing at the camper van. A woman with long blonde hair opened the passenger door, dumping nappies into the bin.

'Err, yeah, keep going along this road, mate. You'll see signs,' Marty said.

'Much obliged.'

Fitting the petrol cap, Marty watched the camper van pull away and raced into the shop. While buying the sweets, sandwiches and drinks and paying for the petrol, his eyes never left the forecourt.

***

'How the bloody hell are you supposed to open these?' Ethel was struggling to tear the packet of family-sized mint humbugs. 'It'd be quicker getting into a bank vault.'

Marty turned his head slightly. 'You genius, Ethel. You bloody genius. I've thought of something, and it might just work. I knew how useful you'd be. I said it to Beth. I said, "Your mother will be a great help – having her with us is a blessing."'

'No you didn't.' Beth laughed.

'What's the idea, mate? Share the lightbulb moment.' Davey pushed his body forward, eager to learn of Marty's plan.

'I need someone great with computers. A hacker. Who do we know?'

'Michael's older brother's an incredible hacker,' Abbey stated. 'I've been to the house a few times, and Michael showed me all his equipment. Says he can break into anything in a matter of seconds.'

'Maybe he could get into these frigging humbugs.'

'Oh, give them here, Mum.' Beth grabbed the packet, tore the corner off and handed them back to Ethel.

'Can we speak to him?' Marty pushed.

'Yeah, I can text Michael and ask him to call. I don't know his brother, but if you don't ask, you don't get.'

Again, both Marty and Davey's phones pinged at the same time.

Davey clicked into The App. His eyebrows dropped deep on his forehead and his mouth fell open. 'Oh shit.'

Clicking the notification, now inside The App on Marty's phone, Beth tapped the latest link, seeing a road appear on the screen. The footage was hazy and jumping. Her heart raced, her voice shaky. 'Someone is streaming.'

Balancing the phone on the dashboard, they listened as the person began speaking—the nervous, timid voice pelting through the speakers.

'I hope you can hear me. I think I'm the first on here today; not sure if anyone is watching. It's a bit like a DJ on a pirate radio station, unsure if there's an audience. I've watched the streams, dreading my time. I haven't found Abbey Benson yet; I guess she's in a vehicle travelling along this road. When I saw the notification, I got out of bed, raced out of the house and made my way over here. I don't live too far away. Granted, I'm premature, but I need to get the hang of streaming. My family don't know I'm here, trying to murder someone to save my son's life. They think I'm at work. Christ, if they only knew. This is the final day to take part. We're going away next week, the three of us – my wife, son and me. We've booked...' His voice drifted off, presumably realising he was giving too much information.

'He's behind us,' Beth pointed out.

Davey turned, facing the back window and scanning the road. 'There's no one behind us.'

In the corner of the screen, Beth saw a row of shops, then the Italian restaurant they'd passed minutes ago. She spoke, almost robotic, her voice stunned as she stared at the screen. 'He can only be moments away. He has the registration plate.'

'OK, nothing is going to happen. It's one man – there's five of us,' Marty confirmed.

'I want to get out.' Abbey's voice was raised as she tried to open the back door. 'Please, let me out. I can't be here.'

'Abbey. You got this. Listen to my voice and look towards the front.' His daughter was trying to pull the handle of the door. 'Abbey.'

Her thoughts were disjointed, and it felt like she was imprisoned in a cell, the walls closing in. She stamped her feet as adrenaline coursed through her body and her eyes darted from left to right, looking for an escape route.

'Abbey, listen to me, please.' Marty glimpsed his daughter in the back as Beth reached behind, holding her hand. 'We are not letting anyone get to you, OK? Take deep breaths and listen to my voice. I'm here – your mother, nan and Davey too. We are all going to protect you. Nothing is going to happen, you hear?'

Abbey nodded, bringing her knees to her face, and began crying.

Again, Marty spoke. 'Say it, Abbey.'

'Say what?' Her voice was muffled as her mouth rested on her thighs.

'Say nothing is going to happen. Say it slow and loud.'

'Nothing... Noth-nothing will happen.'

'Again.'

'Nothing will happen.'

'Louder, Abbey.'

'Nothing will happen.'

The voice began pushing through the speakers. The stream showed the road, almost in fast motion. Then they saw the petrol station.

'Oh shit. He's close,' Beth whispered.

'Like everyone else, I don't want to be here. It sounds like a cliché, something you say to appear normal and win people over, but I'm not a cold-hearted bastard. I look out for my family, and my wife and I have spent every waking hour devoted to our son. We were lucky enough to be able to send him to private school, an outstanding education, and he made it to university. That was our proudest moment.

'I don't know why I'm talking so much. I suppose I'm trying

to paint a picture, to drill home my morals, values and the type of person I am. I adore, absolutely adore my family. We have the best holidays, a huge detached house close to where I am now and want for nothing. My work has paid for it all. I shower my wife and son with love and affection. Time. I think that's the most crucial part. Giving your time to listen and nurture.

'Thinking about it, I know it's possible that these recordings will reach the police, someone will know my voice and see what I'm about to do. The narration will seal my fate. But I signed up for The App; it was my mistake. When they send a picture of your children, it does something to you. It hits home harder than anything in this world. A button is pressed, your world collapses, and you'll do anything to keep that person alive. Please understand that. They've forced me into a corner.'

Her voice was loud and harsh as Beth covered her ears with her hands. 'I can't listen to any more.'

'Yeah, isn't there anything else on?' Ethel asked. 'Change the channel.'

'Look, we have the upper hand – like in poker, we're able to see the opponent's cards. It's such an advantage. We have to listen – it's the only way we can beat them.'

'Man, I like your way of thinking. Good analogy, Marty, boy.' Davey kept glancing behind, observing the road.

'Any word from the hacker, Abbey?'

Checking her phone, she looked for a message. 'No. Nothing.'

Marty glared at the road, watching the surrounding vehicles, scrutinising everyone. He felt sick; his face was hot, his skin clammy. Wiping his forehead, he listened to the conversation behind him. Ethel was asking Abbey where they were going, his daughter doing her best to pave over it so as not to concern her nan. Davey asked if Abbey felt better, finding a bottle of water in the footwell and giving it to her. Next to Marty, Beth's feet stamped on the floor of the Sorento, her hands placed between her thighs.

'I have them in my sight. I can see the car, the correct registration plate. Oh my God, wish me luck.'

'Marty, he's right behind us.' Turning her body, Beth saw a black pickup truck gaining on them up the inside lane, so close she could see the guy in the driver's seat.

'OK, listen, everyone turn to the front,' Marty ordered. 'We can't give away that we know, understood? He's watched the links, people selected from social media, knowing how it works. As far as he's concerned, we know nothing about what's happening. It will make it easier for us to escape. Keep looking ahead.'

Adjusting the rear-view mirror, Marty looked at his daughter. Her pale complexion, and the way her body shivered, indicated how she felt. 'Abbey, say it in your mind: nothing will happen.'

Her eyes slowly rose to him, almost in slow motion, and she nodded.

Wrenching the steering wheel, Marty pulled the Kia Sorento into a country lane, everyone leaning hard to the right.

'Christ, I've never seen a worse driver. There are such things as indicators, Marty. At least give us a warning. Bloody pillock.' Ethel adjusted her body, gripping the back of Marty's seat.

The pickup truck turned in behind them, racing along the country road. Marty watched it gain on them, so close he could see the driver's face. He wore glasses, and his black hair was combed to the right.

'I'm not sure what's going on here. The car is packed – this will make it so complicated. I think they know. The driver pulled

sharply into a narrow road and is speeding. I'm sure they're on to me. I don't know what else to do.'

The pickup truck hit them from behind as Marty watched the sharp bend ahead. Everyone jolted forward. Beth screamed.

'Hold on, everyone. This maniac behind is trying to ram us off the road.'

'What on earth? Stop the car, Marty. I think you've hit the vehicle behind.' Ethel tried to turn around, but there was no room to manoeuvre her body.

'Sit tight, Mum. Marty knows what he's doing.'

'Yeah? He couldn't drive a nail into a piece of wood.' Ethel began hitting the headrest of Marty's seat. 'Stop the car. I want to go home.'

'Please, Ethel. It's not safe.'

'You can say that again.'

'They're not stopping. I've rammed the Sorento. They're onto me. What am I supposed to do? I'm trying, for Christ's sake. I'm doing my best here. You can't come for me. Please don't come for me. I'm taking part – I'm doing it. Please don't kill my son.'

They approached a sharp bend. Marty jabbed the brakes and ripped the steering wheel left, hearing the tyres screech. Glimpsing into the wing mirror, he saw the pickup truck inches away. In the distance, red lights blinked—a railway crossing. The gates were still vertical.

'Marty, you have to stop,' Beth ordered.

'Don't stop. Please, don't stop, Dad.'

Fifty yards ahead, the gates began to drop. The small truck hit them from behind again.

As his body thrust forward, Marty slammed his foot on the accelerator, grasping the steering wheel, aware their lives depended on it.

'No! Marty, what are you doing?' Beth screamed.

Ten yards from the gates, Marty could see the train in the distance, approaching the crossing from the left, the small truck inches away, and the gates a few feet apart. They clipped the vehicle as Marty sped through the gap, making it with seconds to spare.

The loud horn of the train bellowed around them as Marty pulled away, leaving the pickup truck on the other side.

38

FRIDAY MORNING

The alarm beeped from Gary Miller's mobile phone on the bedside cabinet, and he jolted in the bed. He'd been dreaming of the moment he'd killed Cass Carter, the knife plunging into her neck. Opening his eyes, he tried to focus on the ceiling, blinking hard in the hope to stop the spinning room caused by his hangover. For a moment, he'd forgotten where he was. Turning his long, lean frame to the right, he saw two women lying under the sheets. The taste of red wine was harsh on his lips, his throat was dry, and his head ached.

Now he remembered. Last night had been incredible, when he'd finally reaped the rewards of participating in the hunt. Twice he'd taken part, and twice he'd won a hundred thousand pounds.

Excitement rushed through his body, his skin tingled, and he felt so alive.

He recalled the lap-dancing bar, the bottles of expensive champagne and red wine, the private dances, flashing the cash and eventually paying a large sum of money to bring the two hottest women home to his one-bedroom apartment for a cocaine-induced orgy.

Gary's mind reflected on last Sunday's events. How he'd waited patiently in the van and watched the other guy race out of the restaurant and along the street. Going in the back door, hiding in the toilet and waiting for the guests to spill out onto the street. How, when he grabbed the knife from the kitchen and crept towards Cass Carter, there were only pound signs in his eyes as he plunged the knife into her neck.

Suddenly, it dawned on him. It was Friday morning. There'd be a new target, more money on offer. Gary reached for his mobile, the bright screen testing his fatigued mind, his hands shaking as he sniffed the remnants of cocaine from his nose into his throat.

Seeing the links which had been posted, Gary slammed his fist on the bedside drawer, greed causing frustration. He'd set his alarm, intending to wake early, decode the clues and get a head start. The snooze button was activated two hours ago, and it was almost 11 a.m.

Looking at the clues and trying to focus, his eyes blinked hard and his fingers pressed the ache in the side of his head. Gary ripped the sheet away from his body, and, after ordering the women out, he got dressed and left his apartment in Dulwich, East London, ready to find Abbey Benson.

39

FRIDAY MORNING

'Can you see the pickup truck?' Marty had his foot pressed to the floor and was struggling to steer the Kia Sorento along the narrow country road.

Beth twisted in the passenger seat, looking out of the back window, her breaths sharp and harsh. 'No. I think we've lost him.' Turning back around, she frowned at her husband. 'That was too much of a risk, Marty – we could have all been killed.'

'What choice did I have?'

Beth hesitated for a moment, holding onto the grab handle above, her body thrown around as Marty took the sharp bends, then relented. 'I'm sorry. I didn't mean to have a go.'

Marty placed his hand on hers. 'It's OK.'

'No, Marty, it's not. You're amazing. I don't know how you're keeping it together.' She sniffed hard, tears falling down her face. 'It's too much. I can't deal with this.'

Removing his hand and placing it back on the steering wheel, he said, 'But you are. Look how strong you are. All of us, in this together, fighting to keep Abbey alive. You're all incredible.'

'Amen, brother,' Davey announced. 'Beth, you're an amazing woman. Marty, my man, never seen bravery like it.'

Beth brought her feet onto the seat; a shiver ran through her body as she thought about the train, certain it was going to hit them, all of them dying on the side of the railway tracks. 'Do you know where we are?'

'No.' Marty laughed, trying to lift the sombre mood.

Beth grabbed her phone, opened Waze and typed in their destination. After a few seconds, it loaded. 'According to the satnav, we're on Church Farm – the road goes on for around ten miles, look.'

Glimpsing the screen, Marty saw instructions written above the map to turn off in 10.3 miles. 'OK, please be on alert. Let me know if you see anything suspicious, anyone acting out of the ordinary or weird behaviour.'

'Look no further,' Ethel said.

Ignoring her sarcastic remark, Marty said, 'Remember, anyone could be a threat. Abbey. How are you holding up?'

'I'm OK.' His daughter turned her head to the side, watching behind.

Marty glared at the barren fields, the grass a bright yellow from the recent heatwave. Bushes clipped the wing mirror, the strong smell of manure in the air, and the sound of stones crunching under the tyres was intense.

The beeps rang in sync. Beth grabbed Marty's phone from the dashboard, tapping in the PIN number to unlock it. 'Oh, shit.'

'What?' Marty enquired.

'Another clue.' Beth began reading. '"A long country road. A building for worship, marriage and death. Old

McDonald had one.'" Looking at Marty, she stated, 'He knows we're on Church Farm.'

* * *

'Check your phones, make sure the Wi-Fi and location settings are off – this is madness. He knows exactly where we are?' Marty pulled into a ditch, dropping his head into the palms of his hands.

'Mine's off, Dad.'

'Mine is too, and yours,' Beth confirmed, checking Marty's phone.

Ethel didn't own a mobile phone.

Opening the driver's door, Marty stepped out, assuming they'd lost the pickup truck, as there hadn't been a notification. Leaning his body over the car, he placed his finger and thumb into the corner of his eyes to work at the stress. He turned, looking along the deserted road behind. '"There has to be a tracking device. As far as I'm aware, no one can watch your phone if everything is off. I don't even know what it would look like. Beth, keep watching behind. Shout if you see anything.' Lying on his back, Marty crawled under the car, patting around the tyres and pulling himself under the frame. The underside was mainly plastic panelling, with a fuel tank, thick springs, the rear lower arms and a spare wheel towards the back. Pulling the wheel arch liners and removing a plastic covering, Marty found it. 'I have it.' He pulled it away, replacing the arch liner and manoeuvred out from under the car, hurling the tracking device into the field.

As Marty got into the driver's seat and pulled away, the phones beeped again.

'Someone's streaming,' Beth announced.

'Oh shit. This is relentless. What can you see?' Marty asked as he pulled away.

Placing the phone on the dashboard, they watched the screen, a camera focusing on bushes across a narrow road.

'Hello? I... I don't know what to say. It's new to me, all of this. If I'm honest, I'm petrified. I clicked the link sent to me on Facebook Messenger. A friend, raving about how you could win a hundred thousand pounds. I signed up, waited, and when nothing happened, I left the phone to the side and carried on with my day.'

Marty couldn't help thinking it was a similar story to what had happened to him. He felt an instant connection. The guy sounded so frightened; his voice was quivering through fear, and the camera shook as he adjusted its position.

'Later that evening, I was sent a photograph of my dear, beautiful mother cooking in the kitchen. The bastard who took it had got inside. She was unaware someone was behind her. My hands were tied, drawn into a wicked void with only one way out. To murder an innocent person. Christ, you people are evil beyond anyone's imagination. I hope you die a slow, painful death. When you meet your creator, I hope you're cast to the depths of hell.

'I haven't slept since clicking the link, seeing the hateful acts committed within this app, and what you're making people do, turning on each other like an evil horror movie. But it's real. And it's happening to me.

'I'll kill Abbey Benson. I'm hiding out now, about to do it. There's a vehicle coming along the road. I'll film it for you depraved bastards and follow your orders. I'll be back on in a few minutes. God have mercy on my soul.'

His sobs echoed through the speakers as the stream finished.

As Marty drove, the chilling wails stunned everyone into silence. Marty, Beth, Abbey, Davey and Ethel glared through the windscreen ahead, watching the narrow country road twisting in front of them.

Breaking the silence, Marty whispered, 'Is it wrong to feel for him? A man who's trying to murder my daughter? It could be you, Davey, or myself, waiting, forced into something we want no part of, and only one motive, to save his mum.'

'I understand, but we can't let our guards down through emotion, mate. It's one thing feeling for this guy, but remember what he's trying to do?'

Beth took a deep breath, trying to push away the reality of what Davey had just said, and looked at the satnav on her phone. 'There's a turning around a hundred yards ahead. We need to slow down.'

'How many do you think there are? Dozens? Hundreds?' Marty asked. 'Is this our life now, running, hiding from the world?' Seeing the turning, he pulled the car up beside a ditch. 'Wait here?'

'What are you doing?' Beth asked.

'He said there's a vehicle coming along the road. He has to be close. If someone is waiting, I need to surprise them? They won't expect it.'

'Please, this is ludicrous. It's not safe,' Beth stated.

'What's the other alternative? Have him pull out of the turning, come after us and ram the car off the road? I need to see if anyone is there.'

Beth rubbed the sides of her face with her fingers and inhaled deeply, listening as the driver's door opened and Marty got out.

'Dude, hang tight. I'm with you.' Davey got out of the car and stood on the side of the road with his friend.

Leaning into the car, Marty looked at Abbey, Ethel and finally Beth. His mobile was on the dashboard; Beth's was on her lap. 'Honk the horn if you hear a notification. Jump into the driver's seat and lock the doors. Pull away if you see anything,' Marty ordered.

Beth stepped out of the car to swap seats, the strain evident on her face, Marty stepped towards her, holding her tight. He could hear her weep as she gripped his clothes in her fists.

'Just stop the bastard from killing our daughter.'

'I'll do my best.'

Beth climbed into the driver's seat, locked the doors and watched the two men stroll along the quiet country road.

* * *

'How are ya holding up?' Davey asked, walking side by side with Marty.

'I'm numb, mate. I can't show my fear, but I don't know what to do. It's like we're in hell and living a nightmare you couldn't make up.'

'I'm with you, mate.'

Marty turned, facing his friend. 'Thank you.'

'For what?'

'You know. This, what you're doing. Helping us.'

'You're my best mate, man. I adore your family. Why wouldn't I help? Abbey is like a daughter to me, and Beth is one in a million. There's no question.'

'And Ethel?' Marty laughed.

'Ethel is... in her own world. Always has been, but I like her. She's harmless.'

They continued walking. Marty stared down the road through the heat haze. The sun beat down through a clear sky as a plane roared overhead, and miles of fields stretched on either side, with sheep high on a hill in the distance. His legs felt so frail, like matchsticks supporting a large building, fearing he'd collapse at any moment and jeopardise his family. Glancing behind, the Kia Sorento was around twenty yards back along the road; Beth was sitting in the driver's seat, her body pushed forward and her face tense with anticipation.

Ten yards from the turning to their right, Marty stopped and looked through the bushes, able to see the road.

'What's the plan?' Davey whispered, standing beside him.

'He could be waiting, either in his car or standing out on the road. He doesn't know we have access to The App, so he won't expect us to be here. He's listening for our vehicle.'

'So let's take the son of a bitch out.'

'That's the idea.'

A large crow took off from the bushes, squawking loudly and causing them to jump. Marty went first, reaching the corner of the road. Electrical cables looped across the sky between large pylons in the next field, a telegraph pole planted in the grass verge leant to one side and hay bales lay in the field opposite, constructed into almost perfect circles.

Marty leant his body forward and around the bush, pulling it back with his fingers to see along the road. A warm breeze pushed against his face and caused dirt to rise off the tarmac and hit him in the face. Wiping his eyes, he said, 'There's a vehicle, parked along the road, but I can't see a driver.'

Davey joined him, staring along the road. 'Where is he?'

'I don't know.'

'Do you think he got out?' Davey's heart throbbed under his T-shirt, his hands shook, and an ache developed in his stomach, like a fist twisting inside, working through his body.

With his voice low, Marty whispered, 'I'm going to walk to the car. Keep watch and shout if you see anything?'

'I think we should go together.'

'Please, Davey. If he's in the car, I'll tackle him. You run to the Sorento and help keep Abbey safe.'

The men hugged. Then, Marty braced himself and walked along the road towards the parked car.

The stones crunched under his shoes. His body felt drained, as if every ounce of energy had dissolved, and only a broken frame was left. Images swirled in his mind: his parents held captive and gagged, a knife to his mother's throat. How would he get out of this? How would it all end, and would he ever see his mother and father again?

Twenty yards from the vehicle, Marty glimpsed the Vauxhall badge and the empty interior. Could he be lying on the seats, hiding in the back?

Lowering to the ground, he glimpsed back at Davey before reaching the driver's door and placing his hand on the lock. Counting to three, Marty pulled it. The door resisted. Locked. He moved to the back doors, which were, again, locked. Standing, Marty cupped his hands and pressed his face to the glass.

The car was empty.

Marty turned and waved to Davey standing on the corner of the road. 'There's no one inside.'

'Coolio,' Davey shouted. 'Well, let's get out of here.'

As Marty stepped backwards, eyes on the blue Vauxhall Nova, he heard a twig snap inside the field.

He stopped, his body static, hesitant to breathe or take another step. A man jumped out from the bushes and charged towards him. His arm was outstretched, pointing a handgun at Marty. He looked mid-forties, around five foot seven, and his hair was long and unkempt.

'Where is she?'

Stepping back along the road, Marty held his hands up. 'I don't know who you mean.' He watched the man's hand shaking violently, his eyes squinting as if the strain was too much.

'You know who I'm talking about. The girl. Where is she?'

Marty stopped. The man stepped closer, still pointing the gun to his face.

'Put the gun down and we'll talk.'

'I have to get to the girl – you don't understand.'

Marty desperately tried to make eye contact in the hope he could get the guy to listen. 'I do understand. That's where you're wrong.' He could hear footsteps sounding behind him. 'Davey, get out of here. You need to leave. Don't come down here. Run.'

'Who's that?' The guy stepped to the side, pointing the gun at Davey. 'Don't take another step.'

Davey stopped.

Pointing the gun back at Marty, the guy continued to speak. 'No one understands the predicament I'm in. But I have to kill her – they're forcing me. I have no choice. They'll murder my mother. You have to tell me where she is.'

Marty stepped forward, closing the gap, now around ten yards from where the man stood. 'You'll never take my daughter. You'll have to kill me first.'

'Then you leave me no choice.' He raised his arm higher, pointing the gun at Marty's face and bursting into tears. Screaming like a baby, he turned it on himself and pulled the trigger.

40

FRIDAY MORNING

Marty's mother, Gracie Benson, struggled to move; the rope around her legs and wrists was so tight it cut into her skin. Her tongue wrestled with the cloth around her mouth, and her husband, Peter, lay whimpering next to her. She tried to speak, but only muffled sounds came from her mouth. If only she could comfort her husband, hold his frail, ailing body and rock with him on the bed, tell him everything would be OK and that they'd get through this together.

Her eyes glanced along the walls of their three-bedroom semi-detached house in Shepherd's Bush. The large crucifix opposite and the corner table filled with religious artefacts; a statue of Mary, rosary beads, a painting of Jesus, and a photo of the current pope and Mother Teresa set in black frames. Praying silently, Gracie whispered the words of the Lord's Prayer, over and over, pleading to God to help them out of this awful situation.

Earlier, she'd washed her husband, made breakfast in the kitchen and set out four pieces of buttered toast on a tray. After bringing the food to the bedroom, she'd returned to the kitchen, placed two teabags in a pot and filled it with hot water just boiled in the kettle. As she dabbed the teabags, watching the water turn a dark brown, a shadow appeared at the kitchen door.

Confused, Gracie let go of the spoon and strode along the hallway into the living room. The TV standby button illuminated a bright red colour, and an ornament perched on a shelf clicked loudly as the cat's paw waved side to side. The sounds of her husband coughing from the upstairs bedroom were apparent, and the smell of the recently purchased three-seater sofa was pleasant.

Gracie stood by the window for a moment; a gap in the heavy curtains allowed her to see onto the street. She edged a corner of the material back, but it seemed the person had gone.

Back in the kitchen, she placed the pot of tea and two mugs onto a tray, slowly walked along the hallway and climbed the stairs, before hearing a key twisting in the front door.

Now, lying awkwardly in the bed, her hands tied on her lap, she listened for the intruder who'd burst into their home. Gracie peered at her husband, his eyes closed, his skin a deathly yellow colour, face gaunt and cheeks so hollow it was as if he were sucking them in. Tears rolled down her cheeks, unable to relieve his discomfort, and she began kicking her legs, furiously trying to free herself and get help. Panic ripped through her body; the ropes burned her skin as she struggled to free her hands, desperately trying to pull them apart.

The moans spilling from her mouth filled the bedroom. A rush of blood seemed to burst inside her body, racing through her veins, and Gracie cried uncontrollably on the bed.

41

FRIDAY MORNING

'Marty! Oh my God, Marty. Please. No, Marty.' Beth threw open the driver's door of the car, her heart beating so hard it vibrated through her ears. The gunshot moments ago caused visions to play in her mind: Marty, lying dead on the road, the man hiding, waiting for them, holding the gun to Davey's face.

As Beth reached the corner of the road, her body tense in anticipation of another gunshot crack to tear into the air, she saw her husband leaning over a ditch and vomiting. Her body flooded with relief until she saw the body lying on the ground further along the road.

On his knees, Marty turned his head to the side and called out, 'Don't come down here, Beth.'

She stopped. Davey was standing over the body too, his face one of utter shock.

The sounds of footsteps rushing along the road caused Beth to turn.

'Is Dad OK?' Abbey was breathing hard as she approached.

Grabbing her daughter to stop her from seeing the body, Beth said, 'He's fine. Davey is too. But don't go down there. Please, Abbey.'

'I thought... When I heard the gunshot...' Her words faded.

'It's OK. I know. I know, Abbey. But your dad and Davey are fine.'

Trying to catch her breath after sprinting from the car, Abbey broke down, the palms of her hands resting on her thighs as wailing noises spilled from her mouth. She wanted to run, to escape into the fields, race across the long grass and bask in the sense of freedom. But she couldn't see a way out of this hellhole they were in.

Her mother reached her arms out, cradling Abbey's trembling body as she pulled her close, letting her cry into her chest.

Beth looked up as the two men walked over to them. Abbey's face still pressed into her chest. 'What happened?'

Marty explained how he and Davey had rounded the corner and saw the parked car. How the man waiting to kill their daughter pointed a gun at Marty's face, then shot himself. As he placed his arms around Beth and Abbey, Davey joined them. The four of them trying desperately to gain strength from each other.

Beth looked at Marty. 'How are you feeling?'

'Numb, I thought it was over. I can't explain how I felt as he pointed the gun at me; I saw my life flash. But I felt for him, his pain, his grief; I could see it in his eyes. He was so frightened. I don't think he intended to kill himself, you know.'

'I know, Marty.'

'We can't just leave him here,' Marty pointed out.

'Mate, it was him or Abbey,' Davey insisted. 'We have to keep moving.'

* * *

Back in the car, Ethel was dipping into the bag of mint humbugs. She watched Beth, Marty, Abbey and Davey walking towards the car with their heads down. As they opened the doors, she said, 'What was all that racket? It sounded like a bloody gunshot. I don't know what you're all doing, but I'm missing my shows.'

'When we get to the lodge, you can watch all the shows you like,' Marty announced as he started the car.

As Marty drove, his mind relived the moment when the hunter pointed the gun in his face. He was sure he was going to die, slumped on the side of a country road in the middle of nowhere. His throat ached as he tried to gulp the swelling at the back of his mouth and his eyes shifted between the road and the fields on either side. Adjusting the rear-view mirror, he looked at Abbey and glimpsed the winding road behind, his mind so addled he thought his head would explode.

'Oh my goodness,' Beth shouted.

'What?' Marty asked, hearing her shocked tone. His phone was erupting with streams, so many people out there with one thing in mind: to murder his beautiful daughter. Marty gripped the steering wheel, the veins protruding in the backs of his hands, his fingers aching as he thought about the knife held to his mother's throat and what his parents were going through. Sweat emerged on his forehead, seeping down the sides of his face; his body felt weak with pain as if it would fold in on itself. Marty willed himself to keep going, to somehow find the strength to deal with it all.

Voices rang out from his mobile as Beth watched the streams.

'What can you see?' Marty asked.

'Well, I don't think anyone is on this road. That's a good sign. There's a woman who is streaming at the moment and hasn't left the house. I can hear her voice. Another woman is getting inside her car, saying how she has been forced into this. Someone has their mobile resting on the dashboard, and the picture keeps cutting out. I can see a busy motorway. Hold up, let me see the others.' Beth clicked the latest link, watching the stream. 'Another guy is talking; it's hard to hear what he's saying through the noise of the traffic and the screen is blank. So far, I think we're safe.'

Davey leant his body between Marty and Beth. 'It was a good call, man, checking under the car. The fucker will never find us. We're in the clear.'

'You think?' Marty asked. 'Abbey, is there any way they can watch us through our phones?'

'I don't think so. I'm looking on Google now. It's a grey area. Some say with Wi-Fi and location services off, you should be invisible. Other people have commented and aren't so sure. I think we're OK, but I can't guarantee it, Dad. I think it depends how technical The App is.' Abbey's mind was confused, so busy with the events unfolding and she struggled to concentrate, unable to process the information.

'Yeah, I haven't seen any clues posted since you found the tracking device,' Davey pointed out. 'He's probably pounding the floor as we speak. Shit, I'd love to see that.'

'We're nearly there.' Beth announced, eyeing the satnav. 'Another couple of miles.' She turned her body around to face Abbey, who was looking at her phone screen.

'Michael's just messaged. His brother is going to help us.'

Her face lit up as if all the tension was pouring from her body. She typed a message back.

Fantastic news. How does it work?

A few seconds later, Michael responded.

Michael: He'll call you from a burner phone. Should be a bit later. How is everything? So sorry you're going through this.

Abbey: Thanks. We're holding up.

Michael: Shaun will speak to you in a bit.

Abbey: Thanks

Abbey finished the message with three kisses.

As they drove, the phones continuously beeped, like an annoying toy, grating in their ears, as more people joined the hunt. Marty tried to imagine what was going on in their minds, some of them leaving their families, telling them nothing of what they were trying to achieve, fearful of the outcome and knowing the consequences if they failed.

* * *

Reaching the end of the narrow country road, Marty saw a sign for Hatfield. He stopped the Sorento, wondering if the lodge was the correct move. They couldn't keep driving and needed somewhere to hide, but were they safe? His mind was addled, and as Marty turned right onto the main road, he didn't see a blue Jeep that had to swerve around him.

'Sorry,' Marty shouted, holding his hand up.

Beth clutched the grab handle with her fingers as she watched the Jeep slow ahead of them. 'Why's he stopping?'

'Bloody idiot. I hate inconsiderate drivers,' said Ethel, dragging Beth's thoughts away.

'You tell them, Mum.'

'I was talking about Marty. My Ted never went over the speed limit.'

'Didn't he drive a milk float?' Marty asked.

Davey and Abbey laughed, a much-needed respite from the constant tension, and Beth struggled to stem the smile, holding her hand over her mouth.

'Yeah, you may laugh. Fifty years he sat behind the wheel. Never once had an accident.'

'Did he ever manage to start a car?' Marty fired back.

Ethel playfully pushed Marty's arm, tutting loudly as she sucked on a mint humbug. 'Could he drive! When Ted had control of the wheel, it was like I was floating, my body drifting in mid-air. I never feared he'd crash because he was careful. He could go all day.'

'Viagra, was it?'

More raucous laughter filled the car.

'Oh, believe me, he had no need for that—a waste of money.'

'Mum, please,' Beth said awkwardly.

The blue Jeep had now stopped in front of them. As Marty pulled around it, they saw the driver grabbing his phone.

'Shit. Go, Marty,' Beth ordered.

Panic filled the car as Marty pressed the accelerator. The Jeep pulled out after them.

'Is there a new stream?' Marty yelled.

'There's been loads. Let me check.' Beth grabbed her phone, pressing the most recent links. 'Hang on. I see a motorway. Another person is walking along a drive, getting into their vehicle.' She pressed all the recent links. None of them resembled a live feed from the driver of the blue Jeep.

It was gaining on them, getting closer. Marty had to do something; the lodge was only minutes away. He couldn't risk the driver following them and blowing their cover. In a moment of madness, Marty pulled the car over, seeing the Jeep pull in behind him. Opening the driver's door, he raced towards him, banging on the window. The driver looked shaken, the phone quivering in his hand. As he opened the window, Marty grabbed his T-shirt.

'What the fuck are you doing?' Marty yelled.

Stunned, the driver clearly hadn't expected such aggression. 'I'm sorry. It was a stupid thing to do. You came out in front of me, and I wanted to film you and let others know of the dangers on the road. I'll delete the footage. I'm sorry.'

'Is this what you do? Go around filming people, aggravating them? I didn't mean to pull out in front of you, but you're scaring my family.'

'I got it. It was stupid.'

Standing on the side of the road, staring at the middle-aged man behind the wheel, passing vehicles blaring in his ears, Marty saw the embarrassed look, verging almost shame. 'Pull out ahead of us. We'll leave once you're gone.'

'Will do. Again, I didn't mean to scare you or your family.'

The window closed, and the driver drove away, disappearing along the main road.

* * *

'Here. This is it.' Beth pointed. 'Turn in, here.'

Marty jabbed the brakes, gently pulling the Sorento onto the drive. He rolled the car forward, taking in the scenic landscape around them. Stones crunched under the tyres, and a plume of dust rose around the vehicle.

'Wow, it's amazing,' Marty confirmed, suddenly guilty for finding beauty in their situation. He peered along the narrow track that wound deep into the valley. The smell of newly cut grass was thick in the air as fields stretched for miles in front of them, with cows, sheep and chicken coops. Waist-high fences extended around the outside of the fields, and as Marty steered the Sorento along the steep path, a strong smell of paint was noticeable. To their right side, bushes were trimmed and shaped into an array of sculptures: a small garden chair, a wheelbarrow, a couple holding hands and a park bench. Just behind, a tall, strong-looking fence gave adequate privacy and security.

As they turned the bend at the bottom of the path, they saw the accommodation, isolated and breathtaking. A sign dug into the ground declared the name. *Apple Lodge*.

It was a large, two story building, elegant looking, with plant pots sitting on the deep window sills to add extra brightness and colour. The gate looked newly painted and opened to a stony path leading to the front door. Brightly coloured plants and flowers adorned the front garden – roses, tulips and daffodils, all cut and manicured, and the soil was wet, indicating they were recently watered.

Marty parked the Sorento to the side of the lodge and got out.

Beth, Abbey, Davey and Ethel joined him.

'Oh, this is nice,' Ethel stated. 'Where's the TV?'

'Mum, let's get settled first.'

Abbey stood, glancing over the lodge. It felt like she'd aged twenty years in the last week. Her legs were trembling, and the pain behind her eyes that had developed earlier was now like an explosion working around her face. Placing her hands on the side of the building and running her fingers along the wood, she turned to her father. 'Is this going to be enough to keep me alive?'

'See this. See this man here.' He pointed to himself.

Abbey struggled to nod her head.

'This man will fight to the bitter end and with his last breath to keep you alive. That's a promise.' Marty saw the tears suddenly develop in his daughter's eyes, and he reached forward, pulling her close. Whispering in her ear, he said, 'Abbey. Listen to me. Nothing is going to happen to you. We're going to keep you safe. Please understand that.'

'As will this man,' Davey insisted.

Abbey laughed through her tears.

By the front door, Beth rolled the digits on the lockbox pinned to the left side of the front door into the sequence she'd been sent via email. She lifted the button, and the flap dropped, revealing a large, single key. Placing it in the door, Beth twisted the key, hearing a loud clunking sound, and stepped inside, standing on the wooden floorboards.

The smell of damp wood was overbearing. The interior was dark and murky-looking, which Beth hadn't expected – a significant contrast to the outside appearance. Gazing towards the living room on her right, she flicked on the light switch, noticing the open fire, a carbon monoxide alarm on the wall, a pile of wood, neatly stacked and firelighters in a box sitting on the mantlepiece. The walls were painted a stark white, with rooms on either side of the hallway.

Marty joined her, followed by Abbey, Davey and Ethel.

'This is nice,' Marty stated. He walked along the hallway and into the kitchen; the smell of coffee was welcoming. 'Yes. There's a security monitor.' Turning to Beth, he declared, 'This will mean we can see anyone approaching.'

He watched her face drop.

'Do you think they'll find us?'

'We have to keep focused. Remember why we're here. We can't let our guard down for a second.'

'I feel sick,' Beth whispered.

'Me too, but we have to stay strong for Abbey.'

A fist thumped on the kitchen window, causing them to jump. It felt like the room shook.

'Duck!' Marty shielded his wife and daughter. As he looked towards the window, huddled over a whimpering Abbey, he saw an elderly man standing in the garden.

'Sorry if I scared you,' he shouted. 'I'm Rufus. I work here. If you need anything, I'm a mile along the road. Just holler. See you now.'

Marty watched as he trampled along the field and out of sight.

Placing his hand on the rickety-looking table, Marty sighed deeply before helping Beth and Abbey to their feet. 'Christ. He frightened the life out of me. Are you both OK?'

Beth and Abbey nodded, too stunned to answer.

* * *

Once they were settled in, Davey sat at the front window in the hallway of the lodge, peering through the net curtain and out towards the front entrance. He checked his phone, thankful there hadn't been any further clues posted since Marty had found the tracking device under the car. The TV was loud in the living room, and he could hear Ethel calling out for tea.

Marty, Beth and Abbey sat in the kitchen. The security monitor perched on the sideboard displayed the front path and out towards the fields.

Suddenly, Abbey's phone pinged.

Marty kicked the chair back and stood, his body tense as blood rushed through his veins, ready to run or fight, whichever the situation demanded.

'Calm down, Dad. It's Michael.'

Marty sat back down, the adrenaline fading.

'Sean's going to call in a minute.'

'Excellent,' Beth said. Looking at Marty, she grabbed his hands and kissed them. 'Please, God, he can help us.'

Abbey's phone rang. The kitchen fell deathly silent as the mobile buzzed on the table. Looking at her parents, she steadied herself, hoping with every fibre of her body that Michael's older brother could help. It felt like all their hopes rested on the following conversation.

'Hello?'

'Beth, It's Sean. Are you OK to talk?'

'Yes. Absolutely.'

'Great. Hang up and call me from a phone box. I'll be waiting. Don't say another word.'

The phone call disconnected.

'Well, that was helpful,' Beth stated. 'I feel so much better now. We're free.' She slumped her elbows on the table and slammed her face into her hands.

'He's taking precautions. It's a good sign. He knows what he's doing,' Marty confirmed. Looking at Davey sitting by the front door, he called out, 'Anything?'

'Huh. No, nothing to report, dude. All's quiet. Here's hoping it stays like this.'

Turning to Beth and Abbey, Marty stated, 'We need to find a phone box. Let's go.' As they passed the living room, Ethel was sitting forward on the sofa, her hands clasped together, delighting in a DIY programme. 'Ethel, will you come with us?' Marty asked.

'Sod off, I've only just got here. Wild horses won't drag me away. Leave me be.'

'She's OK, man,' Davey said from the chair by the front door. 'If I see anything, we'll hide. It's not us they're after.'

Watching his friends getting into the Sorento, he hoped it wasn't the last time he'd see them.

* * *

'How are we going to find a phone box? I don't even think I've ever seen one in real life.' Abbey leant her body between her mother and father from the back seat, gazing through the windscreen.

'They do exist,' Marty stated. 'But as everyone's got a mobile now, they're scarce. A lot of them have been turned into libraries.'

'There has to be one somewhere. Christ, years ago, they were dotted on every street corner. Take a left,' Beth ordered. 'There's a sign for a local town.'

Marty gripped the steering wheel and pulled a hard left, almost missing the turning. He drove for a couple of miles and into Hatfield town centre. There were market stalls along the pavement, and the streets were bustling with people. In the distance, they saw a phone box on a street corner.

Marty prayed it was working.

The red door was heavy and awkward to pull; the smell of urine inside was almost unbearable, and Marty instantly felt claustrophobic. Reaching into his pocket, he pulled out a handful of pound coins; Beth added more from her purse.

'Put the money in, dial the number and then speak,' Marty confirmed.

'Thanks, Dad. I'd never have worked that out.'

Beth shook her head, smiling at Marty's naivety.

Abbey looked at her phone, placed a pound coin into the slot and carefully dialled the number Sean had called from.

He answered on the third ring.

'Hi, it's Abbey.'

'Hey, how are you doing?'

Looking at the nervousness on her parents' faces, she answered, 'Oh, I've been better.'

'Sorry you had to find a phone box – I'm on a burner phone, and it's not safe for you to talk in case they've bugged your hiding place.'

'I understand, but we've only been there a short while,' Abbey confirmed.

'You'd be amazed at what people can do. Michael explained everything briefly, so I kind of have a picture. What's happening?'

Abbey looked out of the phone box, seeing people standing at market stalls, children playing, a couple sitting on a bench outside a pub, enjoying a drink. She fought with her emotions; her body tingled with angst, and the ache in her head was getting worse. Taking a deep breath, she began talking, telling Sean everything that had happened, from the moment her father received The App, to the picture of her mother and nan shopping in Oxford Street, to the attempted rescue of Cass Carter and ending up on the run and hiding in the lodge. Lastly, she told him about her grandparents being held hostage. When she'd finished, Abbey only heard silence, imagining Sean hanging up the phone and wanting nothing to do with it.

'Shit. Wow, err... that's deep. Oh my God.'

'Yep, you could say that.'

'OK, ask your father to forward the link to this burner phone. I'll see what I can do. There should be a way to get into The App, but I can't make promises. I'll do my best. If this lunatic is still with your grandparents, we need to trick him. There is a way, but it's risky.'

'Go on,' Abbey asked.

'Well, it might work. I need you to drive for as long as possible. Film the road and don't say anything. Nothing at all. Don't make a sound. Make the recording as boring and monotonous as possible. It sounds like this guy knows what he's doing. The App will have taken over your father's phone, so he needs to get rid of it.'

'You mean he knows where we are?'

'Yes, absolutely.'

'But we've turned everything off.'

'Regardless. The App is probably fitted with malware. A file which infects and allows the creator of the App to watch his every move. Even if Wi-Fi and location services are shut down. If your father has his phone, he'll know your exact position. He needs to dump it instantly. Film the road with another phone, keep deathly silent and send the recording to me. If I can hack into The App, your father can go back and get his phone. Retrieving it will probably help with what I have in mind. For now, he must hide it.'

Abbey hung up, Sean's words echoing in her mind. Turning to face her parents, she said, 'They know where we are. You need to hide your phone, Dad.'

'Hide it? Why?'

'The App has probably taken over your phone. Even though everything is turned off, Sean said that they'll know where we are.'

'Oh, shit. How? This just gets worse.'

'That's how viruses work, Dad. I know nothing about them, but Sean is adamant The App's creator will be able to locate us.'

Marty thought about last Sunday, how he'd downloaded The App, never thinking in his wildest dreams all the complications it would bring, and how it was almost breaking his family. He turned, dropping his phone in a public bin outside a police station. *It couldn't be in a safer place,* he thought.

Then he remembered Davey and Ethel were alone in the lodge.

His friend still had his phone, watching for notifications.

42

FRIDAY AFTERNOON

Parking the Sorento at the side of the lodge, Marty forced the driver's door open and thumped on the front door. With his face pushed to the glass, he banged again.

A figure appeared in the hallway.

'Ethel, it's us. Open up,' Marty insisted. He watched as she strolled along the hallway and opened the door.

'You won't believe what's happened,' she said, her hand over her mouth.

'What? What's happened?' Marty's heart was in his mouth. 'Where's Davey?'

Stepping back, Ethel answered, 'He's taking a dump. Been in there a while. I can only imagine the stink. Guess what happened. A couple were on that DIY show, doing up their new house. They've only gone over budget. Poor sods, it's so difficult nowadays with the house extensions and fancy brand names. Serves 'em bloody right. Greedy gits.'

Marty darted up the stairs, along the hallway and banged on the bathroom door. He heard the toilet flush and Davey declaring he'd be out in a second.

As the door unlocked, his friend saw the worry on Marty's face.

'What's happened?' Davey asked.

'You need to get rid of your phone. The App has probably got a virus that can track our whereabouts. Michael's brother reckons the people behind The App can trace us, even with our location turned off.'

'Fuck. I wish I understood technology. That's deep, mate. So what, are you saying he knows where we are?'

'I think so. We can't take the risk.The fuckers can watch us even with our phones off. I've been ordered to film the road. Not sure why yet, but I'll do it from Beth's phone. Michael's brother has a plan. We all need to be together. It's not safe.'

'And tonight? Are we staying here?'

Marty looked at Davey's phone. So far, nothing else had been posted in regards to their whereabouts. Maybe Sean was right, but the lodge was the only place they could hide. 'We have to take the chance. While we're out, dump your phone in a field, there should be no way of tracing us. Then we can come back here and watch for any intruders.'

* * *

Marty tried to balance Beth's phone on the dashboard as she sat in the passenger seat. Abbey, Ethel and Davey got into the back.

'OK, the volume is down, I think. I'm going to pull up to the top of the road and drive. We're doing what Sean has asked, filming the road. It was Ethel who gave me the idea and caused the lightbulb moment as she tried to get into her mint humbugs. Hacking The App. I have an idea what he's thinking.'

'What?' Beth asked.

'I need a way to get to my parents' house without this lunatic knowing we're coming.'

'Right. How are you going to do that?'

Marty turned, watching Abbey struggle with the seatbelt and said, 'Your friend's brother is a genius. I think he plans on us recording, so he can put it on a loop and load it onto The App. That way, he'll never know we're coming.'

Beth sat, open-mouthed, stunned at the idea. 'Wow, you think he can pull it off?'

Abbey answered, the excitement evident in her voice. 'Michael reckons that Sean is insanely good, like one of the top hackers in the country. Reckons he can get in anywhere. People pay him to avenge companies who've sacked them or done them wrong. He has loads of stories.'

'Remind me never to get on the wrong side of him,' Marty said. 'So you all know the plan. I'll drive as slow as possible, filming the road. It goes without saying, keep a lookout for anyone acting suspiciously. Don't make a sound.' Marty braced himself, and they pulled away from the lodge.

'Three, two, one, go.' Marty signed for Beth to hit the record button.

They sat, their bodies tense, exhausted, watching Beth's mobile filming the road ahead.

'Would anyone like a mint humbug?'

'Oh, for Christ's sake, Ethel,' Marty shouted.

'Mum, please keep quiet. We can't make any noise.'

'Go again,' Marty insisted.

'Three, two, one, go.' Again, Beth pressed the record button.

'I am sorry.' The rasp of the sweet packet rang out in the car as Ethel placed them in the footwell. 'There, I've finished them. No more noise.'

'Right, let's go again.' Beth confirmed.

Abbey grabbed her nan's hand, feeling her cold, dry skin. 'Just keep quiet for a few minutes. That's all we need. Then you can make as much noise as you like.'

They watched the screen recording the road, all of them aware of their shallow breaths, trying desperately not to make a sound.

* * *

Marty stared out through the windscreen, gently tapping the brake as he rounded corners, touching the accelerator and careful not to make Beth's phone fall onto the dashboard. The atmosphere in the car was tense, the strain on everyone's mind almost seeping into the vehicle. Fields on either side of the road gave a sense of tranquillity, calm and soothing, but inside, there was only hysteria, like being trapped in a box underwater.

Glimpsing at the dashboard, aware they'd been driving six minutes, Marty could sense the pressure and imagined a balloon, constantly filling with air and about to burst. Twisting the rear-view mirror, he glanced at Abbey, seeing the softness in her eyes, her beautiful face; a sudden hope had replaced anguish. She smiled, blinking, a subtle way they told each other everything was OK. Beside her, Ethel's eyes were closed as she dozed. Thank goodness for small mercies. Davey put his thumbs up, a motivational sign that it would all work out.

Ten minutes had passed; Marty thought about his parents and if they were still alive. The image of the knife held to his mother's throat continually plagued him, haunting his every thought. He wanted to scream, to pound the dashboard, open the windows and yell until his throat hurt, imagining what he'd do to the person putting them through this.

Watching the road, he wondered if they'd ever make it, if Sean's plan would work. His brother Michael was Abbey's best friend; she'd done so much for him, helping with his exams and constant anxiety. Never wanting anything in return.

Well, Marty wanted something now. The biggest favour of his life.

He hoped Sean hadn't forgotten about them.

* * *

Twenty minutes had passed on the dashboard clock. Marty eyed Beth, first pointing to the time and then drawing a horizontal line in the air in front of his throat, a signal to end the recording.

Pushing her arm forward, Beth tapped the screen with her forefinger.

'And relax,' Marty said. The heavy sighs in the Sorento were a testament to the strain everyone was feeling.

'That was bloody difficult, mate,' Davey announced. 'I've never had to keep quiet for so long.' Looking at Ethel, he gently nudged her. Her eyes were still closed, and her mouth a perfect circle. 'You can speak now.'

Opening her eyes, Ethel's expression was one of perplexity. She said, 'I don't want to bloody talk now. I was enjoying the silence. Not having to listen to that pillock in the driver's seat.'

'What now?' Beth asked.

Marty parked the car beside the ditch; they'd circled the road a couple of times and weren't far from the lodge. With his hands over his face, he pulled down on his skin, easing the strain. 'I say we go back and keep hidden. The lodge is our safest bet. We just have to hope no one knows we're there.'

'Sounds like a plan.' Beth turned, looking at her daughter in the back seat. Her face looked swollen from lack of sleep, her eyes puffy, and her cheeks were a glowing red colour. 'Are you all right?'

Abbey nodded, controlling her emotions by swallowing hard and taking deep breaths.

'This is as good a place as any to dump your phone, Davey,' Marty insisted. He watched his friend getting out of the car and returning a few seconds later.

Marty turned the car around and steered the Sorento along the quiet country road, heading back to the lodge. But it suddenly dawned on him. Now, their advantage had gone.

There was no way of knowing if someone was coming.

43

FRIDAY NIGHT

It was beginning to get dark outside. Davey guarded the hallway by the front door, glaring towards the entrance of the lodge as he had before.

Marty was in the kitchen, standing by the window, looking out over the fields. Behind him, Beth and Abbey sat at the table, their demeanour tense and nervous. Abbey had loaded the footage of the silent drive on WhatsApp and sent it to Sean.

Ethel was in the living room watching TV. They'd practically begged her to join them, but she'd recited a list of programmes she'd miss if she sat in the kitchen.

'Anything?' Marty called along the hallway.

'All quiet, amigo. Nothing to report this end.'

'Do you think we're safe, Dad?' Abbey's voice was weak and hoarse.

'I think so. It's getting dark outside, but I can still see into the fields. They look empty. Have you heard anything from Sean?'

Abbey grabbed her phone from the table, shaking her head and placing it back down.

'OK, we just need to sit tight until he messages. I'm sure he's doing his best,' Beth stated. She straightened her back and stood. 'I need a coffee. Who wants one?'

The screen from the security monitor blinked, showing the outside of the lodge.

'Why has that come on?' Abbey asked anxiously.

'I don't know. Davey, you see anything?'

'Nothing.'

Reaching for the monitor, his hand shaking, Marty twisted it towards him.

'I think something is out there. It could be a fox or other wild animal,' he said. The screen showed the edge of the fields and the path leading to the lodge; the gate was closed, and the grainy image appeared calm and serene.

Lifting the monitor, Marty continued watching, looking for a sign that someone was out there.

'Dad!' Abbey screamed, pushing her chair back and standing against the wall.

'What's wrong?' Marty asked, placing the monitor back on the worktop.

'I saw a shadow pass the window. Someone was there.' Abbey placed her hand on her chest, trying to cope with the sudden rush of adrenaline, her heart racing, her body disorientated as the kitchen became a blur.

Racing across the room, Marty flicked the light switch off and pulled Beth and Abbey down to the kitchen floor.

'Did you see something?' Davey called out.

'Yeah, Abbey saw a shadow. The monitor kicked in a minute ago – I think someone is out there,' Marty said.

'What should we do?' Davey asked, his voice quieter. He crouched down by the front door and crawled to the kitchen, keeping obscure.

With a hushed voice, Marty spoke to both Beth and Abbey. 'I want you to go into the living room with Ethel and lock the door. I'm going outside. I need to know if we're being attacked. I don't have my phone, and we have no way of knowing if there's a clue to our whereabouts or if someone is streaming, attempting to get Abbey. Please, go quickly.'

They kissed Marty on the cheek and crawled along the cold, tiled floor into the living room.

The key turned a moment later as the door locked.

'I have to go out there,' Marty hissed. 'We're too vulnerable.'

'I'm with you, Bro; we're in this together.'

The two men hugged, and Marty walked to the back door, Davey to the front., Placing their fingers on the handle, Marty gave the go-ahead. 'OK, let's do this.'

Davey left the lodge from the front entrance, and Marty from the kitchen.

As they walked around the side of the building, they met in the middle and stood for a moment, staring into the bleakness. They turned together and walked to the gate at the front and out onto the path.

The fields opposite cast sinister shadows under a bright full moon. The air had turned cold, and an eerie stillness surrounded them, as though the trees were watching, whispering under their breath.

The distant sound of a vehicle cut through the silence and slowly disappeared.

Marty looked around him, searching for a phone torch, a light in the distance, or voices narrating a live stream, anything to confirm they were being attacked. 'You see anything?'

'Nothing, mate. You?'

'No. Let's go back inside.' Marty opened the gate, closing it as Davey walked through, and the two men went back inside the lodge.

* * *

'Is everything OK?' Marty stood by the locked living room door, the monitor in his hand, listening to the footsteps shuffling on the other side. The key shifted in the door, and Beth opened it.

'Did you see anything?' she asked.

'Nothing. I think it may have been an animal.'

'It would have to be a large one, Dad – it moved across the window.'

The monitor stirred, the grainy picture appeared, and the camera pointed to the path and the edge of the fields.

Bringing the monitor closer to his face, Marty asked, 'What is going on?'

'Has it come on again, Dad?'

'Yeah, I don't know if there's a fault—'

Suddenly he saw a shape; a figure crouched down beside the gate. It was too dark to make it out; only a shadow ducked low at the end of the path by the road.

Marty charged along the hallway and opened the front door. Davey ran behind him.

'If there's someone here, move away from the property. We have a shotgun, and we'll fucking use it. You've been warned.' Marty walked along the path, his body stiff, his mind swirling with scenarios plaguing his thoughts; the only sounds were Davey's heavy breaths on his neck.

Reaching the end of the path, he peered over the gate,

placing his hand on the low wall and stepping to his left along the lawn.

A branch snapped close to where they stood.

Marty's body instantly chilled, as if the blood had drained from his veins, and he stepped backwards, listening hard for another signal. 'Leave us alone,' he shouted. 'I'm warning you.'

Across the road, a light flickered in the fields and went off. Marty held his breath, Again, it came on, pointing in their direction, the brightness blinding them.

Off.

On.

Off.

'Quick, we need to get inside and lock the door.' Another branch snapped close to where they stood, and the bushes clattered in the field next to them. 'Go!' Marty shouted.

Sprinting to the lodge, they stepped into the hallway and slammed the front door behind them. Davey twisted the key in the lock and slid to the floor, leaning his body against the wood.

Marty banged on the living room door. 'You need to keep the door locked. I think there's someone out there. Maybe a few of them.' Beth and Abbey screamed. 'Keep away from the window. If you see anyone trying to get in, run upstairs.'

The security light blinked, and the monitor kicked into life again. Another grainy picture appeared, this time, the camera pointed along the path at the front of the lodge.

Someone was standing there.

Marty felt the hairs rise on his arms, and his heart seemed to stop.

He tried to catch a breath, but his throat felt blocked. The hallway began spinning, the voices from the living room, so loud in his ears, turned to muffled screams. The image of his parents penetrated his brain, and he began having hallucinations, his mother kneeling on the floor wearing a white night slip, begging her son to help them.

Finally able to breathe as the panic began subsiding, his surroundings had stabilised, Marty looked again at the monitor, bringing it closer to his eyes. A person, standing still, motionless, looking at the camera outside. They wore a white cloth over their head, protecting their identity, which gave them an even more terrifying appearance. They remained frozen, peering in the direction of the lodge.

Marty rushed into the kitchen, checking the door and windows were locked. As he ran along the hallway, he checked the living room.

A loud thump boomed from the front door, almost jolting Davey backward as he lay against it. 'Shit, dude, what are we gonna do? We've got to make a run for it.'

'It's not safe,' Marty shouted. 'I don't know how many people are out there.'

'We can't hold them off for—'

The kitchen window smashed, and a large rock landed on the floor.

Marty charged along the hallway, grabbing a knife from the kitchen drawer. Stepping to the window, he held it in the air like a trophy. 'The first person to get into the house gets this in the neck. Just fucking try me.'

A loud buzz reverberated over the lodge as the power went down, plunging them into darkness.

More screams rang out from the living room.

Sinking to his knees, Marty crawled along the kitchen floor, pawing at the bleakness. More thumping sounds on the front door echoed through the hallway. 'Davey?'

'Yeah?'

'We need to get everyone upstairs. It's safer if we're all together.'

Tapping his knuckles on the living room door, Marty listened as the key fumbled in the lock. A moment later, he heard Beth's voice whispering into the darkness, her phone torch in her hand.

'They've cut the power, haven't they?'

With his arms outstretched, Marty touched Beth's shoulder, pulling her close and holding her body tight to his. 'We're not going to die,' he whispered, 'But you all have to go upstairs. It's safer. I have to get the power back on. I saw the main fuseboard outside.'

'Marty, you're not going out there again. Please.'

'I have to. Otherwise, we may as well surrender.'

The lodge was silent.

Abbey turned on her phone torch while Marty helped Ethel off the sofa.

'Forgot to put money into the meter, have we? I was enjoying that show. By the way, turn the radio down – I can't stand that bloody racket. All that banging.'

'I will, Ethel. I'll do it as soon as you go upstairs.'

'It's not my bedtime yet.' Ethel grabbed her handbag, placing the strap over her shoulder.

Taking her by the arm, Marty led Ethel up the stairs and into the main bedroom, guided by the light from the phone torches. Beth and Abbey joined her.

'OK, keep the door locked and don't open it under any circumstances. 'I'm going to try and get the power back on.'

'Please, Marty. It's not safe,' Beth insisted.

'I'll be back before you know it. The only way we'll see them coming is by getting the light back on.'

'Take my phone torch – we have Abbey's mobile – and please be careful.'

Marty closed the door and waited until the key turned in the lock.

As he crept down the stairs, shining the phone torch, he saw the front door open. 'Davey, what's going on? Why's the door open? Davey? Davey?'

44

FRIDAY NIGHT

Earlier, Gary Miller had left his Dulwich apartment, and as he drove, watching the clues within The App, he ended up at Church Farm in St Albans. He was sure the clue was right, but he'd driven back and forth for a couple of hours, searching for Abbey Benson to no avail.

A migraine had developed as frustration built in his mind, and he'd already popped six Nurofen, but the ache still worked across his head.

Eventually, his tired mind and the monotonous winding roads were too much, and Gary pulled over into a ditch, waiting for the next clue. Hours passed as he stared at his phone, willing something to appear. Watching the live streams, he wondered if there was a glitch, something he didn't know. Had he been ruled out of the game? Eliminated due to his greed?

The more he sat, waiting in his transit van, the more frustrated he became. Agitation festered within his body, turning to anger, his skin tingling from the copious amounts of cocaine he'd snorted last night; the ache worked over his face, crushing his skull, and he felt sick. Closing his eyes, giving in to his feeble, weak state, Gary fell asleep.

His body jolted when Gary woke, peering outside. It was almost dark; the engine was off with the keys in the ignition. He opened the driver's door, stepping out and stretching his tall, lean body. A shiver powered through his veins with fatigue, and he spat saliva on the side of the road.

The moon glistened in a clear sky decorated with millions of stars.

How he'd love to lie in a field, a bottle of whisky by his feet and a long joint in his hand to dull the tension.

Stepping back into the driver's seat and looking at his phone, Gary realised he'd slept for hours.

A notification had come through moments ago, possibly the reason he'd been awoken.

Two words. A scarecrow throws this item to the ground. What is he standing in?

'Boom, Easy one. Hatfield. Let's go,' Gary said to himself.

As he drove, adamant he was back in the game, the final clue came through.

The name of a lodge. Keep the doctor away.

'Apple Lodge, Hatfield, baby!' he shouted. The hairs stood on his arms as his body tingled with excitement. This was gonna be so easy.

* * *

Hiding in the grass, peering at Apple Lodge in the distance, Gary waited. The silence was tranquil, almost pleasurable. Patience would win the game and bring him his third monstrous payout.

Shadows swept across the windows, movement; a sudden panic, as if the people inside knew they were under threat. Keeping still, hidden and low in the field, Gary saw the security camera blink to life, the front door open and two men walk along the path to the gate.

Shit. This makes it more difficult, he thought. Behind him, the fields glowed as a torch swept through the air, moving towards him.

One of the men standing outside the lodge called out, making a threat. They knew someone was out here. The two men raced back inside, slamming the door behind them.

The light from a torch blinked behind him, and Gary crawled along the grass as footsteps approached. They were almost upon him; Gary could see the phone in their hand, narrating. He sprung to his feet, punching the figure hard in the face. The man now lay on the floor, and Gary kicked him in the head for good measure, listening as he squirmed in agony.

One opponent down, Gary quickly raced through the fields and hid behind the wall at the front of the lodge. A bush rattled next to him; someone was pushing through the branches. Again, the security light blinked into life, and Gary saw a man creeping along the side of the lodge, kneeling and turning off the power. His surroundings plunged into darkness, save for the man's phone torch.

Coming behind him, using the only light as a guide, Gary rammed his face into the wall and waited for him to drop by his feet.

Through the window, as he crept to the front door, Gary saw the shadows shifting on the stairs and moving to the first floor.

His initial concern of how to go about getting into the lodge was easily solved when the front door opened and a man stepped out, looking towards the fields. With no time to hide, Gary leapt on him, covering his mouth and punching him unconscious. He dragged his body to the gate and rolled him under a bush. Gary had to be quick; it wouldn't be long until others came to claim his prize.

As he stepped into the lodge, he heard voices coming from above, footsteps on the stairs and someone calling out.

Opening the closest door in the hallway, Gary hid.

45

FRIDAY NIGHT

'Davey. Where the hell are you?' Marty stood in the dark hallway by the open front door, shining Beth's phone torch. 'Davey? For Christ's sake, answer me.' Marty held his breath for a moment, trying desperately to listen for his friend's footsteps, a voice, anything to indicate he was OK. 'Keep the door locked, Beth,' he shouted up the stairs. 'Davey has gone AWOL.'

Marty held the phone at arm's length as he stepped outside. Looking into the fields, seeing only bleakness, he wondered how many people were out there, waiting, wanting to murder his daughter. Taking a deep breath to clear his head, Marty pressed his body against the outside wall and stepped along the lodge.

The light he'd seen in the fields a few minutes ago had disappeared and the rustles in the bushes next to the lodge had ceased, but Marty braced himself for an attack. At this moment, he'd never been so frightened. Was this where it all finished?

He held the phone torch in front of him, his body pressed against the wall, as he shuffled along. His foot touched something lying on the ground. Marty flicked the light towards it and jolted at the sight of a man on the floor, blood from a head wound running down his face. He was still breathing. Had Davey done this? He doubted it.

Marty felt guilty stepping over his unconscious body, but he had to get the lights on and keep his daughter alive.

Shining the torch against the wall, Marty saw the lid open to the main power controls. He flicked the switch upwards, and the lodge was, once again, drenched with light. He sighed, relief washing over his body.

Until, a scream pierced the stillness of the night. Abbey.

As he raced back to the lodge, he yelled, 'Abbey, I'm coming.' The sound of wood breaking resounded in Marty's ears as he charged up the stairs. The bedroom door was open, the flimsy lock broken, and a tall, muscular man was standing over the bed. His arm was outstretched, and a mobile phone was in his hand, pointing at Abbey.

It was the same guy from the restaurant, the one who'd murdered Cass Carter.

'Get the fuck away from my daughter,' Marty ordered, but his words were lost as the guy began speaking.

'This is the girl everyone is after. Abbey Benson. I'm here with her now. I'm going to stream her death. Watch and learn, assholes.'

Beth screamed, her body pushed in front of Abbey's, shielding her daughter; Ethel was under the covers, her body hidden.

Marty charged forward and grabbed the guy by his jacket.

Anticipating an attack, in a Judo-style manoeuvre, Gary twisted his arm under Marty's, swinging his body with ease and throwing him against the wall.

Straightening his body and wincing in agony, Marty

pulled himself up from the floor and ran across the room. He jumped on Gary's back, his arm around his neck, and pulled hard with everything he had. He listened as Gary began choking, ferociously twisting his body as the phone dropped to the floor.

'You stupid bastard. You... you... can't help but interfere.' Thrusting his arm back, he caught Marty in the ribs; again, he swung his arm, catching him in the same spot.

Losing his grip, Marty stumbled backwards, writhing in agony. He watched as Gary picked up the phone and began pointing it at Abbey again, live streaming.

With one hand holding the mobile phone, he reached his other hand forward, batting Beth away like she was a fly, and grabbed Abbey around the throat.

As Marty watched his daughter choking, Beth thumping his arm with little effect, again, he drew himself up and yanked at Gary's jacket, feeling like a tug-of-war match, a lone person pulling against a row of people, making no difference.

The blood drained from Abbey's face, her tongue hanging out of her mouth, as she gasped for breath. She scratched and pulled at Gary's hands, but his grip only got tighter.

She could hear her parents screaming, but as she struggled for air, their voices grew quieter. Her vision blurred, and all she could make out was the look of pure evil in Gary's eyes.

Behind her, from under the sheets, Ethel threw back the covers and let out an almighty shriek. She raised her hand up and sprayed Mace into Gary's eyes.

'Arghhhh!'

As he covered his face, he dropped Abbey onto the bed, but Ethel kept spraying, listening to the horrible intruder's screams as he stumbled across the room and lay in agony on the floor.

'Serves you right, you old brute. No one messes with my granddaughter. Mace, very useful – my Ted said I should always carry it.'

'Your Ted is a bloody legend,' Marty said. 'Quick, everyone out. We need to leave.' Marty put his arm around his daughter; she was deathly pale and so fragile. She coughed, turning her body and vomiting on the bed. He helped her up again, easing her across the floor. Beth took Ethel by the arm, helping her out of bed and all of them hurried out the door as Gary continued to yell in agony.

As they reached the front door, the security light shone on a figure standing on the drive, startling them.

'Yo, is Abbey OK?'

'Davey. Thank God. Where did you go?' Marty asked.

'I'm unsure, amigo. I was sitting in the hallway, then I woke up under a bush—' Looking past them, Davey saw a figure at the top of the stairs. 'We have to leave now.' He slammed the front door shut, and helped Beth usher Ethel to the car.

Marty followed, still supporting Abbey.

Once they were in the Sorento, Marty started the car and locked the doors.

But looking up, Beth saw the front door open; their attacker was stumbling around like a drunk person, staggering towards their vehicle. 'Quick, Marty, he's coming. Go.'

At the sound of the engine, Gary jabbed at the air with his hands, his vision still blurry, and stepped in front of the car, pounding his fists on the bonnet. He couldn't let them get away.

Inside the car, Abbey screamed, 'Quick, Dad. Drive!'

Marty reversed, then rammed his foot on the accelerator,

hitting the intruder and seeing Gary's body twist in the air and land hard on the ground. He watched the figure in the rear-view mirror as they pulled away. A torch in the field opposite shone towards them as they steered out of the grounds and onto the main road.

46

SATURDAY MORNING

With all of them exhausted, needing to keep hidden and under the radar and awaiting Sean's instructions, Marty pulled the car over on a country lane a few miles from the lodge, and he and Davey took turns. One to sleep with Beth, Abbey and Ethel in the Sorento, the other to keep watch. They swapped halfway through the night.

Hours later, as the sun rose, the passengers gradually awoke, their bodies fatigued and minds addled with stress and exhaustion. Although the sky was heavy with dull grey clouds, it was bright, and the light stung their tired eyes.

They sat in the car, the windows open and a gentle breeze caressing their skin. Tall bushes blocked their view of the fields, and the sound of sheep in the distance soothed their state of mind.

Abbey's phone pinged.

'Who's that?' Marty asked.

'It's Sean. Michael's brother. He's got into The App.'

'Oh my goodness, that's incredible,' Marty's voice indicated his excitement. 'What now?'

'Hang on – he's still texting.' Abbey read aloud what Sean typed.

Sean: Sorry, it's a little technical. The easiest way is to hack into the middleware of The App. Unfortunately, that's almost impossible because the machine will probably be at the person's home. Without breaking into the property, I can do nothing on that front, as I can't pinpoint the exact address. Both the front end and back end are constantly communicating with each other in order to make sure that the user experience is optimal at all times. While the front end sends client requests to the back end, the back end retrieves the needed information through an API, and sends it back to the frontend.

The long and short of it is I've managed to hack the server where the database is stored. If your father can retrieve his phone and start a stream, The App owner will see it. Get him to say something about your situation and have him plead for mercy. I can then attach the loop, making him think it's live. It should give you all enough time to get to your grandparents' house. It's the only way. I can turn The App off, but it will only raise suspicion. You have more of a chance this way.

Abbey: I can't thank you enough for your help.

Sean: It's not a problem. I was helped with a blip in the security system. It was in the news last week. Hackers were able to run riot, getting into people's phones and companies' systems. It made my job a hell of a lot easier to get inside. I can usually hack systems in seconds. But this guy is good. I wouldn't have had a hope, only for the software crash. It affected thousands of companies. Once your father has his phone, get him to stream for a couple of minutes. I'll attach the loop. I've disarmed the location tracker so your father can leave his phone on. This way, if he checks, he'll assume it's a blip or there's no signal. Good luck.

After reading the message aloud, Abbey placed the phone on her lap. 'Dad, you need to get your phone and stream.'

'Sounds like a load of shit,' Ethel stated. 'A back end was always an arse. Excuse the pun. My Ted said I had the best back end he'd ever seen.'

Marty eyed Beth, seeing the shock on her face at Ethel's last statement, suddenly turning to relief, the message from Sean possibly paving a way out for them all.

As Marty pulled up to the bin outside the police station to search for his phone, he fought the sick feeling in his stomach. What if it had been emptied, or someone had taken it? His mind whirred with possible outcomes, knowing how much he needed the phone to make the plan work.

Stepping out of the driver's seat, his body tense, he walked towards the bin, glancing along the empty street, which had been bustling only hours ago with market stalls and people shopping. Peering back at Beth, he saw her nod, coaxing him to keep going and be positive. Standing over the bin and leaning it towards him; the smell of rotten meat was pungent, Marty dipped his hand in, swirling it around, feeling the wet, soggy takeaway bags, the damp tissues, old food and beer cans from Friday night revellers. As his arm stretched further down, he felt the leather case and breathed a sigh of relief, pulling his phone out of the bin. His face beamed, and his body relaxed as he got back into the driver's seat and turned it on. After a minute, it pinged into life. Ignoring the countless notifications, he looked at Beth. 'What do I say?' Marty asked.

'Whatever you feel. Just be honest. Sean said to stream

for a couple of minutes. You can do this, Marty,' Beth insisted.

Plugging the phone into the charger and resting it against the dashboard, Marty clicked into The App and began streaming.

The Kia Sorento was silent, only for Marty's hoarse voice. 'OK, I'm live. Not to hunt, but on the contrary, I'm here to try and plead with the people running this barbaric hunt to stop. I won't give my name or any clue as to who I am, but I'm on the run with my family. We've been constantly targeted, almost killed many times and are living in constant fear as more people join in. Even as I speak, there are new notifications.' Marty peered at Beth. Taking a deep breath, he continued. 'We've watched the live streams, the torment of others forced into this wicked game, how they struggle with their emotions, forced to kill for fear of their loved ones. Now, we're in the same predicament. I don't know how it will end. I don't know what is in store for us as we continue to fight off and hide from the constant threat. So I'm pleading with you, to the creators of The App, please stop. For the sake of my family and others in the future who will no doubt find themselves in this cruel position. Listen to me. Please end it now.'

As he drove towards his parent's house in Shepherd's Bush, West London, praying it wasn't too late, Marty left the stream running and filmed the road ahead, hoping that Sean had managed to add the fake recording.

47

SATURDAY MORNING

Standing at the window of his penthouse flat, the living room filled with marvellous light, Jonathan gazed over London. A few die-hard staff members arriving early to the office buildings opposite hung their coats and bags on swivel chairs and turned on their computers while sipping on their re-usable coffee cups and chatting to their colleagues.

His anger spread, like a rash through his body, as Jonathan thought about last night. He'd left Marty Benson's parents' house early, intending to return home and watch the terror unfold. Instead, nothing happened. Like watching a Z-movie on a Sunday afternoon.

The streams were all so promising as people traipsed through the grass, closing in on the lodge and Abbey Benson. But something had happened. And someone was going to pay. He suspected Gary Miller. What the fuck had happened to the other participants? How could they drop out, their phones lying on the ground with blank screens and moans seeping through the speakers?

Grabbing his own phone from the bedroom, Jonathan

opened WhatsApp, looking at the message he'd sent late last night.

Find Gary Miller. End him.

There hadn't been a reply. Gus and Stevo, the idiots who were supposed to clean up the mess, had gone missing.

It was obvious the Bensons had found the tracking device under the car, as it had been stationary since yesterday afternoon and it was impossible to track Marty as his phone was stagnant outside a police station in Hatfield.

Grabbing the remote control, he fired up the wide-screen TV and went into The App.

'Oh hold on a second, what's this?' Stepping away from the screen and sitting on the sofa, he clicked a link showing Marty's phone and watched as it rested on the dashboard, the country roads vanishing under the Sorento with Marty narrating, telling everyone his sob story.

Jonathan clicked out of the live stream, watching others join the hunt inside The App.

He grabbed his phone and dialled Gus's number. The phone picked up after four rings.

'Where the fuck are you both?'

'We're at the lodge, awaiting instructions.'

'You didn't respond to my message. Did you find Gary Miller?'

'Yes, his leg is broken. Marty Benson knocked him over as they left. He was crawling along the ground, screaming in agony, close to the lodge. He's tied up in a field as we speak. Stevo is watching him. We were waiting to hear from you.'

'OK, get him in the van, bring him somewhere secluded. You know what to do. I can't have him disrupt the hunt anymore. The fucker is too greedy. Make sure his body is well hidden.'

'You got it.'

'Then get to this address in Shepherd's Bush. I'll text you. Kill both of Marty's parents. Move.'

Jonathan ended the call.

* * *

'Turn on.' The shower instantly sprayed hot water over Jonathan's body as an eighties album he'd selected from Spotify played out over the speakers behind him. First, Michael Jackson, then 'Give It Up'. Singing at the top of his voice, the water invigorating as he massaged shampoo into his hair, Jonathan felt everything was back on track. Since The App went live a couple of months ago, there'd been the odd blip – the system crashing, losing coverage as people streamed within The App, clues which couldn't be deciphered. It happened. But Marty Benson had got under his skin. From the moment Jonathan had seen him at the restaurant and how he'd helped Cass Carter, he knew there would be problems.

When he disobeyed the rules by not sending The App to someone, it was a red rag being rubbed all over a bull's face. Jonathan was furious. During the hunt, Marty tried to use his advantage by turning off Wi-Fi, location services and then dumping his phone. Jonathan was going to make him pay. Not only was his daughter going to die – it would only be a matter of time before someone, somewhere, got to her – he'd watch Gus and Stevo break into the house in Shepherd's Bush and murder his parents too. All from the comfort of his living room.

'Turn off.' The water stopped, and Jonathan stepped out of the shower, towelling his body dry and slipping into a clean dressing gown.

In the living room, he grabbed the remote control,

pointed it at the TV and connected to the camera in the bedroom.

The picture was hazy at first; it jumped, a white, horizontal line gliding up the screen, and then he saw them. The look of fear was priceless. Jonathan laughed, more boisterous than he'd expected, realising he sounded insane. Laughing again, he clicked the remote control and zoomed into their pitiful faces; the gags tied tight around their mouths, their bodies bound with strong rope, the muffled cries, which yesterday were so assertive, had now turned into dull groans. It reminded him of his aunt Joyce, seeing them struggle, their helpless, destitute expressions, and a sense of abandonment.

When this part was over, he'd watch the recording again and again, placing it on the shelf, right next to the footage of Aunt Joyce.

Jumping out of the bedroom in Shepherd's Bush and into The App with the press of a couple of buttons, Jonathan flicked through the recent streams. So many people had joined; it gave him a sense of pride and accomplishment, this ability to command so many with manipulation.

And, of course, the money. But it was a small price to pay for the joy he felt.

He pressed the link showing Marty's stream. He was still driving along the vacant country road.

Something didn't feel right. Before taking a shower, Jonathan had watched the stream. On the side of the road, he'd seen a sign stuck into the earth, declaring London was twenty-two miles. Now, sitting on the sofa, a half hour later, he'd seen the same sign.

London. Twenty-Two miles.

Grabbing his mobile, his hand trembling, he dialled Gus's number.

'Yeah, boss.'

'What's going on?' Jonathan shouted. He tried desperately to stop his body from shaking; his skin was itchy and sore from the shower, his eyes watering with fatigue.

'What do you mean?'

'You fucking know well what I mean. Where are you?'

'We're about to dump Gary. Then we're heading over to Shepherd's Bush.'

'Get Stevo to FaceTime me.' Jonathan hung up, a minute later, his phone rang. 'Hello. Point the phone at Gus.' Jonathan watched the screen as the camera turned to Gus sitting in the driver's seat, looking at the camera.

'Don't you believe me? What do you think we're doing?' Gus asked.

'We have a humongous fucking problem. Marty Benson has somehow hacked The App.'

'There was a blip in the security network last week,' Gus said. 'Companies were getting hacked from all angles. Everyone was told to update and change passwords.'

'I did update and change the password. You know I'm stringent when it comes to security.' Doubting himself, his mind plagued and about to burst with pressure, the living room began spinning, and Jonathan worried that he'd used an old password or the update didn't load correctly. 'I fucking updated everything. Are you listening?'

'Boss, I believe you—'

A loud, crunching noise reverberated through the phone.

'What's going on there?'

Just out of shot, Gary Miller kicked the driver's seat. He'd managed to free his hands and feet and grabbed the steering wheel, trying to force the van to stop.

Stevo turned in his seat and punched Gary in the face.

Gary yelped in pain, but despite his injured leg, he still tried to clamber over the seat into the front, blocking Gus's view of the road.

Through the video screen, Jonathan watched the van as it rounded a corner, heading straight for a huge articulated lorry.

'Gus, watch out!' Jonathan yelled. But it was too late. The van ploughed into the lorry head-on. The screen went black.

'Hello? What's happened? Gus? Stevo? Answer me? Hello?'

48

SATURDAY MORNING

The Bensons, Ethel and Davey had been driving for just over thirty minutes since they'd stopped streaming. Beth had been watching the recent live footage on Marty's phone within The App; the number of people who'd joined the hunt last night was harrowing.

'Christ, there must be dozens of people taking part.' A chill worked up her back. Every vehicle they saw aroused suspicion, and every person could be part of the twisted game.

Marty glanced in the rear-view mirror, grateful to see an empty road behind them. Rotating it slightly, he saw Ethel, her eyes shut, mouth open, and her lips vibrating. The Mace had saved their lives, and Marty had a newfound admiration for her.

Davey had looked somewhat out of it since waking up under a bush, still unable to recall what happened. Perhaps he was concussed. When this was all over, Marty would insist that everyone was checked out at the hospital.

Turning the mirror once again to reflect his daughter,

Marty smiled at Abbey. She peered back at her father, her lips curving into a smile, her eyes wide, and she blinked. Marty was so proud of her bravery.

Beth was curled up in the front passenger seat, her feet tucked under her body, her beautiful eyes peering at the screen. Marty asked, 'Have there been any updates?'

'Nothing so far? No one has streamed since last night.'

'He doesn't know where we are,' Marty said, the sudden hope becoming a reality. 'No one is streaming because they don't know our location.'

He reached for Beth's hand and glimpsed briefly into her eyes as he drove, seeing belief and optimism, her smile was dazzling, and her high cheekbones became more pronounced.

'We're not over the line yet,' she said. Looking at the satnav on her phone as they approached St Albans, Beth's heart sank, realising there was still another twenty-five miles to go to Shepherd's Bush. The satnav approximated fifty-two minutes.

'Are you OK in the back, Davey?' Marty asked. 'Sorry we didn't have time to get your phone.'

'It's no bother. Keeping Abbey alive is the priority. Man, my head is sore. It feels like I've done ten rounds with Tyson Fury.'

'Only ten?' Marty laughed. 'You reckon you could last that long?'

'The way I feel, I couldn't last a round with Ethel. So what's the plan, mate?'

'I need to get to Mum and Dad before the bastard realises we're com—'

Beth's gasps cut Marty's sentence short. 'There's a WhatsApp message,' she said.

'What does it say?' Marty asked, sick with dread.

Beth began reading. '"I know what you've done. Your stupidity knows no boundaries. I'm going to murder your parents."'

'What is wrong with this guy?' Abbey yelled from the back.

'Put your foot down, mate. We need to get there before he does.' Davey placed his hand on Marty's shoulder, letting him know he had this.

It felt like Marty's world had crashed in on itself, the last few days a blur; the streams, the wicked acts of cruelty this evil bastard was instigating, the kidnap of his parents and the attempts on their lives last night were too much for his mind to take. Marty wanted to give up, wave the white flag and surrender. But the visions of his parents and his family kept him going. Marty didn't see himself as a hero, he didn't feel courageous, but if a child was under threat, every parent would do all they could to keep them alive.

His phone pinged from the dashboard.

Beth looked at the notification and pressed the link inside The App. 'Shit.'

'What is it, Beth?' Marty asked, his body tense as he straightened his back.

Her voice was hoarse and feeble. 'There's a stream. How do they know where we are? This isn't happening.' Beth pounded the dashboard again, shouting, 'How do they know where we are?'

Glancing in the wing mirror, Marty saw a vehicle approaching. 'Bloody hell. It's the idiot from yesterday.'

'Which idiot from yesterday? There were a few,' Beth screamed.

'The black pickup truck. We lost him at the level crossing, remember?'

Beth's head was addled with confusion as she tried to think. Suddenly she recalled the train. Undoing her seatbelt, Beth knelt on the passenger seat, seeing the driver following them, a mobile phone resting on the dashboard. The small truck was only yards away and gaining. 'He must have been waiting all night, hoping we'd come back this way.'

'Man, what a fruit loop – in a sick way, you've got to admire his persistence.' Davey turned, looking at the driver. 'I think we should pull over and confront him.'

Marty was tempted. 'It's too dangerous. He may have a weapon. I can't believe this shit is happening.'

They jolted forward as the truck hit the back of the Sorento. The force of the impact caused Marty to swerve. The country lane was busier than yesterday and a flow of oncoming vehicles came towards them. Visions flooded his mind, the Sorento ending up wrapped around a pole or crushed in the side of a ditch. Pressing hard on the accelerator and gripping the steering wheel, Marty watched the speed rise to over forty miles an hour, and a gap developed between the Sorento and the pickup truck.

Beth gripped the grab handle above her with her left hand, while her right hand covered her mouth.

Abbey was cowering in the back seat next to Davey, who had his arm around her, and Ethel was somehow still asleep.

In the distance, Marty saw a turning two hundred yards in front. *Should I swerve sharply and risk the small truck following, or keep going?* he thought.

A sudden lifeline appeared as a tractor stopped at the junction. As Marty slowed the Sorento, flashing the full lights, the driver slowly pulled out, towing a long trailer and gradually turning towards them. At the last second, Marty saw a slight gap between the tractor and the ditch, narrowly squeezing through and watching the driver give him the V sign.

The pickup truck skidded, hitting the side of the tractor, and the two men got out, arguing on the roadside as a line of vehicles honked their horns.

* * *

As they drove along Goldhawk Road in Shepherd's Bush, silence clung to the inside of the Kia Sorento, the atmosphere tense, the strain evident in the air.

Struggling to stem the rush of adrenaline flooding his body, his fingers stiff from gripping the steering wheel, Marty was petrified of how events would play out. The WhatsApp message he'd received over an hour ago charged through his mind as he pulled into a parking space outside his parents' house.

I know what you've done. Your stupidity knows no boundaries. I'm going to murder your parents.

Forcing back the lump in his throat, struggling to deal with his emotions and aware he could break down at any moment, Marty battled with the negative thoughts racing through his mind. Taking a deep breath and looking towards the three-bedroom semi-detached house, he opened the driver's door, stepped onto the road, and peered at the bedroom window on the first floor. The curtains were closed. *What did that mean?* Marty just hoped they'd made it in time.

As he walked to the gate, listening to Beth's voice, pleading with him to be careful, Davey got out of the back.

'Bruv, you're not dealing with this alone.'

Davey strode towards him and Marty said, 'He could be in there, waiting. It's dangerous. I fear we may be too late.'

'I know, but I'm with you, mate. Let's do this.'

As he pushed the gate, the hinges screeched loud in his ears. Marty ran to the front door, eyeing the lock for any signs of damage, and thrust his body against the wood. The door was solid, and there was no way he'd open it without the keys, which he'd left at home in their haste.

Stepping back, Marty turned towards the windows at the front and slid his fingers against the frames. 'I'm making too much noise,' Marty whispered. 'If he's inside, he'll know we're here.'

They walked to the side entrance, inching along the cracked paving slabs towards the garden. Marty tensed his body, ready for whatever was waiting.

The lockbox hanging on the wall by the back door was smashed open, and the key was missing. The kitchen door handle was stiff as Marty tried to drive it downwards, again, checking for any open windows. He looked to the first floor, all the windows were closed and with no signs of damage.

Grabbing a large stone planted in the soil, Marty covered his eyes with his left hand and asked Davey to stand back as he smashed the window. The sound was deafening as the glass shattered, heavy fragments spilling to the ground. Once he'd pushed most of the glass out, Marty grabbed a small ladder leaning against the shed and climbed through, opening the kitchen door for Davey.

'Is everything OK?' A bare-chested, middle-aged man with a shaved head looked over the fence, and the smell of weed was overbearing. Clothes flapped on the washing line, and a dog continually barked.

'Yeah, we're good,' Marty said. 'My parents have locked themselves in the bedroom.'

'Oh, I've never met them. I hope they're OK. Back inside, Hugo.' The door closed, and the dog stopped barking.

Marty stood in the kitchen, his arms cut and his T-shirt ripped. The smell of damp was strong in the air and flakes of glass crunched around his feet. At this moment, it felt like his body would explode with tension. He looked at Davey, placing his hands on the greasy worktop to steady himself, then left the kitchen and climbed the stairs.

'Mum, Dad, are you OK?' Marty listened for their whimpering sounds, a cry in the darkness, something, anything to denote they were still alive.

The crashing glass in the kitchen put him at a disadvantage; if The App creator was here, he'd be waiting, hiding somewhere in the house. 'Mum, Dad, it's Marty. Where are you? If you can hear me, bang something.' Pausing on the stairs, he turned to Davey, placing his finger over his mouth.

His friend nodded, interpreting the signal.

As Marty reached the top of the stairs, he peered along the hallway to his parents' bedroom. With a huge breath, he raced along the wooden floorboards and charged through the bedroom. As he stood at the door, elation saturated his body, seeping from his skin. The exhaustion clinging to his frame like a web around a fly dropped instantly as Marty saw his parents tied to the bed, a replica of the picture he'd been sent on WhatsApp. Racing across the floor, he knelt on the bed, untying the thick rope that bound them.

Davey stood behind. 'Man, you made it. You're a freaking hero.'

As Marty held his parents, feeling their frail bodies against his, wiping the tears from his mother's cheeks and seeing the look of confusion on his father's face, he heard footsteps pounding the stairs. Suddenly, a figure stood by the bedroom door.

'Are they OK. I've put the dog away. I had to check as I was concerned.'

Looking at the neighbour who they'd seen while breaking in, Marty proudly announced, 'They're safe. Thank you. It looks like we got here in time.'

49

SATURDAY NIGHT

'We all need to stay together tonight while he's still out there. It's safer that way.' Marty and Beth stood at the living room window of their house in Dollis Hill, looking out at the darkness. A streetlamp flickered across the road filling the room with eerie light.

Behind them, the TV was loud as Ethel sat on the sofa, her feet resting on the coffee table as she sucked on a mint humbug.

Abbey and Davey sat at the dining table; Gracie and Albert, Marty's parents, were next to them, his mother insisting they didn't want a fuss.

Stepping across the floor, ignoring Ethel's moans as she passed in front of the TV, Beth crouched beside them and held their hands. 'I really think you should both get checked out. You've been through a terrifying ordeal.'

Gracie turned to look at Beth. 'Albert has fought in a war; he's been through tougher situations than this. He's most frightened when he's kept in a hospital bed, staff poking and prodding him with sharp needles and having all those strange faces peering at him. We're fine, love. No ambulance.'

'My Ted fought in the war. When he came back, he was always humming that song, "The White Cliffs Of Dover".'

'"We'll Meet Again",' Marty said.

'I bloody hope not. After all the shit you've put me through the last week. Pillock.'

'What are you watching?' Marty asked. He looked at the bottom of the screen, the UK Gold logo showing in the corner.

'*Coronation Street*. It's a scene with Ena Sharples. I haven't seen her in it for years. She hasn't aged a day – it's good to see her back.'

'Ethel, you do realise that's a rerun from the sixties.'

'Shush, I can't hear it,' she snapped.

* * *

Everyone had gone to bed. Gracie and Albert were in the main bedroom. Ethel was in the spare room with Beth, and Abbey on the pull-out sofa bed.

Marty and Davey were in the living room, sitting at the table with the TV on low.

Wincing with discomfort, Marty popped a couple of painkillers and swallowed them with a glass of water.

Once the neighbour had left, Marty helped his parents down the stairs, assisted by Davey and brought them out to the Kia Sorento.

As he opened the back doors and helped them into the seats, feeling a slight victory, he thought about The App and the hellish nightmare that had been brought to their door.

'How you holding up, man?'

'I've had better days.' Marty stood. 'I need a drink. You fancy one?'

'Christ, do I. Yes. A large whisky if you have it.'

Smiling, Marty walked into the kitchen, grabbing two tumblers from the unit above the sink and adding ice from the fridge. In the drinks cupboard, he found an unopened bottle of Jack Daniels which he kept for special occasions. Marty guessed this was one of those times.

Back in the living room, he stood by the table and opened the Jack Daniels, pouring half a tumbler each into his and Davey's glass. 'To keeping my family safe and the rescue of my Mum and Dad.' Marty lifted his glass.

'Amen to that,' Davey said as he clinked Marty's glass, and they slugged the alcohol.

Marty closed the living room door and sat. 'I have to tell you something.'

'Go on.'

'Earlier, I... What was that?'

'What?' Davey asked.

'The vibrating noise.'

'I didn't hear anything.'

Reaching into his pocket, Marty pulled out his mobile and looked at the screen, expecting to see a new message. There was nothing. 'Have you got your phone?'

'Of course not. I threw it away.' Davey poured another half a tumbler of whiskey into his and Marty's glasses. 'What were you going to tell me?'

The vibrating noise sounded again. Davey's cheeks glowed red, and he looked towards the ground.

'Get up?' Marty ordered.

'Huh? Tell me what you were going to say. I'm intrigued,' Davey pushed.

'I said, get up.'

The App

'Marty, don't do this.'

Kicking his chair back and standing, Marty grabbed his friend, lifted him to his feet and reached behind him, feeling the phone in his back pocket. 'I thought you threw it away. What the fuck is going on?' He whipped the phone from Davey's pocket and tapped the screen. 'Who's messaging you?'

'No one. You're being paranoid. Tell me what you were going to say.'

Holding the phone in front of Davey's face, the screen opened, and he tapped on WhatsApp, seeing the most recent messages from Davey's phone to the unknown number.

Davey: At Marty's house in Dollis Hill. We're having a drink. Everyone is gone to bed.

Unknown: OK. Keep me updated.

'What the fuck?' Marty looked at an earlier set of messages.

Davey: On side of road. Not sure of location. Been here a while after leaving Apple lodge. They'll be awake soon so I won't be able to text.

Unknown: Is he coming to the house in Shepherd's Bush?

Davey: Yes, on way now. Estimate around an hour.

Unknown: I can't get there in time.

Davey: Well I can't hold them off.

Marty thumbed downwards, reading earlier messages.

Unknown: He's dumped his phone. Where are you all?

Davey: Still at Apple lodge in Hatfield. Marty thinks I got rid of my phone so I can't let him see me texting. I have to be careful.

Near the top of the page, Marty read another message.

Unknown: I will abstain you from the hunt if you keep me updated on the Benson's movements.

Davey: Who's this?

Unknown: The App creator.

Davey: OK. But don't ask me to kill Abbey. They're like family to me. Once you keep me out of any future hunts, I'll let you know their exact movements.

Hurling the phone on the floor, Marty shouted, 'Why?'

'I'm sorry, man. He said he'd pardon me from the hunt. That If I helped him, I wouldn't have to take part. I'm so sorry.'

'You put my family at risk to save your own skin. All the time I thought you had our backs. That's how the hunters knew where we were. You kept him informed.'

'I'm so sorry. I would never hurt Abbey.'

'Get the fuck out of my house.'

* * *

Marty stood by the living room window, watching his best friend stroll along the pavement and out of sight. Clutching his fists, he thought about Davey, the link he'd sent last Sunday, drawing him into the hellish game within The App. How he'd pretended to care, coming over to the house and going on the run with them, only to deceive him and his family and stab them in the back. Had Davey wanted to help them? Had he intended on protecting Abbey? Marty would never know. But to betray him as he did was unforgivable.

Slumping forward, his head against the glass, Marty rubbed the tears from his eyes, his back aching and his body sore. He was so tired and in need of sleep.

There was movement in the hallway. Marty was certain he'd heard something. Turning, he crossed the wooden floor of the living room, the TV muted and the picture casting shadows across the walls.

Opening the living room door, he peered along the hallway to the bottom of the stairs. 'Hello?' Marty whispered. He turned, looking towards the kitchen. 'Hello?'

When there was no response, he moved back into the living room and sat on the sofa, pushing out a heavy sigh, thinking about the nightmare of the last few days.

His phone beeped from his jeans pocket. Marty felt an icy chill rush through his body. He fidgeted, wiping the sweat from his face, his skin hot and clammy.

The screen of his mobile phone showed a notification from The App. Marty clicked it and pressed the link, opening up a new live stream.

'I'm at the address. I have him in my sights. There's a shadow in the hallway. I can see him as I look through the kitchen door. He's lying on the floor and curled into a ball. It's the first time I've taken part in the hunt. I've been forced into it, but ask yourself, wouldn't you? To save a member of your family? If your child was threatened? Your partner? Wouldn't you? I've smashed the window and opened the kitchen door. I'm inside and stepping towards him. I have Jonathan Rushmore in my sights.'

* * *

On the way home from her grandparents' house, with everyone in the seven-seater Kia Sorento, Abbey asked if Marty could take a detour, stopping off in Kilburn, a few miles from their home in Dollis Hill. She'd left her AirPods at Michaels's house and wanted to collect them before he went on holiday in the morning.

When Marty pulled up outside the two-bedroom terraced house off the Kilburn High Road, Abbey got out of the car. Marty joined her, telling everyone to wait, and locked the doors. It was a considerable risk, but one that needed to happen.

Inside the house, Marty was introduced to Sean, who was in his bedroom. Abbey and Michael walked into the living room, chatting.

Once they were out of ear shot, Marty thanked Sean, saying he'd saved their lives and asked to see how it all worked. The genius in action.

Firing up the computer, Sean plugged his phone in and showed Marty how easy it was to manipulate The App once you were inside.

As Marty watched, he pointed to a small flashing square which appeared to move slowly across the screen, asking Sean what it meant. After tapping a couple of keys and zooming in closer, it showed the current location of the person who'd created The App. Essex. Sean was able to watch his exact movements.

After Sean selected a picture, the latest photo on his camera roll, and writing a line of text, everything appeared on The App's main page. He could even choose a time the post would appear. Sean had total control. And it was so easy. Then Sean left, running out of the house, late for an appointment and leaving everything turned on. He shouted to Michael that he wouldn't be home until the early hours.

He'd been ushered out of the bedroom when Sean left, but as Marty stood in the hallway outside the bedroom door, he had an idea.

Listening to Abbey and Michael in the living room, Marty stepped back into the bedroom, closing the door quietly behind him. He opened the WhatsApp message he'd received a couple of days ago, with the knife at his mother's throat. In the reflection of the mirror was Jonathan Rushmore, his face so clear.

Marty zoomed in, took a screenshot and cropped the photo. Plugging his phone into Sean's computer, with The App still open, Marty opened a new page, loaded the picture and set it to be delivered to The App's main page at precisely 10.45 p.m. Underneath the photograph, he added an address. The slaughterhouse in Essex where Cass and Ed Carter had been set alight. While Marty had watched a live stream of Ed, standing in front of the full lights, he remembered a road sign. Chigwell Row. And the name. Dag cottage. A tribute to Dennis and Gnasher. Marty remembered the conversation. The men hadn't realised the stream was live.

At the top of the page, Marty wrote a message.

Due to unforeseen circumstances, Abbey Benson should no longer be hunted, and no prize money will be paid. Anyone who breaks this rule will be dealt with accordingly.

Now, Marty continued watching the first stream.

People were banging on the front door and barging against it. Suddenly, it burst open, and mobile phones pointed at a man crouching in the hallway, everyone narrating.

'Leave me alone,' Jonathan screamed, begging for his life as they moved towards him. 'Please, don't do this. I'm the creator of The App. Please. Help me. Someone help—'

50

EARLY SUNDAY MORNING

'Just here's great, by the lamp post. Much appreciated.' Sean opened the back door, paid him and thanked the taxi driver.

'No problem. Have a good one. Take care.'

Watching as the black cab pulled away, feeling light-headed from alcohol, Sean thought about his evening and the first date with Tiffany. He'd taken a chance, contacting her through Tinder, and arranging to meet at a plush restaurant in London. The conversation flowed, the food was excellent, and the date couldn't have gone better. She shimmered in a black cocktail dress and high heels; she was intelligent, well-educated and stunning. The conversation was sophisticated, and she listened. Tiffany spoke a lot about her family, something important to Sean. He definitely wanted to see her again.

As he walked towards the two-bedroom terraced house off the Kilburn High Road, the silence serene, the early morning air still dim, he smiled with expectation after the date.

Sean glanced towards the house, noticing the front door

The App

open. Pushing it back, he peered into the bleakness. 'Michael? Are you awake?' The lights were off, the house drenched in darkness. Something was wrong.

Placing his hand on the wall, Sean flicked the light switch. With blurry eyes from the wine he'd had earlier, he tried to focus, blinking to clear his vision. Michael was going on holiday in a few hours. Could he have left already? But why was the front door open? It didn't appear to be damaged and there was no sign of a break in.

Walking along the hallway, he opened his bedroom door, seeing the computer was still turned on and the screensaver showing a recent selfie of the brothers.

Sean pulled the swivel chair back and sat, pressing a key to fire up the screen. 'No. What's happened?' Inside The App, he saw a picture, the image of a man loaded from a mirror reflection and an address in Essex. Links had been posted only a couple of hours ago.

Live streams.

At the top of the page, was a message.

Due to unforeseen circumstances, Abbey Benson should no longer be hunted, and no prize money will be paid. Anyone who breaks this rule will be dealt with accordingly.

Sean sat, open-mouthed, unable to comprehend what had happened. Earlier, he'd left in a hurry, running late for his first date with Tiffany. He'd left the computer on, with Marty still in the house.

What have you done? Please, no. This isn't fucking happening.

As Sean minimised the page, the software had attached to another upload. While showing Marty how everything worked, Sean had plugged in his phone, loading the last photo from his camera roll, a picture of his brother, Michael.

He'd tapped in their address in Kilburn, showing Marty how easy it was to post, never thinking that Marty would come back into the bedroom and load a new picture with the address in Essex.

The software had loaded Marty's post to the main page of The App at 10.45 p.m, and in a cruel twist of events, by accident, automatically loaded Sean's fake post, which he'd created to show Marty how it worked.

His hands were shaking, his body trembling violently. Sean pushed the chair back and raced into the hallway. 'Michael? Where are you? Michael?'

As he charged along the hallway and into the living room, his heart beating so fast he thought he'd collapse, Sean gasped, his legs unsteady and weak, the room spinning out of control.

His brother was lying dead on the floor, a bag full of clothes beside him, ready for his holiday in Tenerife.

'Please, God, no.' Sean crouched, kneeling in the blood and cradling his brother. 'Wake up. Please, Michael. Wake up.'

The End

FREE SHORT STORY.

Click the link for a free short story, by me, Stuart James.

The Intruder.

A chilling short story from my horror collection, The Macabre.

https://dl.bookfunnel.com/dj3p3s18oq

If you're reading the paperback version, you can go to my website and download The Intruder there. You can also sign up to my newsletter, find more info on my thrillers and get a free copy of Creeper.

https://www.stuartjamesthrillers.com

ABOUT THE AUTHOR

Stuart James is an award-winning psychological thriller and horror author and all his novels have been Amazon best sellers.

His thriller, The House On Rectory Lane, recently won The International Book Award in horror fiction.

Make sure to click the link below and sign up to my newsletter to keep up to date with everything I'm working on.

https://www.stuartjamesthrillers.com

Books by Stuart James.

The House On Rectory Lane.
Turn The Other Way.
Apartment Six.
Stranded.
Selfie.
Creeper.
The Macabre.
The App.

ACKNOWLEDGMENTS

Thank you so much for choosing The App and I hope you enjoyed it.
You can sign up to my mailing list and keep up to date with other projects I have planned.
Just go to:
https://www.stuartjamesthrillers.com

Firstly, I'd like to say a huge thank you to my family for your extreme patience and listening to my ideas constantly. I love you so much.
I feel you know my thrillers as well as I do.

I want to thank a few people who helped immensely with the research of The App.
To my wonderful friend Ali Hickman-Jameson who is a retired Police Sergeant and is always so very helpful with the police procedures. You really are an amazing lady.
My good friend Jack Howe who is an expert with cars, especially the Kia Sorento. Great talking to you, Jack.
Edward Jex and Susheel Arya who are expert app developers and have been absolutely incredible with their knowledge and help. I couldn't have written this without your support. You are both completely wonderful.
To finding an incredible publisher in the wonderful Rebecca Miller. Thanks for everything.

Thanks to Thea Magerand for the wonderful cover design and for being so amazing to work with.

A huge thank you to everyone on my Facebook arc group for your ongoing support. I can't thank you enough. I can call each member of the group a friend and I'm so glad you're a part of the team. Thank you for being there.
We have almost 140 members and I'm so, so grateful to you all.
Please get in touch if you'd like to be a part of it.

Special thanks to the Facebook groups who continually promote my works and support me so much.
The Fiction Cafe.
Tracy Fenton and her wonderful book club, TBC.
Dee Groocock's wonderful book club, Book On The Positive Side.
The Reading Corner Book Lounge.
UK Crime Book Club.
Donna's Interviews, Reviews and Giveaways.
Mark Fearn. Book Mark.
Also to the incredible book bloggers who have supported my journey so much and to all you wonderful readers and authors.
Also massive thanks to Adam Croft, Alan Gorevan and Lindsay Detwiler.
And lastly, special mention to Susie at Prescription Books, Zoe O'Farrell, Chloe Jordan, Kate Eveleigh, Donna Morfett, Emma Louise Bunting, Emma Louise Smith, Michaela Balfour, Kiltie Jackson, Mark Fearn, Wendy Clarke, Debbie Schutt and Chloe Osborne for the support and your friendship.
I'll be forever grateful.

You really are amazing and I can't thank you enough.

Make sure to keep up to date with projects I'm working on and sign up to my mailing list at:
https://www.stuartjamesthrillers.com

Also, you can follow me on social media.
I love to hear from readers and will always respond.
Twitter: StuartJames73
Instagram: Stuart James Author
Facebook: Stuart James Author.
TikTok: Stuart James Author

That's it for now.
Once again, thank you so much for choosing, The App.
Hopefully, I'll have a new adventure with Billy Huxton and Declan Ryan from Creeper, coming soon.
Love to you all and keep safe.
Stuart James.

Printed in Great Britain
by Amazon